Sentient Conspiracy

Sentient Conspiracy

MICHAEL J. BOSSÉ

RESOURCE *Publications* · Eugene, Oregon

SENTIENT CONSPIRACY

Resource Publications
An Imprint of Wipf and Stock Publishers
199 W. 8th Ave., Suite 3
Eugene, OR 97401

www.wipfandstock.com

PAPERBACK ISBN: 978-1-6667-3718-9
HARDCOVER ISBN: 978-1-6667-9637-7
EBOOK ISBN: 978-1-6667-9638-4

JANUARY 19, 2022 12:29 PM

To, Jesus Christ, my Savior,
Rocky, my beloved wife of 42 years and counting,
Bertha, my mother,
Sarah, Michael, and Mallory, my daughter, son, and daughter-in-law,
Erin and Beverly, my granddaughters,
Denise, my sister,
Romeo, Serge, and Andrew, my deceased father and brothers,
My many friends through the decades, and
All my students through my career.

Additional thanks to Randy Rasch and Rolf Kleinfeld, who led me
to the Truth, and Ronnie Stevens, who first discipled me. In various
forms, they are in this story. Oh, sure, now they will want free copies
of the book.

Prologue

As part of my research for this book, I watched many documentaries on UFOs—possibly too many. Through these documentaries, I learned of five theoretical types of close encounters (CEs):

CE1: visual sightings of UFOs;

CE2: physical evidence of UFOs (e.g., crop circles and scorched earth);

CE3: occupants of UFOs observed;

CE4: humans brought into UFO crafts; and

CE5: proactive human-initiated communication with extraterrestrial beings.

This story is about a higher dimension of CE. I call it

CE6: humans having direct and continued contact with sentient extraterrestrial beings.

Chapter 1

"Hey, Hon. I've got to run to Wilkesboro for a few minutes. How about if I pick up dinner at Olive Garden on the way back?" asked a clean-shaven, somewhat portly Caucasian man of average height in his mid-forties. He would have been described as average, typical, or ordinary in far too many ways. Nothing unusual about him caught anyone's attention. He often used this to his advantage as he preferred to disappear in a crowd. His hair was an average brownish with an expected amount of natural graying. He was neither attractive nor unattractive. While he cared about his health, he rarely paid a great deal of attention to his appearance; it was simply not that important to him. Even his attire was commonplace for the September mountains of North Carolina. He wore jeans, hiking shoes, and a thick, plaid flannel shirt. For this dress, possibly the most distinguishing feature was not wearing a baseball cap. He was known to love his family deeply; he would do all he could to make a great life for them and protect them. He had a solid career which gave the family stability.

His comparatively overly-beautiful wife was fair-skinned, tall—about three inches taller than him—thin, athletic, with jet-black, shoulder-length hair. She was exquisitely beautiful. Now, as a stately, dignified, and successful realtor, she still evidenced a past tomboy childhood, particularly when she put her hair in a ponytail for a jog in her neighborhood, in Mount Jefferson State Park, or on the greenway in Boone. Her competitive nature often took hold when running near twentysomethings or during not-so-friendly community volleyball games. She still took pride in being able to whip 'young-uns' twenty to twenty-five years her junior. Almost all recognized—but dared not say, that she was way out of her husband's league. He gleefully showed off his arm-candy wife wherever they went. Recognizing the disparity in their appearance, he and his wife would tell others that she married him because he had potential. Even her son's friends enjoyed coming over to sneak a peek at her, hoping that they would catch such a beauty in their futures.

His eighteen-year-old son followed the lead of his mother. He was very athletic and played in as many sports as fit into his schedule. He was near six feet tall and built like a tank. He also shared her dark hair. Everyone looking at him knew who his mother was, but few could see any likenesses to his father.

His fifteen-year-old daughter was in a darkened bonus room, in some position between sitting and lying down, with a laptop illuminating her emaciated face. She had been struggling with juvenile leukemia on and off for a few years. It had taken a toll on her body which should now be robust and healthy, rather than gaunt with deep-set eyes and hollow cheeks. She was videoconferencing with a number of her 'LeukBuds' around the country.

As good as his medical plan was, it was insufficient to care for all the needs of his daughter's long-term disease. To meet her needs, he had bled his retirement dry, and then his wife surrendered hers, their family savings was spent, and the debt added up to what he perceived was an insurmountable amount—and there were still possibly hundreds of thousands of dollars to go. Lately, as the financial desperation grew, he and his wife had debated selling their log cabin. "As much as we love it," he said, "it is only a *thing*. It can't be compared to the value of our daughter."

From his living room chair, the small log cabin efficiently transmitted his information and question to his wife in their bedroom and his eighteen-year-old son in his bedroom.

"You're gonna go to Wilkes?" his wife verified.

"Yes. I need some things, and I could use a drive alone to think. And Olive Garden would be a nice treat." *I need a drive. Time to think. Not sure what's going to happen. And Robert?* His wife had noticed that he had been agitated for a week or so. A drive alone might help alleviate some of his tension. He loved the mountains and always found them calming when driving through the country.

His wife had long recognized him as occasionally acting somewhat irrational, if not foolish. While he was very bright, as demonstrated by his employment, he was equally capable of making unwise decisions. Not being a mechanic, he once bought a clunker. It was a disaster from the first day, and she made sure that it never happened again. He occasionally desired to purchase items that he could not afford. Although he rarely followed through on these purchases, he may have spent them into poverty had she not intervened. She occasionally thought, *How can someone so cautious in what he does do such foolish things?* He once took a significant financial beating many years ago after bailing a less than trustworthy friend out of jail, who skipped out on bail only to commit another crime.

She saw him as an ever-loving and always well-intentioned Ralph Kramden. She was glad that he was a great family man, making all the time possible for his family. His quirks were his own—apart from when they negatively affected the family. She loved him dearly, despite his faults. Their love was true, and they recognized that opposites attract. She had learned to interpret most of his actions through the lens of good intentions and that, on minor issues, it was less effort to let slide his more minor misdemeanors against wisdom. Indeed, many of his antics became the substance of comic relief for family and friends.

Today was such a case. The weather was not the best for a drive off the mountain. While it was not a foolish gesture, the weather made it less than fully wise. However, she would let him have his way and save any disagreements for more significant issues.

"Well, actually, Olive Garden sounds good," she responded.

"Yeah, Dad, I want some lasagna," came a call from a cavernous teenage stomach.

"Same here, Hon, and some breadsticks."

"Okay, I'll get that. I'll call it in on the way. Be back by six. Be ready when I get back." The trip would be rather ordinary. He would travel down his road, intersect 221 South between Fleetwood and Deep Gap, and take 421 South off the mountain and toward Wilkesboro. The one-way trip would be just under thirty minutes.

"We caught him on the bug. He's heading to Wilkesboro . . . alone," came an announcement on a radio.

"Roger. We will begin pursuit at 221," responded another radio.

In the late afternoon, the clouds had descended thickly upon the mountains, and the rain had started about thirty minutes before his drive. Although the visibility was somewhat diminished, he was very confident driving the steep, curvy mountain roads. His forest green Subaru Outback had excellent traction and control and was perfect for the mountains. Turning onto 221 South, the driver paid no attention to the two full-sized, black SUVs which began following him.

"When?" came a question on the radio.

"Not here. Too flat. He's going to Wilkesboro. Between the Blue Ridge Parkway underpass and the Watauga runaway truck ramp. Make him go off the side of the mountain. You can use the intersections at either Stony Fork Road or Mount Zion Road. Or, if you need to, Chestnut Mountain Road. You know what to do. An accident."

"Roger."

Minutes later, the Subaru took the exit to 421 South, went under the Blue Ridge Parkway underpass, crested at the Continental Divide, and began the curvy five-mile descent off the mountain toward Wilkesboro. The car radio played the XM Seventies channel—Carry on Wayward Son by Kansas. *Mmm mmm mmm my mmm mmm son. Mmm mmm peace mmm mmm mmm done. Lay mmm mmm mmm mmm mmm rest. Mmm mmm cry mmm mmm.* The tune rang in his head, and there was a comfort and relaxation that came from hearing the tunes that his parents played in the car when he was young.

The fog was dense but certainly not as enshrouding as it could often be. He knew that it might clear out as soon as he hit the flat near Fall Creek. He was driving cautiously but in a relaxed manner consistent with mountain experience. Deep Gap was notorious for some heavy fog which could diminish highway driving to 30 mph. When the fog was that dense, it was dangerous to go full speed and probably equally dangerous to slow down and be hit from the rear. Hazzard blinkers helped to keep from getting tailgated. The safest following distance seemed to be far enough behind another car to just barely see its taillights. This provided sufficient reaction time while imagining the invisible road's curvature based on the vehicle ahead.

In what seemed like an instant, one of the black SUVs passed him on the left and pulled in dangerously close in front of him. *Too close!*

Idiot! Tourist!? Simultaneously, the other SUV pulled up and paralleled him on his left. *Whoa. Too close. Back off.* His visibility immediately went from mediocre to very limited by the size, proximity, and spray from the SUV directly ahead, and the opaque mass obliterated all visibility to the left. *Can't see. Can't . . .* His Outback, dwarfed by the SUVs, he grasped his steering wheel firmly. His sense of comfort was instantaneously replaced by helplessness, realizing that if either SUV did something stupid, there could be an accident. He tried to calm himself, thinking, *this won't last long. These idiots will keep going in a few seconds.*

But five seconds led to ten and fifteen. Little was visible apart from the taillights of the forward SUV. A tightening started to form in his stomach. *Can't see. Get out of the way! Get out of the freaking way!* He glanced at the SUV beside him and shook his hand to inform the driver to give him some room. *COME ON!* However, the elevated windows of the larger SUV and the tinted glass gave him no confidence that the driver noticed his gesticulations. *He can't see me.*

In what felt far more like frustration than fear, he could feel his anxiety rising. With no option to fight, he opted for flight. He decided to slow down and escape out the back of the formation. However, with the lack of visibility, he did not want to slow too abruptly and be rear-ended by another vehicle.

Between the decision to slow and the first tap of the breaks, the mammoth SUV on his left began to creep into his lane. *STAY IN YOUR LANE, MORON!* The Outback driver nudged his car to the right to avoid a collision, and his lane departure warning began to beep. The SUV came further, halfway into his lane. The Subaru now straddled the line on the right-hand side of the road, sufficiently clearing the line to confuse the safety system and silence the beeping. *I'M HERE! I'M HERE! SEE ME?!* As the SUV kept forcing him further right—even outside of his lane—the SUV ahead slid right also, continually blocking his vision. The Subaru inched closer to the guardrail.

Instantly, the front SUV darted left, revealing the guard-railed entrance of Mount Zion Road directly ahead. An instinctive, optionless reaction caused the Outback driver to jerk hard to the left, hitting the SUV beside him. The size differential between the two vehicles caused the Subaru to merely careen off the heavier undeterred object. All options for escape instantly evaporated. In the last millisecond, there were no flashes of the reliving of his life. There was no time to contemplate death.

There was only the driver's realization of the inevitable accident before him.

Some mixture of road engineering and physics elevated the Subaru before its lower chassis forcibly struck the guardrail near the top, pole-vaulting the car into summersaults until it landed unforgivingly in an ugly mass at the bottom, well below the road. The two large SUVs sped away, recognizing full-well that there was no need to check on the survival of the car's driver.

"Sir," one spoke into a cellphone. "Yes, Sir, it's done . . . No, Sir . . . Absolutely, Colonel. Copy, Sir. Martin out."

Chapter 2

DAY 10: SUNDAY

> There is no other God but one. For even if there are so-called gods, whether in heaven or on earth (as there are many gods and many lords), yet for us there is one God, the Father, of whom are all things, and we for Him; and one Lord Jesus Christ, through whom are all things, and through whom we live. (1 Corinthians. 8:4-6, NKJV)

THE Pastor, Alex Spencer, read with passion and conviction. His fifteen years in the ministry had not been overly kind to him. Just barely forty years old, he had become weak and flabby—far from the ruggedly handsome man he was in college. Of medium height with professionally cropped sandy hair, he had developed an academic paunch from too many hours in sedentary counseling and study and not enough time exercising. He sported a neatly trimmed beard, more so because it covered an already forming double chin. He loathed being in public in just a tee-shirt. *Too much belly and too little arms*, he thought.

He had practiced through his sermon the day before. By page length and experience, he knew it would take thirty minutes, plus or minus two. He was well-schooled and, after five years leading his congregation, knew when sermonic crescendos, decrescendos, gesticulations, and embellishments would prove most effective at maintaining the attention of the congregants. His sermon notes occasionally included reminders to perform hand claps and finger-pointing to accent essential points.

Grace Unity Church was a medium-sized church in Boone. It had about 350 members. It was nowhere near the 1500 membership of Alliance Bible Fellowship or the 800 at Mt. Vernon Baptist, but it was a very respectable size, particularly for a nondenominational church. Most of the congregants remained dedicated to the church due to solid and decades-long connections with family and friends. Unlike many denominational churches, Grace Unity Church did not rotate a pastor every three or four years. Alex could stay as long as he or the church board wanted. On Sunday mornings, the sanctuary was usually about two-thirds full. The pews were very traditional—two rows of long pews down each side with a generous width between the rows and along the outsides. The building contained a few offices, a conference room, a library, and classrooms for smaller meetings.

Alex was not one to attempt to whip his followers into emotional frenzies. However, he did find it essential that he was personally sufficiently stimulated—or at least demonstrating such. One of his seminary profs had frequently stated, "Enthusiasm is infectious, but so is boredom. If you are enthusiastic about your topic, you may turn some people on. If you come across as bored with your own talk, all others have little choice but to agree with you."

While he recognized that some degree of showmanship was necessary for effective public speaking, his goal was not to stoke the embers of emotionalism to flame. His goal was to preach 'Truth'—not his own, but truths directly from the Word of God. With a degree of satisfaction and possibly a modicum of pride, he openly stated time and again, "What I think and believe is trivial at best. What God says is paramount." He sometimes used this to hint at his superior knowledge of, and submission to, the Bible than some of the other pastors in town.

He made it a practice to mention other churches in town only rarely. Even when there were disagreements in practice between the churches, or one focused on minor doctrinal differences, Alex believed it essential to demonstrate Christian unity. His focus was on Christ and helping his flock live out their callings in Christ in a fallen world. Other pastors respected him because he knew his place—as a pastor of a medium-sized church—and as one who quickly befriended others. He always sought partnerships, agreements, and collaborations among churches and never dealt with rivalries. As with all towns, he had lost congregants to other churches and received others from them over the years.

His wife of twelve years, Jenny, had occasionally reminded him that God loved a humble heart and not to minimize or judge other pastors. "God has revealed to them what He wants them to know for their congregations. You must always try to work with other pastors and appreciate what they bring to the community." Jenny recognized that other pastors occasionally made questionable decisions and took dubious liberty with biblical interpretation. *Nevertheless, their hearts were usually right, and they cared greatly for their congregations*, she thought. But, most of all, fracturing a community through squabbles among pastors was always disruptive to the community's view of the faith.

Jenny was tall, but not unusually so, five foot eight. Her beyond-average female height and Alex's average male height allowed them to see each other eye to eye. She still retained a chiseled nose and chin and shoulder-length blonde hair, but the raising of her two children had metamorphosized her college size 6 to an unfit, toneless, size 12—not large, but not where she was satisfied at being.

Jenny had grown up in church and, upon graduating high school, had gone to Moody Bible Institute in Chicago to study music. She loved music and could play piano and sing for hours on end. She chuckled when her friends called it Moody Bridal Institute. She, too, had secretly hoped to find her partner at the college. She had often thought that having musical skills could come in handy for a pastor's wife. Indeed, there were rumors that some new pastors had not been selected for positions if they did not have an accompanying wife who could also minister in the church, particularly with music.

Jenny wrestled with the many aspects of desiring to be a minister's wife. She wrestled with her identity as a modern Christian woman. *I would love to be led and fed by a deeply spiritual man, but this is antithetical to the secular view of 'I am woman, hear me roar.' I must ground my identity in Christ. But how will people look at me? How can I tell people that this is what I believe in and what I think God wants me to do? I'll probably have to keep a side career so that I don't look bad to the many women of a church and community who are expected to work. Will the people in the church expect that the pastor's wife is a position with expectations within the church?*

Alex and Jenny first caught sight of each other at a freshman orientation session in Torrey-Gray Auditorium at Moody Bible Institute. She was seated a few rows ahead of him and diagonally to his right. For a fraction of a second, she had looked to her left to talk to another student. She brushed aside her hair to clear her visibility. Alex could see her profile. That was enough. She was stunning—fair-skinned with a captivating profile. *Cut it out*, he scolded himself. *Cut it out. She is amazing. She would never be interested in . . . How can I meet her?*

Alex attempted to focus on the orientation speakers, but his mind was lost in imaginations of her. He looked intently at the back of her shoulder-length blonde hair. He could imagine it in a ponytail when she exercised or was deep in thought. He hoped deeply for another look at her face. *Come on. Just turn once. Just a glimpse.* It happened. She turned almost completely around to look toward a student behind Alex who was asking a question. She had to look almost through Alex to observe the questioner. Alex could not help but to look at her intently. *Does she see me? Is she . . . ?* Involuntarily, Alex donned a wide-eyed smile. Jenny had no choice but to notice him staring at her and smiling. Alex waved at her with two fingers—hoping to accentuate the eye contact but not appearing to be overly apparent if he were not seen. She politely nodded in return, noticing his smile and his long flowing hair. Alex had a mane of curly dirty blonde hair that most women envied. *She saw me. She saw me. But it doesn't matter; she won't be interested.* He was mesmerized by her beauty.

She turned back to face the front of the auditorium and did not turn around again. *Cute smile. Nice hair. Don't fall for the first cute guy. There will be dozens or hundreds more. Ignore him. Focus on the talks. I wonder if he is still looking at me.*

The orientation session came to an end. Both stood up, attempting to observe the other without being obvious. Jenny turned right to exit the auditorium. Alex followed her lead, but more slowly so they would end up at his end of the row simultaneously. *Can I time this right? Can I get a little closer?* He hoped for one more glance before he went his way, only to dream of her in the future. Just as their paths intersected, as he had planned, Alex's foot got caught in the frame of the auditorium seating, and he tripped full force into her. Realizing that he was falling, his arms flailed in the air seeking something to grasp. To his utter embarrassment, his only handhold became her shoulder and arm. This was sufficient to topple them both over in the aisle—she on her backside atop her backpack and he on her with his backpack between them. *Stupid klutz! That is the end of that.* Neither were injured, and Alex scrambled to his feet, humiliated. Jenny recognized the accidental nature of the trip that neither were injured and Alex's complete mortification—in total, a comic storybook event—that she had no choice but to laugh out loud. *What a story when I get home.* Relieved by her laughter, he offered her a hand and stood her upright.

"Well, you might as well give me your name and phone number," Alex said, shocked that those words came out of his mouth. But they were now out. "It was meant to be that we bumped into each other."

"Or you fell into me," she said with a smile and a sense of humor. And within moments, not knowing where this might go, the two were intimately connected by ten digits each. More than a decade later, they still chuckled when relaying the story, realizing how superficial and stereotypical it sounded. Nevertheless, it was *their* story.

Of the two, Jenny was more gregarious than Alex. She would naturally work a room and meet everyone. She liked to immediately break the ice with those around her. Alex was more standoffish. He would speak with anyone who talked to him first but was hesitant to initiate a conversation. He believed that he was called either to pastoral ministries or to teach. Regardless, he anticipated a life of ministry. Still, he was unsure how to master his shyness to be the effective minister he saw in others, including his father and grandfather.

Alex's grandfather lived five years after retiring from pastoring and then passed away, encircled by as many of his family and congregants that the hospital would allow. Due to his prominence in the community, this was a greater number than most were allowed.

His father was still actively pastoring a church in Indiana, Pennsylvania. Some of the towns in Pennsylvania were named after other locations such as Indiana, California, Moon, and Mars. Like military brats, pastors' children were often not 'from somewhere' as much as they were 'from everywhere.' Alex grew up in Indiana but went to Moody Bible Institute to prepare for ministry. His education was funded by a generous giver at his father's church who felt called to support Alex to get to the ministry.

As soon as he graduated and began his first job in ministry, Alex knew that the family would call him 'Number 3,' or 'the third,' or some other moniker designating him as third in line in the ministry. He accepted this; he was proud of his pastoral lineage. However, he was also intimidated by it. *Can I do as well as Dad and Grandpa at leading the flock? Can I do this for thirty or forty years? Can my future family and I survive with the meager salary of most pastors? Will my wife need to work? Should I align myself with a mainline denomination? There is usually better pay there. Should I even be focusing on money as much as I am?*

After meeting again at some gatherings and Bible studies, Alex and Jenny began dating. Once very committed to their futures together, they decided to get married the summer before graduating. This accomplished multiple purposes. First, they would be allowed to enjoy each other intimately. Second, this would give her Alex's last name, and she would not have to change it after they arrived somewhere. If she taught music at a school, she did not want the students to struggle with a name change.

Through their relationship, Alex grew more confident in front of people. Unbeknownst to him, some situations in which he found himself—where he needed to meet people and often had to speak extemporaneously—were orchestrated by her. She knew that experience would breed skill which would then lead to confidence. In their case, the familiar adage, 'a good wife makes her husband into a better and more complete man,' was undoubtedly true.

Although Jenny now only infrequently played piano at church, Alex saw their marriage as a true partnership in ministry. She ministered to the women in the church and some youth, particularly those befriended by their children, Jordan, eleven, and Bella, nine. He saw her primary responsibility as being a supportive mother and wife. While this role was disparaged in more secular realms, neither Alex nor Jenny cared; they did what they believed that God wanted. They knew many young ladies in college and then in their church with other career goals who would whisper that they wished nothing more than to be married and raise a family. But, since this was taboo, these desires remained whispers among only the most deeply trusted friends, as they sought careers as backup options.

As a partner in ministry, Alex often looked to Jenny as his most trusted confidant — even beyond the elders in the church. He had long ago learned to listen to her wisdom. Sometimes the same wisdom, when directed toward him, smarted. However, after taking time to lick his wounds, he never doubted her motives to support him and want the best for him and his ministry.

"In our text, Paul is making some interesting points," preached Alex. Some are expected, but others may not be. We know of Old Testament pagan gods such as Baal, Molech, Ashera, and others. We know that many cultures followed their gods. However, repeatedly, we see that Jehovah, Yahweh, the I Am, defeats these false gods. Elijah, at Mount Carmel, embarrasses the priests of Baal. The worshipped statue of Dagon falls in humility before the Ark of the Covenant. The people of Jericho recognize and fear the God of the Hebrews, knowing that He has destroyed all who have come against the Jewish people."

"Paul is clearly stating that, while there may be so-called gods," Alex motioned with his index and middle fingers on each hand in air quotes for emphasis, "apart from the One True God, these other gods are false gods."

Sitting in the fourth row on Alex's left, Robert Forsythe slightly, and almost imperceptibly, involuntarily shook his head. This was unusual even for him. He was usually disconnected from church. A decade before, he had agreed with his wife, Emily, that he would uncomplainingly attend the church service and Sunday school each week, but he was not a willing victim. His only sign of disapproval was his usual silence during these meetings. He wanted people to witness his silent boycott, his martyrdom to Sunday mornings. His protestations were most often relegated to squeezing Emily's hand at the most cringe-worthy instances. Interestingly, the moments he felt most cringe-worthy were often equated to moments in which the topic most blessed her.

Far more frequently, Robert remained stone-faced at anything Alex stated *ex-cathedra*. However, today's barely perceptible shaking of the head caught the attention of both Alex and Emily. In concert, Robert and Emily squeezed each other's hand—he in apparent disagreement, and she to scold him. *Caught. Gotta behave. Play the game. I might pay for this one.* He looked past her disappointed face, pretending to check on his eighteen-year-old daughter, Abigail, seated on Emily's other side. She had not noticed his signaling of defiance. His daughter, Grace, fifteen, sitting on his other side, had not seen him shake his head either; but she did notice him checking on Abigail. Grace knew that she was the good child, the one rarely wrong. Abigail was another story altogether.

Abigail and Grace were notable opposites. Abigail, a high school senior, was tall—taking after mom—seemingly fit without exercise and always fashion conscious. To the extent that she could afford, she wore trendy clothes—the right brands from the right stores with the right logos. While naturally beautiful with mid-back length, very straight auburn hair, she always wore makeup, but not too much. Among her friends, she was vivacious, lively, and fun-loving. However, around her family, she was moody, almost brooding. She invested most of her time in knowing her friends and being known.

Fifteen years old, Grace was fun-loving, freckled with dark red, shoulder-length naturally curly hair. If not for grandma Bertha, no one could explain the curly hair. Her hauntingly beautiful, bright, blue eyes fought for attention with her vibrant-colored hair. She was shorter in stature, cute, and moderately heavy for her age; she loved spending time with her parents and with Abigail when Abigail was in a tolerable mood. Grace had little concern for fashion. She was comfortable with anything she grabbed from the drawer that day. Her hair could be down on any given day, in a working ponytail, or amusing pigtails. Life was simply too short to worry about those things. She took great joy in her freckles and hated the thought of hiding them under makeup.

Robert looked back toward Alex, who had continued his message without a step. "There is but one means of salvation for man, through the Savior, Jesus Christ. There is only one God, Who has formed all; all that is or was or ever will be."

At this, keeping his head motionless, Robert furrowed his brows, silently voicing his disagreement with the thought. *He doesn't know that there is so much more.*

Still maintaining his composure, Alex continued with his theme, slightly sidetracked by Robert's unusual and unexpected facial gestures. He wondered what could be bothering his friend. Almost weekly over the years, Robert had proffered some version of this central tenet to the Christian faith from the pulpit.

"To ascribe to the existence of other gods, possibly co-equal with the Godhead, leads to countless implications contrary to the Gospel. Scripture is clear that there is no salvation but through the name of Jesus. This is the salvific economy under which man resides, and since God has created this economy, man cannot alter such."

Alex loved to both employ and have everyone hear him use dense and rich theological verbiage. At first, the church interpreted this as braggadocios. Once asked publicly why he spoke and taught at such an elevated level, he responded, "If I teach at a higher level, the people will learn at that level. They will elevate their thinking and communication to this level. If I teach at a lower level, I have tacitly indicated my lessened expectations of them, and that is where they will stay." After five years of Alex's sermons and lessons, many others in the church freely employed similar phraseology, particularly when in church-related speaking roles. The depth of ideation in the more sophisticated nomenclature often brought about an economy of words. Much could be succinctly communicated by properly selecting the most precise theological terms. "After all, while Christianity is a faith, theOLOGY is a disciplined study, a science if you will," Alex had stated.

"The doctrine of the uniqueness of God is central to the Christian faith. Departing from it can place one in eternal jeopardy." With this, Alex ever so slightly formed a pointing finger. While waving it about the congregation, he paused for a millisecond longer directly toward Robert (he saw it) for emphasis that could be detected only by the intended. Both knew precisely what Alex was communicating: 'There are ideas which are sacrosanct.'

Alex remained uncertain as to precisely why Robert seemed to be silently perturbed on this day. *What's going on? Problems? He can't disagree with this message. Can he? Even Robert would agree that there could be no more than one God. He may question if Jehovah was that God or if all the monotheistic faiths shared the same God, but by another name; but only one God it must be.*

Emily, Robert's wife of twenty-five years, had become a believer in Jesus Christ about fifteen years prior when she was thirty, and he was thirty-one. When Abigail was young, Emily decided to raise her daughter in church. When Grace was born, Emily's commitment to church was deepened. Abigail made a personal commitment to follow Christ at age eight, and Emily implored Robert to join them at church every week. She knew that he did not share her faith and that he would do little to encourage the girls through Bible reading or prayer, but possibly, his attendance in weekly Sunday school and church would have some softening effect. She knew that her roles were to model Christ in the home and pray daily and fervently for God to change the heart of her husband.

Overall, Robert was a kind man, an attentive and supportive husband, and an involved parent. While Emily pined for her husband to independently show interest in church and the truths it espoused, she greatly valued her husband as he was. She had decided that she would exemplify the faith without making him feel belittled by it. She hoped that Robert's involvement with some of the men of the church would eventually influence him.

Alex and Robert were deeply caring but cautious friends. While they cared deeply for each other and genuinely enjoyed the other's company, they were guarded about what they discussed. Their wives, although about ten years apart in age, were best of friends. Alex would share notions of the faith with Robert, but he would not be so aggressive as to shoo him away. He was always slightly concerned that if Robert ever felt ostracized, so would Emily, which would affect her relationship with Jenny, and then he would hear it from his wife. Alex was in an impossible position. Both wives hoped he would lead Robert to Christ. However, neither wanted him to push so hard that it would harm the existing friendships.

Robert, too, was relationally trapped. He enjoyed being around Alex if Alex did not 'go too far.' They would hunt and fish together and toss around a football at times. He enjoyed goading Alex into philosophical arguments but did not appreciate being cornered by an effective parry.

Alex's sermon went on, but Robert was lost in thought. *There are so many things that he doesn't know.* Emily recognized it and gently squeezed his hand to bring him back to attention. They often reciprocated this gesture when one got weary and fought off falling asleep during the sermons. For some reason, no matter how interesting was Alex's sermon, one or both would struggle to stay awake. They credited this to the fatigue of the week catching up with them. Neither wanted the other to be embarrassed by falling asleep in church. They saw the squeezing of each other's hand as a discrete, loving gesture of partnership and support. Robert's attention was brought back to the sermon. He looked over at Emily with a thankful eye. *I love this girl. I'm lucky.* She smiled.

"The Christian faith is a fine balance of unwavering faith and humility in what we do not and cannot know." Alex continued. "The height of arrogance is to claim an opinion on all, particularly those things which are extrabiblical. But this we can claim with full confidence and biblical authority, there is no other God but one." With this, Robert sighed and ever-so-slightly lowered his head in disagreement. Fortunately, it was only noticed by Emily and Alex—and Grace. Grace gave him a friendly and teasing elbow. *Caught again, and now by a fifteen-year-old.* He nudged her back and smiled wryly. He loved her deeply and did not want to disappoint her, but his newfound objections to Alex's sermon were profound.

Near the back of the church sat a new visitor. Alex noticed him as he preached. He had slipped in unnoticed, even to all but one of the ushers. He sat in the back-most vacant pew. He would possibly have gone unnoticed if he was not an adult Black man. Occasionally, Black students would visit the church seeking somewhere to worship. They were usually from Appalachian State University and often student-athletes. The visitor was a tall man in his early fifties. He was conspicuously well-dressed in a well-tailored suit. People living in Boone were notoriously underdressed. Even in church, jeans were more common than dress slacks.

Alex made a mental note of the visitor and intentionally planned to meet him before leaving. He believed it was important to make the few minority visitors feel comfortable and safe in his church. Unfortunately, in a predominantly white community, many local pastors made such a considerable fuss of greeting and welcoming minority attendees that the visitors themselves felt singled out and uncomfortable.

The man had a calm and powerful presence. He was clean-shaven, with a neat haircut. There was a soothing formality about him, something high-brow business or governmental in form.

He sat silently. When the congregation stood to sing, he stood also but remained silent. When the congregation greeted one another, they all turned and shook hands with the people closest to them. Mainly, due to habituated seating, those closest were those regularly greeted. Yes, Miss May and several others went out of their way to exit their row and meet others up to two and three rows away, but these people were unusual, and most of them belonged to the church's Greeting Committee. Greetings were shared, and people returned to their usual seats. Miss May was always the last to get back to her seat.

Bill Teek, alone, shook the visitor's hand and exchanged—or at least attempted to—greetings with him. Bill was always positioned in the back of the church. Church members did not know that he unofficially acted as the church's security and was packing a 9mm HK P30. Pastor Spencer was on a don't-ask-don't tell policy with church members carrying a weapon. He suspected that a few men who had prior law enforcement backgrounds had weapons on them. He appreciated that because he knew they were well trained. He was less comfortable with others who may be packing without sufficient training. There were also a few ladies in the church with suspiciously heavy purses.

Bill thrust out his hand toward the visitor, who reciprocated. "Good morning," Bill offered. The visitor only nodded in response, with little change in facial expression—and indeed no smile. *Leave me alone. Don't make a scene. No attention . . .* He seemed to be focused on—well, something—to give much heed to Bill. From the pulpit, Alex had noticed this exchange. He was discomforted that so few went to greet the man. However, for others to do so would have been equally awkward, as most of the congregants were in the rows nearest the front of the church.

Upon reseating, the visitor was steady and focused. But his attention was less on the message than on one of the congregants. The visitor sat near the left rear of the church. Robert Forsythe and his family were in the front right. The visitor had a clear sight of Robert, and his gaze was fixed on Robert's every move.

Chapter 3

G RABBING his cup of coffee, John Tate, who from childhood had just gone by 'Tate,' pressed 'confirm' to agree to transfer the entire content of a large directory from the new system Z-drive to his local work drive. He had casually looked at the amount of data on the drive a few minutes before copying to estimate how long the transfer would take. He estimated that he could finish his cup of coffee and continue examining a spreadsheet of data to find any anomalies.

At a birthday party of a mutual friend, Tate met his wife, Sarah Melida, after they graduated from the University of North Carolina in Charlotte—he with a major in Accounting and a minor in Computer Programming and she with a degree in Small Business Administration. Following her mother's lead, Sarah began working in real estate. Tate was grabbed by an accounting firm and his work investigating the books of the firm's clients. Soon, his skills at discovering anomalies were recognized by his supervisors and those above them. Not too long later, he received a clandestine note to contemplate working for CCTech. He followed up and made a career there.

In their third year of marriage, Samuel was born and grew up to be a star high-school athlete in football, wrestling, and basketball. His eighteen-year-old, six-foot, muscular frame defied that he was Tate's son. However, in a masculine sense, he mirrored his mother's perceived athleticism. His high school and college plans were to enter law enforcement.

Allie was born three years after Sam. From childhood, she was the physical antithesis of her older brother. Sam was bounce-off-the-wall active, and she was weak and sickly. While juvenile leukemia was diagnosed and, through the years, the disease and its treatments ravaged her now fifteen-year-old body, she remained a fighter. Occasionally discouragement set in, but she fought it whenever it reared its ugly head.

Since nothing was beyond the worth of their daughter's life and health, unbeknownst to the children, Tate and Sarah had sacrificed almost all liquid and hard investments and reserve assets to meet Allie's medical expenses. Debt exceeding their combined annual income had grown to a crushing demand. Their lack of hope for financial recovery was exasperated by seemingly no end in sight to future treatments and costs. In their own manner, each family member fought their respective battles against some form of discouragement regarding Allie's health.

Both the cup of coffee and the transfer ended almost simultaneously. The screen said, 'Transfer Complete, 1,056GB.' *This is wrong. Doesn't make sense.* Tate had recalled that 972GB were on the folder just moments before he asked for the transfer. He wondered where this additional 84GB of data was from. *84GB? From where? Just checked before. Doesn't make sense.*

Tate knew that system administrators could make some classified files and directories utterly invisible to users. Even the data display would not recognize the additional files. However, these hidden files were coded so that they could not be transferred without specific security clearances on the part of the computer user. Regardless of this and many other file protections in any facility with top-secret files, the process inexplicably transferred 84GB more data than anticipated. This warranted more investigation.

He examined the new directory on his drive containing the system drive. The upper levels of the directory tree seemed quite regular. He drilled down, folder after folder. Everything seemed normal—unusually normal, considering that an additional 84GB was sent. There were no stray files outside of their respective directories. He investigated more intensely and stumbled upon a deeply embedded subfolder, SETL. In theory, all the files on the entire copied drive, including those in the SETL folder, were benign. Classified folders and files would not have been allowed to be transferred without sufficient authorization. Unless Tate were assigned to a particular project with an associated level of clearance, he would not have permission to transfer classified files.

Curiosity led Tate to investigate the SETL folder. For no conscious reason, he opened the directory titled 'Videos' and randomly opened the directory '2013.' Then, for again no discernable reason, he selected the file ATS-2013-09-16v. The file contained a blurred video that was frighteningly apparent despite the blurring. *UFOs and aliens? On CCTech systems? Can't be a gimmick or fake news.* He recognized that the blurring was a sophisticated encryption method, only remediable using a decryption key. The file would be defragmented and completely clear with the decryption key code.

With a shake of his head in disbelief, he felt compelled to investigate further. He backed out of a few directories and opened the directory 'Analysis.' He again went to the subdirectory '2013' and opened the file ATS-2013-3-26a. Despite the blackened redacted portions of the document—again, only fully readable using its unique decryption key—his experience with governmental files gave him insight into the contents he encountered. He investigated a few more files from each of the directories in SETL: 'Videos,' 'Analysis,' and 'PublicResponse.' While incomplete or blurred, each file provided more bits of information, more pieces of a puzzle. Intersecting directories across years, he investigated the files associated with the same date. He noticed that for every date for which there was a file in any directory, there was an accompanying file in the other directories with a similar date. He immediately thought to himself, *these files should have never been in the same complete folder. Even if someone accidentally finds a particular file, that person should not see the accompanying files. The conjoining of the Videos, Analysis, and PublicResponse folders under the SETL folder probably broke numerous security protocols.* Tate reached up and rubbed his forehead and temples hard and then ran his hand through his hair. *What has happened? Why do I have these files?* He looked over his shoulder to see if anyone had stepped into his office and may be looking at his screen. No one was there. *Before I report this, I better make sure that I know what I have.*

Tate had fifteen years of experience as a forensic accountant. His primary role in CCTech was to analyze the books of the numerous external companies and entities with whom CCTech had various governmental security-level contracts, regardless of the project. He was not concerned about the nature of the project CCTech was completing for the company.

His primary focus was on determining whether these companies might be participating in some financial illegalities. Procuring a government contract with CCTech required that a company submit the totality of its books to CCTech for an audit. In addition to investigating possible fraud and illegalities, Tate was astute in finding hints that the submitted materials were incomplete.

Once, back five years ago, based simply on the file naming structure provided with a batch of data files, he was alerted that a company was probably committing fraud or illegality. The company thought they had used a system that would probably not be recognized as having a pattern. The files we named XYZ0002, XYZ0007, XYZ0019, XYZ0043, XYZ0079, XYZ0139, XYZ0281, etc. Tate spent days analyzing each file for anomalies. None were found. However, in either a stroke of luck or brilliance—even Tate was unsure—he noticed both a pattern and some omissions: all the numerals in the filenames were prime. Making a list of primes, he recognized: <u>2</u>, 3, 5, <u>7</u>, 11, 13, 17, <u>19</u>, 23, 29, 31, 37, 41, <u>43</u>, 47, 53, 59, 61, 67, 71, 73, <u>79</u>, 83, 89, 97 101, 103, 107, 109, 113, 127, 131, 137, <u>139</u>, 149, 151, 157, 163, 167, 173, 179, 181, 191, 193, 197, <u>199</u>, 211, 223, 227, 229, 233, 239, 241, 251, 257, 263, 269, 271, 277, <u>281</u>, . . . Not only were they all prime numbers, but there was also a skip of prime numbers by the prime numbers in order. Prime 2, skip 2nd file, prime 7, skip 3rd file, prime 19, skip 5th file, prime 43, skip 7th file . . . However, following this pattern, file XYZ199 was missing. This would be a nearly impossible 'coincidence.' Someone had too meticulously efforted to have developed such an elaborate pattern that they would never have missed one. The case was blown.

When Tate demanded file XYZ199, the company in question was shocked that it had been determined that a file was missing from the batch sent for investigation. Company officials were so certain that the file would not be noticed that they did not bother to alter file XYZ199 or delete it. They felt an even greater surprise when the precise file was precisely named, leaving them no time or opportunity to corrupt the data in the file. When the file was turned over to CCTech, evidence of foul play was discovered, and Tate had solved it! Not only did the company not get the contract with CCTech, but they soon were also indicted on serious federal charges of various sorts. Tate was immediately famous.

Since then, his friends still would occasionally call him 'Mr. 199', 'minus 1' (for being one short of 200), or—Tate's Favorite—'007' (as in James Bond or for finding the missing 7th number in the sequence). Even his wife, Sarah, would occasionally chime in and affectionately alter the catchphrase 'Bond, James Bond' to 'Tate, John Tate.'

Tate watched ATS-2017-9-2v and comparatively read ATS-2017-9-2a and ATS-2017-9-2pr. Substantial discrepancies existed between the analysis of the video and the proposed public response. *I know how this works—seen too many 'governmental responses' on hundreds of other concerns.* Through semi-blurred issues and redactions, he understood that this was governmental evidence of extraterrestrial life on earth, the analysis of such, and the sanctioned response to the public if the evidence was ever released.

As alarming as this revelation was, Tate was immediately struck with concern regarding an even greater potential for danger—personal danger. His gut wrenched tightly. He had not previously noticed that all these files had the 'ATS' prefix. *These are 'Above Top Secret.' I'm not supposed to be able to see these. What happened? Why were they on the Z-drive in the directory I needed?* While he did not have the security clearance to view any files above the secret classification—and even then, only in the realm of forensic accounting—he had been trained about the filing nomenclature. Occasionally, he encountered files with prefixes of 'C' and 'S.' However, most of the files he investigated were unclassified and had no such prefixes. He instantaneously realized that he had been investigating files far above his clearance. If he were caught doing this, there would be hell to pay—discipline, loss of confidential clearance, firing, and possibly other ramifications, including incarceration. *How do I undo this or get out of this?*

Sitting at his computer, Tate instinctively spun entirely around in his seat to see if anyone could see him. He was alone in his office, but panic was quickly taking hold—a panic about his career, his security clearance, and possible imprisonment. *Don't know how I got these. Wasn't my fault. Wasn't my fault. If I tell, they will see that this is not my fault. I need to . . .* Confusion set in. Tate could not process through the complexities of the situation. *What if they don't believe me? Why should they? I don't even know how this happened. But, if they track my computer, they'll know what I have seen; but they will also know that I got the files accidentally. Gotta count for something.*

Tate could feel his heart pounding ferociously. He noticed his sweaty hands and wiped them on his pants. He wiped his forehead with his sleeve, and oily sweat stained the fabric. His office felt unusually hot. *In all my years, this has not happened before. What is the proper protocol?*

Warring against the terror of the situation, his curiosity was piqued. Thoughts flowing faster than he could process clouded his judgment. Despite the possible harm to his career, he was too engrossed in the investigation to let it drop so quickly. He felt driven to investigate at least one more video file. *Just one more.* He decided that it should be a more recent one. At the same instance, he thought, *if they catch me, I can use what I know as leverage for protection. Been in this biz long enough. Information is power.*

He opened ATS-2020-10-5v-alpha and was dumbfounded at what he saw. Behind some blurring of the picture was a still discernible conversation between a man and what appeared to be an extraterrestrial. This communication was in an indiscernible interlanguage combining English words and sounds of alien origin, each member sharing some articulations from the other species' language. Most noticeable was the fluency shared between the two communicants.

Tate watched enough to understand the big picture of what was preserved in the files. *Evidence of a government coverup of alien research. Wait . . . Why the disparity? Are these actually ATS files? If so, how did I get them? If not, why the prefix? Because of the aliens, it is more likely that they are actually ATS files and got transferred over accidentally. But how? Transfer of classified files needs the proper clearance. What do I do?*

Tate was a cautious man. He invested cautiously and took no pleasure in gambling. He was never one to take a leap of faith. Safety was his guiding principle. Not only would he not chance to do something ill-advised, but he would also wrestle with avoiding those thoughts altogether. However, he now found himself contemplating the chance for a once-in-a-lifetime windfall—this imagination alone greatly disquieted him. This opportunity took hold of him in an unanticipated and inexplicable manner. He did not know the person in his skin who was contemplating monetizing the windfall. *Bet this is worth a lot of money to some people. A LOT OF MONEY. Millions! TENS of millions. Could pay for her leukemia treatments. Rebuild our finances. That's enough. Don't need to be rich. Just need to recover, pay for the kids' college. Maybe rebuild our retirements. Some would pay to get this information, and others would pay to keep this covered up.* He was again struck with an earlier concern. He wondered how he could protect himself from future reprisals from the company or government if it were found out that he opened the files. *They will find out by the next full data audit. Would need to work this fast. I would have the leverage.*

He expected that few would believe his verbal testimony about his observations of alien life without proof. He rummaged around in his desk and found a casually tossed and semi-discarded USB flashdrive in the far reaches of his top drawer. Quite a while ago, he had forgotten its existence. Since CCTech did not allow the use of flashdrives, and Tate's computer had no USB ports, it was easy for everyone to overlook an abandoned flashdrive in the back of a desk drawer. *Archaic technology. But can't copy to the cloud. Building's intranet won't allow access to the internet. Computers are blue tooth disabled. Old tech, but workable.* The flashdrive was 256Gb; it would do. *Have to make it work. But how? Am I really doing this? One shot's all I have. Now or never. Chance to get money to recoup all we have lost, or everything will stay the same for the rest of my life.* Again, Tate wondered who he was and what was driving this reaction. This contemplation was utterly antithetical to his nature. However, His daughter's disease had taken its toll on him as well. The many financial losses had beaten him down over the past few years. He could easily justify that this was his act of teenage rebellion, which had never manifested until now, or maybe a midlife crisis. Nevertheless, he was strangely empowered by the notion that his ship had come in, and it was time—probably his only opportunity—to cash in.

Tate contemplated how he might gain access to a computer with a USB port. Tracie Bryant, a close friend and a network administrator at CCTech, had such a computer. Regulations would not allow Tate to use her computer, but he believed that he could gain access. From her computer, he could go back door to his computer's Solid-State Drive and copy the files. A network administrator had access to all computers and all drives. She had both the authority and ability to gain access to his computer in his office at any time. He did not have to be present at his computer for her to access it, but he would need to get her away from her office for a few minutes. *How can I get her away? Only need a few minutes. I need a tech problem for her to investigate. I need for her to come here so I can go there. Gotta be something physical, which she can't diagnose from her office.*

He bent down and loosened the computer's power cable from the receptacle so that it would barely make a connection and could potentially disconnect. He then did the same to the other end of the power cord to the back of the computer. With this, the slightest jostling of the power cord, even from light movements of hands or bodyweight against the desk, could intermittently disconnect the power from the computer. He then opened several applications on his computer to look very active and cover his tracks of investigating classified files. The battle of fear from knowingly doing wrong against the hope for financial recovery waged on—both uncharacteristic of the mild-mannered man, husband, and father. He fought himself with every agonizing step he made in the direction of completing the task. *What would Sarah think? And the kids? Maybe I can keep it from them.* He would never be able to keep this information from his wife, Sarah—at least not for long. The muse of potential was both encouraging and corrupting his problem-solving reasoning. Panicked creativity superseded judicious cautiousness.

Cellphone in hand, Tate walked the halls toward Tracie's office. *The closer I am to her office when I ask her to go to mine, the more time I will have at her machine.* He walked one hallway, then two, up a flight of stairs, then another hallway, and another. Passing by her office, he glanced in to verify that she was in and working. He stopped at the corner of the next hallway and called her cellphone.

"Tracie, any chance you can come down and check my computer? It keeps shutting down and rebooting. I have never seen this before. It is really bugging me."

"Sure, I'll be right there," came the reply from the other end. She knew that Tate was sufficiently competent at computers that this would be an unusual situation. He could troubleshoot everyday issues. "Why are you calling me on your cell and not the desk phone?"

"Ah," Tate fumbled for a response, "I guess that I wasn't even thinking. Just grabbed a phone."

"Okay."

"Hey, if I'm not there, I'll be in the john. Just look at it. It might be on its last legs."

"Okay."

Waiting for Tracie to leave her office, Tate stood at the corner of the hallway, attempting to look nonchalant. Thirty seconds. Sixty seconds. His heart was pounding out of his chest. Every breath was a fight for survival. His chest cavity felt too small to accommodate both a powerfully beating heart and sufficient breath to remain conscious. Compounding all was his need to appear calm to any others passing by. *I hope that I don't see anyone I know.* He looked at his shirtsleeve and noticed the wet spot where he had wiped his brow. The wait was interminable. *What*

is she doing? She said that she was on her way. With that thought, a renewed fright came over Tate. Tracie could take just seconds to check on
the network to see if his computer had been shutting down and booting
back up. She could know everything about the hardware and software
performance of the computer by simply running some algorithms from
her desk. *She could . . .* She finally exited her office and began down the
hallway in the opposite direction of Tate.

Tate began to pull out of his hiding place toward Tracie's office
when, in an instant, Tracie pivoted and went directly toward him. He
reciprocated and spun back to his spot in the other corridor. *Her head
was down. Her head was down. She didn't see me. She didn't see me.* She
went back into her office and, within two seconds, was out again. *She
must have forgotten something.* Tate decided to let her round the hallway
corner before again proceeding toward her open office door.

Tracie exited her office and disappeared down the corridor. Tate entered her office and closed the door. Another fear befell him. *I didn't think
this through. Not a very good criminal. Criminal? What am I doing? Just
finish the job and figure those things later. If she logged off, I won't be able
to get on.* Tracie's machine was a networked computer configured so that
only she could log on. However, with her assigned network privileges, she
could remotely log on to any other computer under her user account or
the employee's account. Thus, she would be able to troubleshoot computer glitches. Tate hoped that she had not logged off. For security purposes,
all CCTech computers were set up to lock up after a frustratingly brief
period of inactivity from the users' perspectives, after which users would
need to log on again. If Tracie had logged off, this venture was over; Tate
would not be able to log on. If she had not logged off, which could be the
case, since she had complete confidence that the system would be secure
after the brief period of inactivity, Tate would have only minimal time to
move the mouse and keep the computer awake.

As Tate reached for the mouse, the screen blinked to a screensaver.
No. No. He flicked the mouse indiscriminately, hoping that any motion
would supplant the logoff processes. The screen went blank. *Too late.*
With a microsecond flicker, it flashed on again. The system was active
and still logged on as Tracie. *Oh, man! Lucky. Just in time. Probably just
by a fraction of a second.* Tate easily navigated to a directory structure
that showed all drives on the network system. He found the drive named
after him and clicked to open the drive. The system then asked him to log
on with his account to open the drive. With a few keystrokes, he did so

and gained access to the Solid-State Drive on his computer. He inserted his flashdrive into an available USB port and initiated the file transfer process. A fear erupted in his thoughts. *What if she jiggles the power cord and knocks off my computer? It will kill my computer and not transfer the files. Just hope not.*

It would take very little time for the files to be transferred, and he had very little time. In a panic, he remembered that he had not checked the flashdrive to see if there were sufficient space left on the drive for the files he needed. It was now too late. It would either work or not.

Unlike in suspense movies, the file transfer occurred well before he would be in jeopardy and probably even before Tracie arrived at his office at the other end of the building. He grabbed the flashdrive, closed the file transfer program, and left the computer to timeout and log off automatically. He exited Tracie's office and went toward his own. An entire hallway and a half from her office, he was greeted by Marty Keeler. This was far enough from Tracie's office so that even Marty would not suspect that he had been in Tracie's office. A casual greeting was exchanged between them, each carrying a countenance that denoted their mutual busyness.

Walking down the hallway, Tate looked up. The fear he felt in Tracie's office was replaced with novel anxiety. *Cameras!* So accustomed were employees of CCTech to the ubiquitous existence of security cameras that most employees became numb to them and ignored them as little more than a part of the building structure, lightwork, or furniture. *Cameras in every corridor. They must have recorded me walking toward her office and back. Well, it is too late now. Gotta deal with the consequences later.*

Returning to his office, Tracie was still sitting at his desk facing the open door. "You are such an idiot," she said teasingly. "Your power cord was loose on both ends. If you jiggled it, it would kill the computer. The cleaning staff might have loosened it over time as they cleaned around your computer. It is all fixed now."

"Thanks so much," replied Tate. "I don't know what I would do without you."

"Well," responded Tracie. "These are the easiest of my concerns today. It was a pleasure helping you." Tracie rose to leave but seemed willing to be delayed by small talk.

"Thanks again," Tate replied as he returned to his seat at his desk, indicating his unwillingness at this time to share more time. Tracie left without insult, understanding that all employees were heavy with work.

Realizing that he still had the flashdrive in his hand, Tate bent over and shoved it far down in his sock. There was only an hour left to the workday. Distracted by what he had seen in the files and the danger in which he had placed himself, little more work was accomplished beyond recognizing how slowly the clock would turn. Feigning to work on his computer, he continued to look over his shoulder at his office door, wondering when security would enter his office and escort him away. Sweating had not stopped, but his panting and palpitations were replaced by forceful handwringing.

Chapter 4

THE sermon ended, and the congregation rose for a final hymn and prayer. Along with a benediction, Alex usually tied the final prayer to ideas in the sermon. Knowing that the congregation had their heads down and eyes closed, Alex scanned the auditorium as he prayed. He had long had an unknown practice of usually praying with his eyes open. It reminded him for whom to pray during the week. *The Wallaces. Smiths. Bob Cramer. Little Tommy Warren. The Sprakers and Pierces.* He noticed Robert looking at him. Robert had changed from a visage of disagreement to being overwhelmed and lost in thought. Their eyes locked. Alex pointed toward the door seamlessly while praying. Robert knew that Alex meant that they would meet at the door. Robert nodded in acknowledgment. He had no other response at his disposal as his right hand held Emily's hand and his left hand held Grace's.

Upon dismissal, church members had a tradition of fellowshipping together for a few minutes on their way out. Families shared friendly greetings with others. These conversations were socially understood to be pragmatically brief. While chatting with others, all the members were heading toward the doors that would provide egress to the parking lot, the cars, and the destinations of a local restaurant or home. Some of the older couples dared to remain in more extended conversations, but they knew to stand in safe locations out of the direct paths of those with a focus.

Alex stood at the main door, shaking hands with congregants. While many were happy to get their one to two seconds of attention from their pastor, others saw him as an obstacle to their exit. One option was to use a path to another door and exit.

Emily and Jenny, long-time friends, were chatting about their upcoming week. Both would be back on Wednesday evening for Bible study. Each had parental responsibilities for their respective two children. Emily worked part-time at Robert's business and part-time as a teacher's aide at the middle school. This led to a busy life. But her part-time status at both jobs gave her more flexibility to manage the home and family. Jenny had turned her musical training into a cottage industry, providing music lessons for students in the town. While piano was her primary instrument, she was also effective at teaching violin. She had never felt sufficiently strong at woodwinds and brass to teach those for private pay. Between their jobs, husbands, kids, and the prayer needs of many friends and church members, they were never at a loss of things to discuss.

Alex and Robert met at the door.

"You seemed disappointed with the message today," Alex charged.

"No, no, that's not it," Robert responded, attempting to protect his friendship with Alex more than truly address the concern. *Please don't get into this now.* "I just have a lot on my mind." *Leave it.* "You just don't understand." *He can't possibly. Who could?* Robert gestured with his hands as if pushing Alex away. "No one understands."

Alex immediately became more concerned for his friend. *What's going on?* "Is everything all right?" *He probably won't tell me here. Chet and Judy are coming up behind him. Won't have much time for a discussion here.*

"No, it isn't." *Shouldn't have said that. Just lie.* Shaking his head. "I can't talk about it right now."

"What do you mean?"

Robert held up his hand. "I'm not allowed . . . " Robert's voice trailed off as he saw Emily and Abigail approaching. It was clear to Alex that Robert did not want to continue his conversation in front of his wife. This sent Alex's mind reeling with countless options of what Robert's problem might be. *Were Robert and Emily having difficulties in their marriage? Was he having an affair? Was his business failing? Was he in financial distress?* One after another, thoughts arose and were dismissed. He knew Robert very well, and none of these ideas were worthy of further consideration.

Today, something else must be bothering him. What could it be? He's never been standoffish like this before.

"Lunch on Tuesday?" Alex asked.

"No, no . . . I don't know." *He knows I can't get out of this. It'll look even more suspicious if I beg off. Touché. I'll agree, and then I'll be evasive at lunch.*

"It really wasn't a request," Alex stated both a little forcibly and yet with a cautious, friendly tone. Alex and Robert had a history. While guarded, their relationship was simultaneously mutually challenging. They had developed a great respect for each other. Their challenges often removed options and escape routes for the other. Some challenges were humorous, while others, at times, were serious and deeply personal. Nevertheless, they both recognized that challenges improved each other and willingly participated. Both understood this and accepted his role when the challenge came his way. Robert would reciprocate later.

With a slight nod of confirmation, Robert simply said, "Tuesday." They both knew that they would meet at Our Daily Bread, a small restaurant on King Street, at 11:45, just before the lunch crowd arrived. This crowd included university faculty and students from ASU and tourists who had just finished their first round of shopping at Mast General Store and some of the antique stores on and about King Street. At Our Daily Bread, the two men could talk and share a meal.

Emily did not comment but noticed an unusual, albeit unidentifiable, discomfort in the communication between the two men. The line of the last congregants to exit the church, including the Sluter sisters, was pressing up behind them. It symbolized that the interaction at the door was expected to be brief. It was programmed church communication: 'How are you?' 'I am well. And you?' 'Great. Really blessed.' Often the communication was as predictable as it was hollow, meaningless, and often tinged with half-truths. Occasionally, the compliment, 'Great message today, Pastor. Great message,' was heard. There was a social understanding that this was not the time to get into more detail.

Taking a step ahead, Robert sent his hand behind him, indicating to Emily to take hold. Instinctively, she did. They walked hand-in-hand more often than most couples. Others admired them. While wives would privately scold their husbands to be more like the Forsythes, in truth, neither the husbands nor the wives made the necessary attempts to accomplish this. On the walkway to the parking lot, Emily squeezed his hand just a little more tightly, providing a silent communication that he

was both walking too fast and that she was with him throughout whatever he was struggling. Without a word, he slowed his pace and felt the
assurance of their partnership, but this time, it was different. He could
not share the depth of his concerns with her—not because it was private,
but because it was forbidden.

The line of congregants greeting the Pastor dwindled. Alex noted
the curious absence of the visitor. *Where did he go? In the sanctuary?
Gone?* So often, visitors would like to meet the pastor on their first occasion at a church. More truthfully, they did not want to meet the pastor as
much as they wanted to become known by him. If they remained at the
church, they wanted him to remember them personally. It was an all-too-
common egocentric maneuver.

Alex wondered if the visitor were still in his seat and peeked back
inside the sanctuary. It was empty, apart from the worship team members
still packing up their instruments and chatting about music. There was a
tug on his sleeve. "Mom wants us to go, Dad," nine-year-old Bella stated
emphatically. Jenny always wanted to get out quickly after the morning
service. Whether they were all going out to lunch or preparations needed
to be made for evening ministries, Sunday was far from a day of rest. It
was hectic, and, most often, within minutes after the service, the church
was almost empty with everyone else being like-minded—not to mention the hustle to see the kickoff. Occasionally, a parishioner would want
some of the Pastor's time. When this occurred, Jenny would wait quietly,
knowing that this was a valuable time for the congregants, as most people
worked during the week and had limited access to her pastor-husband.
Monday was the day off and usually just about the only full day off for
the church staff.

Jenny and Jordan were only feet behind Bella. Jenny had sent Bella
as a scout to forward a message. Turning toward Jenny, Alex asked, "Did
you see the visitor sitting right here in the back?"

"No."

"He was a well-dressed Black man."

"A student?"

"No. Mid-fifty-ish. Ah, maybe older." *Not sure. Too far away, in the
last row.*

"No, I didn't see anyone. Did you meet him?"

"I didn't get a chance. He just ducked out. He must have used the
side door."

"Maybe he will come back."

"I hope so." *It would be nice to have more diversity.*

The Forsythe's car ride had a sense of unresolved tension. Grace was in the back seat, but Abigail had gone off with her friends who would catch lunch somewhere then go back later to church for ministries geared toward high school and college students. The Forsythes would grab lunch somewhere, but there were always moments of indecision: Cracker Barrel, Troy's, Pedalin' Pig, among many others. The Boone and Blowing Rock area had plenty of eateries. The decision was usually based more on the restaurant's availability of seating rather than the food options. Any restaurant would suffice, and each person had their menu preference at the various establishments. Often, they would go to lunch with another family. However, this time, Robert had been too preoccupied with his secretive concerns to interact with other families.

Red Onion was their choice this time. Upon seating, Grace was the first to cut the ice. "Dad, what's wrong? What was wrong with the sermon?"

"What do you mean?" *No breaks today. Brought this on myself.*

"You seemed upset while Pastor Spencer was speaking."

"Was I?" *She knows.*

"You know you were," interjected Emily.

"It's just something I came across at work." *Tag teamed. This will be tough.*

"About there being only one God?" asked Grace.

"No. Not really. About other things." *Let it go, please. Change the topic, quick.* "What do you want to eat?"

Emily looked at him quizzically, not willing to dismiss the topic so quickly but also not feeling the need to pursue it *at the moment. The sermon was great. All stuff we had heard many times before, but really solid. What's he having trouble with. Just a little too obvious. He's such a great guy. I just wish that he would come to know the Lord.* More time and opportunity would arise after they arrived home. Robert could feel his wife silently interrogating him with her bright hazel eyes. Her chiseled face resembled a woman ten to fifteen years younger. Her shoulder-length red hair, now bearing a few streaks of gray, did not make her look old as much as refined, dignified, and comfortable with her natural aging. She had gained only fifteen pounds or so since her college days but, after pushing herself too hard in any one day, could be seen walking with a noticeable limp in her right leg—the result of decades of running. Robert still very much appreciated her beauty but, at this moment, having something to hide, could not look directly into her eyes. *She'll see right into me.* Emily, too, appreciated Robert. He was still tall, thin, and dark, with a streak of silver flashing through his tidy goatee. He hesitated on growing a fuller beard for fear of how much silver might appear.

The family ate their meal. Emily, very predictably, had the chicken fajita. Robert liked that she ordered it since it was too large for her, and he would always be offered at least a quarter of it to eat there or take home for later. Grace had ordered a hamburger. She was not yet old enough to realize that she could order something a little more expensive since her parents were paying. Robert had the Mauney's Club; it was always more than he could eat.

Grace talked about her girlfriends and school. Tenth graders had so much to discuss. Shows on Netflix and Amazon Prime, music downloads, YouTube videos, Instagram, Snap Chat, TikTok, and much more were available fodder. Suzie was getting braces. Cindy was considering dating Brian. Rocky had a new cellphone. On and on, the trials and tribulations of her friends were recounted. So many of them seemed trivial to the adults, but she was worth listening to. Most noticeably missing were Grace's more personal and intimate concerns about herself. These she was careful to keep private. More so than Robert, Emily knew that Grace was interested in a boy named Tim, but they knew too little about him to be either enthusiastic or concerned.

The Spencers—Jenny, Jordan, Bella, and Alex—had chosen to go for a simpler and quicker lunch at Barbaritos. Sundays were far from a day of rest for either a pastor or a pastor's family. The family of four ordered their meal and sat at a table near the door. Alex always liked to sit at a seat facing oncoming people. This allowed him to greet friends and acquaintances. They could not sneak up to him, and his position would often let him see others before they saw him, providing him time to remember their names and concerns before interacting with them. Everyone knew how important it was for a pastor to see a person and know their name whenever they met. So emotionally frail were some people that, if a pastor forgot their name, they would use that as an occasion to indicate how little the pastor cared and leave the church for another. The family understood his choice of seating and purposely surveyed the table and the room to allow him his requisite arrangement.

While the Spencers were eating, Ralph Wilson and his wife Joyce walked by the table and greeted the family. Ralph ran a technology company, CC Technologies, in Charlotte and another branch somewhere in South America. Although his business seemed to ebb and flow, he always appeared to do very well. If there were significant pressure from his work, no one would ever know. He was always upbeat and personable.

Ralph was on the shorter side if among NBA players but almost freakishly tall in respect to all others. Knowing that his six-foot-seven-inch frame made him stand out in public, he admitted to only six-foot-five inches when asked. For such a tall man to be under two hundred pounds was even more remarkable; he was rail thin. His clean-shaven head often sported a hat that matched his outfit. When in the mountains, he frequently wore a cowboy hat, boots, jeans, and a stylistically matched large belt buckle adorned with a bronco or bull. At CCTech, he wore business suits. On occasional Fridays at CCTech, would he mix the two and wear a suit with a bolo and boots.

CC Technologies was little more than a coding farm. Depending on the workload generated from client contracts, the employees went from the dozens to the hundreds. CCTech was recognized as 'programmers for hire.' Various companies would contract with CCTech for projects to be coded and tested. Occasionally, a company would want a project from another coding farm to be inspected for efficiency and security. CCTech had specialists in business, finances, testing, robotics, military, and numerous other applications.

By external perception, CCTech was housed in an old unassuming multi-floor warehouse building. Inside, however, the building was wonderfully refurbished. The renovation had retained the look and feel of the old building, including some brick walls and exposed plumbing. Still, it had wholly modernized the interior to be a bright and welcoming work environment. Many offices were constructed with glass walls to allow visibility and encourage collegiality and collaboration, attempting to avoid a closed-in feeling. The glass walls allowed light from the enormous windows in exterior offices to filter into more central areas of the building. Several inner conference rooms and a few personal offices—depending on the nature of the professional responsibilities of the occupant—had glass walls which, upon the flip of a switch, became frosty and translucent to keep meetings and materials secretive. For the most part, each floor or wing of the building was dedicated to one type of application. For some reason, it always seemed like the robotics people were having more fun than all others.

The building was too large for the usual number of employees. Each had their own office, and there were conference rooms aplenty for groups to collaborate. When the number of employees swelled, there was still adequate room so that employees never felt on top of each other. They had breathing room and, more importantly, they had thinking room. Ralph Wilson would instead give up on contracts than sardine his workers into uncomfortable working conditions.

Joyce seemed to know very little about Ralph's company and work. While he made a generous salary, she lived a humble life that was commensurate with a wife of someone making one-eighth as much. At five-foot-two-inches, Joyce was almost unnoticed when she was with her husband. As much as Ralph dressed up, Joyce dressed down. She was always comfortable in, at most, a simple dress, or more often, jeans and a casual blouse. Still shy as an adult, she never wished to bring attention to herself. She was a behind-the-scenes person. Ralph knew that he would never have accomplished as much in life without her. She knew it too but never mentioned it.

The Wilson's wintered in Charlotte and summered in Boone. However, even during their Charlotte season, they would make frequent trips north. This was early September, and they had not yet made their move off the mountain to the warmer hills of Charlotte.

It was probably too well known in the church that the Wilsons were big givers supporting the church. In addition to supporting the church's general fund, Joyce often spearheaded everything from small renovation projects to the support for drilling water wells in third-world countries. Although a profoundly spiritual man, Ralph had never desired to serve as an elder or deacon. His service was through giving. He believed that if he were also an elder, people would see him as having too much power in the church.

"How are you doing, Alex?" asked Ralph. "And Jenny and ah . . . ?" There was a slight hesitation which Joyce immediately punctuated with, "Jordan and Bella." Ralph looked at eleven-year-old Jordan and shrugged, half apologetically. Jordan shrugged back as if to say, 'It's okay, that's how older folks treat kids.' Jordan knew how to play the game of the pastor's kid.

"We are well," responded Alex, fully realizing that to be the appropriate response. "How's the business going?" *Usually a safe question.*

"Busier than ever, but all good."

"That's a good problem to have."

"Better than the alternative. Well, we don't want to interrupt your meal. You guys have a great day." The Wilsons disappeared around the corner.

Waiting to ensure that the Wilsons were out of earshot, Emily said, "I heard that his company has some gigantic government contract. Something top secret."

"If it's top secret, then how do you know?"

"What it is, is top secret. That it is, is not," Jenny responded.

"Well, whatever it is, he is always very tightlipped about everything his company does," stated Alex.

Alex and Jenny purposely did not mention anything about Ralph's finances in front of the children.

Chapter 5

"Mr. Wilson, we had a breach." A tall, lanky man in his early thirties entered the large reception area outside of Ralph Wilson's office.

Ben Tusk always moved and walked quickly. It was said that he moved so fast and continually that fat never had time to grab hold of him. Everything was done quickly. On rare occasions, his haste led to mistakes—but only rarely—and these were acceptable due to his expeditious and copious accomplishments.

Upon seeing Ralph Wilson's office door open, Ben pealed his announcement. Ralph had insufficient time to react, let alone process the statement, and Ben unceremoniously entered his office and repeated his information. Ralph stood up from his desk and began a barrage of questions trying to cover the entirety of who, what, when, where, how, and why, but the answer to nearly every question was unsatisfactory.

Deduced from Ralph's staccato inquiry and Ben's efficient, mostly monosyllabic responses was that someone transferring data from one drive to a new Z-drive temporarily declassified some files for ease of copying. Simultaneously, however, someone was transferring a batch of unclassified files from the new Z-drive to their work folder. The classified files were inadvertently grabbed up in the transfer process during the few seconds they were declassified.

The system always made users jump through hoops of security verification for the movement of any classified files—online forms listing each file to be transferred and describing why it had to be transferred, paperwork requiring approval by many levels of bureaucracy. It was an onerous task. Quite illegal and improper, it was easier to declassify files in bulk, transfer them, and then reclassify them in bulk. Unfortunately, from the time that the files were copied to the new drive until they were reset as classified, they were left open for all to see. It was assumed that no one would notice this file transfer activity before the reclassification could be completed. The entire process usually took less than thirty seconds by someone experienced who knew precisely what they were doing—far less time than the hours of completing the forms for permission would take.

Classified files were distinguished as 'classified,' 'secret,' 'top secret,' and 'above top secret.' The latter were denoted with the prefix 'ATS.' Indeed, so patrolled were these files that, usually only those with the equivalent clearance knew what ATS files were. Only a few subjects ever had such classifications: China, Russia, the Middle East, Weaponry, and such—topics of grave national security. On rare occasions, files that had little impact on national security but were deemed necessary to conceal inappropriate or embarrassing activity of high-ranking politicians were given such classification. There were innumerable files labeled as ATS from the Jeffery Epstein case, which placed many prominent people in compromising positions. Even under the most aggressive Freedom of Information Act requests, these would never see the light of day. The argument was that if this information were released, influential people could be blackmailed, affecting national security.

"So, Ben," said Ralph, "do we know where the files went?"

"Not yet, sir. We were monitoring activity on the Z-drive. We only know that the files came in declassified, went out declassified, and then were reclassified after getting on the Z-drive. We do not yet know where they went. We do not know who copied them. But we are working on that."

"Is the problem resolved? I mean, are the files reclassified?" *We need to get this under control at once.*

"Well, yes, Sir. The files are reclassified. Only those with ATS clearance can access them, and, even for them, if they do not have the decryption key, they can only see fragments."

"Who else knows?" *I hope no one. Easier to manage. I'll have to inform Colonel Poriss, but I need to know as much as possible first.*

"Of course, the person who was transferring the files to the Z-drive knows. We will know who that was soon. There is the possibility that they do not yet know that they circumvented the correct procedures. Otherwise, only Bobby, in IT, who monitored the drive activity, you and me, and, of course, the person who received the files. However, it still remains the possibility that they don't even know that they pulled down classified files. It was a bulk copy of files. It would be unusual to notice a small directory named SETL among all the others."

"SETL?"

"Yes, Sir."

A quick shudder went down Ralph's spine. While he made it a personal practice never to swear or curse, he came as close to a profane utterance as ever he would. "Do you know what those files are?" Ralph asked Ben, whom he knew also had among the highest clearances.

"No, Sir."

"Be glad you don't. You wouldn't be able to sleep at night," warned Ralph. Even Ralph knew very little. Although he had himself earned among the highest clearances, he only suspected what was precisely in those files. He had heard rumors. He did not have access to the decryption keys. Even among those who had ATS clearance, only a tiny fraction of those had access to SETL files, and even a smaller number possessed the decryption keys. *No one would ever be able to sleep at night.*

"Do our suited brothers know of the breach?" asked Ralph. Everyone knew that the 'suited brothers' or 'suits' meant the government agents both overtly and covertly among them.

"No, Sir. They won't know until the end of the month technical audit."

"No," interrupted Ralph, "They must know soon, as soon as possible. I want to know as much as possible before I inform them. All the information, if possible. How soon can we know everything?"

"Well, Sir," pondered Ben, "it depends how we investigate. An audit will tell us everything. However, anything above a Level-One Audit will raise red flags. Everyone would know what is happening, or at least that we are probably investigating a breach. If we go with an L-O-A, we will know everyone who transferred any files. That would probably give us the information we need."

"So," recapped Ralph more for himself than for Ben, raising his index finger, "we know that someone, let's say Person A, transferred some ATS files from one drive to the Z-drive." Ralph raised another finger. "To do this without authorization, they had to declassify the files, at least temporarily. This is illegal." Ralph raised a third finger. "However, we don't know if they declassified the files in order to do something nefarious with the files or simply for the ease of transferring. Nevertheless, we need to know who did this immediately." Ralph added another finger to the tally. "Someone, could be Person A or Person B, copied the ATS files to their machine over our intranet." He included his thumb to the count. "These people may or may not be working together." He added a finger from the other hand. "Person B may not yet even know that these files were transferred." Another finger was raised. "The files were then reclassified. Was that from Person A, Person B, or even a Person C?"

"Yes, Sir. All those questions and more." interrupted Ben. "Just give us a day to do a Level-One Audit, and I believe that all these questions will be answered."

"We can't wait." Stated Ralph. We need to get on this NOW."

"Yes, Sir." Ben continued, hoping that he was not about to overstep his authority. "I, I, I already got it started. I didn't think you would want to wait."

"Excellent," assured Ralph. "Great job, Ben."

"Thank you, Sir. We should have almost all of that information by early morning. I even have it ready to immediately lock down the facilities. No one in or out during the audit."

"No, Ben," interjected Ralph. "We don't want people involved to know that we suspect anything until we know who was involved." *Also, I don't want the suits to know anything until we know everything. If this is all accidental, I want to know. If this is criminal, I want to know.* "So, they don't know that among the files transferred were the SETL files," Ralph commented rhetorically.

"Ah, we don't know that yet, Sir." Ben wished to be precisely correct regarding what was already known and what was not yet known.

Redirecting his comments to Ben, Ralph said, "Okay, let me handle informing the suits." *Hopefully, I can.*

"Yes, Sir." With that, Ben disappeared out the office door. Unfortunately, that left Ralph, the owner and CEO, alone to strategize how to best inform the government agents. While he knew who some of the suits were, he was certain that he did not know all of them. Through the sparse grapevine of other executives of companies with top-secret contracts, he heard that suits infiltrated the company a good year or two before a company ever earned such a governmental contract. His knowledge of the data transfer before the suits gave CCTech time to covertly investigate for problematic personnel and processes before running up against the inevitable barrage of questions from the government inquisitors.

Ralph contemplated the least problematic way to inform the governmental agents; it had to be done, but how and when was slightly more at his discretion. It did not matter what was to be discovered. There was going to be hell to pay. Ralph hoped that, if he quickly had the answers, he could mitigate negative ramifications to the CCTech. He did not wish CCTech to be seen as a security risk and possibly lose lucrative government contracts. Colonel Poriss was the higher-up who would eventually be informed and bring the information to the Pentagon. Ralph considered if he should directly contact Colonel Poriss or contact Marcia Commander as an intermediary. In either case, communication with one of them did not need to happen until he had more answers—which would preliminarily come in just hours. It was Friday, mid-afternoon; he would know something, possibly everything, by early morning.

A few minutes before midnight, Ralph's cellphone rang. He was at his desk in his home office working—or more so, worrying about work. There was no need even to try to sleep until events were more resolved. The caller ID indicated that it was Ben Tusk.

"Hey, Ben. What did you find?"

"Well, Sir," replied Ben, "we have almost everything figured out. We know who copied the files to the Z-drive and how and we know . . . " The line went dead.

"Ben? . . . Ben?" The call dropped. *Bad cell connection? Was he traveling? He'll call back. Or I will.* Minutes passed. Ralph tried to call back. No answer. Ralph tried again. An automated answer came from the phone provider that the number dialed was no longer in service. *This is not good.*

The early hours led to a Saturday and then a Sunday of silence—an ominous silence indicating that Ralph was cut out of the loop of secrets than a lack of information regarding the investigation. Repeatedly, Ralph attempted to call Ben on his cellphone, and each time he encountered the same system response. He also called others in whom Ben would have confided and used in the investigation. These contacts led to cryptic, non-informative communications. *I've been cut out of the loop. Purposely. Suits. Someone has taken this to the suits. Ben?* While Ralph had the authority to go to CCTech at any time, he wrestled with what would be best. *If I go in, particularly if the suits have taken over, that will set off more alarm bells. Plus, the audit has already begun and may be over. If suits wanted me to know the results, they would have told me. Expect some kinda mess on Monday.*

Chapter 6

B REAKING a long monologue about friends and school at Red Onion, Grace returned to her former line of inquiry. "Dad, in the sermon, Pastor Spencer read, 'even if there are so-called gods in heaven or on earth.' Are there other gods?"

Robert was caught off guard and felt immediately and impossibly cornered. He well knew the correct Sunday School answer, but he was wrestling with his own concerns. He looked over at Emily. She furrowed her brow and gave him a look that communicated that he better get this correct for the sake of his daughter and Emily's curiosity regarding his position—particularly after his affect during Alex's sermon. *Better get this right. Sunday school answer.* Robert palpably felt the pressure and was willing to lie to protect his daughter and marriage. He could always tell Emily the truth later.

Robert was in a strange position. While he regularly attended Sunday School and Sunday services out of his agreement with his wife, he did not agree with some essential tenets of the faith. Since being more interested than he anticipated in a college philosophy class, he was very studious and enjoyed working through philosophic inquiries. He found church a valuable incubator of ideas to debate and exercise his mind. Far more deeply than most would suspect, Robert listened intently to opinions and variants of positions. Without orally stating any opposition, as an intellectual exercise, he often pit one person's opinion against another's.

After a decade of attending church, he now found most of his closest friends among the congregation. His friends in church were quite heterogeneous, including doctors, lawyers, small business owners, and laborers. They recognized he did not share all their beliefs, but many of the men cared for him, and he reciprocated.

"Paul was saying that there is only one God," Robert said, pointing one finger to the sky for emphasis. "He was arguing that, even if there were more gods, it doesn't matter; for us, there is only ONE God. He is not saying that there are other gods. He is saying that if there are, it doesn't matter for us. *I better say this right. Now, how did Alex say this?* God has given us the plan through which we can be saved." Robert glanced toward his wife for a nod of confirmation of the correctness of his statement. She provided the acknowledgment for which he hoped. While Robert had not committed to the Christian faith, he was a solid student and knew most answers. "Paul was a philosopher. He liked looking at hypothetical scenarios to show the strength and importance of his position." *I hope that worked. Subject over?*

"So, Paul is not saying that there are other gods, but our God is supreme," Emily interjected. "He is saying that EVEN IF there were other gods, ours is supreme."

"I get it," said Grace, and, as fluidly as any faucet of words, she returned to her recitation of issues with friends and acquaintances. Robert was glad that the situation was diffused, but it forced him again to be distracted by the problems which he alone knew. *They can't know. Not yet. I need to work through this. I need time to process, time alone.* As the meal continued, Robert silently stared into space. He answered questions posed to him. But his answers were clipped, and he provided little more than the essential response. He did not seem tired or in an ill mood. Instead, his thoughts were preoccupied. Emily noticed. There was a time and a place to address this, and she knew that Sunday lunch at the Red Onion was not it.

Grace went back to her monologue about friends, consistent with the life of a fifteen-year-old. Once, months ago, in the middle of one of Grace's self-centered speeches, Robert out loud said to Emily, "Zing." Grace didn't skip a beat and went on with her oration. A few minutes later, still within Grace's less than tantalizing soliloquy, Robert again said, "Zing." This caught Grace's attention but not sufficiently to cause even the slightest pause. She went on so fervently that it was difficult to see when and if she ever took a breath. After another few minutes, Robert again said, "Zing," but a little more emphatically, this time including his index finger pointed upward and rotating.

"Okay," snapped Grace, fully aware that something was going on. "What does 'zing' mean?

Emily chuckled a little. Without having previously discussed this with Robert, she knew exactly what 'zing' meant.

"No, I'm serious. What does 'zing' mean?"

Robert chuckled and responded. "I'm fine. Work is going great. I met a new client. My friend Rick is getting married." He turned his attention to his wife. "Honey, how was your week? Did you get to see . . . ?"

"Cut it out," Grace interrupted. "What does 'zing' mean?"

Robert, although attempting to take a more serious tone, continued chuckling. "Zing is the sound of the universe revolving around Grace. You have gone fifteen minutes barely taking a breath, only talking about yourself, not even asking us one question about how we are doing."

Needless to say, 'zing' was not one of Grace's favorite words, but it was a valuable life lesson. Now and then, when Grace talked about herself too much, and at the minimization of everyone else, Robert or Emily would simply say "Zzz," and that would snap Grace back to a consciousness of the importance of others in the room. Occasionally in a public situation, in a loving parental manner, and to not embarrass Grace openly, Robert or Emily would whisper "Zzz" into her ear to keep her from possibly humiliating herself through self-centeredness.

Today, Emily and Robert let Grace talk freeform, in a never-ending stream-of-consciousness. Robert had other things on his mind. Allowing Grace to talk allowed him to pay attention to her with one-third of his mind and work on different problems with the other two-thirds. Emily occasionally listened to Grace to glean a nugget of spy-worthy information regarding Grace, her life, and the lives of her friends. With the recollection of an elephant, Emily often remembered tidbits from Grace's orations which Grace herself did not recognize that she had ever spoken.

After their meal, the Forsythes returned to their home on the outskirts of Boone. Upon the death of his grandparents—both within the same year—while Robert was a Sophomore in college, he found himself the beneficiary of their three-bedroom farmhouse and a few acres of land. It had previously been part of a large farm, primarily raising Black Angus cattle. After the sale of most of the acreage a decade before, a respectable tract remained. The house needed considerable renovation, but, Robert thought, *the price is right.*

Robert's father and mother, Todd and Sally, considered renovating the old homestead to be an excellent investment. Todd said that he was willing to invest $20,000 toward materials for renovation if Robert was willing to partner with him in the sweat equity. The agreement was: if Robert ever did sell the home, he would reimburse his father or mother the costs of the materials.

Whenever possible, after school, on weekends, and during school breaks, the two worked together to fix up the old home. "It had solid bones," they often said. In the mountain coolness and moderate humidity of Boone, this house had very little rotting and, to their surprise, had almost no termite damage.

The floorplan was very slightly altered, with the minor expansion of the kitchen. Since $20,000 certainly wasn't much, Todd and Robert learned numerous skills needed for the renovation: plumbing, electrical, wallboard, painting, and many other crafts associated with the work.

The work continued at every mutually spared moment. An unspoken agreement was that Todd would not help with the work unless Robert were there as well. Todd recognized all aspects of the renovation as training for his son. He involved him in every financial decision regarding materials and work. Both oversaw the $20,000 budget. When Todd invested another $10,000 out of his well-funded retirement into the renovation, Sally was never told. Todd figured that his son would eventually inherit everything anyway, so another $10,000 would not matter. Robert knew and was appreciative, but no mention was ever made outside of the two. The funds were sufficient to add an unfurnished office, which doubled as a game and music room, in the basement.

Upon completing his senior year at AppState, Robert's house renovation was completed. He immediately began his first real job at an insurance firm in town. While the pay was low, his living expenses were manageable without a mortgage.

The year after his graduation was a tumultuous year. In May, Robert graduated and started his job at the insurance firm. In June, he attended his friend's wedding and met his wife-to-be. By August, he and his girlfriend were deeply committed. Both knew how unusual this was for their generation and saw their full-speed romance as a sign of a promising future. Unfortunately, Todd and Sally died in a car wreck before Christmas, traveling on 321 past Blowing Rock, going down Lenoir Mountain to visit an ailing friend. While the roads were icier than they had anticipated, and they would not usually have been out apart from feeling the need to minister to their friend, it was not overly problematic for the locals accustomed to mountain driving. Sadly, a twenty-something from the University of North Carolina in Charlotte was visiting friends in Blowing Rock. She was unfamiliar with the mountain weather, the road conditions, and the roads. She was driving far too fast for the weather conditions on tires designed for dry weather. She lost control, panicked, overcorrected, and slid sideways into the left-hand lane. Her right-side tires hit a dry spot, caught solid traction, and catapulted the car into a roll inescapably in front of Todd. There was no opportunity for defensive avoidance. The seconds flashed in slow motion before everyone's eyes with full recognition of the inevitability. On the car's second revolution, the two vehicles fatally collided.

Robert was glad that his fiancé could get to know his parents before their death. While it had not been enough time for Sally, Emily, and Todd to become very close, Emily greatly appreciated the time she had gotten to know them. She was also glad that she could be there for Robert through his season of mourning. Within a few years, Robert had lost his grandparents and parents. Emily would now be his only family. He married her the following May. Fortunately, Emily was still accompanied by her parents, grandparents, two sisters, and a brother. She was close to all of them, and so was he. They were his new family, and they readily adopted him.

Performing his responsibilities as the only child, Robert worked through all the legal documents regarding his parents' estate. However, he was to inherit everything with the proviso that he had no access to any cash from their accounts until he was thirty years old. He decided to continue living in his grandparents' renovated house and make his parents' house into a student rental until he could make more permanent decisions. He felt fortunate that he and his dad had spent considerable time renovating the house and getting closer to each other.

While Emily was sad about Robert's losses, she greatly appreciated that they would not be burdened by a mortgage or rent. The rental income from Robert's parents' house would be significant since that home had long before been paid off. Indeed, they were a young couple with two homes, no mortgage, and rental income from one. This Emily saw as a great blessing. Robert recognized it as hauntingly fortuitous. There were many memories in the two homes, and almost everyone was very positive. To demonstrate to his wife that he recognized the worth of both houses to their early marriage and that each home had its specific value, purpose, and memories regarding his upbringing, Robert insisted that he carry his wife over the threshold of each home. Emily saw this as a highly romantic gesture.

Robert immediately went into the living room and sat on the couch. *Need some quiet.* During the workweek, he might work in his basement office, but, on the weekends, he tried to stay upstairs to be more a part of the family. He often enjoyed the movement about the house and the occasional two-sentence communications with his wife or daughters as they passed by. His mind was split between watching his Carolina Panthers play and choreographing his upcoming weekly work schedules. He had been a Panthers fan since they began to play in the league in 1995. He had seen some bad years, some good years, and even some great years. He remained a Panthers fan because it was his local team.

Each Sunday, it took hours for him to plan for the weeks ahead—a month out if possible. Robert was perennially busy. He owned a web development company, WebMark, which provided a sufficient, albeit modest, income, demanded an inordinate investment in time. Apart from his income, Robert prized two things his career brought him: mainly that he could help others with employment and that, with his flexible schedule, he would meet many people and spend time with friends and acquaintances. He probably undervalued the fact that he knew so many local and statewide businesspeople and that his business gave him broad and ready access to so many social networking platforms. He had developed a sophisticated understanding and ability to use these platforms. In moments, with just a few keystrokes, he could disperse advertising and information around the world.

It could be said that there were some similarities between Robert's website and advertising company and Ralph Wilson's significant corporation. Both employed people who could code in various forms. However, Robert's people had more expertise in HTML and Ralph's people in countless programming platforms down to assembler language, which communicated directly to each chip in the computer. The comparisons were more like an ant and an elephant. If so inclined, Ralph's CCTech could easily take over Robert's WebMark, but Ralph had no intention of doing so. He had plenty of business. His clients, often corporations and government, had far more resources to pay CCTech.

Working on his computer with one hand, Robert petted the family Goldendoodle, Foxtrot, with the other. The large, cream-colored dog was friendly and ever desirous of being petted. He was often the center of attention. Robert was not a dog person. Indeed, Robert was not a pet person at all. While he tolerated them, took care of them, and never abused them, he had very little feeling for them one way or another. Robert petted Foxtrot, not because he desired to, but because he felt that Foxtrot needed it. Since Foxtrot was Grace's dog, Robert was not 'expected' to do anything for him. Nevertheless, since Robert got up well before the others, the dog would be let out and fed by him, but he refrained from walking Foxtrot without either his wife or daughter accompanying him.

Today, Robert had much to consider. *Just too coincidental. How'd he know? That sermon? Now? This week? He'd not been looking at those chapters recently. Beyond freaky. And no way Emily's gonna leave me alone on this. Just need time to figure things out.*

Chapter 7

U PON arriving at his office on Monday morning, Christie McAlister, Ralph's administrative assistant, gave him an ominous look. She had been working for him for almost ten years. She knew the ins and outs of the business, his schedule, and his life. Christie spent more time with him every week than did Joyce, his wife. Fortunately, Joyce appreciated that Ralph was cared for at work. Christie made sure that Ralph ate, drank, and rested. None of these would he do if he was not prompted. With complete respectfulness, Ralph often called Christie his RH. Both knew that meant his 'right hand' at work. When Christie answered Joyce's phone call, Joyce would say, "Hey, RH. What's going on?"

Christie was loyal to both Ralph and CCTech. She knew when he needed a heads-up. She nodded toward his office door to warn him that someone was inside. The glass wall between Ralph and Christie's office was already switched to frosted and translucent by whoever was within. He expected a meeting to occur upon his morning arrival—this morning was preceded by three unslept nights. She tried to mouth the name 'Colonel Poriss' with her nod, but Ralph could not read her lips. He wanted to go closer to her to understand better, but he did not have the opportunity. Yet a full three yards from his office door, and a call came from inside.

"Come on in, Ralph." It was the voice of Colonel Poriss, inviting the entrance into Ralph's office as if the Colonel had taken possession of it. Marcia Commander, 'The Commander,' was at his side. "We have a problem."

"Good morning, Colonel," replied Ralph, knowing that the Colonel never bothered with such formalities and always got directly to the point. *As if I don't know what this is about.* Ralph towered over the Colonel's nearly average height of five-foot-eight inches. Whenever possible, Ralph would stand close to the Colonel to use his height to mitigate the Colonel's authority regarding military and classified issues.

"We had a breach on Friday," announced the Colonel.

Ralph was both experienced and wily enough not to respond too quickly. He knew that if he admitted that he knew, he would be questioned why he did not report it. Simultaneously, he knew that if he denied knowledge of it, they would challenge his leadership and competence for the position. Silence might be his best weapon—or defense. Plus, he did not know if Ben, who had a couple of days before informed him of the breach, was a suit and had forwarded the information to The Commander.

This was a game of cat-and-mouse, or, more precisely, monkey-in-the-middle with Marcia Commander in the middle. The Colonel was fully aware that Ralph knew what was going on. Ralph expected the same from the Colonel. Their relationship may have been more adversarial in many high-security situations, but each had come to respect the other and recognize that each held CCTech and government security paramount. However, the Colonel was less trusting of The Commander. Two men knew that a game had to be played before her.

Ralph stood tall with his hands behind his back. He portrayed strength and calm authority. He knew this to be necessary. Although the Colonel held absolute authority and could instantly shut down all government contracts, he was a gracious man and only wielded his clout when necessary. Collaboration was always his preference. Authority was employed only when collaboration failed. Ralph knew this well and was thankful that he and the Colonel had so often collaborated in discussions in the past few years.

However, before The Commander, the game was different. She was more erratic and would quickly use her authority to steer the ship where she wished it to go. She would gladly invite others of higher authority into the situation simply to be seen as being in charge.

Marcia Commander had a long history of friendlessness. Tina was her best friend up through eighth grade. Tina's family moved away, and in time the relationship dissolved. In tenth grade, Danny, Marcia's boyfriend, was killed in an unfortunate hunting accident in the fall of their junior year. The following spring, Marcia's mother left home. Marcia and her younger sister were left alone with a father who had deeper relationships at the local bar than at home. Through high school and college, Marcia visited with her mother and new stepfather only once or twice per year. She then ended all contact when her stepfather made some questionable advances. Relationships, Marcia learned, required a great deal of effort and often led to pain. *The more you care, the more you get hurt. So much easier to go it alone. No one will hold me back.* She never married.

Since high school, the self-described perfectionist had no meaningful relationships. As a solitary singleton, she sought to develop her career. Few people invested much in her since they quickly recognized no reciprocation. She was left as alone as she wanted to be and eschewed the notion of the value of a confidant. While pained by the thought of being an Eleanor Rigby, she self-soothed with the idea that she was the master of her destiny. Sadly, she was blind to her self-imposed enslavement to her career and determination to succeed.

The game continued. In a well-choreographed performance, the Colonel acted more harshly than usual before The Commander. He knew that Ralph would collaborate to determine what had happened and what must be done. However, having far more at stake, the game was more tenuous for Ralph, who knew that if he ever crossed the Colonel, CCTech could be destroyed in a moment. Ralph's confident thespian recital masked a trepidation of the always ominous potential for CCTech to be closed down, lose its government contracts, and have to let go hundreds of excellent employees. One misstep from Ralph and CCTech could quickly revert to an old, dilapidated, and empty warehouse.

"Tech has algorithms which automatically monitor any new drives added to the system. On Friday, we saw classified files get declassified and copied to the new Z-drive," the Colonel reported. Ralph stood, seemingly unphased by the previously known information. He could not allow The Commander to recognize his foreknowledge. *Silence,* he repeated to himself. *Just look calm.*

"That person has been terminated from the firm and all clearances permanently rescinded," The Commander added.

Ralph knew how serious this was to the fired person and his family. Not only had the person lost his income, but he had also lost his clearances to do classified governmental work. At the very least, this would be devastating to any future position he might apply for or hold. Some in his situation had been so dejected, so despondent, that they felt no other option but to end their own life. If they could be captured in the hours of greatest peril by a loved one and encouraged that there was life after that job, they could be saved. Others could maintain a strong facade for weeks, months, or even years, but the loss occasionally was too great.

Ralph still had much to learn about how and why the person had declassified the files for transfer. Was this person part of a conspiracy of just trying to cut corners for expediency? Both were malfeasances of the highest degree punishable minimally by termination and maximally by prison. Nevertheless, Ralph wished to know the perpetrator's rationale and intent. Suppose the act was one more of poor judgment than criminality. In that case, Ralph could surreptitiously reach out to the family to encourage and support, if not even help find the person a non-security-related position in another firm—possibly even one of his competitors. However, if the act were criminal, Ralph would toe the line and willingly seek prosecution. Ralph believed that he ran an excellent company that provided excellent pay with a supportive and encouraging working environment. Ralph recognized only two unpardonable sins among his employees: lying to Ralph or stealing from CCTech.

"For the moments that the files were declassified on the Z-drive," continued the Colonel, "they were simultaneously copied by someone to another system drive. The computer to which the files were transferred will be known soon—possibly even within minutes." With that, Ralph felt slightly more empowered. He realized that the Colonel and The Commander were nearly at the end of what they knew. Ralph was pleased that he knew almost as much as they did, even after two days.

"When this activity was flagged, Ben Tusk initiated a Level-One Technical Audit," dispassionately continued The Commander.

"Excellent man, that Tusk is," added Ralph. *Ben could still be a suit. Need them to think that I have no clue either way.* While a positive statement about any person was usually dismissed as unheard by The Commander, she looked at Ralph with eyes and a snarl which denoted that Tusk was not to be discussed or inquired about. Whatever 'they' had done to Tusk would not be addressed at this time. Ralph would need to wait. *What did they do with him? He did the right thing with the LTA. Re they trying to keep us apart?*

"When I was informed late Friday evening, I ordered a Level-Three Audit." This last claim came with a more pompous air, connoting that she alone—apart from Colonel Poriss—had the immediate and undeniable authority to call for a Level-Three Audit while bypassing Level-Two.

Ralph knew the extensiveness of a Level-Three Audit. A neophyte may have naively interpreted such as a company-wide investigation of computer use down to every keystroke performed on any computer on the system since the last technical audit. No, it was far more. Within the entire CCTech intranet, every byte and bit of code was scrupulously examined, including every bit of data passed among all the computers, whether the user knew this had happened or not. Codes and subcodes were investigated and reinvestigated for bots and trojan horses, even if having possibly infiltrated the system years ago.

The internal computer system was connected to the internet only through a few highly isolated and guarded terminals used by operators with need-only clearances. When manned, these were often utilized by two simultaneous, peer-checking operators. These terminals contained an exceptional amount of highly sophisticated security to block any external attempts by hackers. Another minimal number of computers on the system had any ports to attach a USB or other type of drive. Nevertheless, the security system was only as robust as those entrusted with correctly doing their work. If some internal person with a high-security clearance wished to bypass security protocols, they could—but only at their possible later expense.

The Commander's claim that she instituted a Level-Three Audit without informing Ralph evidenced the actual power that she wielded. Ralph's previous confidence in pre-owning Marcia Commander's information was quickly waning. He knew that many innocent employees could be quickly caught up in a Level-Three. They could be accused of data breaches and misuses without doing anything wrong. The Commander could have people dismissed with no trial, jury, or means of due process, and she would gladly do so to remind others of her authority. Ralph was becoming rapidly concerned for his employees more than anything else. *I need to save everyone I can. She may be more dangerous than any data breach or audit.*

"By tomorrow morning, we will know everything that happened here," continued The Commander. "Things you should already know." This last dig was pointed and purposive. Ralph knew that The Commander had long despised him. He was too civilian for her likes. Although she, too, was a civilian, she acted as a governmental wannabe. She wielded much power. Behind the scenes, she had a say in most new hires, and a very open say about firings. She wanted to be seen as someone to be reconned with. Still, Ralph did not take the bait and remained silent.

Ralph knew that, although the data would be collected from the audit very soon, there remained an extensive data analysis process to interpret all that had transpired on the system. The Level-Three Audit would collect the data, analyze it, and then synthesize the results. This would all be disaggregated into a report which flagged dubious activity. Then the report had to be analyzed by some suits to determine appropriate punitive actions. Once this human element was introduced, the process often slowed significantly. The Commander, however, could circumvent this protraction by her unilateral decision.

The Commander had a long history of government service, including the FBI and CIA—of which she all-too-frequently reminded everyone. It was deliberately out of Ralph's purview to know precisely which of any half-dozen three-letter organizations currently funded her position. In her early 50s, she had worked her way up the ranks and was now well-positioned. She was tough and focused. Her greatest weapon was intimidation and fear born from her position and not her relatively diminutive size.

Realizing that nothing more could be done at that moment, Ralph chose to regain possession of his office. He walked to a position behind his desk and sat in his chair. "Would either of you like a cup of coffee?" he asked, declaring ownership of his office through control over coffee services. His subliminal act accomplished its purpose. The Commander immediately toned down a shade or two and became less aggressive.

"No thanks," simultaneously responded Marcia and the Colonel. Ralph knew that would be their response. He knew that she never drank coffee, and the Colonel rarely ever drank anything outside of at a meal or in his office. Nevertheless, the twofold moves of taking his seat and offering coffee had their hoped-for effects. The Colonel and The Commander began to move toward the door.

"Colonel," continued The Commander, "we may need to inform Colonel Peterson of the breach." With this, Colonel Poriss visibly bristled. He had a long-standing disdain for Colonel Peterson. Peterson had retired from the military decades ago but insisted on retaining the title among military personnel and civilians alike. Additionally, Colonel Peterson was a 'full-bird' Colonel. If both were still in the military, Poriss would outrank Peterson's Lieutenant Colonel. Colonel Poriss knew that Peterson had been passed over for promotion. Moreover, Poriss had long known Peterson as one who bent the rules with liberality to accomplish his goals. Peterson's current civilian position was not well understood by military and government personnel alike, and even less so by civilians and civilian contractors like The Commander. Nonetheless, while all assumed that Peterson had a direct line to the President, the Joint Chiefs, and possibly the NSA and other organizations, all contacts in these directions were situated in plausible deniability.

"Yes, of course," Colonel Poriss stated in an emotionally lukewarm tone. Although he knew it was inevitable at times, he preferred to interface with Peterson as infrequently as possible. In front of Marcia Commander, Colonel Poriss muted any animosity toward Peterson. He knew that she was all too willing to play one against the other to maintain her position of authority inside the walls of CCTech.

All too vividly, Colonel Poriss recalled an argument between the three of them more than a year ago. None doubted that, within the confines of CCTech, Colonel Poriss had ultimate authority. However, before data or people arrived at CCTech, the roles of superiority and submission were far murkier. The Commander focused on personnel issues more than the data itself. Colonel Poriss concentrated on processes and data. Colonel Peterson took charge of whatever he could, whenever he could.

The argument centered on a suit being transferred to CCTech with some top-secret information and who was authorized to vet the entire process. The suit was not yet officially part of CCTech—but soon would be. Was his vetting the responsibility of Colonel Peterson since the suit was not yet on the premises? Since he would soon be working in CCTech, the Commander insisted that she would need to investigate his background. Simultaneously, there were disputes about the data. While it was unclear if either of the Colonels had the authority to look at the very compartmentalized top-secret data, they both had some responsibility regarding its transfer and safekeeping. Thus, the two squabbled over the correct processes for this precise set of data.

Altogether, the argument became heated, with unprofessional language exchanged all around. Colonel Peterson hated when anyone challenged him. Colonel Poriss was frustrated that Peterson—of all people—would put a chink in his armor and cause him to react less than appropriately. The Commander held on tightly to every vestige of authority and power she could hold within the three-way rows.

This had been their more recent argument, but it was memorable to all. In this case, the winner was as ill-defined as was the argument itself. Nevertheless, they all worked together to the best of their abilities. They all recognized that, at any moment, a frustrating situation could arise to rekindle animosity never fully resolved.

The Colonel and The Commander exited Ralph's office, and Ralph reached for his office phone. Taking a breath of relief, he spoke into the phone, "Christie, could you please ask Ben Tusk in here . . . Thank you." In minutes, Ben burst into Ralph's office. His abrupt entrance would have been comical if not so usual.

"L-3-A?" Ralph acknowledged. *Glad he is still around, and they are not keeping us apart for some reason.*

"Yes, Sir, Level-Three."

"Do WE know anything yet?" Ralph knew that he was taking a great gamble. He was still far from certain whether Tusk was a suit. The result could be catastrophic. If the government knew that Ralph was circumventing the Level-Three Audit by getting inside information before the audit was complete, he could lose his security clearance. This would cripple his company by canceling all the government contracts which required clearances. He thought to himself, *I'm not affecting the audit. I simply want to know what we can.*

"Yes, Sir. I was hoping that you would ask," replied Ben. With this, Ralph was more confident that Ben was not a suit. "We are certain that whoever copied the SETL files from the new Z-drive did it accidentally. We have confirmed that the files were transferred during the minutes that they were declassified, and they were copied in bulk with a far greater number of files, all of which were not classified. So, it seems that the SETL files just got caught up in a bulk transfer. We truly believe that the person who copied these files does not even know what they have. The SETL directory was only about one percent of all the files transferred."

"Do we know yet who copied the files from the drive?" Ralph continued.

"No, Sir." Ben looked around the office and outside the door for a moment to ensure that no one was within earshot. Then he reminded himself that hidden microphones could be anywhere. If suits wanted to plant a mic anywhere, they could get away with it. They probably even had personnel among the janitorial staff with access to the entire building. He had no option but to trust that Ralph could protect him. "We know to what wing the data was sent. We are narrowing the search to a particular computer. Then, through access codes, we will be able to tell the exact user at that time." With that information, Ben's non-suit nature was confirmed.

"Well, keep working on it, Ben. Maybe we can get that information before the suits do." Ralph paused for a moment. "By the way," continued Ralph, "who was the employee who declassified and transferred the files and was terminated?"

"That was Troy Billows. He made a mistake—a grave mistake, but he was a great employee. He left here absolutely devastated." Although nothing was ever said between Ralph and Ben, Ben had heard an occasional rumor that Ralph could work the system to get new positions elsewhere for good employees who had to be let go. While far from confident, Ben was hopeful that, if all went awry, Ralph would take care of him as well. "I will keep working on this, Sir. Is there anything else you need?"

"No, Ben. That's all for now. Let's just try to get ahead of this." *Not sure how long that's possible.*

"Yes, Sir."

"Oh, by the way," Ralph interrupted Ben's departure, "do we know if, after the files were copied to the other computer, they were opened or copied again?"

"No, Sir. Not yet. We will be better able to determine that after we know precisely to which computer the files were sent. It will be in the L-3-A report."

"Okay. Thank you."

As Ben exited the office, Ralph approached Christie's desk. "Troy Billows?" he began and was immediately interrupted by Christie's nod of confirmation. Neither could articulate neither the question nor the answer. This protected both. Christie would not tell Ralph that she already had a plan to call Tanisha at Bryan & Company. Tanisha could talk to Tim, the CEO, and see if Troy could be provided a position as soon as possible—at least before depression could set in.

"You're the best," Ralph said to Christie. "A real right hand."

"And maybe even a little better," she teased, hoping to ease the tension. "I'll help him every way I can." She had heard everything said in Ralph's office.

Ralph returned to his desk and chair. He was left to himself to contemplate the potential outcome of events. Hopefully, the files were copied accidentally and had not been copied again or taken outside the company.

Ralph also knew of Colonel Peterson. Moreover, he knew of the Colonel's reputation. He knew full well that calling in Colonel Peterson could lead to some deadly results for someone. There was no end to the Colonel's reputation for prying information out of people. This is far from over. *Wish I knew how this is going to end.*

Ralph sat, numbed and fearful—more so for his employees than for himself. Events were quickly spiraling out of his control. He could deal with Colonel Poriss and The Commander but adding Colonel Peterson to the mix would exponentiate his difficulties.

Chapter 8

E MILY and Robert had been introduced to each other soon after graduating from college. Emily had a degree in Literature from the University of North Carolina at Greensboro. Robert was a dual major in Business and Computer Science from AppState. The two were introduced at a wedding between Emily's friend, Susan, and Robert's friend, Chris.

Robert did not find himself attractive, but women seemed to. They always smiled at him and were comfortable with him. Many felt safe when he was around. Unfortunately, Robert suffered from being self-professedly 'profoundly un-funny.' He had no ability or timing to propose a joke. He called it 'anti-rhythmic jocularity.' His only sense of humor was in the form of sarcasm, his timing of which was impeccable. All too often, a sarcastic line emerged with such instantaneous automaticity that it surprised even him. "Did I *actually* say that?" he would ask aloud. His sarcasm was rarely biting. Instead, he often teased others to their strength rather than their weakness. He would call unusually tall people 'shorty,' connoting a sarcasm that shed light on the all too obvious. He often teasingly wondered if he should write a book on the bane of being un-funny. While he was happy that others could not read his mind, his sarcasm may have provided others with more of a window into his thoughts than even he knew. Somehow, in a way that even he could not explain, others interpreted his sarcasm toward them as indicating that he genuinely cared for them—and this was most often the simple truth.

Emily was short, redheaded, freckled, and ruggedly thin. Her beauty came from her flaming hair—envied by all—and her undiminishable self-confidence. She was a runner and loved to exercise. Until the children arrived, Emily inviting Robert to go with her for a run was a continual joke. He was thin but never from running. He was 'allergic to running.'

There was a strength and vigor about her, which was attractive to men and intimidating to women. Even male gym rats were threatened when she could do more pull-ups than they. However, she could quickly win over both genders with her naturally ebullient nature. She was a 'people person,' readily befriending everyone.

While neither had previously considered the reality of soulmates, they had each found their soulmates in the other. At their third meeting, they were surprised that they spent almost ten hours together at the same table in the student union, talking about their respective pasts and answering the other's questions. After half-a-dozen protracted outings discussing life, love, and dreams, they compared their relationships to the many silent examples they witnessed and wondered if they had already completed ten to twenty years' worth of communication. After only a dozen dates over the course of five or six weeks, they very quickly fell in love—so quickly that even respective families were concerned. They were thoroughly committed to each other, and marriage seemed inevitable.

After college and marriage, although there were far more job opportunities for each in Greensboro, they chose to move to Robert's hometown of Boone. Emily had always loved visiting Boone with friends. It was a small town, and the university and tourism gave it unusual energy and opportunity to enjoy the arts. Besides, Robert had a free house—no two—in Boone. They would save a mortgage or rent payment by moving there. It only made sense.

Robert's employment with a local insurance company was not what he loved, but it paid the bills of a single man. He remained in his position when first married, hoping that the opportunity would lead to promotions and a position that would eventually better support a family. His job became one of many topics of conversation in preparation for having children. He decided to start his own company, developing a web presence, marketing, and advertising for business clients. He believed that this would best use his training and give him a good occupation that, after the initial investment of some years of dedication, he could enjoy every day and provide a respectable living.

Emily was equally a part of the employment discussions. Through friendly connections and advice, she decided that a lecturer's life at the university would well meet the needs of their family—particularly when children came. As a university lecturer, she would have an adequate second income for the family and still have almost four months off per year without the pressure of the research and committee service required of tenure track faculty members with PhDs. To become a lecturer, she would need to earn her Master's degree.

Altogether, they would both be investing in their careers simultaneously—he on developing a new company and she on graduate studies. They both knew this would be demanding on a young marriage but a necessary season to build the familial infrastructure needed to support the children they anticipated having. To further complicate this season, Robert would need to keep working his job at the insurance company while building his own company, WebMark—the concatenation and abbreviation of 'web' and 'marketing.' He negotiated a four-day workweek to meet with potential WebMark clients for his business on Wednesdays. In what was left of his evenings, he would be coding and developing websites. All too often, they felt like ships passing in the night. They placed a planned time frame of two years to complete their respective investments in their careers and the frenetic pace to cease, or at least subside.

The couple discussed how to meet their financial needs while pursuing a graduate degree, working a job with limited pay, and trying to develop a new company. They debated selling either Robert's home—inherited from his grandparents and renovated—or his more recently inherited parents' home. This would provide an immediate sum that they could parcel out in a controlled manner as needed over the two, three, or four years it would take to get firmly established. But, if they chose this option, they realized that they might permanently end their future potential for making rental income and might never be able to again buy a rental home. They decided to keep Robert's current home and use the other as a rental unit until they ran into dire straits. If they budgeted carefully, they would hopefully make it through their season of personal investment without selling either of the properties. Indeed, they could even take out home equity loans on the house if needed to help them through the most challenging times.

Prior to the burdens of children or a job, Emily completed her graduate program in two years. She had made such an impression on faculty members in the department that she was immediately in line for a potential lecturer position. Through a friend in the department, it was also beneficial that she came into more frequent contact with Dr. Kronbach, the Chair of the Literature Department. He became aware of her work ethic and willingness to go above and beyond to succeed. She was an occasional sitter for Dr. Kronbach's home, dog, and children. She was trusted by all who came to know her. Even more impressively, Emily completed her Master's program with a thesis rather than the more commonplace research project. The latter, while respected, was considered an easier route. She had gone the extra mile in all her academic endeavors.

When a lecturer position opened, the department performed its obligatory internal and external search, with the tacit understanding that the position would go to Emily unless she did poorly on the interview or another candidate far exceeded her qualifications. Neither happened. Contemporaneous with graduating in May, Emily was offered, and gladly accepted, a one-year appointment as a lecturer. She would receive her first paycheck in September. A lecturer's position was coveted. Although only a one-year appointment, few lecturers ever lost their positions unless they wished to move away. Unless there was a cutback in positions due to state budgets or low enrollments, only those lecturers who were very poor at their responsibilities had their contracts not renewed. So, if desired, it could become a lifetime career.

The couple decided that, as soon as Emily received her first paycheck, which was already more than Robert was making at the insurance company, he would quit at the insurance firm and pour himself full time into the further development of WebMark.

The process was not easy for Robert. He worked ten-hour days at the insurance company doing mindless paperwork to ease and expedite the workload for the brokers. Often, he did all the necessary work for a particular client, only for the brokers to take all the credit. In the evenings, he would use his computing skills to develop websites for the companies of people he met on his days off in the name of WebMark. He recognized the necessity of working through the weekend to get established. So, Wednesdays and half-days on Saturdays were put aside to meet new and potential clients, and Sundays and every evening were dedicated to building websites. Moreover, Robert used his business acumen to attract more clients. He would state that many could build websites, but far fewer understood marketing and advertising to increase the company's visibility and business. Many clients were impressed with his sales pitch and came on board. Robert's early goal was to meet three companies on Wednesdays and two on Saturdays.

Within six months, Robert could see demonstrable growth in Web-Mark, but not enough to abandon his regular work and trusted paycheck and to strike out on his own. Another year-and-a-half passed with continual growth to the point of nearly matching his pay from the insurance firm. However, Robert knew that WebMark's development was stifled by his limitation in going out to glean more business. He simply did not have time to pound the pavement for clients and then develop their websites as well.

By November of his second year, Robert recognized the need to hire his first employee. It would diminish his pay significantly but allow him to beat the streets to drum up business. He hired Tyrell as an investment in WebMark. For a few months, Tyrell was making more money than Robert, the owner. However, soon after, the investment paid off, and WebMark exploded with clients and potential. It was not much longer, and Robert hired his second employee, then a third. Unfortunately for the company finances, that is also when Emily demanded that WebMark find a facility other than the basement of their home. After some hunting, Robert found a small building on West King Street which could easily be upfitted for offices and a reception area.

Juggling finances, school, and career development, their early marriage was not easy. Both committed to the unity and strength of their marriage. Their love was undeniable and admired by couples both their age and much older. They held hands and openly praised each other among their mutual friends. Theirs was a relationship in which neither ever publicly diminished the other even in jest.

In their sixth year of marriage and to the great thrill of both Robert and Emily, Abigail was born. The couple was now a beautiful trio. For months, Emily had already loved the child in her womb. Robert's reaction was delayed until just moments after Abigail was born. Minutes after he saw the miraculous relationship of a newborn in her mother's arms, he had the opportunity of holding his daughter and the miracle revivified in his heart. Both parents felt a sense of love never before recognized. It was a joyous time.

In their tenth year of marriage, Emily became a believer in Jesus Christ when she was thirty-two, and he was thirty-three. Emily decided that she needed to raise her daughter in church. The same year, Grace was born. Emily's commitment to church was deepened. At age eight, Abigail made a commitment to follow Christ, and Emily implored Robert to join them at church every week. She knew that he did not share her faith and that he would do little to encourage the girls through Bible reading or prayer, but possibly, his attendance in weekly Sunday school and church would have some softening effect. *I love him so much. He's such a great husband and father. If only . . .*

Overall, Robert was a kind man, an attentive and supportive husband, and an involved parent. While Emily pined for her husband to independently show interest in church and her truths, she valued her husband as he was. She had decided that she would exemplify the faith without making him feel belittled by it. She hoped that Robert's involvement with some of the men of the church would eventually influence him.

Unspoken to anyone, including Emily, Robert held a seething animosity toward God for taking his grandparents at a relatively young age and taking his parents when he was only twenty years old. He harbored anger at God for his daughters never having the opportunity to meet their grandparents. He struggled to forgive a God Who could allow all this pain to happen. Emily knew this of her husband, but not to its fullest extent.

Robert had once shared his feelings with Alex, but Alex's response was wholly unfulfilling. "You are having trouble forgiving God, precisely because you cannot forgive Him. He does not need us to forgive Him. He is righteous and holy, incapable of sin or wrong. We cannot forgive Him because He has not done anything wrong. He has not wronged us. We can forgive people, but we cannot forgive God. In the vertical direction, the only path for forgiveness is from our heavenly Father down to man and not vice versa."

Over twenty-five years of marriage, Robert and Emily's bond grew stronger. They enjoyed almost every minute together. Although arguments occasionally arose, Emily's fun-loving personality seemed to morph tension into laughter in only minutes. They learned to rely on each other's strengths and simply either avoid or build each other up to overcome weaknesses. Often, if they were in the same room, one would have their hand holding the other's. Even in public, they would often walk hand in hand or hug. He would often guide her through a door with his hand on the small of her back. In the past few years, her knees had weakened through decades of running. She had once calculated that she had run the circumference of the Earth more than two times over, and now she felt it with almost every step—but she was not yet ready for reconstructive surgery. Now, when they went from sitting to standing, he would often offer her a hand, and she would accept it. He would put it out solidly, and she would use it to support herself and help herself up. Physicality meant much to both. Through touch, they communicated care for each other in innumerable ways.

Robert was not much of a romantic man; there were few flowers and gifts. Emily recognized that stability and profoundly committed love were more valuable than fleeting moments of romance, but both would think privately and speak openly of their love for each other. Words of affirmation were never absent for long. Indeed, men were occasionally annoyed at how openly Robert spoke lovingly of his wife, and many women were jealous, wishing that their husbands did this more.

DAY 10: SUNDAY

After decades of marriage, Robert and Emily remained very committed. Both had individual interests, and they shared others. They were together as often as possible. Emily loved that Robert had no concern about public displays of affection. Twenty years of marriage brought with it the ability to read the other's moods and thoughts from the slightest cues.

Emily saw Robert in the living room. She recognized his distraction and disconnectedness at church and lunch. She hesitated to interrupt him. She knew that Sunday afternoons were busy for him and a mini respite between working from morning until evening to drum up more business for his company and complete tasks for his immediate clients. While he could do most of the work electronically and virtually, he still felt that few things were as valuable as a personal visit and a handshake. However, this time, she felt compelled to address what she did not understand. While there was a chair opposite him, she chose to sit gently beside him on the couch. She took his hand from his laptop keyboard to emphasize that she needed his complete attention for a moment.

"What's wrong?" she asked in a comforting tone.

"What do you mean?" *She can see right into me. Always has.*

"Cut it out. You know what I mean. I saw it in church, with you shaking your head every minute. I saw it last week when you were disconnected from the kids and me." She looked in his eyes in a manner that demonstrated enduring and undeniable care.

"Nothing is wrong." *Doesn't matter what I say; she will know what is not the truth. Can't tell her.* He tried to divert his gaze from her eyes, but with one hand, she gently touched his face and guided his head to look straight at her.

"Last chance."

"You don't understand. It's nothing bad."

"So . . . Then why not tell me?"

"No, I can't. Please. Not right now."

"What!?" Emily was transitioning from comforting to demanding.

"I can't tell you." *Please leave it alone. I don't want to lie.*

"Can't tell me what?"

"I'm not allowed . . . " With the instantaneous reflexes of a frightened cat, Robert silently rebuked himself with a cussword and immediately cut himself short. He knew that he had said the wrong thing. He knew that she would immediately pick up on it. There would be no escape. "I mean, I can't." *Too late.*

He was right; she instantly caught it. "Well, which is it?" she asked. "You are not allowed to, or you can't tell me? Sounds more like you won't tell me." Emily's demeanor morphed from comforting to more emphatically demanding.

Robert pulled his hand away. He could not tell her the truth. It was too dangerous. "Honey, no matter what I say, I can't make you understand what I barely understand myself."

"Understand what? Are you in trouble? Are you having an affair?" Robert could see some fear rising in his wife's eyes. As if to protect herself from a possible body blow, she recoiled her arms to her chest.

"No. NO. I'm not having an affair. It's something else . . . " Again, he realized that he had said too much.

"What else?" Emily was so persistent in questioning that Robert was unable to keep up. He knew that if she continued, he would accidentally give her too much information—information that could endanger her. He felt horrible that he had to keep such a grave secret from her. *It is for her safety.* Although his silence may temporarily harm his marriage, he realized that it could protect her life.

"I can't tell you. Please trust me and let this go for now. I'll let you know when I can. PLEASE." Robert finally became more insistent in ending the conversation than Emily in continuing it.

Emily disappointedly ended the chase. It was clear that she could not penetrate his defenses at this time. Trying more forcibly might lead to someone saying what they shouldn't. His silence had sparked an ominous feeling that she had only once before sensed—the day Robert's parents died in an accident. She felt some anger at his refusal to share with her. This was not the type of marriage they usually enjoyed. She would later have more opportunities to breach his defenses. She would follow up at a strategic time.

"Okay. If you're not in trouble, I'll let it go for now. I do trust you, but you will need to share with me SOON." Robert could see that his wife was crestfallen.

Emily walked into the kitchen to do some work, and Foxtrot followed her, knowing that there was more hope of getting food scraps both in the kitchen and from Emily than from Robert. Robert was momentarily relieved, but he knew this was far from over. Emily would not let this go until she had answers.

Chapter 9

"I'M so glad that you agreed to meet," Tate said to Robert.

"My pleasure, friend. What's up?"

The waitress approached and asked, "Hi, I'm Kayla. Is this your first time at Sunrise Grill?"

Both men chuckled a little, "No," responded Robert, "I, I mean we, have been here a number of times."

"Great. Well, welcome back. Are you ready to order your drinks?"

"I'll have a coffee, black," said Robert.

"And a half and half iced tea," said Tate.

"Will do. I'll be back with those and to take your meal order in a few minutes."

Tate sat, but he was hardly still. He fidgeted, looking left, right, and behind. He was far from calm.

"Hey, buddy, what's going on," Robert gently prodded. Robert was suspicious that Tate was in Boone rather than in Charlotte at CCTech in the late morning on a workday. *He's nervous. Never seen him like this before, other than after he shot a deer on the hunting trip and didn't know what to do next.*

Robert knew Tate for well over a decade. They had met at a mutual friend's cookout at his home in Hickory. While in other dimensions in the world of computing—Tate in accounting and Robert in marketing, advertising, and web design—they hit it off with a mutual appreciation for business applications of computing. Their friendship evolved, and a few times per year, each would meet the other either in Charlotte or Boone. Tate had as much a sense of humor as Robert did not. Tate was generally good-natured, if not sanguine. Their wives also grew fond of each other but rarely spent time with each other, apart from when the guys were around.

The men found that they had much in common. They loved sports, their respective jobs, computers, and their respective families. Both were family men. Possibly by coincidence, and maybe as part of convincing Robert to attend Grace Unity Church, Tate and his family attended 'Grace' on the weekends when they were at their cabin in Fleetwood. They saw each other at church meetings.

"Robert," replied Tate, "I don't know if I have much time. By now, I'm sure that they know . . . "

"Know what?" asked Robert. "And who?" *Okay. Strange. This isn't like him. He's usually funny and relaxed.* "Okay, we've been here for less than a minute, and this is already getting weird." *At least.*

"Yes, I know. And I can't give you much information right now." Tate again looked around nervously.

"And what are you doing in Boone on a weekday?" Robert asked.

"I had to get away. So, I called in sick." Both rang incredible to Robert. However, evidence belying the latter sat directly before him.

"You don't look sick."

"I'm not. I just needed to get away. I left work on Friday and came straight to the mountains. Sarah and the kids are home in Fleetwood. I just needed to get away. *Did I just say that?* I think better and relax better out here." *Not quite sure it is working this time.*

Robert knew that Tate had a second home between Deep Gap and Fleetwood off route 221. It was a small log cabin that the family enjoyed on many weekends. Tate and his wife had purchased the cabin from her parents' friends a decade or so before for an amazingly low price. Tate or Sarah, and sometimes together, would pop out to their mountain home at almost any time for a day or two, and sometimes even for only half a day.

"When you called this morning to set up lunch, I was surprised but happy to meet with you," Robert said with cautious enthusiasm.

Tate continued, "Look, I need to talk to you about something. I have something for you which will change your life and the lives of everyone."

"Everyone? Who is everyone?" Robert feigned a chuckle. He knew that Tate was always good for a gag.

"Everyone on Earth," Tate claimed emphatically, yet with a voice that barely exceeded a whisper. *That sounded stupid but real.* His voice was generally robust, but his now subdued voice made it difficult for Robert to hear amidst the level of noise, voices, servers, and the kitchen of Sunrise Grill.

"Okay," smiled Robert. He was ready to believe that Tate was setting him up for a coming huge joke and an even larger punchline. *But he is not acting right.*

"Yes," responded Tate, "the entire world. The whole world will be rocked. It may never be the same, and even more so for your family and mine." *No one is going to believe this without seeing the files.*

"Okay, Tate, what the hell is going on. You need to spit it out. What's the joke?" *I sure hope that there is a punchline.*

Tate looked at him very seriously. Hissing in frustration through his partially clenched teeth, Tate stated emphatically, "This is NOT a joke. This is serious. Deadly serious."

For the first time, Robert understood that something was truly seriously wrong. This was not Tate, and certainly not the Tate he knew well. *What is going on? Serious. He even seems scared.*

Tate fumbled in his pocket and took out a USB flashdrive. He showed it to Robert for only one second and then closed his hands around it, holding it securely. "I have information that will truly change the world and how we see things."

"Ah, what information?" asked Robert, recognizing the humorless situation and that Tate's continual scanning of the room was not a choreographed component of an elaborate ruse. Developing a gag that would evolve over minutes or even hours was not beyond him.

"Here are your drinks," interrupted Kayla. Tate was a little startled and took his clasped hands from on top of the table to under it as if there would be another layer of concealment of the flashdrive.

"Thank you," said Robert.

As if reminded to be polite, Tate looked up with what he could force as a smile and thanked the waitress.

"Are you ready to order?" asked Kayla.

"Um," hesitated Tate, realizing that he had not yet even picked up the menu. "Can we have just a few more minutes?"

"Of course," answered Kayla. "Just flip your menus upside down when you are ready."

"Okay," responded Robert, and Tate agreed with a nod. Kayla disappeared into the din of activity surrounding the two men.

"I don't think that I can eat," Tate announced. He remained visibly agitated.

"What is going on?" Robert asked, attempting to force Tate to open up. Robert had quickly transitioned from expecting a joke to becoming annoyed that Tate's delivery was slow and disjointed.

"I got some information at work."

"Okay?"

"This is big."

"Okay?" Robert responded while providing a small gesture indicating, *just get to it already.*

"No, you don't understand; this is really big." *Okay, I've probably said 'big' too many times already. Synonyms could help. Use your words, Tate. Use your words.*

"Okay?!" responded Robert more emphatically, with a more exaggerated hand gesture connoting, *I'm starting to get annoyed.*

"Do you know what we do at CCTech?" Tate asked.

"No, not really."

"Well, in addition to commercial programming, we also have some governmental contracts. Some of these are secret, and even top secret, regarding programming for various weaponry and dozens of other projects."

"That's pretty cool," Robert responded, "but that is far from a secret."

"It is not a secret that we do some classified work," replied Tate. "Many people know this. It is only secretive what those classified projects are. Sometimes the secret simply entails that we are contracted to store files for the government. Files that should stay out of Washington's eyes."

"Okay," replied Robert. Tate again scanned the room to see if anyone was listening to their conversation. No one was noticed. However, the cloak-and-dagger tone finally caused Robert to check the room as well.

"Some of these files need to be made public," said Tate. "People need to know."

"I suspect that some of these files are on that flashdrive?" asked Robert.

"Yes," responded Tate, with a finger to his lips to indicate to speak more quietly.

"About military? Weapons? Governments?" Robert asked more quietly. *Obviously supposed to be secretive.*

"No. This is far more concerning than weapons and international relations. These files will change much of what we believe about this world."

Robert was on the verge of frustration. He felt as if he was being teased. "Are you going to tell me what is on the thumb drive?"

"If I told you, you would not believe me. You need to see it yourself." And with that, Tate placed the flashdrive deliberately in Robert's hand and forced Robert's fingers closed to conceal it again. "When you look at these files, make sure your computer is NOT connected to the internet. If you are connected, they can detect that these files are opened and on which computer in just minutes."

"Why are you giving this to ME?" asked Robert. "I'm not sure that I want this. I don't have any security clearances." *What are you getting me into? This can't be legal.*

"You don't want this. Very few would want to see what is on this drive. But everyone needs to see this. I understand, and I agree with you. You really don't want to get involved in this . . . but you must. To help me, to help everyone, and even to help your own family, you will get involved. To be fully transparent, or a much as I can be at this time, you know that my wife and I have sacrificed everything—our retirements and savings, and even gotten deeply into debt—in order to pay for my daughter's leukemia treatments. I need money to recover. This is my ticket. However, even if this was not for the money, this information needs to be out there."

"What makes you," asked Robert, "the arbiter of what secretive government information needs to be made public? Are you a self-proclaimed reincarnation of Edward Snowden?"

"No, no. This is different," continued Tate. "This information has value to us as human beings. This is not about the military or anything like that. Plus, you have the opportunity to make millions off of this. I'm gonna make some too. But I just need enough to recoup from her leukemia and get my kids through college. You can make as much from this as you want. I suspect that this is worth millions. I know that you and your family can use the money. Everyone can. However, if you don't want money out of this, give the money to others."

"I don't want anything to do with this. This is crazy." Robert pushed his hands back toward Tate, indicating he was returning the flashdrive. *He's losing his mind. Something's really out of whack.* Tate pushed Robert's hands away, countermanding the refusal. "Why me? Why me?"

Tate replied, "I need you to take this because you are not connected to CCTech or to the government in any way. By the time I get back to Charlotte on Wednesday, they will know that I copied these files, and I am sure that I will be terminated from CCTech. If someone outside of CCTech has these files, when others see the files, the files will have more credibility."

"When others see the files?"

"We need the timing to be right. Someone—that's you—has got to get these files out to a wide audience. They would say that any insider of CCTech was simply a disgruntled employee who put together some imaginary files to discredit the company. That is not what I want to do. I want this information to get out."

"Still, why . . . ?"

"Why you, Robert?" Tate finished his friend's question. "Not just because you are not in CCTech, but also because you have the technological sophistication and infrastructure to accomplish it rather quickly. Also, you have the expertise to keep it covered until the very last moment. We need timing. We need it to all happen quickly, but not until we want it to. We want them to pay for the information." *He wants ME to disseminate these files? ME?* Robert quickly transitioned from being concerned about the welfare of his friend to grave concern for himself.

"Wait," thought Robert, "do you want money for not sending this information out, or do you want to get this information out for the good of humanity. This seems like doublespeak."

"Well, I guess it does." *I might not have thought this out thoroughly enough.* "To be completely honest, I want both."

"If you get paid for keeping this information secret, and then you make it public anyway, aren't you playing with fire?" *And now he wants me playing with the fire as well. I don't want to be involved. Too many ways this can go wrong.*

"Possibly, but I need the money, and the world needs to see this stuff. So, yes, I guess I do want both." Tate recognized that there were some problematic concerns regarding accomplishing both. *We'll figure that out. Not sure how, YET.*

"How do YOU want ME to get this information out?" Robert was curious regarding any methodology that Tate may have had in mind.

"Use your technology skills. Look, I'm only a forensic accountant. You are the real guru on social media and information dissemination."

"Will I or my family be in danger?" Robert inquired with deep concern.

"At this time, I do not believe that you will be in danger. Getting this information out will be your protection, our protection, everyone's protection. Once it is out, they will not be able to stop it."

"Who is the 'they?'" Robert asked.

"Actually, I can't exactly tell you. It's not that I won't. I just can't. I'm not sure. Maybe nobody. Maybe the FBI or CIA. Maybe some para-governmental group. And, again, maybe no one. *I must sound insane. Paranoid.* I'm not really sure who might be charged with the oversight of these materials. As far as how to get this information out, I'm sure that you will figure it out." Tate was not all that certain that Robert's family could be perfectly protected. Still, he had confidence that the more information became public, the safer all were who had a role in disseminating it.

Robert began to loosen his grip on the flashdrive to look at it. "Put it away, in your pocket," Tate ordered. Robert obeyed.

With an abruptness commensurate with his nervousness, Tate stood up, grabbed his wallet, and threw a $20 bill on the table. "I'm sorry. Get whatever you want. I've got to get back to my family."

Robert was left with far too much to ponder and too little time to accomplish it. In his hand was trouble for Tate and possibly for anyone else who encountered it.

Kayla returned to the table. "I'm sorry. I see your friend has left."

"Yes. He was in a hurry."

"I could tell by how he busted through the front door."

Robert grabbed Tate's $20 bill, placed it in his wallet, and gave Kayla a $10 instead—far more than the cost of the drinks and a very generous tip for taking the table. "Keep the change."

"Thank you. Have a great day."

Robert left the restaurant and drove off, wondering how his immediate and future life might change from the events of the past few minutes. He wondered if there were anything truly of importance on the flashdrive or if this were the concoction of a friend under too much pressure. Tate had been clearly unnerved regarding files purported to be from CCTech. There was a sense of credibility to the entire situation.

Events with Tate had occurred too quickly. Robert had no time to process the situation. In the quiet privacy of his car, he attempted to piece together the puzzle. The free flow of thousands of thoughts made him visibly shake. His heart pounded, and his stomach was tight. Conjoined with grave concern for what could happen to him and his family—let alone the Tate family—Robert also felt betrayed by a close friend inviting, *no, forcing*, him into such a scenario. *This was completely unfair. He is willing for me to share any money from this . . . but he didn't ask my permission. He didn't ask if I wanted to. He forced me. He used our friendship. No, he betrayed our friendship.*

Within a few hours, Tate was back in Charlotte. He had planned to return the next day but was driven to return to CCTech and see what was happening—to see if there were obvious ramifications of his deeds. Plus, he was now delighted that the drive was both out of his hands and in the hands of another person, a trustworthy person, a person who knew about technology.

Robert carried the weight of the burden of the unknown. While he was oblivious regarding the drive's contents, they were undoubtedly important, or Tate would not have acted so strangely. Robert began to wonder where he could safely investigate the flashdrive. He knew to avoid his family or business computers. While they could be disconnected from the internet, he was concerned that they would eventually lead investigators back to him, his family, and his employees. He thoughtfully retraced his daily and weekly paths to determine where he could safely open the flashdrive. Exhausting the possibilities of his most usual haunts, he considered the next concentric ring of encounters—those places where he went less consistently. He then remembered that his family members went places which he visited only infrequently. While he attended church almost every Sunday, he was quick to leave. However, his family went to church regularly on Wednesday evenings while he regularly avoided going. *Ah, the church.* On some occasions, he had been down a few of the corridors beyond the sanctuary. *The library, the library. There is a computer in the library. I'll ask to use it. Alex shouldn't have any problem with that.*

Later in the day, an announcement rang on Robert's cellphone. To his surprise, it was a text from Tate.

> I'm sorry that I got you involved in all of this. I shouldn't have. *But seemed to make sense. Share millions. Help Allie.*

No problem. *You betrayed our friendship, and I'm pissed.*

No. It really is a problem. I should not have involved you. My job could be in jeopardy. Hell, I could go to jail.

Let's hope not. *You got me into this. Now you are worried!?!*

But my daughter is worth this. You will understand everything when you open it.

Ok. *Not sure that anything will be worth this. Well, Allie is. My children would be.*

When will you get a chance? *He needs to do this soon. This is OUR only protection.*

Not sure. Certainly not today. Busy day. *I'm only human. I can only do so much.*

I need whatever you can do with it. *We need it.*

I understand. *I think. Not yet sure what.* Depends on what it is.

You'll see.

Chapter 10

ROBERT was startled by an incoming text to his phone. He had been lost in thought, and the ding of his phone brought him back to the reality that the day before he had been given a flashdrive together with a dire warning. He looked at his phone. The number was unknown. Robert read the text and began a series of replies . . .

> Remember, no internet

> > Who is this? How did you get my number?

> Tate. Burner phone.

> > Burner? *This is getting even more strange.*

> Trying to be safe.

> > Gotcha. No internet. *I got it already. Burner? He's getting more paranoid. Yeah, you got a burner to be safe, but you're texting my phone. You don't care about me.*

> Got back to work, but things feel strange. Feels like something's up.

> > Paranoid? *Stressed out.*

Don't think so. Feels too real.

How so? *Right now, not quite sure how much I care about what's going on at your work. I'm stuck in the middle.*

Big boss just stopped by my office to say hi. Never happens.

Hmm. Coincidence? What did he say?

Nothing much, really.

Just asked me how my weekend went.

He was glad that I got a long weekend. He'd never done that before. *More than coincidence.*

Hmm. In trouble? *Hope not, but not sure that I care all that much right now. If this wasn't for Allie, this would be over NOW.*

Don't know. *Hope not.* Don't know if they figured it out. They did a Level-3 audit over the weekend. Wasn't previously scheduled. They would have access to EVERYTHING. But might only notice if they specifically looked for it.

Need to get out? *Get out of there. Could be bad.*

Don't think so. YET.

Should I ask? Family safe?

Why did I ask that?

Will do my best to make sure.

Both men knew enough to make sure nothing about the files was explicitly mentioned in their texts. Big brother could be monitoring their texts—and everyone's texts, emails, and calls. Their texts were simultaneously cryptic and informative—albeit, hopefully only to one another.

I don't know yet where or when.

> Will try to open the package tomorrow. *Wonder what it is?*

Probably the sooner the better. *SOON. Very soon.* But dissemination is more important. When for that?

> Not sure. Depends on what I find?

> What is this stuff?

Trust me, you will be shocked. (long pause) Everyone wants to know this, but some would do anything to make sure no one does.

> Is it legal? *What have you gotten me into?*

You asked that yesterday.

> ? *Well, answer the question.*

Really can't say.

> Or won't? *Playing a game . . . If only he wasn't so stinking serious about all of this.*

Doesn't really matter.

> *Why haven't YOU done it?*

You have access and skills with technology and social networking that I don't have. You can accomplish this quickly. (pause) Can you hide your identity when you do?

> (pause)

I don't know yet. *Haven't yet thought about how I might do this yet. I need to know what are in the files to know how to do it.* Will try.

Gotta run. Now regretting that my friend is involved. *Hate it more than you can know. But gotta protect and inform everyone. And be able to keep helping Allie.*

Not too involved yet. Don't yet know the contents. Will do what I can. *Nervous.*

And with that, the texts ended, and Robert began texting his wife.

Hey, Lover.

Hey, Babe. How's things going?

Busy, but good.

You usually text before this. Everything ok?

Yup. Just preoccupied. Just want to say I love you.

Ditto, Babe. (pause) You tossed and turned a lot last night.

I didn't notice. *I can't get her involved in this.*

You wouldn't

Guess not. lol.

Much on your mind? Work stuff?

More like friend stuff.

Someone I know?

Yup. But not now . . .

Ok. Trust you. Let me know when you can.

Yup. Have a great day. I'll check in later.

Ok, Hon.

Day 6: Wednesday

Wednesday evenings were always busy at Grace Unity Church. While not a church service per se, there were numerous ministries for children, parents, college students, and the like. Robert often remained home as Emily and Grace attended various ministries. He had promised his wife to attend on Sunday mornings, but not Wednesday evenings. This time, to the family's surprise, Robert tagged along.

Entering the church, Alex spied Robert and immediately made his way to him.

"Hey, Robert. How are you doing?"

"Well . . . I'm here," Robert said with a grin. "I'm here, aren't I?"

"Yes, but some people come because they are well and others because they need help." Alex knew that Robert could be one for some drama and theatrics. So, his response was not all that unanticipated. Indeed, more unanticipated was his presence at church.

"Hey, can I use the church library?" asked Robert.

"For?"

"There is just something that I need to look up."

"Book?"

"No, on the computer."

"Sure. Let me unlock the library for you." Alex was so pleased that Robert had come to church on Wednesday that he did not further question why. If he were using the church library, that would be great. There were plenty of great books on the shelves. *Maybe he'll find what he needs. Great to see him here midweek.* While asking to use the computer was unexpected, Alex was again confident that the sanctifying environment of the church could lead Robert to positive and helpful information. There was the possibility that he would investigate grief and forgiveness and take steps toward God through that. *Eventually, he needs to get over his anger at God for his parents' deaths.*

The two walked down a hallway. Robert had not thought about it before a few days ago. The church had security cameras, but they were mostly outside and in the sanctuary. The church monitored who came in and left the building, and, if there were ever to be any significant trouble, it would probably be in the sanctuary where most people congregated. There were no cameras in the hallways going toward the offices of the pastors and staff. Many conversations within a church building were meant to be private and confidential. Too many security cameras located in too many areas in the church could cause people to doubt the validity of their privacy and could thwart some aspects of ministry. No cameras observed this hallway or the library.

Alex unlocked the library door and flipped on the light. It was a small room with bookshelves along the entire usable perimeter, with a small wooden desk in the middle of the room. It had a small lamp in one corner. On the other end was a return with a solitary out-of-date laptop computer.

Nodding toward the computer, Robert asked, "This hit the internet?" *Wow, what a relic.*

Examining the computer for a moment, Alex responded, "Yes, the ethernet cable is connected. Looking up anything special?"

"Don't worry, no porn on church computers," Robert joked.

"Good. Stay as long as you need. Your girls' activities will be done at about eight."

"Thanks."

Alex returned to his responsibilities which always began in the foyer and moved to various rooms in the church. This time, he led a Bible study for anyone who might attend—usually men in their 30s and 40s. However, he would still monitor activities in most of the group meetings.

Robert sat at the laptop and, remembering what John Tate had told him, 'You CANNOT be on the internet when you open these files. Computer algorithms used by big tech and the government continually scouring the internet can instantaneously find that computer.' Robert immediately pulled out the ethernet cable. *Can't have them—whoever THEM is—see that I opened these files,* he thought. He booted the computer. It was old, with an old operating system, but it worked and would be sufficient for what he proposed. A moment of concern arose. *Does this old thing even have a USB port?* He looked on the side and spied a single unused USB port. *Can't even remember how long USB ports have been out there.*

He inserted the flashdrive, found it on My Computer, and opened File Manager to investigate its contents. The flashdrive contained a list of folders named by year, beginning with 1957 through 2020. Opening a folder 2016 as a random selection, Robert found three subfolders named 'Videos,' 'Analysis,' and 'PublicResponse.' Before opening any of these folders, Robert fumbled around the parent and child directories. He noticed that all the yearly-numbered folders had the exact similar structure: the same three folders per folder year. He returned to the folder 2016 and opened the subfolder 'Videos.' This folder had video files named by nothing but dates with additional letters if there were more than one video for a particular date.

He clicked on the file named ATS-2016-9-20v-a, and it opened immediately in a browser window as a static picture with a video play arrow centered on the page. The image was fuzzy. Either the camera or the action was moving during this still frame. He hesitated, remembering that he had received this flashdrive from Tate. Tate worked for Ralph Wilson's CCTech, a firm doing very well and growing even before receiving some top-secret government contracts only three years ago. Since then, security had been upgraded with armed guards at the company parking entrance. While Charlotte was a large city, some noticed an ever-present slew of official-looking government types in the restaurants and hotels nearest CCTech.

While entirely unaware of the contents of the flashdrive, Robert sensed that his next click would irrevocably change his life. Tate was so serious, so frightened, so concerned when he gave Robert the flashdrive. With as few words as possible, he warned that the contents were top-secret and the information would change the world. *Will it more change THE world or MY world?*

Robert clicked the play icon, and the video started to play. The contents were blurry and very shaky. There was no audio. The shakiness of the video seemed to be an artifact from the person initially filming; they were obviously very nervous, jerky, and was moving very quickly. The blurriness, however, seemed to be artificially created, purposely distorted. It was akin to a particular lens used to film and distort the picture, which caused the center of the picture to be more blurred than the periphery. In the lower-left corner of the video screen, a code was continuously depicted superimposed on the video: ATS-T-kX9HzD7e. This code was clearly displayed and not blurred like the rest of the video.

What little could be discerned in the video was of what seemed to be a large metallic object of which Robert was unfamiliar. The video must have been taken on a farm; a barn, roughly the same size as the object, floated in and out of the video frame. The object, too, randomly entered and exited the video frame. It was an effort for Robert to watch and interpret what was occurring on the screen. To better make sense of it all, Robert stopped the video on a few occasions when the object was best captured. While each frame was purposely distorted with blurriness, he considered the object's shape and contours more deeply. *Round? Smooth. No hard curves. Not wood. Metal? That big?* At best, he could only relate it to cartoonish depictions of alien spaceships, but that was too absurd to contemplate further. *Tate gave me THIS? There have been UFO videos out there for years. Decades. He threatened his career for THIS? Doesn't make sense.* The entire video lasted only about forty-five seconds.

Robert clicked on the file denoted, ATS-2016-09-20v-b. The file opened to its first static frame and indicated that this video was only five seconds in length. This video had the superimposed code ATS-T-CtY857rA clearly depicted and not distorted. Another click brought similarly-programmed fuzzification, faintly showing two similar objects hovering above the first for just a second or so and then flying off and disappearing into a clear sky.

"No way," Robert unintentionally said aloud, pounding his fist down on the desk in frustration. Muffling himself and decorating his silent language with expletives, he thought, *This can't be. Another video about freaking UFOs? Flying saucers? Come on. Tate gave me files about flying saucers?! And I'm supposed to be afraid of what I find? This is supposed to be serious? The government doesn't want us to see this stuff? It's out there everywhere on the internet. Conspiracy theorists have always been out there. This is total garbage. He must be losing it. Schizophrenia? Doesn't Schizophrenia usually begin in the early twenties? I should talk with his wife about my concerns.*

ATS-2016-09-20v-c was entirely different, it was better filmed, but only in that it was less shaky. As in the other cases, the video remained purposely fuzzy, and the code was clearly depicted on the bottom left of the screen. This video captured scenes that appeared to be from inside a barn. *Must be the same barn as in the first video.* The centralized fuzzification of the footage again provided more clarity along the outside of the frame. What could best be observed was seemingly accidentally captured on the frame's outer edges as the video panned through the recorded environment. A faint figure was sitting on the floor, collapsed against a piece of *farm equipment, I guess.* It was human, no, humanoid, no, it was uncertain. The blurring made it challenging to interpret. The panning periphery of the video frame revealed a semblance of clothing, but the blurriness made the fabrics indiscernible—not that Robert would have known one fabric from another. The torso—or so it seemed, as there was no discernible change of girth from what might have been shoulders to where hips could be imagined—was clad with an open vest of sorts. A wrap of equally unknown fabric began at what could only be interpreted as a waist and covered parts below. The fuzziness of the video disallowed Robert from distinguishing with certainty whether the figure even had two arms and two legs, or more, or less.

With more investigation, blurred shadows from the figure's mid-torso caught his attention. *Is that an extra pair of arms? Shorter arms? Aliens? Come on, aliens? This is crazy. Government files? Tate?! Are you crazy? Do you really believe this conspiracy trash? What did you do? Your career for THIS? What did you do? What did you do to me?!?* These possible appendages seemed to emanate from his sides, midway between what would be considered armpits and hips. These extra limbs seemed just long enough for the 'fingers' on one 'hand' to touch those of the other when stretched to full length in front of it. If not for what vaguely appeared to be an extra pair of arms, Robert may have recognized the figure as a very badly burned human being. Before being satisfied with what he could glean from the video, it abruptly ended after 43 seconds. The video was inconclusive and unfulfilling but compelling. *I've got to see more. Have known him for a long time. Give him the benefit of the doubt.*

After more investigation and thought, Robert recognized that the creature on the video was no human being. It was clear that the purpose of these videos was to record a case of space aliens on earth. But this was nonsensical. Robert just shook his head, wondering if he or Tate was being gaslighted. *Someone out there is crazy. Or are they trying to make me—or anyone else who sees this—crazy? Seemed to have made Tate a little crazy . . . unless he's in on this gag as well. Or . . . the government could have purposely placed these hoax files on their servers to see what would happen. This could be a government experiment on people.* He looked back at the list of files in the directory. ATS-2016-10-2v, ATS-2016-02-13v,

ATS-2016-07-06v-a, and UTS-2016-07-06v-b had similar themes: videos of possible aliens.

Robert skipped to another year, 2009, then 1985, then 1977. In each year, he sampled some videos. They were all thematically similar: alien vehicles, alien bodies, or footage from military aircraft, and all programmed to be blurry with a code positioned on the screen. Some videos were complete with observer narrations, often very emotional in nature. Robert estimated that he had sampled only a small subset of the videos on the flashdrive. In some ways—*no, many ways*—they were becoming increasingly compelling, possibly due to the seemingly large number of them. They created a narrative that extraterrestrial life had visited earth. However, this still could have been merely a compilation of collected hoaxes. Robert had seen enough of the videos. Since each video was relatively brief, his total viewing time had been less than ten minutes.

Worrying that someone would enter the library, Robert thought it prudent to stop playing videos. He checked the door behind him and re-positioned himself and the laptop so that he would have an earlier visual warning if someone were to enter the room. He better shielded the laptop screen so that no one would be able to see it before he could quickly shut the cover. He clicked on the 2020 directory and unintentionally, or by rote through previously investigating different folders, again clicked on the video folder. The file list opened, and he immediately spied a different file name from the rest, ATS-2020-9-17v-alpha. *'Alpha,' why 'alpha,'* he thought. *The other files had only 'a,' 'b,' or 'c.'*

He opened ATS-2020-9-17v-alpha and began to play the video that he immediately regretted seeing. It was not simply of an alien cadaver. It was a live interview with a living alien. Three men, fuzzified beyond recognition, were in a room with an equally blurred alien creature. One of the men was communicating with the alien. Some of the words were English, some in German, and some in a seemingly African dialect. More so, some of the words were indistinguishable from any human language. Again, expletives adorned Robert's thought language. *No freaking way. No WAY. This is impossible. No, this is bigger than impossible. This is . . .* Robert had previously witnessed occasions of linguistic code-switching among Hispanic families at church and work, but never when intermingling so many languages and inhuman sounds, so seamlessly, even fluently. Nervously, Robert spun around in his chair, ensuring that no one else was in the room and that the door was securely shut. *No one can see this. This is BIG.* Then another thought crossed his mind. *And dangerous. Game changer.*

While a human speaking to an alien was undoubtedly shocking, the next event was even far more so. The alien responded! *What? What?! Did I see that?! Back up. Play again.* The alien used a similar concatenation of human languages and alien sounds, emphasizing the latter. *Communication . . . with meaning. No wonder this is secret.* The man and the alien seemed to have created an effective interlanguage. A conversation that Robert could not interpret continued. *Wish I knew what they were saying.* Robert looked at the video timer. It read sixty-three minutes, far too much time for Robert to watch while sitting in the church library. He stopped the video and thought for a moment. *Wait, there was something I saw. What was that? It was . . . It was . . .* He looked back at folder 2019/videos and noticed ATS-2019-4-30v-beta. He opened this file and observed more examples of human and alien communication. This was equally so with ATS-2012-11-17v-gamma, ATS-2014-12-3v-alpha, UTS-2015-10-2v-beta, and half a dozen more files with the Greek alphabet suffix. He viewed each of these files for only seconds, taking snippets out of the middle or near the end of each video. *Ah. . . I see what Tate wanted me to see. I get it. Can't be a government hoax.*

Robert cradled his head in his hands, wondering about what he had seen—enough for this time. Enough to freak him out. Enough to mesmerize and entrap him into needing to see more. It was an instantaneous addiction. He had seen what only the scarcest few had ever encountered. He saw what some government personnel had kept under wraps from congressmen, senators, and even presidents for decades.

Ah, wait, ah, what about the 'Analysis' and 'PublicResponse' folders? He opened 2017/Analysis. It had files coded directly to the videos. He returned to the folder 2016/Analysis and looked for files associated with the first three investigated videos. There it was, ATS-2016-09-20a.pdf. He opened it. The document had an official government agency letterhead. While the agency may have been important, Robert was much more interested in the document's content. Many lines in the document were blurry and illegible. Some entire paragraphs were redacted, and others had only sporadic words concealed. He only took the time to scan a small subset of the entire document. Particularly catching his attention were words like 'aliens,' 'extraterrestrial,' 'interaction,' 'understanding,' 'God,' 'planet,' 'uncertain,' 'dangerous,' 'sentient,' and 'eradicate.' Of these words, 'sentient' immediately hit Robert hardest. However, he wondered why such important words would be legible with a great body of unintelligible text. He wondered if what was concealed was of even greater importance—or danger. Notably, on the top right-hand corner of the page was the completely legible code UTS-T-gkJL29D3.

Robert opened the parallel file from the folder '2016/PublicResponse.' *There it is,* he said subconsciously as he found file ATS-2016-09-20pr.pdf. Simultaneously, he formed a Gestalt and recognized a more extensive coding system. The initial numerals in the filename were the year and date of the alien observation—that was only too apparent. The second prefix of 'a,' 'b,' or 'c' allowed for the association of numerous videos for a particular date. The first prefix of 'v,' 'a,' or 'pr' connoted whether the file was a video, analysis, or public response. *What is a public response?*

He opened ATS-2016-09-20pr.pdf. It again had official-looking letterhead, this time with the positioned code ATS-T-67RDw7Bg. While some paragraphs, sentences, and individual words were wholly obscured, other terms were recognizable. What could be read seemingly painted an incomplete story of what the government would say to the public if the information ever escaped. The report differed significantly from its respective analysis file, forming a counternarrative palatable to the general public. It obfuscated findings and painted the government-sanctioned story of crashed military aircraft, charred crew members, radar software blips, and the like.

Robert was psychologically undone. His heart raced at the consideration of what he had seen. His world was turned upside down. *Tate was right.* In a nonlinear and iterative manner, unanswered questions revolved in his mind. *Could this be true? Extraterrestrials? Government knew all this time? Misinformation? Sentient?* All of this could have been rationally discounted as a hoax if it was not that Robert knew that Tate worked at CCTech and that the company had some top-secret government contracts. The origin of the flashdrive gave it more credibility than Robert could tolerate. *That's why Tate thought he could get money from someone or the government for these files. Extortion, yes, but what amazingly valuable information. Many would pay for this. However, no matter if there was no money involved, he's right that the world should know this information. It is only classified because the government wanted to keep this from us. Now I know why he is scared. Some who are willing to pay for this may also be willing to kill. Okay, Tate was right about all of this, including the danger of it. Now I'm in this as well. Up to my knees. Maybe up to my neck.*

Robert sat at the laptop, staring blankly through the screen rather than at it. His mind was a million miles off. If respiration had not been an involuntary act of the nervous system, he would undoubtedly have forgotten to breathe many minutes ago. *Feel like I'm in an episode of Ripley's Believe it or not.* He considered so many movies that he had seen over the years with aliens. *Is it possible that the creators of those shows knew more than we do today?*

Forcing himself to bring his focus back on the screen, he noticed a small icon that he had previously overlooked. He immediately panicked. *No, no, no. NO. Idiot. Stupid IDIOT.* He grabbed at the fabric of his pants about the thighs, scolding himself for not previously noticing. *No, no, NO.* The Wi-Fi icon showed that he was connected to the church's wireless network. He had disconnected the ethernet cable but had not given a moment to consider that the old laptop may yet be connected to the church Wi-Fi system. Angry at himself and unforgiving of his oversight, he slammed his hands on the desk. The self-imposed sting snapped his consciousness into ultra-awareness, prompting him to immediately rip the flashdrive out of the port. He had been warned not to be connected to the internet when he opened the files. Now he wondered if the government truly could see if particular files were opened anywhere and anytime.

Maybe, I pulled it out in time, he desperately hoped. He again spun around to ensure no one else was in the room. "What do I do? What do I do?" he asked aloud. To leave and quickly was the only possible solution. *I've gotta get out of here. I've gotta . . .* He shut down the laptop as soon as the old operating system would allow—when in a grave hurry, it was never fast enough—left the room, even remembering to turn off the lights, closed the door, and headed toward the more populated parts of the church. For some inexplicable reason, being near people seemed that it would be safer in some manner. He returned down the hall toward the sanctuary. Some people were talking in small groups. Some had not attended a particular ministry; they attended church on Wednesday evenings to meet with friends seen only once per week. Others had participated in a ministry group and were preparing to leave.

Robert saw Tom and Marsha Cleef. Tom ran security for Samaritan's Purse, an extensive ministry off Bamboo Road in Boone. Tom always had a concealed weapon on him, and he was very well trained in security and self-defense. *Will be safe with him. Need some small talk, ah some small talk*, Robert thought. *I only need to come up with some small talk . . . The*

Panthers, the Panthers . . . Kuechly retired . . . Newton to the Patriots and back.

Robert approached Tom, but a panicked thought forced him to alter his path away from Tom and others in the foyer. *If THEY know that someone has seen the files, they may be after me, but they may also come after anyone I contact. Got to keep as many people safe as possible. Big groups or nothing. Big groups would be safe. Small groups could jeopardize others.* Robert turned toward the exit door, trading the safety that Tom could provide him for the security he could provide Tom for not associating with him. He could wait for his wife and daughter in the car. His family would almost expect this from him. But he also did not want to be alone. His option was to pace around the foyer, waiting for his wife and daughter while avoiding as many people as possible.

"Hey, Robert," called out Tom. "So nice to see you here."

"Hey, Tom," Robert responded while continuing to walk to an empty space in the foyer. He pulled out his cellphone and started looking at it, pretending that he was doing something important. *Good excuse for being alone in a corner.* Emily and Grace would be there soon. He only needed to stall for a few minutes. "Hoping all is well with you," he answered Tom in a tone that he hoped was not too dismissive. Pacing and as alone as possible, he attempted to consider his options, but his imaginations were blinded by fear. He paced, trying to avoid eye contact with anyone to avoid needing to speak with them. *Play the rabbit. Play the rabbit.* Robert remembered stories about hunting rabbits. He was told that they would often face away from a hunter, in full sight, as if, when the rabbit could not see the hunter, the hunter could not see the rabbit.

In just minutes, his wife and daughter entered the foyer from different directions. They all spied each other and intuitively met at the circumcenter point.

"Can we get a milkshake at Cookout on the way home?" Grace asked.

"No," replied Robert. "We need to get home." *Got to get out of public.*

"Honey," Emily teasingly scolded her husband. "I could use one too. Or we could split one."

"Not tonight."

His wife and daughter did not understand his intractable response but could tell that he was not in a mood to debate the point. Possibly, he had a disagreeable conversation with someone. Maybe, worked had called.

The three walked toward the exit. The coast was mainly clear. A path had organically formed between groups of people to escort them out. Robert took his wife's hand and placed his hand behind Grace's back to hint at the need to move on through. They complied, but only feet from escape, Alex blocked the way.

"So, what did you find?" Alex asked Robert.

"Nothing really." *Shut up. Shut up. Leave it alone.*

"What were you looking for?"

"I'm not even really sure." *Come on. Give me a freaking break.*

"What were you doing, honey?" asked Emily. Robert thought, *Really? You too? Not now.*

"He was in the church library. I think using the computer," Alex answered for him.

"What were you looking for?" she again asked her husband.

"Nothing special." Robert knew that he needed a response. His previous partial thoughts of the Panthers crossed his mind. "I wanted to see check out the Panthers' quarterback situation. Darnold has a broken shoulder. Newton is back but not first string. Walker was backup. He's had a good past but mostly untested in Carolina. Lots going on."

"Is that it?" Alex interjected. "You could have found that news anywhere."

Robert immediately knew that using the church computer for searches that could have been as easily investigated on his smartphone was almost implausible. *Stupid excuse. Caught off guard. No choice, gotta run with it now.* "Well, I wanted to see it on a bigger screen. Sometimes a computer is still easier to navigate."

"You did that instead of going to one of the church meetings?" Emily's tone was a mixture of joking and annoyance.

Robert did not verbally respond, but he did look at her with eyes that stated that she had crossed a long-ago agreed-upon line. She knew it too. They had agreed that she would not require spiritual activity from him. The Forsythes continued their advance toward the door.

"See you later, father," Robert teased Alex.

"Bye, Pastor Spencer," said Grace.

"Bye, Grace. See you on Sunday."

The Forsythe's drive home was quiet. Emily had a strong sense that something was wrong with Robert, but it was not the time to press the issue. Grace, too, recognized that her father's attitude coming out from church was different from when he went into church. Unexpectedly, Robert turned onto Blowing Rock Road and turned into the drive-through at Cook Out. *Been a jerk. They deserve a milkshake.* Each ordered a milkshake: mocha for Emily, strawberry for Grace, and double chocolate for Robert. Double chocolate was not on the menu, but Robert knew that, upon request, they would put an extra shot of chocolate syrup in the milkshake. Emily and Grace understood Robert's milkshake run as a gracious act, silently asking for forgiveness for his mood.

Upon arriving home, Robert immediately went to the living room to further consider the situation. His mood still communicated 'leave me alone.' Refusing the obvious, Emily followed him to the room. He sat on the leather loveseat, and she in a chair opposite him.

"So, you want to talk about it?" she asked.

"No, thank you." *I thought I had escaped this. She's gonna pester me.*

"Are you sure?"

"Yes." *Please.*

"You know I love you."

"Yes, I do."

"Please share with me when you can."

"I will." After a pause and a securing glance toward his wife, he assured, "I will, I promise." *Escaped, at least for now. She won't let this go. But at least I have some breathing room.*

Emily departed to the kitchen to do some work. Robert sat pondering his situation. *Okay, okay, calm down. Right now, even if they know that the files were opened, they won't know who opened them. I'm okay for now.* In addition to fear of being caught by the government, Robert harbored anger at Tate for giving him this information. *Why me? Why did he give this to me? He knew that whoever he gave this to would be in jeopardy. He must have been even more desperate for money for his daughter's treatments than I knew.*

Chapter 11

"COLONEL Peterson, Colonel Peterson, Sir." A jacketless suited man in his early thirties burst into the Colonel's office. His name was Randy something. The 'something' really did not matter, particularly to the Colonel. Even though he occasionally brought information to the Colonel, the Colonel did not know his full name. For a decade or more, everyone affectionately and respectfully called Randy 'Rabbi'—for no reason that anyone could remember. Randy wasn't Jewish, but he was an effective teacher of those he supervised. The Colonel rarely knew the names of people if he could not see how they would benefit him and his position. Those whom he minimized by not taking the time to learn their names despised him. Some would attempt to curry favor with him to springboard their own career, but this often fell short. When the Colonel realized he was being used, he quickly cut those people off. He had no difficulty in using others but refused to be used himself. Little did he know how poorly he was seen in the eyes of almost everyone.

Randy had known Carla since nineth grade. They began dating in eleventh grade and continued dating in college. In their junior year, he proposed, and she accepted, and they married in June after their graduation. It did not take long for both to realize that Carla's biochemical engineering degree had higher earning potential than his, still respectable, computer science degree—particularly if she followed it up with her master's degree and went into the private research sector. Their mutual early marital goal was to promote her toward her career, and later he would follow up. They followed this plan, accentuated with the birth of their first child in their third year of marriage, almost immediately after she completed her graduate degree. During Carla's graduate pursuits, Randy opted for a more stable position with the federal government. He would never make as much money as would one in the private sector. Still, the positions were almost guaranteed for life if he continually kept up with ever-evolving changes in hardware, operating systems, software, and coding techniques. The stability of the government position allowed them to plan for their second child in their fifth year of marriage. Professionally, Randy could have accomplished much more, but he wished to put his family before his job.

The Colonel was married relatively young. He and his wife met in a chemistry lab in their first week at college. She was immediately smitten by his good looks. She was an exceptionally beautiful eighteen-year-old. She melded beauty with sophistication. She had poise unseen in most her age.

After some weeks of study sessions and a few more cups of coffee at the student union, she grew an admiration for his drive to succeed and make something out of himself. He did not want to be just another student seeking employment after college. He wished to make a name for himself even during college. He joined 'the right' fraternity, which would give him a leg up in specific career fields. He joined the debate team. And he made himself known to the professors who seemed to have the most political and business connections. After a year as a business major, he spoke with a friend who was a criminal justice major. He was immediately enthralled with the notion of possibly working for the FBI or CIA—subconsciously, any position with authority. Whenever he could not enter various groups, he would have his girlfriend, fiancée, and wife join the organization and then bring him in with her.

Unknown obstacles hindered the Colonel from entering one of his preferred governmental agencies immediately after college. Some believed that recruiters saw him as too aggressively determined to get a position. They interpreted this as potentially troublesome down the road—a person driven to succeed, possibly even at the expense of others, not a team player. Armed with a bachelor's degree in criminal justice, the Colonel applied for Officers Candidate School, which, upon completion, would provide him a position as a commissioned officer in a branch of the service. He would enter as a Second Lieutenant—a butter bar—and would do his utmost to fashion his career toward working in the intelligence realm.

After only a few years of marriage and watching her husband wheel-and-deal to advance himself, his wife soon realized that his greatest blessing was a two-edged sword. He was ruthless in using those above him and abusing those below. His drive to succeed, which was initially his most attractive attribute, soon became most ugly. She often wondered if she were simply a tool for his advancement, and the divorce proceedings confirmed as much. He wanted nothing and made no arguments contesting her desire to leave. He had gotten what he needed from her, and now that he could not see in her any more value that he could exploit, she was expendable. Anyone hindering his advancement was expendable. He never married again.

After completing twenty years in the military, he earned the rank of Lieutenant Colonel. He relished that both Lieutenant Colonels and full-bird Colonels were called Colonel. Thus, without others looking more closely into his history, few would know that he was an O5 rather than an O6. In his twenty-fourth year, he was passed over for promotion. Those who oversaw his promotion noticed his dogged determination to advance—even at the expense of those below him—and his utter willingness to bootlick those above. He was not a team player and was more useful to those above when working alone. Apart from using those around him, he was too unpredictable in how he would accomplish his tasks to remain in roles where those above him could be held responsible for his actions.

As expected, when the Colonel was passed over, he immediately began plans to retire from the military. He was unaware that some of the people involved in his being passed over were working with a clandestine group focused on intelligence but outside of the military's continual oversight. The Independent Intelligence Initiative, more cryptically denoted 'I3,' included mavericks such as he.

Within minutes of returning to his home on the day of his retirement, the call came. As anticipated from an amorphous entity such as the I3, the offer was vague, even secretive, but enticing. He would be given various assignments regarding investigating and protecting intelligence outside of the military, CIA, NSA, or FBI at three times the salary of others in those agencies. He would develop his own team and act mostly independently in I3. In addition to any operations handed down by the deeply hidden I3 chain of command, he could pursue any operations he deemed valuable. While the Colonel appreciated his independence, he also recognized that the structure of I3 was to protect the organization from rogue individual decisions and actions.

While entering without knocking and being welcomed in was strictly forbidden, Randy knew that the importance of his message warranted any intrusion and breaking of rules. He would be forgiven for his faux pas. "Someone has opened some ATS files," he continued.

"Which ones?"

"The SETL files."

The Colonel swallowed an expletive. "How many?"

"About a dozen or so—so far. I'll get an official count and list as soon as I can, but I wanted to let you know immediately."

"Do you know who?"

"Not yet, Sir. Just a location and the computer for now. The team is working on it. We do not yet know the person associated with it. I will work with our video people to see if we can nail down a person, but, with the files I have already seen that have been opened, I have a feeling that they have the entire SETL directory."

"Where?"

"In a church in Boone, North Carolina."

"Did they have the decryption keys?

"It does not seem so, Sir. They opened the files, but it does not seem that the translation occurred."

The Colonel thought to himself, *All the images will be distorted, and necessary text will be blackened, but they might still see too much. There is very much to see and understand even without the codes. I keep telling them that too much information is obvious even without the codes. They are such idiots.* He returned to his conversation. "In a church?"

"Yes, Sir."

"In Boone?"

"Yes, Sir."

"I've heard of Boone, but where is it?"

"On the western part of the state, Sir. In Watauga County, bordering Tennessee. Near Blowing Rock. A couple of hours north of Charlotte."

"Get me there, Rabbi. I'm heading to the airport. Have them get the jet ready and reserve a car on the other end. I have my traveling bag in my car."

"Yes, Sir."

"Yes." While curses commonly decorated the Colonel's thought language, he would rarely deign to be heard using inappropriate language aloud. In his train of thought, silent curses were now flowing freely. *This is bad. If I don't get immediate control of this, it could be the end of me. Bob Davis had some trivial files get out, and no one has ever heard from him again. A ghost.*

Before Randy could exit the office, the Colonel had left. Randy knew that this was no ordinary call. Too many files had been viewed. The person who opened the files would be in great jeopardy, and their knowledge could jeopardize the nation. At least, that was what he had been trained to understand. Although he had earned a top-secret clearance to work in this department, he still did not have access to view ATS files. He did not know what was in the SETL files, but he knew they were of paramount importance.

The importance of the files was verified by the Colonel's immediate need to become involved on-site. He had a team of pros always at his disposal. He could call up any number of people to perform many tasks, from legal and illegal surveillance and investigation to acts that would certainly be considered illegal in any society.

Although drivers were always at his disposal, the Colonel preferred to drive himself. It gave a feeling of additional control. Often his pleasure came from controlling others. However, having control over himself also generated satisfaction.

As the Colonel drove to the D.C. airport, he received a text from Rabbi.

> The Sec Def needs the Jet. You will need to go commercial. *He'll never know better. Serves him.*

Randy had his unique and subtle manner of revenge. The jet was perfectly available and ready for the Colonel. Making him fly commercial was certainly discomforting and inconvenient. Only Randy would know about his small act of revenge. Even the Colonel would never know. But that was enough for Randy. *He'll never investigate this. Too busy with other things. He's never checked behind me before.*

Commercial?!? (The Colonel refused to text all the
expletives he was thinking.)

Yes, sir. (While Randy wore a wry grin, he avoided
adding a smiley emoticon.) United.

First class.

No, sir. At this late timing, only commercial was
available. *I'm such a liar.* (Randy chuckled aloud to
himself.) *I'd love to see him in coach.* Tickets are at the
counter.

The Colonel responded with a loathing, thankless silence.

The flight from D.C. was uneventful. The quick ticket purchase disallowed the Colonel to be assigned a first-class seat. In economy seats, he was surrounded by ordinary folk. Nearest to him were two large men who talked incessantly about sports. They seemed to be in some business affiliated with sports memorabilia. It was clear that they had found employment in the field of their greatest passions. *I hope they shut up soon.* A row ahead was a man who wore far too much cologne. Despite any attractiveness in his profession, appearance, or attire, the heaviness of his cologne made no one wish to be near him. Two rows behind the Colonel were a woman with a crying child. *Certainly, that kid is old enough to have the discipline to be quiet*, the Colonel thought. *Poor parenting.* Everyone within four or five rows of the screaming toddler was annoyed, and some showed it more than others. Although discomforted more than the others, the Colonel camouflaged his frustration. He had long ago learned to stifle his emotions. The less attention he could bring to himself the better.

The Colonel continually scanned his surroundings. He observed everyone and everything. He was programmed to assess people and situations for possible danger. Unfortunately, in many ways, his training dehumanized his subjects. They simply became targets of observation. He looked around and cognitively recorded information regarding different passengers. *Blue shirt, black pants. Had a tie on but took it off. Asian, probably Chinese. Heavy sweater, must be cold, or going somewhere colder. Teenagers, but traveling where on a weeknight? Trying too hard to look like a professor. Ah, pretending to be sleeping to not be disturbed.* In moments, he assessed—rightly or wrongly—everyone within eyesight.

He endured the flight encapsulated with others who were oblivious to grave dangers that perennially surrounded them. Terrorists were hell-bent on destroying the lives and livelihoods of others. Nations threatened war against the U.S. Biological and chemical warfare and cyberattacks were diagnosed and thwarted daily. Still, the Colonel believed that nothing rivaled the danger posed by a possible alien invasion. Too much was unknown—their communication, their transportation, and, most importantly to the Colonel, their weaponry. *How thankful these people are to not know all the dangers which surround them*, the Colonel thought. *While ignorance is bliss, ignorance is also ignorance*, he would say to himself. He despised the 'ostriches' who would bury their heads in the sands of ignorance and the 'lemmings' who would mindlessly follow others to destruction. His knowledge of the aliens, which the government kept so quiet, gave him a feeling of superiority and power over others—this fulfilled his itch for authority.

Many of the passengers took a nap on the evening flight, hoping to sufficiently rest before their arrival to engage in activities at their destination. The Colonel stayed awake, hypervigilant. He had trained himself to stay awake whenever he was not specifically in his own home or somewhere unequivocally safe. Sometimes, he would stay awake, with almost superhuman determination, for seemingly days on end until he found the right opportunity and place for equally dedicated sleep.

The Colonel checked his phone within seconds of the plane's wheels touching down at Charlotte Douglas Airport. It had been in his hand prepared for use for the last thirty minutes. He had always hated the dreaded airplane mode of silence, which separated him from valuable information. He switched the airplane mode off and immediately received one single text message. 'We have a source.'

The message had come from Rabbi, the underling messenger in the Colonel's office. The Colonel did not wish to lose the valuable time the plane took to taxi on the runways. He immediately phoned the messenger.

"Good evening, Sir," came Rabbi's automatic response to the Colonel's call. At this moment, even this two-second greeting bothered the Colonel. Time was of the essence. *Just get to it.*

"Sir, go directly to CC Technologies. I'll text you the address. The owner is Ralph Wilson. The files were copied from one of his servers. We believe that a 'John Tate' copied them on Friday afternoon. By the time you get there, we will have exact confirmation of this. We have some guys on the inside who can check the data leak."

"Don't spook Tate." The Colonel communicated with the messenger in sparse words. *These guys are so quick to jump that they often alert their quarry. We need to know as much as possible before we interrogate. We need to know far more than he does. I work with idiots most of the time.* He did not want others on the plane to understand anything regarding the conversation.

"No, Sir. Our guys will make no contact with him until you get there."

"What do we know about Wilson and Tate?"

"Wilson is very safe. He was vetted repeatedly and deeply before CCTech was ever able to get our contracts. They do some programming for us. Some targeting. Some war simulations. Their front is in developing software and interfaces for medium to large-sized companies." The Colonel recognized the distinction denoted by a deep vetting. All people, even tangentially associated with secret government information, were vetted. Those few associated with top-secret information had a far more extensive vetting reaching tentacles into immediate and extended family members and past financial and business dealings. However, the rarified few involved with the above top-secret information underwent the highest and almost continual vetting. An office within the National Security Administration worked continuously with other agencies to vet and re-vet these people.

"And Tate?"

"He too has been vetted, but he was just one of the business programmers. He did not have direct access to the files, to any ATS files."

"But he got it," the Colonel responded rhetorically. *I have repeatedly told them that there are loopholes in the security. I'll figure out this one too. Breaches have got to stop, and SETL is among the most important.*

"Yes, Sir. We are looking into this as well. We will have much more information before you get to CCTech."

"Send everything that I need immediately to my text. Then, send everything to my email. EVERYTHING." The Colonel looked around to ensure that no one was paying particular attention to his conversation. Travelers near him were annoyed by his phone conversation on the plane, but no one seemed to be intentionally listening. Indeed, some were purposely not listening.

"Already working on that, sir. By the time you pull into the parking lot, you will have all that we have, and by this evening, you will have everything."

The Colonel immediately ended the call with no salutation. His habit was similar to Jack Bauer's character on '24,' who always ended calls immediately with only a click. Within a second or two, he received a series of texts with CCTech's full name and address, Ralph Wilson's name and picture, and the same for John Tate. Also included were the names, pictures, and descriptions of three men and two women who worked at CCTech, who were also undercover employees for the NSA, FBI, and other governmental agencies. The texts noted that Peter Tippet and Josh Hawley might have the most pertinent information and best follow-up position.

The Colonel texted,

> Have Tippet or Hawley contact me about where to meet. Don't let Wilson know that I am coming.

> Will do.

Chapter 12

TATE was immediately accosted by the myriad of smells of cleaning supplies. He looked about the basement room in CCTech, to which he had been escorted with no explanation by company security. The room was unexpectedly large for 'Janitorial Services.' Everyone who used the parking deck under the building walked past this room every day, but only the janitorial staff had been inside. The room contained numerous rows of racks and shelving for cleaning supplies, machines, and tools. So profuse were the supplies and shelving that it was difficult to discern how deep the room actually was. A solid eight-person wooden table was against the front wall with two chairs on the exposed side and one on each end. Fluorescent lights in the ceiling illuminated the room. One fixture of fluorescent lights was suspended over the table to assist when the table doubled as a workbench. Upon being escorted into the room, the security guards departed.

Pete Tippet, from Accounts, and Josh Hawley, from Advertising, were already in the room. Tate was confused about why this assortment of people was in the same place. In some indescribable manner, Pete and Josh seemed more discerning of what was transpiring. Pete gestured for Tate to take a seat. Tate obliged and sat on the long side of the table. Tippet sat beside him, and Hawley sat at the end closest to him.

Pete was a huge man, very tall. In his greying, crewcut, mid-forties, he had the musculature of a past bodybuilder or football player. He did not care what people thought of his haircut, and no one dared critique it.

By stature alone, he was an imposing figure. He had always been the quiet type. He did not need to raise his voice or gesticulate angrily to garner anyone's attention. When he walked in the room, the tenor automatically changed—most notably, a heated room would quickly become more subdued.

"Hey, Pete, Josh, what's going on? Why are we here?" *What's going on? I didn't even know this room was here. Why are they here?*

"Don't you know?" asked Pete, in a soft tone, again belying his massive size.

"No idea." *Even if it's about the files and flashdrive, accounts and advertising would not be involved.*

"Someone wants to meet you," Josh declared with representational authority.

"Who?" Tate was perplexed. *Who? In the janitor's closet?!?* Tate's growing nervousness was born from confusion. He could sense an ill-defined tension.

"But," continued Josh, "he says it would be better if you told US what was going on first."

"What do you mean?" *I don't do accounting or advertising. We have nothing in common. Wait, they are talking to me. This meeting is not about us; it's about me.*

"Tate, we know everything." *I'll break him,* thought Josh. *Been trained to break the best.*

"What?" *Don't squirm.* "We know about the data and the flashdrive." *Give enough line to set the hook.* "What data?" *Deny. Don't give up anything. Play dumb. Find out what they really know. But . . . they must know something, even a lot, if they play this card right off the bat.*

"Look, Tate," interjected good-cop Pete, "We know about everything, every keystroke, every bit of data, every nanosecond of copying data. We know everything."

"Pete, Josh, you're from accounts and . . . "

Josh pushed what looked like a bifold wallet in Tate's face. All Tate had a chance to see was Josh's picture and a very formal-looking government-issued ID card on one side and a badge on the other. He did not have the opportunity to verify if it was from the FBI, NSA, or some other acronym which all spelled trouble.

"Wait, you're from . . . " Tate's inquiry was cut short. He hoped to clarify the events. In an instant, he wondered: *Do they really work here?*

What was on the ID badge? Are they both working for the government? I'm really in trouble!

Neither Josh nor Pete seemed willing to give Tate another look at the badge. They recognized the fear mounting in Tate and were trained to make full use of it. Indeed, fear was building. Tate felt the tension of copying the files all over again. He was not sweating . . . yet. It would not be long, and his involuntary sweating would indict him.

"Whenever a company has a top-secret contract, some of us take roles in the company. Often, even the company management doesn't know who we are. Where is the flashdrive?"

With this, a great fear came over Tate. He knew that he was caught— completely caught—and he silently acknowledged, *They probably do know everything. They already know too many details: the file transfer and the flashdrive. They must know about Tracie's office. Better tell them as little as I can. No cops here . . .*

"It's gone. I don't have it anymore." *Might as well confirm what I cannot deny, and they seem to have proof about. Tell them what they know.* He hoped he could give them just enough information to get free of them.

"We know it is gone. Where?" In an instant, the tone changed from threatening to ominous.

"I got rid of it."

"Define 'got rid of,'" Pete insisted, emphasizing his question with air quotes.

"What does it matter? It's gone. I don't have it."

"Did you destroy it or . . . ?" Pete stopped his question, not wanting to list options from which Tate would choose.

Before Tate could answer Pete's question, Josh asked, "You know what's on it. Right?"

"Yes. Ahh . . . some." Tate regretted that he knew even the slightest of what was on the files. The questions were coming faster than he could invent responses.

"So, you know it matters, right?"

"I guess so," answered Tate, trying unsuccessfully to downplay everything.

"So, where is it?" asked Josh.

"I destroyed it."

"Oops," interjected Pete in a quiet, powerful tone. "Wrong answer. Anything valuable enough to jeopardize your career, your clearance, yourself, and your family . . . No one would destroy that."

"My family? . . . " As highly fearful as Tate had been only moments before—a level of fear that he had never previously experienced—this fear now escalated. His stomach was in his throat, and he could barely breathe. Tate had been in the Army. However, as a computer technician, he never saw combat. His service never included an actual fear of death. He was once in a command facility and had the opportunity to observe strategists planning to eliminate a terrorist cell. There was a palpable tension in the air, a grave concern for the safety of 'our guys' who would be completing the mission. Once, he was in a near-miss car accident that inevitably led to his death and one or more in the other vehicle. It was a close call that left him contemplating the nearness of his death. It was terrifying but short-lived. Nevertheless, it was sufficient to produce flashbacks and thankfulness for life for a year or so. However, at the mention of an overt threat to himself, and much more so, his family, a newer, more agonizing, and more unshakable terror arose. Josh noticed Tate's fear and enjoyed watching his target suffer.

Tate immediately contemplated how he could protect his wife, his eighteen-year-old son, and fifteen-year-old daughter. They were completely unaware of events that occurred only three days ago. His family had found it mildly curious that he spontaneously wanted to go to the Mountains on Friday. While they went often, their trips were usually planned. Their mountain home near Fleetwood was always fully stocked, even with extra clothes, and they could go at any time. They had returned to Charlotte on Monday afternoon.

While in the mountains, Sarah, his wife, had noticed that Tate was distracted. Something had been bothering him. This was unusual because the mountains were his place to rest, relax, and unwind. While it was not uncommon for Tate to meet with Robert Forsythe, it was curious that he did it on a Monday morning rather than on the weekend. Breakfast on Monday in Boone would mean a return later in the day on Monday or Tuesday morning. Either would alter regular travel plans on a non-holiday weekend.

"This is not a game," Josh declared, slapping his hand down hard on the table. Josh was a diminutive man. He was of average height but with a pencil physique, which could quickly be snapped. From shoulder to wrist was a constant diameter, barely thicker than the arms of a prepubescent teenager. His neck was so thin that it seemed physically impossible to hold up his asymmetrically large head. Slapping the desk for attention seemed to be his technique for hopefully generating fear.

This was certainly effective in the current situation. In a less severe situation, the same antics from such a slight man would have been comical if not oxymoronic—like Barney Fife throwing a tantrum. "You know that the materials on that flashdrive could destroy this nation and maybe the entire world." *He doesn't know. Ha, I don't either. No idea what's in those files. He knows more than I do. Just my job to get them back. Wonder if Pete knows?*

"Destroy this nation? More like inform it." *Shut up. Just shut up. Don't give anything away.* Tate realized how bad he was at this game. He had no game face, a real sucker in a poker game. With every sentence, he gave away any semblance of advantage he might have had.

"And to what end?" asked Pete in a soft tone that connoted control and demanded attention. Indeed, Pete's huge gentleness was more intimidating than tiny Josh's slamming of his rake-like hands on the table. "Do you really think that others knowing about this will help them? It won't. Churches will be destroyed; governments will fall; people will lose hope."

At that moment, Josh's question was answered. Pete certainly knew more than he did about the files. Josh was a little demoralized, recognizing that he was at least one rung lower than Pete. *I thought I was lead on this. Maybe he doesn't really know that much. He is as trained as I am to be able to lure prey into a verbal trap.* Their job was simple: get the flashdrive back as quickly as possible. There was no need for them to know the content of the files on the drive.

"And they will know the truth," answered Tate, deciding that he would attempt to turn the tide with an offense. He sat up straighter, trying to show some degree of defiant strength and, if even possible, authority. It was very short-lived.

"Relax," Pete said in a muted manner. "Relax. Everything is fine. No reason to get uptight. Just answer our questions."

Tate obeyed, and the defiance quickly drained out of his demeanor. He again sunk into his chair under the pressure of the situation. How he wished he could be bold and strong like guys in movies being interrogated. They were calm and collected. The prey toyed with the predators and often won. His situation, however, was different in at least two ways: he was the person being interrogated—not an actor—and this situation was not fiction. *At least I recognize the good-cop, bad-cop play.*

"There are truths which they should not know!" Josh slapped the table again, this time with even more force. He had put his total weight into it, and it stung him more than he would ever admit, but the effect was worthwhile—Tate stiffened with trepidation.

Josh continued, attempting to ramp up the pressure, with no concern for whether he was telling the truth. He had but one job to do. "I don't have even a moment to discuss this. I don't care what might happen. The only thing I care about is getting that data back and out of the hands of those who can't stand the truth. This information belongs to the U.S. government. It must be returned."

"I don't have it."

"Where is it?" asked Josh. "It will be easier on Sarah and your children if you just let us know." Josh's threat hit Tate as forcefully as any slap in the face. Threatening his family again took this to a level for which he was unprepared—explicitly using any of their names made this all more real and personal. The reality and danger of the situation instantly elevated. This seemed to be the end of any play-acting that may have been occurring.

"You would threaten my family?" Tate began to stand up. Pete's huge, heavy hand on his shoulder informed him that sitting was preferred.

"No," insisted Josh. "YOU are threatening them! Your lack of cooperation is threatening them." *Getting close. He's breaking.* Inwardly, Josh was smirking as he witnessed the reactions he hoped would happen. Josh took great pleasure in intimidating others. Those on the receiving end sensed in him a sadistic relishing of the psychological pain that he could inflict.

"You guys are from . . . " Tate remembered that he had not entirely determined the governmental organization to which Josh and Pete belonged. "You can't . . . " Tate reconsidered Pete and Josh. They both had a governmental look, but each of a different ilk. Pete had the brawn some would wish for in law enforcement. Josh was the prototypical nerd. Pete could *persuade* people to do even that which they did not want to do, and Josh could use his computing skills to ruin a person's life in many ways.

"As you very well know, this is so big that we can and would," responded Pete, in a voice which could terrorize simply by its calmness. "Losing two or three to save untold numbers and the destruction of our nation that would be worthwhile." This further confirmed to Josh that Pete had insights and information of which Josh was uninformed.

"Losing?"

"Look, it's up to you. We know that the flashdrive was opened in a church library."

Tate remembered seeing some movies where governmental agencies could track the opening of files within seconds. Any internet-connected computer activity could be found in moments. However, he was unsure if this was real or simply the machinations of creative storytellers. *Well, now I know for sure. Must be true.*

"Grace Unity Church," Josh expanded. In an instant, Tate realized that many 'fictional' movies might be based more on reality than he had previously believed. Simultaneously, he knew that many more people were in jeopardy, including Robert Forsythe and his family.

"I want to call a lawyer," Tate declared, half pleading and searching if this were a possibility. *Questioning is supposed to stop immediately.*

"Ha," Josh burst out with an incredulous laugh. *Played this game before. Lightweight.*

"Tate," stated Pete, in a tone that was authoritative while attempting to be as comforting as the situation allowed. "There are no lawyers for this. You are not under arrest. We just want the data back and know who has it."

"No lawyers? I've never heard . . . "

"No lawyers, you moron. This is too big for lawyers, and we need to act too quickly for lawyers. Look . . . " Josh started to hold up his cellphone toward Tate. Pete grabbed his arm to pull the phone away from Tate's view, giving Josh a look, signaling that he thought it was too early to be using this tactic. Josh pulled his arm away to reset what he intended to do. Tate wondered if these were more 'good-cop-bad-cop' theatrics or if Pete were truly more caring than Josh. Pete gave Josh a quick pleading look to delay the play, but Josh gave him no heed, pretending that he was somehow superior in this inquisition.

Josh forced his cellphone into Tate's line of vision. *What is this?* It took a few moments for John to interpret what he was seeing. It was a picture of the front of his Charlotte house. No, it was either a live feed or a recording. Into the frame passed his wife and son as they exited the car in the driveway. They grabbed a few bags from the car's trunk and Sam's backpack. They walked on the cemented path to the front door. Sarah unlocked the door, and they both went in.

"Martin," ordered Josh, "wave to the camera." A hand on the other end appeared, waved, and retracted out of sight. The feed was LIVE, and John's fear felt like a nuclear explosion. He was entirely and inescapably trapped. If the options were fight or flight, neither seemed plausible.

"That's enough," came an unexpected voice from deeper within the room. Tate spun around to see the person speaking. "He got the message."

"Yes Sir, Colonel," responded Josh as he immediately placed the cellphone face down on the table. A tall, slim, official-looking Black man came from behind some racks. The tone of his voice, his well-dressed manner, and the reaction of Josh and Pete immediately indicated that 'the Colonel' was in charge. Pete and Josh were subordinates. The turmoil of the previous minutes had made Tate forget that he was told that someone wanted to meet him. He wondered if 'the Colonel' were this person.

Tate's attention was split between the newcomer in the room and wanting to see on the phone that his family was okay.

"They are okay," reassured the Colonel. "You must help us immediately if you want them to stay that way."

"Leave them alone, and I'll do anything."

"Look, John," continued the Colonel, "I know that you hoped to make some money out of this. Yes, we've had time to investigate. I know that you have been bled dry by your daughter's treatment. I know there are more ahead. It only makes sense." Pete and Josh were immediately aware that the Colonel had access to Tate's family information that they did not have. Josh was jealous of the Colonel's additional knowledge of the situation and thought *we could have gotten more out of him if we had that information in hand.*

"You'll not make a penny out of all of this. Not how the government works." Josh interjected, pretending he knew more than he did—and certainly more than Pete. The Colonel looked harshly at Josh as if to say, *'shut up. You had your turn, and you failed.'*

"Who has the flashdrive?" asked the Colonel professionally and calmly. His composure was different from that of Pete. Pete could remain quiet and speak with his robust stature. The Colonel used calmness to communicate his ultimate authority in the situation.

Tate hesitated.

The Colonel immediately continued. "You don't understand. You don't have five minutes to think about this. You don't have ten seconds. I have one job, and right now, your family is between me and my job. I'm not going to do that old-fashioned technique of counting down from ten. Now, John," he ordered. The Colonel's 'now' was even softer and more emphatic than all the other words.

Tate again hesitated for what seemed a fraction of a moment. He was first taken aback by someone calling him by his first name. Only strangers would do that. The Colonel was both a stranger and a menacing one. Tate dismissed the use of his real first name. *He would have access to personnel files and see my first name as John.*

The Colonel picked up the phone in such a manner as to ensure that he was never in the frame. "Go ahead, Martin. The boy first." The Colonel gave orders, even those possibly associated with life and death, in a matter-of-fact tone.

"NOOOO!" screamed Tate, again rising to his feet in contestation and again being encouraged by Pete's heavy hand to remain seated. "Forsythe, R . . . Ro . . . Robert Forsythe," he stammered, hoping that he had saved his family, but immediately felt guilty that he had betrayed a friend. "I gave it to Robert," he stated apologetically and lowered his head in shame, wondering if he had now placed Robert and his family in similar jeopardy.

"Thank you, John." Turning toward the cellphone, the Colonel ordered, "Stand down, Martin." This resulted in a hand with a thumbs-up on the screen.

"Now, John, I still have one more question. Please answer this completely and quickly, and you will never see me again." Tate looked up with interest. This deal sounded too good to ignore. "Did you discuss what you found with anyone else?"

"No."

"Not to your wife or family?"

"No, no one. No one other than Robert. Well, actually, I barely mentioned it to him either. I just gave him the flashdrive and told him to look at it and see if he recognized what I think I saw." Tate hoped that 'barely' would make them less concerned about Robert. *Oh, no, they knew about the files opened at church. They know that he has seen them.*

"Okay. Thank you. Martin, return to base. John, you seem like an honest person. We know that the initial file transfer was accidental. We also know that you have never done anything like this before in your career. You guys, let John go back to work. John, keep your nose clean. The company doesn't know what happened here or what you did. Only we do. We can all keep it that way. However . . . " Even though stated in a factual and commanding manner, Tate was unsure how much the Colonel said was a truth or a lie.

How can he know and not CCTech? All the information would need to come from CCTech. "I understand." Tate did not spare a second to exit the room, heart pounding, feeling like he and his family had escaped the jaws of death. He headed toward the stairs that would take him back to his office. He found a nook out of eyesight of the janitorial interrogation room. Feeling drained, he leaned against the wall. Thousands of thoughts ran randomly through his mind. He covered as much of his face as he could with his hands as if to separate his consciousness of the world from the notions swirling in his mind. *What is going on? What the hell? How did they find out so quickly? My family? They were willing to hurt or kill MY FAMILY . . . Why weren't any of my supervisors there? Or Wilson? Or even The Commander? Is this more top secret than they are allowed to deal with? Why wasn't I fired? I don't get it. This is bad. Robert is in trouble. I've got to warn him . . . somehow. And Tracie . . . I've really messed this up. I'm not fired. Will they threaten Robert and his family? Sarah, I'm so sorry, Sarah. Sam, Allie, Sam, Allie . . .*

Tate felt like he had gone for hours without a full oxygenated breath. He was tachycardic and dizzy from the stress. He bent over, placing his hands on his thighs, gulping for air. *Calm down. Calm down. It's over. Get a grip. I've got to get hold of Tracie. I hope that she is okay. Slow down your breathing. Heart, slow down. Calm down. Think. You just escaped. It's gonna be all right.* Burying his face in his hands, *but for whom? And for how long?*

Wait. They didn't offer me money for the files. That would have been the easiest way for them and for me to pay for the leukemia treatments. Instead, they threatened me and my family. The files must be invaluable— probably ten times more than whatever they would have offered. Threatening was more expedient than a bidding war. My family was more valuable anyway. They must want those files at any cost, and I need to save our lives.

After a few seconds, Tate decided that he had to go home and hug his wife and children. Without a thought of the ramifications of walking out of his work mid-shift, he went to his office, packed up his laptop and man-bag, grabbed his jacket, turned about, and escaped to the parking garage to his car. *I'll tell them I was sick. I certainly do feel like puking.*

Chapter 13

DAY 18: MONDAY

A LEX was usually off on Mondays. However, this week, he had a scheduled Zoom meeting with Dr. Paul Burns and Dr. Ronnie Blie, both longtime friends and theological allies—and occasionally funloving adversaries. Alex sat at his desk and opened the Zoom session two minutes before its scheduled beginning. Paul was already on the screen

"Hey, Number 3. I got your email."

"Hey, Paul. Or should I call you Dr. Burns?"

Alex had met Paul Burns and Ronnie Blie while he was a student at Moody Bible Institute. The three had become inseparable in their early studies. Many of their earlier, required courses were together, and it only made sense that they studied together, but their connection far surpassed academics. They joined the same Bible studies and social groups. At least four days each week, the three ran together, usually for seven to ten miles at a pace of approximately six-and-a-half minutes per mile. Running, Paul demonstrated a singular, exceptional skill. On the shorter seven- to eight-mile runs, nothing unusual occurred. However, on the more extended nine- to ten-mile runs, an amazing event could be seen. At the seven-mile mark, Paul would take off at a pace which the other two could not maintain. Occasionally Alex would attempt to match Paul's pace, but he could never do so for more than a quarter-mile or so.

Paul's bursts of speed after seven miles of running frustrated Alex. Since the three followed the same fitness regimen, it seemed reasonable that they would all be at the same fitness level. Paul's final kick was simply inexplicable.

Once, immediately after Paul sprinted off, Paul asked Ronnie in a fit of frustration, "How does he do that?"

"You don't know?" Ronnie responded.

"No. I don't get it."

"Well, I don't think that I have the right to tell you," Ronnie said. "All I can say is that you should watch him as we get ready to run and see if you notice anything.

Over the next week or so, Alex observed Paul. The only unusual thing he noticed was that Paul would search the ground for a stone which he would palm in his hand and carry with him through the run. Noting this, Alex again asked Ronnie the purpose for the rock, and again, Ronnie refused to answer and directed Alex to ask Paul himself. It was clear that the response was private in some manner and for some reason.

Alex finally summoned the courage to investigate Paul's profoundly personal activity. Before one run, as Paul was scouring the ground for a small stone, Alex asked him what he was doing, why, and how it made him run so fast.

"I look for a small sharp stone," Paul admitted. I run with it loosely in my hand for about seven miles. Then I squeeze it to make it hurt."

"Ah," continued Alex, assuming that he had come to some understanding, "you squeeze the rock, make it hurt, and you focus on the pain from the rock instead of the pain from the running."

"No," stated Paul emphatically. That is not it at all."

"So, what is it?"

"When I squeeze the rock, it hurts," Paul explained. This makes me focus on the great pain my Savior suffered for me. I do not replace some pain for another pain. I relish in Christ's pain, knowing that it was a necessary part of taking upon Himself the punishment of my sin, leading to the forgiveness of my sin. When I contemplate the extent of His love toward me, that He was willing to suffer and die for me, the thought carries me to another level of joy, a joy only expressible in what I would call 'enraptured running.' The rock does not make me run faster. By squeezing the rock and remembering Christ's sacrificial love, I cannot contain myself from running faster."

Beginning their second year at Moody, the three continued to take the courses they could together. However, they also began to separately take courses differentiated to meet their respective intended career aspirations and God-felt callings. Alex planned to be a pastor, Paul a seminary theologian, and Ronnie a missionary. As much as possible, the trio remained intact. Paul and Alex had found their soon-to-be wives in their first year at Moody. Ashley, Paul's girlfriend, and Jenny enjoyed that the trio of guys had such deep affection for each other. However, nearing the middle of the second year, after Tanisha had captured Ronnie, the women began to vie for their respective man's attention. All three couples were married by the end of the year.

After graduation from Moody, Paul and Ronnie went directly to Dallas Theological Seminary for graduate studies and advanced preparations for their careers. Alex began as a youth pastor in his church in Boone. Regardless of a young man's skillset, there was a tacit understanding that people started their careers in youth ministries—even if that were not what they felt was their specific calling. It did not matter if they were not specifically trained to work with youth or that they may be more gifted to work with adults; they were usually initially hired to work with the youth and provide an occasional, fill-in sermon to the adult congregation until they earned their 'street cred' and the respect to work more with adults. Often children's ministries positions led to positions as a college minister—as if the youngest ministers were best suited to work with the youngest congregants. Promotions came more in line with the age and perceived maturity of the junior pastors, in conjunction with retirements of more senior pastors, than any other characteristic. Assuredly, senior pastors were loath to relinquish their pulpits to future challengers for their posts. Eventually, most college pastors would find a position as a senior pastor—their original dream job and the culmination of their calling. Interestingly, even if a man felt a direct calling to be a senior pastor, the church machinery effectively delayed that outcome.

The trio of men kept in contact through their first decade and then less so in the next. An unspoken circle of envy existed among them—a cycle antithetical to the notion of a career being God's calling. Alex envied that Paul and Ronnie had the opportunity to go to seminary. Paul and Ronnie envied that Alex had quickly gotten a full-time position, potentially leading to permanency in a church. Paul and Alex admired that Ronnie had been called to missions—a position that many felt reserved for only the best and most deeply spiritual. While Ronnie and Alex envied that Paul would probably make the most money as a seminary professor, all were committed to what they believed God had called them.

Eventually, Alex earned a bachelor's degree, Ronnie a Masters, and Paul a Doctorate of Theology.

"Well, if it wasn't for this email, we could go by Paul. But you have put me on the spot."

Chuckling, Alex responded, "Well, it is your brain I'm after this time, not your friendship."

"Maybe, I can give you both. I spoke to Ronnie, and I told him what you asked, 'to make this a serious academic exercise.' We did. I have to admit it was quite fun. Unfortunately, Ronnie could not make this Zoom meeting. We'll just wing it without him."

"Well, if it wasn't for the seriousness of a friend of mine, it would have been a recreational endeavor of my own. I'm really hoping that the three of us can come to some agreement and conclusions."

"Let's just get down to the nitty-gritty," said Paul. "Let's agree to what the question is. I think that you are saying, 'what are the theological implications to Christianity if it is conclusively determined that sentient extraterrestrial life is found to have visited earth?' Is that correct?"

"Correct."

"And no joking, right?"

"Right," confirmed Alex.

"Well, I can't guarantee that some jokes won't slip by my lips, but I'll do my best." Paul was known to, at times, be boisterously comedic.

"I know. Neither can I. In fact, when I first discussed this with a friend, I named the alien Zoot, for simplicity's sake."

"Okay, Zoot, it is," Paul agreed. By the way, is Zoot male or female?"

"Well," answered Alex, "he left his family for an adventure. I'm guessing he is a male. Females tend to be much smarter than that, and if his great adventure is traveling through the galaxies to come to visit Earth, he is even less bright than we could imagine."

"If he could travel across galaxies," added Paul, "surely ZootLand would be far more advanced than Earth. Why would anyone want to visit and maybe even stay somewhere far more primitive than where they came from?"

"Hey, are you kidding? Millions of people go 'camping' every year," Alex said with a smile.

"Okay, Earth is Zoot's primitive campground," said Paul.

"Yup, campground, at best. So, like I said in my email, I've worked through some scenarios, but I didn't want to share that yet, so as not to taint the brain pool."

"Brain pool may be quite shallow off this diving board, but we gave it a plunge. Ronnie and I put together some scenarios. It's easier if we consider some cases."

"Okay?"

"First, we need to consider two passages that guided the discussions with Ronnie," said Paul as he could be seen opening a relatively hefty and well-worn Bible. "They are Romans 8:19-23 and 1st Corinthians 8:4-6. I know that you are very familiar with these. But maybe not in the context of Zoot. Romans 8:19-23 reads,

> 'For the earnest expectation of the creation eagerly waits for the revealing of the sons of God. For the creation was subjected to futility, not willingly, but because of Him who subjected it in hope; because the creation itself also will be delivered from the bondage of corruption into the glorious liberty of the children of God. For we know that the whole creation groans and labors with birth pangs together until now. Not only that, but we also who have the firstfruits of the Spirit, even we ourselves groan within ourselves, eagerly waiting for the adoption, the redemption of our body.'"

"Yes, Alex interjected, "I know it well, but I am not yet seeing your connection."

"Ah, right. The connection comes in the word 'creation.' We must consider whether or not the biblical notion of creation extends to Zoot."

"Yes," continued Alex. "Either Zoot is considered part of God's creation, or he is not."

"Well, more precisely," explained Paul, "it is not whether or not God created Zoot. He certainly did since God is the creator of all. It is whether God's revelation of His creation to us includes Zoot."

"Okay," replied Alex with as much a question as an affirmation.

"Okay," continued Paul, sensing that Alex was not yet tracking with him. He anticipated that distilling what he and Ronnie had discussed for hours may take a few minutes. "Let us first look at the Greek word for creation. It is *ktisis*. Now, let me blow your mind. Do you know what *ktisis* actually means? I mean what it means way down deep in the etymology of the Greek language."

"No," answered Alex. I haven't looked that deeply into the Greek for 'creation.'"

"Okay, here goes," stated Paul with scholarly authority. "The Greek word, *ktisis*, which stands for the English word 'creation', means ... 'CRE-ATION' of 'the CREATURE'. Get it?! Nothing more and nothing less." A smile came over Paul's face, knowing that he had so quickly and craftily teased his good friend.

Alex immediately recognized that he had been baited, hooked, landed, and filleted in one fell swoop. "Okay, okay. You got me. Now, cut it out." *I knew we couldn't go very far in discussing Zoot before this would be a free-for-all.*

"Okay, responded Paul. "I'm sorry. I just thought that would be fun. So often people look for DEEP meaning in the biblical languages when the languages are just what they are—both non-mysterious and simply communicative of the Divine Mind and the Divine story."

"I get it. Unlike for politicians, in Aramaic, Hebrew, Greek, Latin, German, English, and other languages through which the Bible was writ-ten or translated, the word 'is' often means 'is.'"

"Right," interjected Paul. "So, before we consider whether Zoot is part of God's creation, we must wrestle with the question regarding for whom was Scripture written. For the people of the Old and New Testa-ments, or for us as well?"

"Well, I believe that Scripture is God-breathed and thereby, eternal. Thus, while Scripture was written two to three thousand years ago, it is meant for us as much as it was meant for our predecessors."

"Yes, we believe that, also," articulated Paul, "but we also believe that some Scripture was written specifically for some people and simply recorded for all. For instance, when the Apostle Paul writes to Timothy, 'Bring the cloak that I left with Carpus at Troas when you come—and the books, especially the parchments,' Paul is not asking everyone to bring him his cloak, books, and parchments. He is specifically asking Timothy to do so. Thus, while the letter to Timothy was written for Timothy to read then and the world to read now, that imperative was directed specifi-cally to Timothy. So, we must be careful to investigate, concerning any and all passages, who precisely is the primary and secondary audience."

"I got that," stated Alex. "So, regarding 'creation,'" he opined rhetori-cally, "I guess the question is whether Romans 8 considers Zoot part of the 'creation' that Paul wished the intended audience to understand."

"Clumsy, but correct," inserted Paul. The two had a long history of razzing each other as they discussed serious theological concerns. "So, first, was the Book of Romans written singularly for Christian believers of the Church of Rome? Even more precisely, for Jewish-Christian believers, or for a broader audience?"

"Well, I guess that my first off-the-cuff argument would be that there is quite an extensive list of people whom Paul is greeting in chapter sixteen. These people are from the entire Christian world of that day. This even includes Jewish and Gentile believers. So, I would argue that this letter is for a wider audience than the immediate Roman Church. Or, rather, than singularly the Jewish Christians in the Church of Rome."

"Agreed," stated Paul. "Anything else?" he asked, employing his best Socratic method.

"Well, then there is the message of the book. Few books detail the Gospel so explicitly. This is applicable for today. Additionally, we still see the present need for sending the preacher with the Word. That, too, is applicable for today. Therefore, without getting even more specific, I would say that the intended audience for the book is the original Roman Church audience, the entire Church in that day, and even our current and future Church."

"Quite possibly," responded Paul, "but have you considered the distinction and collaboration of the human author, Paul, and the inspiring work of the Holy Spirit? Might Paul have had one audience in mind while the Holy Spirit was targeting a broader audience?"

"Well, that could certainly be the case, but I would not presume to know the mind of God. His ways are beyond our ways. Since the Book of Romans is preserved in the cannon, I would assume that it was meant for all time, for the teaching of all of us through eternity.

"Right," agreed Paul. "Some books were written even to individuals, like Paul to Timothy or Luke to Theophilus, but with a future wider audience in mind by the Holy Spirit, Who inspired the author's pen. I think that we are all in agreement on this. So, back to 'creation?'"

"Well, I would suggest that the notion of creation in biblical times was much smaller than the scientific interpretation of creation today."

"Science, today, does not believe in creation," countered Paul.

"Yes, I know. I know that the Bible is not a science textbook. What we call 'creation,' secular scientists would call the universe. Nevertheless, if the Book of Romans was written for us also, then all the universe is creation. So, Zoot would be part of the 'creation' intended in Romans 8."

"Great job, Alex," stated Paul, "we completely agree with you. However, then we saw another perspective. Let us assume that 'creation' was originally intended to denote the limited world understood in biblical days. Once Zoot enters our world and interacts with our world, he becomes part of our world. He becomes part of creation."

"Like Ezekiel's wheels. They were other-worldly. However, as soon as Ezekiel saw them, they became part of his recorded vision and real to him and us—part of the creation in which we belong." Alex paused for a moment. "And what about us? We were not part of creation when Paul wrote Romans. Nevertheless, we clearly see that the text applies to 'all creation' from the week of creation until now and into the future until the return of Christ."

"Exactly," responded Paul. "Indeed, the biblical authors could not possibly have had a vision for creation which included microscopic organisms or creatures from other planets."

"But," added Alex, "they had a vision for heavenly creatures which we have never seen on earth. Therefore, they, too, are part of creation."

"Thus?" asked Paul, begging Alex to come to a logical conclusion.

"Zoot, and all other extraterrestrials, must be part of 'creation,' whether or not the apostle Paul could envision such."

"That, too, is our understanding," agreed Paul.

Chapter 14

T HE Colonel immediately barked orders to Tippet and Hawley. "Get Commander in here, NOW." The two men jumped out of the room, glad that they could use this as a reason to escape from the Colonel. Within minutes, Marcia Commander entered the room and saw the Colonel sitting at the table deep in thought. Marcia was the chief civilian contact who worked in CCTech and directly connected downward to the other employees or upward to the Colonel and sometimes above. All employees below her and even most above her, less than affectionately, called her 'The Commander,' but the Colonel would never do such. He always dropped the article 'the' when naming her. While her last name was sufficient for him, he even hated calling her 'Commander' for its sheer authoritative inference. Nevertheless, it was her name, and he could not escape that.

Marcia Commander was no more than five-foot-four, with medium-length blonde hair transitioning to silver. Both her presence and her position made others perceive her as significantly taller. While only slightly overweight, she had an athletic physique under her appropriately tailored business suit. She was all government. She held no paid position in CCTech. The government paid her to monitor events at a firm that held top-secret contracts. She was different from most of the suits, many of whom had actual positions and responsibilities in CCTech. Her independence from CCTech allowed her to travel the building at will. She was to watch others, not have them watch her.

No words were required to communicate the tension in the 'Janitorial Services' room. The Colonel peered up from his folded hands. His demeanor was stoic. She stood stiffly in front of him. Hawley had said nothing to her of the situation other than that the Colonel wanted to meet with her. This alone was sufficient to get her full attention and set up her guard. The actual order of superiority or submission was ill-defined between the two. The Colonel certainly had authority outside of CCTech, but it was unclear who had the greater authority within the company's walls. Both wanted the other to recognize that they had authority in this domain, and neither was willing to relinquish such. Thus, the stalemate continued whenever the Colonel met The Commander regarding CCTech. Fortunately for both, the Colonel rarely made visitations to CCTech. His domain was far broader than only one company.

Marcia had no fondness for the Colonel. Beyond the professional wrestling for authority, she saw his disdain for others. She recognized how he could dehumanize those who were obstacles to his trajectory. His fickleness made him unpredictable. At any moment, he could employ a heavy hand upon others, and the limits of which, while secretive, often seemed to be terminal in some manner or another. Unfortunately, Marcia had enormous blind spots. She was oblivious that the dimensions she most despised of the Colonel were precisely characteristics others saw in her.

"Do you even know what is happening in this place?" he asked in a tone so soft that it was even more emphatic and incriminating.

"Regarding?" she asked. She was smart enough to feel out a situation before committing to an ambiguous scenario posed by another.

"John Tate."

"Yes, we began an investigation on Friday night and found out that Tate copied files by Monday afternoon."

"Sir," stated the Colonel, demanding that she address him as 'Sir.' Specifically circumventing his demand—and as an act of defiant refusal—she continued her comments without starting with or ending with 'sir'. She had never been in the military and would only use 'sir' for someone she truly respected. She knew that the Colonel garnered respect from those below by intimidation and those above by sucking up. Unknown to the Colonel, every time Marcia ended a sentence to the Colonel, rather than speaking 'sir,' she silently replaced it with a carefully and creatively constructed curse word.

"He was off on Monday. He returned to Charlotte Monday afternoon and came back to the office on Tuesday morning. We have been monitoring him since to see if he attempted to copy any other files."

"How do you know that he came back to town on Monday?" asked the Colonel.

"The second we knew what happened, I told Colonel Poriss."

"I was not informed!?" snapped the Colonel.

"That, I mean informing YOU, was neither my responsibility nor my concern. I followed procedures." She silently ended the sentence with an invective. "We knew Tate's whereabouts almost immediately after Friday evening or Saturday morning. Shortly after, we put a tail on him. We quickly caught up with him after he had lunch with another person, and we continued to track his whereabouts."

"He had lunch with Robert Forsythe," said the Colonel, filling in the blanks to attempt to regain a sense of superiority of knowledge. "I know EVERYTHING that you know." Although he said this with authority, Marcia doubted that this was true. However, there certainly could be someone who leaked information to him to attempt their own ascent of 'Mount Importance.' Government security was a cut-throat business.

"If you know everything, I assume that this meeting is completed," Marcia countered, hopefully calling his bluff.

"Not yet."

Seeing that she was not to get away so quickly, she also attempted to obtain some information. "Who is Robert For . . . ?"

"Robert Forsythe is one of Tate's friends in Boone." Immediately, the Colonel decided that providing the Commander with any additional information was pointless, contrary to the direction of the proper flow of information, and possibly threatening his upper-hand position. In an abrupt about-face, he disrespectfully dismissed her with only a silent gesture. As she exited with her back to him and hands in front of her, she had a gesture for him as well but kept it out of his eyesight.

Robert was surprised by his cellphone announcing a text but more so that it was his second text from Tate's burner phone. Before reading the body of the text, he was taken aback by its first line.

DANGER!! IT'S OVER

No $

    It was sufficiently alarming that Robert pulled over into the nearest parking lot to concentrate and respond safely. Rather than replying to the text, he pulled out the burner cellphone he had just purchased and set up. He copied the phone number from his cellphone to his burner phone.

> This is R.F. burner. ??? What's going on?

(Tate immediately understood that it was Robert.) They know EVERYTHING. Went to work. They cornered me. It's BAD. REALLY BAD.

> Lose your job?

Not yet. Worse. Threatened LIFE & DEATH. Family threatened. (pause)

And they know you have it.

> What? YOU TOLD?!? *Fool for trusting.*

No choice. Threatened.

> Family more important than $. Safe if we give it back?
> How can we fix this?

I don't know. We know too much.

> I need to look at it again. I think I saw something . . .

Get rid of it. No, I mean get it to everyone. EVERYONE.

> *I need one more look first.* Probably Saturday.

May cost you more than you can afford.

Sounds like that either way. I'll examine the package and then decide how to get rid of it or send it out.

I think that you should. (pause)

Stop. You got me into this. I'll decide how I get out of it. I think I know how.

Ok.

Chapter 15

A LEX continued his Zoom call with Paul, his friend from Moody Bible Institute who went on to be a seminary professor.

"But I was thinking," said Alex, "more important than the notion that all extraterrestrials must be part of God's creation, this entire discussion leads to a great number of implications. For instance, would the existence of Zoot imply the possible existence of other gods? Of course, I do not believe in other gods, but some may see this as a natural implication."

"Other creators, you mean?" asked Paul.

"Yes, but I fully realize that, according to Scripture, this is impossible. This is simply an academic exercise." Alex was concerned that he was treading on thin ice. He did not wish to sound heretical.

"Look," assured Paul, "in theological circles, when we debate ideas, we regularly experiment with ideas which we know are on the fringes of heresy. Often, there are two camps. One camp imagines some notions and then searches for biblical support. Another camp examines Scripture and sees how far they can stretch various interpretations and implications without veering too far from the confines of biblical security. When either camp submits to the authority of Scripture, everything can be corrected. However, if they believe that their ideas—and therefore, really, they themselves—are more authoritative than the Bible, heresies automatically abound, the first one being a misplacement of authority. So, while we may toy with heresy for a moment, as long as in the end we submit to Scripture as having the final unassailable authority, we will be okay."

"We are on the same page," Alex stated. "I looked to the Bible, and I was caught in a thematic series of passages in Isaiah 43-46, where the prophet—and, therefore, God through the prophet—mentions repeatedly that there is no other God." Alex pulled out his cellphone and opened his Bible app. He began to read. "This includes,

> Isaiah 43:10b-11. *Before Me there was no God formed, nor shall there be after Me. I, even I, am the Lord, and besides Me there is no savior.*

> Isaiah 44:8b. *Is there a God besides Me? Indeed there is no other Rock; I know not one.*

> Isaiah 45:5-6. *I am the Lord, and there is no other; there is no God besides Me. I will gird you, though you have not known Me, that they may know from the rising of the sun to its setting that there is none besides Me. I am the Lord, and there is no other.*

> Isaiah 45:14b-15. *Surely God is in you, and there is no other; there is no other God. Truly You are God, who hide Yourself, O God of Israel, the Savior!*

> Isaiah 45:18. *For thus says the Lord, who created the heavens, Who is God, Who formed the earth and made it, Who has established it, Who did not create it in vain, Who formed it to be inhabited: I am the Lord, and there is no other.*

> Isaiah 45:21b-22. *And there is no other God besides Me, a just God and a Savior; there is none besides Me. Look to Me, and be saved, all you ends of the earth! For I am God, and there is no other.*

> Isaiah 46:8-9. *Remember the former things of old, for I am God, and there is no other; I am God, and there is none like Me."*

"Four chapters in a row with a common theme," continued Alex, "that there is no other God. This is important."

"Yes, it is," interjected Paul. "If we stop there, we could not even discuss whether there are other gods."

"Right."

"But, as an academic exercise, we must continue down this path," continued Paul. "You see, we are at an intersection of ideas."

"How so?"

"Well," argued Paul, "we have several crisscrossing ideas. First, for whom is Scripture written? Second, are there other gods? Third, if there are other gods, are any creators of part of the universe? Fourth, we know that salvation on this earth is only through Jesus Christ, but if there are other creator-gods, does salvation have different paths under those conditions? This is where Romans 8 brings us."

"It's quite a puzzle," offered Alex.

"Yes, but at least the various possibilities are limited." Paul began to read from First Corinthians, 8:4b-7.

> "There is no other God but one. For even if there are so-called gods, whether in heaven or on earth (as there are many gods and many lords), yet for us there is one God, the Father, of whom are all things, and we for Him; and one Lord Jesus Christ, through whom are all things, and through whom we live."

"I know that passage well," replied Alex. "I just preached on that."

"Isn't God's work cool," Paul nodded in agreement.

"Throughout the Old Testament, there are mentions of gods worshiped by other tribes and nations: Asherah, Baal, Dagon, and Moloch among many others."

"And there certainly," added Paul, "are false gods mentioned in the New Testament."

"Yes, but first, they are exactly that. All of them are false gods. Ours, Jehovah, Yahweh, is the one true God. More than that, let's even assume that others are real gods. Then, I believe that it simply does not matter if one accepts the authority of Scripture. The only salvific economy is provided to us by Jehovah through Jesus Christ alone. Even those passages from Isaiah state not only that there is only one God, but that He is also our only Savior."

"While I completely agree," continued Paul, "I think that there are many more cases to consider. According to Ronnie, we need to consider whether Zoot has fallen under Adam's fall has affected all of creation."

"Wasn't that decided after we determined that Zoot was considered part of God's creation?"

"In part," answered Paul, "but there are more conditions. Let's go through some of the cases. The first case is that all creation is fallen through the Adamic fall, and Zoot is fallen as a derivative of the fall. In that case, Zoot would hold no special position beyond that of all other non-human creation. Back to Romans 8, 'All creation eagerly waits—even groaning—and will be delivered from the bondage of corruption.'"

"But this deliverance from bondage," added Alex, "is tied to the return of Christ for the redemption or resurrection of the Church. Creation is not redeemed and liberated until all believers are."

"Right. God's revealed salvific system is centered on Jesus and mankind, not any other creation elements. So, just as a dog or cat may be liberated from bondage—although I can't even imagine how any cat could be liberated from its feline pestilence—Zoot would be a part of this redemption, but not in a manner similar to believing humankind." A wry smile came over Paul's face at the comment about cats.

Keeping up with a torrential pace of theology and implications, Alex added to the discussion. "Christ came in the form of man. And each aspect of His life is part of salvation's plan—His birth, life, suffering, death, resurrection, and ascension. Every part of it is connected to the perfect, sinless Godman, taking on human flesh, experiencing humanity in its fullness, suffering, and dying for us. The Pascal Lamb, taking upon Himself the wrath of God for our sin which He bore, being the firstfruits of the resurrection, and ascending to His rightful place at the right hand of the Father."

"Great summary," proffered Paul. "So, back to Zoot. God came in the form of man and not in the form of Zoot. So, while Zoot—he, she, or it—may receive benefits including deliverance from the bondage of corruption, this benefit would fall short of the adoption and redemption provided to believing humanity."

"Therefore, in this case," summarized Alex, "the existence of Zoot would not affect Christian theology."

"Correct," responded Paul.

"You said that there were several cases. What's the next?" Inquired Alex.

"Okay," said Paul with confidence that he had his following line of argumentation prepared, "Let's assume that Zoot is in a fallen state through his action or the actions from earlier Zoots."

"Then," Alex responded, hoping that he could more independently work through this hypothesis, "there are two cases. First, God did not provide a means of salvation for Zoots, or second, He provided a very different means of salvation for them. If God did not provide a means of salvation, then Zoots would be irrevocably lost. There is nothing that demands of God that He provide a means of salvation for anyone. For us, salvation is God's love and grace at work. No one can mandate to God that He must show grace to Zoots."

"Okay," interjected Paul, "Zoots might be lost and unsavable."

"Right. However, if they are to be saved, it would probably not be through Christ, or at least through the human Christ. God would need to come in the form of Zoot and die for Zoots to the saved."

"Well," hesitated Paul, "that's what I thought as well, but Ronnie made me second guess this. He said that I was employing the salvific model designed for us humans. A means of salvation for Zoots may be completely different than for us. Indeed, God has the complete sovereign authority to even create a system of salvation by works for Zoots—as contrary as that might be to our system of 'by grace through faith.' God could have created Zootkind as, how can I say this, to be not as completely depraved as is mankind. In short, God can do anything that God wishes to do. Granted, we have no divinely inspired revelation that God may have done this, but He is under no mandate to inform us of His plans for Zoots."

"I'm with you," affirmed Alex. "Very interesting."

"It really is."

"So, wait," Alex raised his hands, "what would this case mean for us?"

"Actually, for each of these cases—whether the Zoots are fallen or not, God's plan for Zoots could be both different from, and independent of, our means of salvation."

"So, it will not affect us or our salvation," synthesized Alex.

Paul nodded, agreeing with Alex. "I think that there remains one more case," opined Paul. There is still the case where Zoot has not yet fallen from either the Adamic or Zootian fall."

"Then it could be that Zoots were created not to fall," added Alex, attempting to keep on track with Paul and his previous discussions with Ronnie. "Maybe they don't need to be saved because they will never be lost."

"Quite possibly," answered Paul.

"Then, again," parsed Alex, "the existence of Zoot would have no effect, whatsoever, on us."

"Right," agreed Paul. "However, there is one more interesting subcase."

"How so?"

"There is the possibility that Zoot will fall through interaction with humans."

"That would be sad," acknowledged Alex, "that man would cause the fall of an entire other world."

"Indeed, if that happened, I do not know how Zoot would be saved. The human Christ will not be again sacrificed. I just don't know how salvation could be provided for Zoot. However, I do know that it would not matter to us. We have the historic sacrifice of Christ. That can't be either undone or done again."

"Wait, we have gone through a total of one, two, three, four, five," Alex counted on his fingers, "five different cases for Zoot. All of them came to the same result. Concerning the existence of extraterrestrial life on Earth, there really is no implication to Christian theology, at least in respect to the theology of salvation."

"That is the opinion of Ronnie and me. We could be wrong."

"That would be a first," Alex retorted with humorous sarcasm.

"For sure, for sure," Paul said with a chuckle. "In fact, I believe that, if extraterrestrial life were indisputably found on Earth, the greatest implication to Christian theology would not be in respect to salvation; it would be again to demonstrate to us—in possibly, a deeper and more expansive manner—how magnificent God's creation is."

"Amen, brother. Amen. God and His creation are glorious indeed." After a brief pause, Alex continued, "I think I have three more cases," stated Alex.

"How so," asked Paul. "I really thought that we had all of them." Paul was curious and quite certain that Alex's scenarios would fall into the previous cases.

"First," continued Alex, "Couldn't aliens be demonic manifestations aimed at turning our attention away from the One True God?" Alex envisioned something likened to gargoyles perching atop Gothic architecture.

"Yes," replied Paul. "That is a common understanding among those in the church universal." Paul paused for a moment of thought. "However, that would mean that they are fallen angels—within God's creation—but outside of the redemption of creation through Christ. They are lost. Eternally lost. Yes, aliens could be demonic manifestations. Even Satan disguises himself as an angel of light, a roaring lion seeking whom he can devour, and a serpent ready to deceive. Thus, he and his minion can parade about as aliens distracting believers from God."

"Right, but still part of creation."

"So, not really a new case. But an important case for consideration." After a brief pause, Alex continued, "Hmm, since this case is still part of creation, we are back to our previous conclusion that 'it doesn't matter.'"

"Exactly!" exclaimed Paul. "Even if the aliens are fallen angels, they are part of creation, and their existence has no impact on our Christian salvific theology. So, what is your next case?"

"Well, ah, there is the 'Creation Gap Theory." continued Alex.

"There is, indeed. Give me more."

"Well, some believe that there could be a gap of even millions of years between the first creation in Genesis 1:1 and a second creation, or a re-creation, in Genesis 1:2–31. If so, creatures—even humans—could have been formed in the first creation and could have evolved in some manner to be much more advanced than us, traveled off, or even stayed around in some way that they are only infrequently seen by us, then the Earth was destroyed in some manner, and then a new Earth was created, and here we are—and so are they."

"And what do you think about that?"

"Now, after our previous discussions, I think that whether of the first creation or the second—if there actually were two creations—this is all under the umbrella of creation. Thus, again, 'it does not matter.' It has no impact on our salvation and, more precisely, the mechanisms of grace and faith in Christ which brings about salvation."

"I agree," continued Paul. "Now, my dear friend, what is your last case?"

"As I consider it more, it still remains part of 'creation.'"

"How so?"

"Some who dabble in physics believe that aliens could be part of a parallel universe. They seem to particularly believe this when they analyze the flight of UFOs. They seem to fly in ways that contradict our laws of physics. Possibly, our universes intersect at some points—or at some times. I'm not really sure how to say this. These UFOs may be behaving consistently with their universe and its laws of physics."

"Ah," interjected Paul, "the old Star-Trekian 'space-time continuum.'"

"Right. Right."

"So, what do you think about that?"

"Now, I think that all of this would still be a matter of God's creation. Thus, 'it doesn't matter.'"

"I again concur," stated Paul. "It really doesn't matter. In fact, NONE of these options has any real implications or effects on the Christian theology of salvation."

"If a parallel universe exists, it would have been created by the Creator. This could bring even more glory to Him as we realized all the more how magnificent is our God and His creation." With joy for having run the gamut of options and found God ultimately glorious and God's plan of salvation for man secure in all cases, Alex gleefully said, "This type of exercise is fun."

"It certainly is," agreed Paul. "It is even more fun in the theoretical. I couldn't imagine having these discussions if aliens were authentic. It might cause me more consternation. However, I do not believe that the theological results would be any different."

Alex bit his tongue. *If he only knew what might come out soon. The theoretical is now the actual. At least, when it comes out, I'll be ready to answer the questions of my congregants.*

Chapter 16

ALEX'S cellphone rang. The ringer was a modern praise song. The caller ID indicated 'Caller Unknown.' "Hello, Alex Spencer speaking."

"Hello, Alex. It's Tate."

"I'm sorry," continued Alex, "I did not recognize your number. Hey, Tate. How are you?" *Midday? Not at work?*

"Um, I'm using another phone for right now," Answered Tate, not wanting to mention the burner phone. "I just . . . " Even in his first words, Tate sounded halting and cautious. He believed that, for now, his burner phone was safe from government eavesdropping, but he did not know about the phones at the church or even Alex's personal phone.

Alex interrupted Tate's attempt at an introduction. "Hey, I was just talking to someone today, and your name came up in passing."

"Who was that?"

"No one special. Just about your two houses."

"Someone in church?"

Alex was always protective of all those in his flock. "Yes," answered Alex, providing little information about who it was.

"It wasn't Robert Forsythe, was it?"

"No. Someone else." Alex was taken aback by Tate singling out of one particular person from hundreds. "Why Robert?"

"Oh," Tate immediately recognized that he had gone too far. He hoped that he had not inadvertently ignited interest when there was none previously. "Ah, no reason, really."

"Again, it was just a passing comment." Changing the conversation, Alex continued, "But you called. About what?"

"Ah, I don't really know what to say without potentially getting you in trouble also," Tate unexpectedly interjected into the conversation.

"What? About?"

"I may have done something illegal," stated Tate.

"You MAY HAVE?"

"Well, I know that it was illegal."

"Um, what do you want to say?" asked Alex. Caught off guard, he immediately reverted to 'pastor mode.' "Take your time and . . . " Alex added a hand gesture for emphasis, which he immediately recognized that Tate would not see since they were on the phone, "don't tell me anything that I really shouldn't know." Alex wanted to ensure that he could keep the conversation confidential.

Only once in his career did Alex have to report a situation to authorities outside the church. A guilt-ridden man confided that he practiced a particularly vile and harmful compulsion and was within minutes of reoffending. Fearing another child's grave and imminent harm, Alex ordered him to halt his plans immediately. When the man stated that he could control neither his thoughts nor actions and had even less power to stop the immediate offense, Alex decided to report the situation to the police before any more children and families were devastated. Within minutes, the man was apprehended, and the child was returned to his parents unharmed.

"Well, I copied some files from work. I wasn't supposed to. I'm sure that was illegal. I accidentally copied them."

"Wait," interrupted Alex. "Did you copy them accidentally or purposely?"

"Well, first accidentally and then purposely."

"I don't understand. Did you copy them TWICE?"

"Exactly. I accidentally copied them during a mass file transfer. It was absolutely not my fault. On that, I did nothing wrong. When I looked at a few of the files, I saw what they were, copied them all to a flashdrive, and took them out of CCTech."

"If you knew that was illegal, then why did you do that?"

"Well, it was a combination of two things," answered Tate. "First, I saw that the information was important to be seen by as many people as possible. It can affect everyone. It is important but not life-threatening." *The information is not life-threatening, but the people who want to keep it secret are life-threatening.*

"But who makes you the arbiter of what is important and should be seen?" asked Alex.

"Good point." Tate received but immediately dismissed Alex's question. "Second, I thought that I could possibly get money from the government or someone else for these files."

"Extortion?!?"

"Um, I never thought of it as extortion as I was doing it. You know, with Allie and all, my family can use some money."

"I understand," followed Alex. "I understand that very well. Is this the way, though?"

"I'm no longer sure," replied Tate. "I just don't know right now."

"There must be a better way. Something better than extortion. Can you return them?"

"Um, it doesn't work that way. If I turned myself in, I would at least be immediately fired from my job."

"Okay."

"And I might not be able to get another job in IT at any other company. My career could be over."

Alex could sense Tate's fear. It was more than about what he had done. It was about the life-long career consequences he could suffer. He had been in IT for quite a while. Losing his position and any prospects for another IT position would essentially cause him to start all over again with a new career path. It could be financially devastating, at best.

"Look, Alex, I confess that I did it for money. Maybe greed took over. I thought that I could either sell the files to someone or even sell them back to the government. I just wanted to recoup financially from what we have already paid for Allie's leukemia treatments. There are more treatments ahead. We have lost almost everything. I suspected that there could be money in it for me and my family. Now I realize that this is probably not an issue of money; it's about peoples' lives. Maybe lots of people."

"Should I know what the files are about?" asked Alex.

"Please. No. Don't ask. It is better that way." *I can't get him into this as well. I have already jeopardized Robert and Tracie. He may already be in some danger.*

"Okay. Okay." *Some things are better off not knowing.*

"I'm just not sure that it is safe," warned Tate. He wrestled with every syllable he uttered, wondering if he were saying too much or the wrong thing. Flashbacks of the interview passed through his mind. The vision of Martin holding the cellphone and videoing his wife and son at their home was particularly traumatizing. Each memory took hold of his consciousness and made concentrating on his own words difficult. He would have still been terrified if he had not become numbed by emotional exhaustion.

"Are you going to tell the company?"

"Probably." *Someone in authority over there said that CCTech does not yet know anything about this. Colonel could be lying. I think that, if they knew, I would have been fired already.* "I would need to consider how and when to do it, but . . . "

"But?" responded Alex, attempting to draw out a response from Tate.

"Someone in the church. I mean, I told someone in the church."

"Who?"

"Ah, let's just leave it at that. No names." *Gotta keep Robert as safe as I can. Or am I keeping Alex safe from all of this?*

"Okay," said Alex, "but might that person be complicit in a crime as well?" *Not that I would report this. This is not like the imminent danger posed by that abuser.*

"Maybe, . . . but he might be the only way to fix this and protect everyone involved."

"Wait. Aren't you the only one involved, other than, now, this person?"

"Well, yes," answered Tate. *And Tracie.* "But the families too." *That might sound like the families are in jeopardy . . . Um.* "I mean that someone and I could both be in trouble, and this might affect our jobs and families."

"Look, Tate, I trust that you will do what is best. Just do what is right and as soon as you can. Where are you now?"

"I had a terrible meeting at work. They know that I had the files and what I did with them. Well, it is difficult to define who the 'they' are. Some government types, I believe. 'They' certainly want them back. 'They' told me that no one at CCTech knows, but I find that a little hard to believe. However," Tate mused aloud, "If CCTech knew, I believe that I would have been fired immediately." After a pause, he continued, "I have to confess, they scared me, and not just a little. I took the rest of the day off from work. I'm heading home, and we are going to get away for a few days. I just got here with my family." Tate immediately regretted saying where he was—in case *they* were listening in. Then he thought to himself, *If they can hear in on my conversations, then they much more easily can track everywhere I go.* "Look, I have to go. I'll get back to you when I can."

As abruptly as the call began, Tate had hung up. Alex was left with unresolved concerns for Tate, Robert, and who knows who else. Alex immediately bowed his head in prayer for the situation, or at least for the little portion of the situation that he knew.

Alex knew that few would understand the complexity of being a pastor and hearing parishioners' secrets. Some were issues of sin, and others were less clearly so. Some were simply unusual opinions. Some were about lifestyle or biblical life application. Regardless of the type of secret, secrets they were, and secrets had to be kept secrets. This was particularly difficult when Alex realized that the secret had to be confessed to the person's spouse—by the person, not the pastor. He would be available if needed, but the delivery of the news belonged to the congregant.

Adding a layer of complexity, Alex made it a practice to forgive when needed and forget whenever possible. In the case of Barry and Vera, Alex knew that they were unfaithful to each other a decade or so ago. They had repented, confessed to each other, forgiven each other, and had since had a beautiful marriage blessed with three children. Alex thought it to be unfair to permanently hold their pasts against them. As best he could, he focused on more recent and wholesome events. He always sought to define a person by their recent history rather than by one or more single events which occurred years ago. He often thought, *if when we repent God forgives us our sins and casts them into the sea as far as the east is from the west, then I should do my best to do likewise and at least cast the remembrance of forgiven sin across the street, where I won't go looking for it again.*

Chapter 17

I MMEDIATELY upon arriving home from his interrogation at CCTech by the suits, Tate informed his wife, son, and daughter to pack for a long weekend in the mountains. They could do the two-hour drive on Thursday, spend the weekend, and return on Monday. His son could do school online, and his wife had no immediate appointments and was free to travel. His daughter often missed school for health reasons and, more usually than not, learned online. Doing the same for a few days would go unnoticed by her teachers and school. They accepted his invitation— albeit he insisted upon it—with gusto. They always loved their visits to their log cabin.

While they were curious why Tate seemed in such a rush, they also knew that he had far too few days off and had recently been inundated with work. While he had been to the mountains the previous weekend, he now wanted to go back. They took this to signal how desperately he needed time off to recuperate mind and soul. They willingly accepted almost any reason for traveling north. They planned to take some hikes in the Blue Ridge Mountains. They loved trails on Jefferson Mountain or carriage trails at Moses Cone Park, particularly up to the fire tower.

On this drive to the mountains, Tate seemed disconnected and spoke very little on the drive. This was not all that unusual. However, this time there was a darkness to his silence. Sarah, Tate's wife, found this disconcerting but in no way alarming. They drove north on I77 and turned north onto Rt. 421. As soon as the mountains were in view, they felt a sense of calming relief. Life was a little slower and much more picturesque in the mountains. They had room to breathe. The fresh air rejuvenated the soul.

When they arrived at their log cabin near Fleetwood, they entered and immediately unpacked their limited bags. They needed to bring little with them since this was as much their home as was their Charlotte residence. Tate immediately turned on the news, irrationally wondering if his situation would be broadcast. Almost at the same instance, Sarah gently scolded him, "You don't need that, do you? You need to relax for a couple days. I can see that you have a lot on your mind. That stuff will just suck the life out of you."

Tate agreed and complied. He pulled up a book which he reserved for reading at the cabin. It was usually some nerdy scientific reading or old piece of literature. However, this evening, he only feigned reading. His mind was in a stupor, remembering events of the day and, even more importantly, what that might mean to Robert Forsythe's life. Tate trusted the Colonel and believed that providing Robert's name would protect Tate and his family. *What about the Forsythe's family?* he thought. *Martin has been called off from harming us. Would the Colonel now sic him on the Forsythes? Robert needs to get those files out. This is his, no our, only complete protection. The more people know, the safer all are.*

Hour after hour, Tate worked through the events of the day. He wondered what he could have done differently. But nothing of value came to mind. He wondered how he could now help Robert, but he was equally at a loss. Tate's wife was not fooled by his inattentive reading. "You could at least turn a page now and then," she said to him, acknowledging that little attention was being paid to the book. "Anything you want to tell me?"

"No, Hon. Just work stuff." *Hate lying, especially to her. Sometimes I have to.*

"Well, maybe you should just go to bed. You can get a good night's sleep and get up with a fresh mind in the morning. I'll come to bed in a couple hours."

"Sounds great," Tate replied and, with a small peck on his wife's head, he headed to their bedroom. He had all intention of following her recommendation, but sleep eluded him. He tossed and turned deep in thought until his wife climbed into bed. Her entrance into the bed made little difference. He knew that exhaustion would eventually and unforgivingly force sleep into submission; and that it did.

Upon cracking his eyes open in the morning, his tormenting thoughts returned and tortured the rest of his day. He considered every phrase in the interview, what was said, what was implied, and what might be inferred. He was angry that he did not have better responses to the suits' questions but consoled himself because he was caught off guard. *Why hadn't I been planning answers to questions they would raise? I could have been more prepared.* He had never before done or considered doing anything like he did. Tate was not a man of great courage. He was not one to gamble. *Why did I even look at those files? I knew better. Someone else messed up by transferring those classified files. I shouldn't have looked. Greed made me do it. Greed. Proud of yourself?* He liked the status quo.

Tate looked about the room. His wife, Sarah, was already up. She was probably in the kitchen cooking up something delicious or sitting on the deck with a hot cup of coffee. In an unexpected moment, he remembered Tracie Bryant, a good friend and the network administrator at CCTech. He had commandeered her computer to log in to his account and copy the files to his USB flashdrive. Certainly, they had determined that the files were transferred to the flashdrive from her computer.

Almost like telepathy was at work, his cellphone rang. The caller ID indicated that it was TRACIE!

"Hey, Trac . . . "

Before he could complete his greeting, Tracie firmly interrupted. "What did you do?!" He did not need to see Tracie. Through her voice on the phone, he could feel Tracie shaking with fear about losing her job and loathing for him.

"Um . . . I," Tate stammered to respond.

"I got FIRED today. Fired. All clearances revoked. FIRED." Tracie was livid. "They came into my office and escorted me out of the building. No chance to do anything. Just out of the building. They even checked my purse on the way out. Like I would have the Fagaku supercomputer hidden in my purse? I was mortified." Tate could tell that there were terror and tears on the other end.

"I . . . " Tate tried to interject.

"I heard your name mentioned. They saw you on camera go into my office when I was fixing your computer. Wait . . . " Tracie was finally putting pieces together of the puzzle which had flashed so quickly before her and permanently altered her life. "You messed with your computer, didn't you? To get me there. No, to get me out of my office. WHAT DID YOU DO?" Tracie demanded.

"I copied some files from my account on your computer to a flash-drive," Robert confessed. In a way, he hoped a clean confession would quickly result in understanding. It did not.

"How dare you. We have been friends for more than a decade. I love your wife and your children. How could you do this?" Tate hung his head in shame. It was no use to tell her about his failed notions of coming to some money to help with debts and his daughter's leukemia treatments. There was no justification. The increasingly large circle of people being hurt dispelled any attempt at a rationale. He imagined dropping a pebble into a pond and watching growing concentric rings of disturbance. However, the waves that his stone had formed were also increasing in severity—from ripples to waves to devastating tidal waves.

"I needed copies of some very important files. I know you don't understand, but these files are . . . "

"I don't care what they are. I don't care at all . . . Are, hey, are you a Communist spy? Are you working for another country?" Tracie knew full well that CCTech held and used many classified files at every level. As a network administrator, she was one of the first to get top-secret clearance because of the nature of future work.

"No. NO, I am NOT A SPY." Tate tried to be as convincing as possible.

"Then, why did you copy some files? No, never mind. I don't want to know. I don't care. I lost my job. They first blamed me. They BLAMED ME. Before they saw the video of you going into my office. How will I take care of my daughter? How will I pay my mortgage? How will I make it?" Tracie was distraught and in an inconsolable state.

"I'm sure . . . " Tate again tried to comfort her.

"SHUT UP. JUST SHUT UP," she shouted. Tate reactively pulled the phone away from his ear to protect his hearing.

"Look, I'm sorry, I . . . "

"I said, SHUT UP. You used MY computer. You used OUR friendship. You used ME. I don't want to hear anything from you ever. EVER." A tone sounded, and Tate knew that Tracie had hung up. He tried to call her back. His call went dead. He tried to text, but the text was not delivered. It was clear that Tracie had blocked his number.

Questions swirled through his mind, interfering with normal thought. *Would this be considered corporate espionage? Or governmental treason? How would it be classified? Did it matter? Would he have done it either way? Yes, if not for the threats to his family. He could never have predicted that someone would watch his home and menace his wife and son. What was Martin going to actually do to them? The Colonel seemed sufficiently motivated to get his information that, quite possibly, nothing was out of bounds. People still need to know what is on these files. Even if I get no money out of this, people need to know. I'm not willing to trade my family for the world to know this information. I'm not willing to trade Robert's family either. He's got to get those files out. Or have I already?*

Tate had deep and genuine concerns for Tracie. She was caught up in this mess because of him. He hated that his actions had hurt her. Since Tracie was fired after they—either government goons or CCTech administration—knew some or all of what transpired, including that Tate no longer possessed the files, he knew that there was no undoing of her firing. He suspected they found some obscure protocol that they could claim that she had broken to justify her firing—probably nothing that had anything to do with the network. However, her firing probably sealed his fate at CCTech. *Just a matter of time.*

The circularity of the unanswered questions made them never-ending. The morning led to the afternoon and a rainy evening on the county's east side. Still, Tate remained silent, almost lifeless. "Hey, how about if I run to Olive Garden and get us something to eat?" He asked.

"You're gonna go to Wilkes?" his wife asked.

"Why not? I need a drive anyway."

"Well, actually, Olive Garden sounds good."

"Yeah, Dad, I want some lasagna." . . .

Chapter 18

SATURDAY agendas were often up in the air. On some Saturdays, Robert worked through a fair part of the day. Equally often, he did not work at all and spent the day with his wife or his youngest daughter. His eighteen-year-old, Abigail, was usually off on her own with her friends. But fifteen-year-old Grace still spent time with the family, certainly more so than Abigail did at fifteen. On other Saturdays, Robert simply spent time in some leisure recreation independent of both work and family. This inconsistency in Saturday routines was regularly an area of stress and disagreement in his marriage. Emily wished that he would share all his Saturdays with her and prioritize her on that day of the week.

Robert was usually early to rise every day of the week. This day was no different. He woke up before 5 a.m. and began his morning routine: he let Foxtrot, their cream-colored golden doodle, out, waited for a few moments, and let Foxtrot back in; fed Foxtrot, ate his breakfast, and then performed his morning constitutional while checking his phone for important emails and a few newsfeeds. He then sat in a comfortable chair in his living room, turned on the TV, and began putzing on his computer. This was usually a quiet time before the rest of the family arose in a few hours. He liked this time. It was a typically productive time for thinking and planning.

This Saturday morning, Robert was still reeling from the visions he had seen on the flashdrive half a week earlier. He was overwhelmed by the sight of videos of extraterrestrial life, governmental analysis of each,

146

and the planned governmental response. On Thursday and Friday, Robert was unusually quiet in thought about his findings, and his reticence had not gone unnoticed by Emily. Today he needed to formulate a plan to see more files without endangering anyone—including himself—in the process. He knew that he would need access to another computer that was not connected to the internet. He discounted using either his home or work on computers, as they could be tracked. *A new computer, a brand-new computer, would never have been connected to the internet. I could disconnect my current computer from the internet, but a new computer might be even safer. A few hundred bucks is worth the added safety.*

Robert booted his laptop and investigated the business hours for the Staples store on Blowing Rock Road. There would be a sufficient selection of laptops there. And, at this point, laptops are priced as consumables to be replaced every few years. Numerous choices would be under $400. The website said that the store opened at 8 a.m. He decided that he would purchase a new computer, bring it to his office, never connect it to the internet, and investigate more files from the flashdrive.

It was now nearing 6 a.m.—too early to wake his wife by entering the master bedroom, getting clothes, and showering in the master bathroom. He would wait until 7 a.m., get cleaned up and dressed, and get to Staples as soon as it opened. He watched the minutes tick by—painfully slowly. He attempted to concentrate on a client's project, but focus and purpose were fleeting. Between glances at the clock, a full ten minutes passed. Then the interval between peeks diminished to five minutes, then three, two, and one. The clock seemed to be an enemy blocking him from getting to see more files.

At 6:55, unable to wait any longer, Robert entered his bedroom. His wife would soon be waking. He passed the bed, entered the bathroom, stripped, and immediately jumped in the shower. Emily heard the shower begin and got up. Entering the bathroom, she asked him, "Hi, hon. Did you sleep well last night?"

"Well, enough," he replied. "And you?"

"I slept well."

Robert knew that the inevitable question would arise, and it certainly did not take long.

"What do you have planned for today?" his wife asked,

"Oh, I thought that I would go into work for just a few hours, a potential new client." *I hate lying to her. This whole mess has recently made me lie to her more. I just hate this.* Now came the response he was dreading.

"I was hoping that you would come with me to the outlets in Blowing Rock. I need a few things."

"Can we do that this afternoon? I just need a few hours."

"Sure," responded Emily. "I have to run to the grocery store this morning anyway." Both were slightly pleased that their simultaneous busyness had averted a disagreement.

At 8 a.m. on a Saturday, Staples was empty. Before being pestered by a salesperson, Robert immediately made his way to the laptop section to get an idea of prices. Consistent with a typical Type A personality, Robert was ready and impatiently waiting for assistance after only a few minutes of investigating the display models. He went to the technology service desk and saw a young man getting ready to begin work. Robert looked at his name badge and said, "Hey, Thomas, how are you?"

"I am fine, thank you. How may I help you?"

"I need the cheapest possible laptop with a USB port and which can open PDFs and videos."

"The cheapest? Okay. Any other concerns?" *Cheap? Is that it? He must be in his 40s. Old people are a pain. They don't know anything.*

"I don't think so." *Just get me something simple.*

"Well, we have two options. First, there is a traditional laptop. Most will run $400-$500. Then we have Chromebooks. Some of these are $200-$300. What do you currently have for a computer?"

"I have two HP laptops, one at work and one at home. My daughter has a Chromebook, but I really don't use it."

"Then, based on familiarity, I strongly recommend that you stay with a laptop. I think that you might become frustrated with a completely new machine and platform. I suggest that you stick with an HP. Our least expensive laptop, which will probably do anything you need, is this one. It's $499 on sale right now."

"Okay. I'll take that one."

Chapter 19

Robert brought the smallish box to his office, opened it, and pulled out the new laptop. It certainly was smaller and lighter than his machines. *Technology keeps improving, or at least changing.* He plugged it in and started the setup process. He was careful to enter the least possible personal information. He refused to enter a name or email address when prompted. The computer stated that, without this information, he would not be able to complete the setup process. The computer would run, but he would not access all functions and could not get on the internet. Being wiser than a few days ago, Robert noticed that the Wi-Fi was automatically attempting to connect to any network that could be found and for which permission was given. Robert did not grant this permission and immediately saw the Wi-Fi icon and turned off the Wi-Fi system.

Robert wondered if he had found the sweet spot of providing enough information for the laptop to run while simultaneously avoiding all information that would connect the machine to the internet. He believed that he had satisfactorily completed the task. Nevertheless, with trepidation, he pulled the flashdrive from his pocket. *Last chance. Make sure it is right. No room for mistakes.* He inspected the laptop again to ensure that the Wi-Fi was off. Robert set his cellphone alarm for 11:30 a.m. to ensure that, if he were overly engrossed in the material, he would hear the alarm and meet his wife at noon for their afternoon together. With every step in the process, he became more nervous—not about doing something wrong, but about getting nearer to again seeing the files.

He could describe it no better than as a teenage boy nervously awaiting a chance at a second date.

Robert inserted the flashdrive into the USB port. The laptop immediately recognized a new drive and asked if he wished to open it. He did so and immediately saw the SETL folders again listed by year. Knowing that he had only a little time this morning to investigate more deeply, he decided to focus on video files with the Greek alphabet suffixes: alpha, beta, gamma, and the like. These were the files he had previously noticed, which contained recorded interactions and communications between humans and aliens.

He opened the folder ATS-2015-2-18V-alpha. It opened with a video blurred differently than the previous videos. It showed a man holding a small whiteboard with words written on it: 'Feb. 2, 2015, Zims.' The video panned out and showed a Caucasian man and a Black man sitting in a room with an alien. Only the alien was blurred and not as thoroughly as in other videos. As with all the other video files, in the lower-left corner of the video, a code was continuously depicted superimposed on the video—ATS-V-KLtStG95. The pixelated alien was short with a disproportionately large head and eyes even disproportionately larger. It stood about the same height as the two men who were sitting. They all were adjacent to a whiteboard with markers.

The conversation among the three, in many ways, seemed quite fluid. They included words in English, words seemingly of an alien tongue, clicks, whistles, grunts, and gesticulations. This went on for minutes at a time. Only understanding the words in English and partial meaning of words in other human languages, Robert had difficulty deciphering the communication. It was sometimes problematic to decern a question from an answer. Questions were seemingly raised by the men and responses given by the alien. It seemed that both species had learned enough of the other's language and added an interlanguage through which conversations could occur.

Every minute watching the videos led to heightened anticipation of the following minutes to be seen. Robert felt the suspense of unknown birthday and Christmas gifts altogether.

Along with the communication came periods of silence, after which the two men would respond—not with a question, but with what seemed more like an answer. Then they would articulate a question to which the alien would again respond. This pattern continued through the better part of half an hour. *What is that silence? What is that?* Robert asked himself. *They answer when there is no question raised. They respond to silence. That does not make sense.*

Robert then opened ATS-2015-2-18v-beta. It was the same, with a relatively large collection of words and symbols written on the large whiteboard beside them. For unknown reasons, none of the board was blurred. *Maybe because it wouldn't mean anything special to anyone?* With more careful observation, Robert recognized the vocabulary list was carefully printed on a large piece of white poster board propped up against the whiteboard. The vocabulary list seemed the result of protracted work among the three with English words translated into a simple symbol and then translated into some strange code. The list implied a semblance of organization, as the words were compartmentalized in a table. Robert neither had nor took the time to decipher the categorization of the words into cells in the table.

The two men used a laser pointer and pointed at the line 'All $\Leftrightarrow\forall\Leftrightarrow\grave{U}_m$añi$_{st}$.' The two men practiced sounding out $\grave{U}_m$añi$_{st}$. While the symbols seemed to have some phonetic meanings known to the trio, they were not all sounds natural to any human language known by Robert. After the two men had a second try at pronouncing $\grave{U}_m$añi$_{st}$, the alien was heard making a sound like "HicClick." The men frowned and tried again, "$\grave{U}_m$añi$_{st}$." The alien could be heard making the noises, "HicClick HicClick." The two men chuckled, and one of them said, "Oh, so now you're laughing at us, Zim. Hmm, maybe you should try our word," and he pointed at 'All.'

The alien tried to phonetically sound out the English word 'Ooaaawlll.'

The white man then quipped, "I'm not sure if he is from the South, but He's certainly not from the North." The two men chuckled, and Zim joined in, "HicClick HicClick HicClick." It was as if the alien knew as well as they did how poorly he had articulated the word.

Words, questions, responses, humor? At this, Robert let out a loud expletive. He was dumbfounded. Not only did the alien attempt to speak, but it also even seemed to have a sense of humor. Moreover, there appeared to be a real relationship between the three. *They know each other. Interaction and word list . . . long relationship.* Adding all of this to the extensive vocabulary list, it was apparent that what he was watching was the result of probably weeks of linguistic collaboration.

In only a few seconds, Kathy Hollander, Robert's employee down the hall, showed up at his office door. "Are you okay?" she asked. Robert had been so preoccupied with getting his new computer running and investigating the files that he had not noticed that Kathy was working at the same time in her office, most distant at the opposite end of the hallway leading to all the employee offices. No lights had been on in the office suite's common areas, and neither Kathy nor he had turned lights on in their offices. Kathy had noticed the front door to the suite open and close and had heard Robert shuffling around in his office, but she had paid no attention to him—until she heard him call out.

Robert jumped in his seat and slammed closed his laptop. He was almost as traumatized by Kathy's instantaneous appearance as by the video. "I'm fine," he answered. "I'm fine. Just watched video . . . " Robert slowed down, more carefully watching his words. "It was a . . . a . . . a video someone sent me from an old college buddy. It just startled me."

"What is it? Can I see it?" asked Kathy.

Oh no. "No, I am sorry. It is totally inappropriate. Even for me. I need to tell my friend that I don't want him to send me that junk." *That should be enough.*

"Okay. I understand. It's hard to tell others what your boundaries may be."

"Indeed." *Whew.*

Looking around Robert's office and noting a box for a new laptop and some packaging material, Kathy asked, "Hey, is that a new laptop?"

"Yes, it is," said Robert. "I'm just in the process of setting it up. I'm not very far into the process yet."

"Cool," said Kathy. "Let me know if we are all going to get new machines," she said with a hopeful but doubtful chuckle.

"I will," responded Robert. *Can't afford to get everyone a new one right now. Maybe a couple by Christmas.* Robert made a mental note to make sure Kathy would be one of the recipients. With the assurance that there was nothing seriously wrong, Kathy went back to her office.

Robert put his two hands over his mouth and reminded himself to remain calm. *No matter what, shut up.* He opened the laptop again and found the video that had automatically paused upon the closing of the cover. He took a moment to collect his thoughts. The video was another thirty minutes long. Robert was mesmerized. Even if he wished to, he could not tear himself away from it until its conclusion. There were more episodes of communication among the interlocutors and extended silence broken only by responses from the human participants. Each of the communicants took turns pointing at words or symbols on the board, attempting to extend the ideas discussed through the limited vocabulary. When hindered by the limitations of the lexicon, they seemingly experimented with enhancing the language with additional words and tenses of words.

One scientist spoke to the other and said, "This session will take some time in the lab. He's given us more, much more language, syntax, and ideas to consider."

"Yes," said the other, "I think that he has given us some subtle changes in tense and syntax that we did not have before. I think that there are more aspects of a tonal language than we previously knew. We need to interpret all of this and record what we can on an extended board."

"Yes, but I think that it is time to close out this session. We have so much to decipher." With that, the scientist walked to the camera and ended the video.

Robert faced the crucial decision: investigate file ATS-2015-2-18v-gamma or look at a video in another group. As captivating as this video series was, he opted to consider a video from another series—one even newer than 2015. He decided to go to the latest files, but he could not immediately remember if they were from 2019 or 2020.

Wait, can I get a screenshot of the word list? Robert used his cursor to move the still frames of the video down and then up again in timestamp to find the one frame with the best resolution and the complete view of the word list. *There, that's it. That's a good one.* He took the screenshot and saved it as a jpeg to his drive. *I'll look later.*

Robert looked for another file. He found the file ATS-2019-8-39vpd-alpha. *Had I missed this before? This filename has another letter in the suffix. What's 'vpd' versus just 'v?'* he wondered. He opened the file. He immediately noticed that this file did not have the additional code superimposed on the screen. *Was that a mistake, an omission?* He started the video. It was immediately notable as very different from the others. It began with a title screen: Sentient Extraterrestrial Life (SETL) on Earth. The video was not pixelated or blurred in any way. The camera work was more professional. It zoomed in and out of three men sitting at a table with a microphone in front of each. They each wore some sort of official nametag. When one spoke, the camera panned on him or the presentation screen beside all of them. Robert listened for a few minutes. The discussion seemed to be a briefing from experts to high government officials regarding extraterrestrial life on Earth.

Robert began to play the video. The first speaker wore a white lab coat atop a shirt and tie. He was clean-shaven with a professional haircut. He wore barely perceptible wire-rimmed glasses. He seemed to provide a historical account of what had been found since 1945. He had numerous still pictures of UFOs. He also showed video clips of what he purported to be sightings of UFOs. Most were taken by clumsy video operators of cameras and, later, cellphones. They were shaky and ill-focused. Even when the videos were enhanced by stabilizing technology, they were difficult to discern—and before ten days ago, utterly unbelievable if not farcical. More reliable were videos made by commercial or military pilots. These were trained aeronautical experts who professionally looked to the skies as part of daily practice, who could quickly recognize anomalies.

The discussion of this lab-coated man was mechanical, official, cerebral, dispassionate, wooden. He occasionally provided counternarratives explaining how some pictures and videos could have been of balloons, drones, toys, and spoofs. However, the balance of the presentation was credible—particularly as presented by a seeming expert.

The second speaker provided more of the same: still pictures and videos accompanied by a droning monologue depleted of enthusiasm seemingly from decades of presentations to lifeless audiences. He wore a shirt and tie and sported a well-manicured, reddish, short beard which contrasted his bald head. His presentation was built upon the previous talk. Rather than considering UFOs, this speaker had dozens of pictures and video snippets of alien beings, both living and dead. He droned on about them being seen all around the globe for over 70 years. So impressive was his collection that it seemed his goal was to convince others through exhaustion. Some of his video clips lasted for only a few seconds, while others lasted for minutes. While avoiding explicitly stating that the government had covered up these findings in a circumspect manner, he intimated that some people had been silenced regarding what they had seen or known. Robert wondered to what extent people had been 'silenced.' He imagined much of what he had previously seen or read in spy thrillers. *Were they disallowed from speaking of such for fear of losing employment, positions, and pensions? Committed to mental hospitals and continually medicated into silence? Killed?* The presenter's matter-of-fact tone gave no hint about the meaning or means of silencing; it was left to the imagination.

The third man was a muscular Black man with a thick beard and large, heavy-framed glasses. His clothes—tight tee-shirt above the table and jeans and running shoes below—connoted both his rebellion to those in authority and his rugged build. In some ways, above the shoulders, he looked like a poorly disguised caricature, and below his neck, he looked like a powerful and intimidating person.

His presentation contained videos snippets of scientists having conversations with extraterrestrials. The presenter explained the difference between two different types of aliens with which they had communicated. 'Zims' stood for the short extraterrestrials first recognized in 1994 by more than sixty students at the Ariel School in Ruwa, Zimbabwe. In addition to the unusualness of their diminutive size, Zim could speak both audibly and telepathically. *Ahh*, thought Robert, *THAT'S the silence. That's when, in the video, all are silent, and then the men attempt to answer questions raised by the alien.*

'Gitts' was short for Gittites. These were the tall aliens seen in many other parts of the world. Robert's decade of attending church meetings and Sunday morning sermons and childhood of being taken to children's church and told Bible stories clicked in gear. *Ha, in the Old Testament, Goliath, his giant father, and his three giant brothers were from the tribe of the Gittites.*

Robert thought for a moment and was certain that he had seen the word 'Zim' written on the board in the previous video with the two scientists and the alien. *Got to look at that video again.*

The presenter explained that, while scientists interviewed many Zims and that an extensive and growing vocabulary had been developed for communication with them, the Gitts never seemed to live long on Earth. To date, scientists did not know what caused Gitts to weaken both significantly and quickly. Thus, simultaneously, they were unsure how to preserve Gitts' lives on Earth. *Must have been a dead or dying Gitt I saw in the barn video.* While the presenter acknowledged that no other species of sentient extraterrestrial life had been found on Earth, language coordination between some Zims and scientists seemed more problematic. They were unsure if there were different ethnicities among the alien species.

The video of the expert presentations continued. The third presenter provided more video examples of conversations with vigorous Zims and attempts at such with failing Gitts. He continued his talk with, "Moreover, we suspect that, from the UFOs observed around the world, there certainly may be more species. We have only communicated with Zims and Gitts, but we have observed at least six distinct types of UFOs. They have all been so unique in style, shape, substance, and, we believe, technology, propulsion, and maneuverability, that it would be doubtful to have come from the same planet or civilization. Clearly, the craft that crashed in Roswell in 1947 and the one in Bakersfield in 1986 are entirely dissimilar."

Robert's mind was reeling with questions. *Why are the aliens here? What do they want? What do they eat? Where do they sleep? Why do the Gitts die? If they die, why come here? Are the Zims free or captured by us? Could they escape if they wished to?*

Unexpectedly, Robert's cellphone alarm blared him to a consciousness from which investigations of UFOs and extraterrestrials had taken him. He could not bear the thought of leaving this treasure trove of captivating information, but he knew that he could even less handle the ramifications of being late to spend the afternoon with his wife. As is, he had set his alarm with little time to spare to get home before noon. As quickly and safely as possible, he removed the flashdrive, powered down the laptop, closed its cover, and placed the laptop and the cables back in the box to transport. He had not considered bringing his computer bag with him. With only the quickest call of "Goodbye. Have a great day" toward Kathy's office, he was out the door with his new computer. He juggled whether to bring the laptop with him in the car as they shopped or leave it at their home. He decided to leave it home and lock it up in his gun safe in this closet.

The afternoon was uneventful. Robert and Emily went shopping at the outlets in Blowing Rock. Emily did the shopping and Robert did the toting. Every time she bought something, he would offer to carry the bags and would joke, "Let me take that to maximize your shopping pleasure." Each time, she would chuckle, appreciative that, even though he wasn't all that participatory in her shopping, he wanted to make it as pleasant as possible for her. Robert's strategy had a twofold purpose. He truly wished his wife to have an excellent time, but he also wanted to hold back to have time to process the morning's sights. Fortunately, each offer from Robert to assist his wife came with such a gracious smile that Emily did not notice his distraction; but he knew that had a limited expected duration.

They grabbed an early dinner at Peppers. The Applewood Bacon Cheddar Burger was his favorite. He insisted that it was the best hamburger in town. Troy's Diner had the largest burger, but there must have been some different spices on the Pepper's burger. As usual, Emily had the salad bar and French Onion Soup. No other salad bar in Boone rivaled that of Peppers since the close of Golden Corral. They talked about his work, their family, and the people they cared about in church. They both liked early dinners. They often teased each other about eating when the 'blue hairs' do. They often had their dinner as early as 2 or 3 p.m. This helped them eat only one or two meals per day to maintain the weight each determined appropriate and healthy. Plus, when they ate out, restaurants were far from busy, food was hot, service excellent, and the atmosphere quiet. Furthermore, when they arrived home, they had ample time to accomplish more tasks before the end of the day.

Discussing work and family, Emily also mentioned people she cared about at church. Robert, too, cared about many of the same people. However, his care was for them as friends and acquaintances, not as fellow believers. He was too unsure of his own faith to count himself with the others. He carried a genuine fondness for so many people, and they for him, that it camouflaged his struggle with the faith. Many assumed that his regular church attendance connoted a sincere and heartfelt devotion. He knew better. Emily appreciated that he attended church with the family, but she well knew of his struggles.

Chapter 20

I T was still early when they got home—arguably, late afternoon rather than early evening. Emily disappeared deep into the bowels of the home to perform some of her tasks associated with keeping everything running smoothly. She playfully called her domestic duties 'skirt work'. On Saturday evenings, she would usually talk to her mother on the phone for a while, touch base with her father suffering from Parkinson's—a conversation which generally lasted only a few minutes—and call a friend who needed encouragement. This was her ministry, and Robert had come to appreciate it for what it did for so many others.

Robert retrieved his laptop from the safe and retreated to the privacy of his office. This would allow him to investigate more video files. *No*, he thought, *someone may walk in on me. That could be impossible to explain. Can't look at videos. What about . . . ?* Robert decided to investigate the screenshot which he made of the vocabulary list. He opened the file and investigated the pic.

Statement ⇔ S ⇔ N`òót$_z$	One ⇔ 1 ⇔ ^	Same ⇔ = ⇔ Ss$_s$
Question ⇔ ?? ⇔ S$_h$mo^rït	Two ⇔ 2 ⇔ ^^	Different ⇔ ≠ ⇔ $_s$sS
And ⇔ ∧ ⇔ Pri^	Some ⇔ >2 ⇔ Ēg$_r$t	More ⇔ > ⇔ Dô^t
Or ⇔ V ⇔ ^a$_{sh}$	Many ⇔ ≫2 ⇔ E$_a$o$_{sh}$	
Not ⇔ ~ ⇔ Õg$_r$	All ⇔ ∀ ⇔ Û$_m$añi$_{st}$	
	There is ⇔ ∃ ⇔ S'^a$_h$	

Human ⇔ H ⇔ Human	Earth ⇔ ◎ ⇔ Earth	Birth ⇔ ↑ ⇔ $D_r a{\sim}t$
Zim ⇔ Z ⇔ $T't_h\ddot{\imath}_{\acute{o}}^{\ P}$	Ship ⇔ ⊔ ⇔ $Ba_r{\sim}$	Live ⇔ → ⇔ $\grave{U}_m \hat{o}\tilde{n}i_{st}$
Male ⇔ ♂ ⇔ ^Seq	Have ⇔ ∩ ⇔ K^~in	Die ⇔ ↓ ⇔ $\grave{U}_m \bar{o}{\wedge}^{\wedge}\ \tilde{n}i_{st}$
Female ⇔♀⇔ Seq^	Want ⇔ ∪ ⇔ ~K^in	God ⇔ ⇑⇔ $\grave{U}_m a\tilde{n}\ddot{o}_{st}$
Child ⇔ Δ	Food ⇔ Ā ⇔ $M_n \bar{a}t_s$	
⇔ Clò~^	Drink ⇔ ⊻ ⇔ $Fi_{sh}{}^{\wedge}$	
Adult ⇔ ▽		
⇔ ~^clò		

Robert immediately recognized the 'statement,' 'and,' 'or,' and 'not' as the basic notions of Boolean logic necessary to make cogent statements and arguments. These were elements he learned in computer programming to build his foundation for developing electronic infrastructures for clients. He appreciated that the list provided the symbol with which he was familiar for each. He also noticed that, through the rudimentary nomenclature provided, statements could be distinguished from questions.

The limited word list was simple but efficient to communicate basic ideas and to ask simple questions. Along with English words were symbols for each and some type of phonetic depiction of the word in a language comprehensible by the Zim. Robert could now distinguish a Zim from a Gitt, at least if he did not encounter a tall Zim or a short Gitt or some creature from another species of which he was not yet familiar.

Robert's eyes were drawn to some even more conspicuous list of symbols written outside the chart on the whiteboard. The list included:

$$(1♂∧1♀) ↑ \ Δ$$

$$H (Ā∧ ⊻) ∨ ↓$$

$$?? \ Z ∪ Ā \ ??$$

$$\gg2 \gg2 = ∀Z$$

$$H ≠ Z$$

$$?? \ Z ∩ (♂∧♀) \ ??$$

$$⇑ 1 Z ∩$$

$$?? \ Z \ ⇑ = 1 Z \ ⇑ \ ??$$

With interest piqued, he wondered if he could decipher any of this from the vocabulary chart. He separated the first line and rewrote it on a piece of paper. And he wrote some corresponding words beneath.

(1 ♂ ∧ 1 ♀)   ↑   △

(1 Male and 1 Female) birth child

Robert was stunned. It was apparent that the researchers were indeed communicating with the alien and informing them of our world. Robert immediately attacked the next line of symbols.

H   (⊼   ∧   ⊻)   ∨ ↓

Human (Food and Drink) or Die

Robert found this somewhat confounding. *If this species has the sophistication to travel through the galaxy, wouldn't they know such elementary ideas? Certainly. Maybe this is just the beginning of learning each other's language.*

Robert moved to the following line and immediately recognized this as a question.

?? Z   ∪   ⊼ ??

Zim want food?

He was pleased to see that questions were bracketed on both sides with question marks to demonstrate the beginning and end of a question. He was also pleased that the humans were congenial to the alien. For all he knew, the alien was neither friend, foe, nor captive. He found it difficult to believe that, again, an alien with the technology to ship across innumerable star systems could not easily overpower humans who would be comparative troglodytes.

Robert transcribed the following line.

≫2   ≫2   =   ∀ Z

Many Many Same All Zim

This puzzled Robert. *What does this mean?* The sentence structure had no verb. *Maybe the Zim language doesn't always have verbs.* While the English language necessitated a verb within a sentence's proper construction, he was unsure if that was universal even among all human languages, let alone alien species.

He moved on to the next line. It was simple in form.

H   ≠   Z

Human Different Zim

A confirmation that humans and Zims are different. Hmm, not the same. Isn't that obvious? Different in what way or ways? What's this really getting at? Robert scratched his head. Some of the transliterated sentences were symbolically simple, almost trivial. He again concluded, as in his computer programming classes in college, that the development of the linguistic communication between the two species necessitated the development of, and agreement upon, simple ideas which could later be expanded.

Then he was struck with an epiphany. The scientists were using mathematical symbols to the greatest extent possible. *If ≠ is interpreted as 'different,' could also mean 'not equal to.' Then the previous statement could mean 'many many equals all Zims,' or 'there are many many Zims.' Does that mean on their planet or already on Earth?* Thoughts swam in random directions in his mind. *Could there already be a high population of Zims living on Earth? But wouldn't they have been seen by countless other people? How could they hide? And why would they want to hide? And, wait . . . If there are many many Zims on Earth, might there also be many many Gitts? No, they don't survive here. Did many come and all die? How could the government have hidden this from all of us?*

For the better part of an hour, Robert mulled over these symbolic statements and, more importantly, the possible implications from each. He struggled, wondering why he had access to this information and what he would eventually do with it. He decided to investigate the following line of symbols on the board. It was clearly a question.

?? Z ∩ (♂ ∧   ♀) ??

Zim Have Male and Female?

This was the first question on the list probing into Zim physiology. Robert noted that no responses were recorded for the two written questions. However, both questions were sufficiently simple that they could have been answered with a nod performed earlier in this session which was only recorded in parts.

Robert was caught off guard with the form of the following statement. While the symbols were in the vocabulary list, they were clearly written by another hand. The figures were sufficiently distorted to appear to, at best, be authored by someone other than the person who wrote the previous statements. The writing seemed more like a child copying letters of which he was unfamiliar. *This . . . This is . . . a different handwriting. Could this be from the alien?*

⇧   1   Z   ∩

God 1 Zim Have

'God?' 'God?' 'God 1?' Could that mean 'one God?' Could this mean that the 'Zims have one God?' Could these aliens be monotheistic? Maybe they have a different meaning for 'God' than we do? Strange. Wait, should it be 'God' or 'god?' This statement went far beyond anything that he had anticipated encountering. Robert proceeded to the next and last statement. It was in the same semi-scribbling. It again was a question.

?? Z   ⇧   =   H   ⇧   ??

Zim God Same Human God?

'Zim God same as human God,' 'Zim God same as human God' . . . A question? Yes, this is a question. Is the alien asking if the one God that the Zims have is the same God that the humans have? What is this? Robert was beyond confused. He continued to shake his head in disbelief. He wondered about the significance of the last two of the alien's statements about God. And last was an unanswered question. *Does this indicate that the Zims valued an understanding of God? Maybe more so than the human scientists? What is this all about?*

Recognizing that he could discern no more about these statements and that any more would be mere speculation on his part, he took another look at the vocabulary list. He considered the Zim words. After a few minutes, he noticed some similar-looking words in the transliterated Zim language. 'Ù$_m$añi$_{st}$,' 'Ù$_m$ôñi$_{st}$,' 'Ù$_m$ō^^ñi$_{st}$,' and 'Ù$_m$añö$_{st}$,' all looked quite similar. Possibly some of these words had common roots. The words for 'live' and 'die' were nearly identical apart from '^^', which could mean a negation. The negation of 'live' would be 'die.'

He investigated more deeply. The Zim words with similar appearance were connected to the English words 'all,' 'live,' 'die,' and 'God.' *Could these words be connected by the Zim?* Robert asked himself. *Do the Zim equate 'God' with 'all?' And with 'life?' They look alike.*

"Hey, Hon. Are you nearly finished working?" Emily called from her domain in the house. It shocked Robert back to consciousness. He quickly looked at his laptop screen. He had been in his office for almost two hours. Without an immediate response, Emily poked her head in the door of his office.

"Hey, isn't that a new laptop?" she asked. Robert quickly powered down the laptop, desperately hoping that she would not make a big deal of this.

"Yes," he said. "I was having trouble with my older one. I needed a different one for work."

"Okay, as long as it goes on your business expenses."

"Yes, yes, it did."

"Are you coming back to the family any time soon?"

"Sure am."

Robert had a little spring in his step. He was excited about what he was uncovering. It energized him. He wondered what a linguist could determine from the human-alien communications. Like an addiction, he craved to know more. He desperately wished to share what he was learning with his wife. *Soon. Somehow. Soon. This is fascinating.* He wanted to learn more, but the opportunity to do so was not to come on this day.

However, his jubilation of finding hints into what scientists and Zims communicated was muted by his recollection of the potential danger to those who possessed this information. His wonder warred against his need to protect his family and himself. Additionally, he still harbored resentment toward Tate for involving him in this situation and personal guilt for keeping the whole truth from his wife. The combination of these emotions he recognized—and countless others that he did not—put energy in his life far beyond anything he had felt since the birth of his first daughter. *Would be nice to keep this excited energy minus the fear. But then, would it be the same?*

As the day progressed, Robert found himself unintentionally being drawn back into an unresolvable line of contemplation. Without the file open before him, he could not again investigate details. However, swirling about his head was the reminder of how similar appeared the transliterated Zim words for 'God,' 'all,' and 'live' with the possible negation of 'live' being to 'die.' *Do the Zim believe that 'God is in all' such as in pantheism, or that 'God created all?' Do they believe that 'God created life,' or is it a statement that 'one's life should be in God'? With 'live' and 'die' being so similar in appearance, does 'die' mean 'the absence of life,' 'the loss of all,' or 'the absence of God?'* Countless iterations of other immediately unanswerable linguistic possibilities ran through his mind. He relished the opportunity the words and observations provided him for philosophic wrestling.

Chapter 21

Day 12: Tuesday

O N Sunday, after the service at Grace Unity Church, Robert had agreed to meet Alex for lunch at Our Daily Bread, a small restaurant on King Street in Boone. Today, Our Daily Bread was not busy, but it would be within minutes. Alex was already at a table. He was able to get his favorite table near the window. It was fun to watch the tourists. Boone was a hippie town—in some ways, an Ashville wannabe.

It was still quite early in the fall semester. Some college students took part in what Alex called the 'weird competition.' From strange clothing, hairstyles, and piercings, university freshmen could be singled out; rather, they desired to single themselves out. They seemed to compete for who could look the weirdest. They all wanted to stand out and make their mark as 'different.' Alex believed that the weirder a student tried to look, the more pain they were trying to hide underneath. Unfortunately, the students were often not fully aware of their own pain and the purposes of their devices. However, so many attempted to participate in the weird competition that they all looked the same. This humorously commonized 'weird.' The local folk often chuckled at this. Either interestingly or humorously—depending on the observer's perspective—a transformation usually occurred in their junior and senior year when they had to look professional to get a real job. Suddenly, their appearance was more mainstream. It seemed like getting a job, surviving in the real world, and gaining true independence from their parents' finances became more important than making a statement of unusualness. Plus, being weird took effort, which they could ill afford to compete with completing academics.

Alex glanced at his watch. It was 11:43. Robert would be there at any moment. Billy Thompson walked on the King Street sidewalk and saw Alex in the window. Before getting a table, Billy entered the restaurant and greeted Alex.

"Hey, Alex, how are you?"

"All is good. Really blessed. And you?"

"Work is good. Jill has her last round of chemo on Thursday. It's been rough, but we will make it through . . . I hope."

"You will. So many are praying for you." Alex was encouraging—it was his job, but he was far from confident that Jill would make it. He also wondered about their three kids. These were difficult times for the Thompson family, with possibly even more difficult times ahead. Alex was not concerned that he implied that all would go well for Billy, Jill, and their kids. He believed deeply in the sovereignty of God and His constant goodness, despite difficult circumstances.

Alex believed that whatever God had one go through on this side of Heaven, He remained good, and the experiences made one more heavenly focused. He had once heard a profound statement from one of countless messages he had listened to and read throughout the decades. 'It has been said that so-and-so is so heavenly minded that he is no earthly good. I have never seen this. However, I have seen again and again when so-and-so is so earthly minded that he is no heavenly good.'

Alex knew that people suffered during their temporal earthly inhabitance. He daily balanced two truths: life on Earth was temporary and filled with various forms of suffering, and life in Heaven was eternal and tear-free. He had stolen and often used a phrase, 'This earthly life is the closest any believer will ever get to Hell, and this earthly life is the closest any unbeliever will ever get to Heaven.'

Life was replete with suffering. Alex knew this all too well. As a pastor, he often and deeply empathized with many regarding their struggles of health, finances, and relationships. His wife, Jenny, recognized his propensity to, possibly too often and too intensely, wear the emotions and trials of others on his sleeve. To prepare his flock for forthcoming suffering, he had frequently admonished his congregants, "You must get your theology of suffering in place before your seasons of suffering.

Suffering will come to all of us—sickness, death, separation, job loss. Everyone suffers. Once a season of suffering begins, it is not time to attempt to understand God and His ways. In the middle of a great trial, it is not time to try to determine if God loves you. You must develop a theology of suffering which will sustain you through the trials."

In a past sermon, Alex had said, "Notice that the Twenty-Third Psalm says 'Yea, though I walk through the valley of the shadow of death.' Note that the psalmist is walking THROUGH the valley. That means he gets to the other side. Note that he fears the SHADOW of death. This isn't even death itself. It is the ominous, sometimes paralyzing, feeling of inescapable death." Knowing that suffering was inevitable for all, he often prepared them theologically for that particular season. He always hoped that the theological preparation would lead to spiritual, psychological, and emotional preparation.

The Thompsons seemed to be doing well—or as well as possible given their circumstances.

"I'm meeting with Maurice," Billy said. Maurice did not need a last name. He was a well-known church member and entrepreneur who regularly worked business deals with small business owners. "We're discussing expanding my landscaping business." Billy was pleased that he had a topic to interject to stop the conversation about Jill. He had to live with the notion of a sick wife every moment of every day. All too well, he knew that he might be a widower in less than a year and have to raise his small children. It was overwhelming. Discussing something, anything, other than the obvious was welcome. He had learned the valuable technique of changing the subject.

Looking around, Billy saw Maurice a few tables away. "There he is. Have a great day."

"Take care. We continue to pray."

As Billy walked away, Robert walked up. In passing, Billy and Robert smiled at each other and went to their appointed tables. Both were too preoccupied with their scheduled tasks to make a formal greeting. At this moment, a passing smile and nod would suffice for a greeting. Robert took his seat with Alex.

Realizing that Robert had seen Billy, Alex said, "Billy is going through a really rough time."

"I can only imagine," responded Robert, still with a distant look.

The waitress, a college student, quickly came to their table. The crowd was just about to build, and she wanted to get them served as soon as possible. "You guys have been in here before. Glad you're back."

"How long have you worked here?" asked Alex. He always made small talk with the service staff. He genuinely cared about people and wanted everyone to feel welcome. He wanted the waitstaff to feel valued.

She was slender-built and tall, with her nose pierced with a hoop. Alex noticed tattoos on her arms and peering out from her collar. On her right side, a tattoo went all the way up to her ear. Dragons and butterflies seemed to be the theme. The artist had undeniable talent.

"About two years."

"What's your major?"

"Hospitality management."

"Well, that's great. You are in the right job for now."

"Yup, I'm learning a lot." *Please just let me take your order. I've got other customers and more coming in. Cut the chit-chat.* She attempted to cut off the conversation. She was not there to be pleasant that day. She was there to do a job and, in moments with the lunch rush, that job would become much more challenging. Alex recognized her hurry.

"Just water, please."

"And mine without lemon."

Looking around at the quickly growing queue of people at the entrance, the server asked the men, "Do you guys have an idea what you might want to eat?" *Make it quick, guys.*

"I do, said Alex. "I'll have the Brie BLT with extra Brie."

"And for your side?"

"No side. All good. But please change my drink to a diet Pepsi or Coke, whatever you have."

"Okay."

"And I'll have the ODB Club with potato salad," declared Robert.

"Excellent choices, guys. I'll get those orders right in." *Whew.* And in a flash, the server disappeared to her next customers already seated.

Until the meal came out, Alex and Robert made small talk about the weather and the day. They discussed the growth of WebMark. Robert thought, *yes. Let's just keep to small talk.* They discussed the tourists and a street musician they both passed on King Street—he played guitar and sang some old popular tunes. His guitar case was open, boasting with several dollar bills. By the quality of his performance, it seemed that the musician himself had probably seeded the case with the money in hopes of goading others to reciprocate. Occasionally, there were genuinely talented musicians on the street. He was not one of them. Soon, when the winter mountain weather settled in, they would be gone for the season. Boone was on their summer migratory pattern. The winter cold would encourage them to lower elevations off the mountain.

After a few minutes, the meals were delivered. This was Alex's chance to address Robert more pointedly. *Do it now. No one runs out with a meal in front of them.*

"So, what's going on?" Alex asked. *Something's weighing him down.*

Robert knew exactly what he meant. *Okay, here we go.* This was no longer small talk. All the small talk was just a ruse to get to the crux of the situation. Robert dreaded this moment. *Shouldn't have agreed to lunch. Start with a compliment. Always disarming.*

"Look, there was nothing wrong with your sermon. It was fine, as always."

"No, something is going on. I've known you for a decade. Something was different this week."

"Because we are friends, I will admit that something is different," Robert stated. "But, because we are friends, I will say that I can't tell you what is different. I hope that you can respect that." *Ha, that's not gonna slow down his probing.*

"I respect you," Alex said. "But I don't necessarily respect your silence."

"Look, I'm not struggling with sin or anything. It's a philosophical dilemma."

"A faith issue?" *Another philosophy struggle* thought Alex, frustrated that so many people struggled with philosophical issues. He had often thought, *They struggle with philosophy because they are afraid of it. Paul stated, 'Beware lest anyone cheat you through philosophy and empty deceit, according to the tradition of men, according to the basic principles of the world, and not according to Christ.' That does not mean Christians should avoid philosophy as something menacing. Rather, it means we should study philosophy so that we are not cheated of our Christian blessings through deceptive philosophical applications aimed more toward attacking Truth than genuinely seeking for it.*

"More of an intersection of philosophy and faith and their implications." Robert scanned the dining area to see if anyone was listening. *No one can hear this.* Only a few locals and an abundance of tourists were there. No one seemed interested in their discussion.

"Tell me about this philosophy," probed Alex.

"I really can't. I'm processing it."

"Processing what?" Alex was coming from a genuinely caring heart that sincerely wanted to help.

"Look, Alex. I can't. I just can't. This isn't about you. This is something that I need to process. *It's HUGE. I need time.*"

Okay. Maybe he can't tell me what it is, but he may be able to tell me how it came to be. "How did this come about?"

"Alex. I need to know if you trust me." *Turn it around. Put him on the hot seat.*

"I do."

"No, I mean, really trust me." *Push it even further.*

"Yes. But you sound mysterious."

"Well, it's going to get more mysterious." Robert looked around the room a little, scanning more than staring. *No one is listening.* "It may be a matter of national security, or even life and death. That is ALL I can say." *That should do it. How can he push back now?* "Please don't pursue this any further. I could be in danger, but if we go on, so could you."

Alex could not connect any of Robert's jobs or hobbies to national security issues or any that could be so life-threatening. "But . . . "

"Stop. Please. You will find out, but not yet."

"Does Emily know?"

"Not yet."

The conversation ended as quickly as it started. There was a silence as they each took a few bites of their respective meal. Both men wanted the meal to be over as fast as possible. They both strained to return to fractured and struggling small talk. Students, tourists, and the mountain weather always provided sufficient fodder for chit-chat.

I hope he is okay, thought Alex. *Seems to be a pandemic of cloak-and-dagger secrets going on right now. First Tate and now Robert . . . in less than one week. Strange, but no reason these are connected. I worry about these guys.*

A few tables away sat the visitor from the church. He was camouflaged in plain sight as simply another prototypical tourist. He wore jeans, sneakers, and a light jacket over a heavy shirt. In his casual garb, he was much less conspicuous. He had no hat, and his head was shaven clean. He was noticed, but simply as another African American tourist. Concealed among the crowd, he had come in moments after Robert.

The visitor had again managed to sit where he could observe the two, but Robert more. He was less obvious in a town restaurant than in a predominately white church. Boone had many tourists from the eastern regions of the United States, from all ethnicities. Even from less than an hour away, people liked to visit Boone to get out of the heat off the mountain. For the local folk, there were two distinct regions: 'on the mountain' and 'off the mountain.' Boone claimed to be at 3,333 feet above sea level.

The locals recognized tourists as a necessary evil. Tourists cluttered the streets, caused traffic jams, got in the wrong lanes, did U-turns in the middle of Rt 321, filled the restaurants, and crossed King Street on foot wherever they wished, often without looking for moving cars. They were a hazard to all, even to themselves, but a necessary boon to the local economy.

Without being noticed as observing, the visitor watched Robert and Alex talking. Although he discretely wore a directional mic and earpiece which better allowed him to isolate their conversation, only when either man spoke a syllable slightly louder than others was one of their voices heard by the visitor: 'what's going on?' . . . 'sermon . . . fine' . . . . 'No . . . different' . . . 'is' . . . 'But, because . . . friends . . . I can't tell you . . .respect' . . . 'I respect you . . . silence' . . . 'philosophical' . . . 'faith' . . . 'intersection' . . . 'philosophy' . . . 'processing' . . . 'what' . . . 'Look . . . I can't. I just can't . . . you. . . It's big, and I need time' . . . 'trust' . . . 'really' . . . 'mysterious' . . . 'more' . . . 'national security . . . life or death . . . all.' At 'national security,' he strained to hear more. *What is he saying?* The ambient noise precluded him from answering his own question. With the limitation of hearing, he was more attentive to the men's nonverbal communications.

He ate his meal, attempting to pace himself slightly behind the two men. He could always leave the meal quickly if they left, but he suspected, as was expected, that the men would eat more slowly while talking and that they would linger a little while after eating. He purposely left a $20 bill on the table. It was well beyond the value of the meal and tip. This allowed him to leave very quickly if need be while having generously covered the check.

With a direct line of sight, the visitor observed his quarry. The body language of Robert and Alex spoke volumes and replaced much of which could not be heard by the visitor. Robert was upset, but not overly so. Alex was bewildered and frustrated, but the levels of emotions demonstrated by both were not yet anything about which the visitor was concerned.

The line of people attempting to enter the restaurant made the visitor feel a little pressured and awkward. Potential patrons were looking at him seated alone at a table that could have held four diners. He did not need to avert his gaze from these waiting patrons; he was focused on Robert, principally, and Alex by extension.

Robert and Alex rose to leave. Walking by the visitor, Robert asked Alex, "How well do you know John Tate?"

Hearing that name, the visitor immediately straightened up and stared hard at the two men as they passed by. *Tate?* he thought. *Yes, I also want to know how well the pastor knows Tate. This is getting out of control. Gotta do something.*

"Yes. I know him well. I've been his pastor when he is in the Boone area for more than a decade. I wish he was here more often." Alex responded. "Anything wrong?"

"No, no. Never mind," Robert responded, regretting that he had ever brought up the name.

The visitor thought, *Need to shut this down . . . before another person knows, or another person is within reach of knowing.* He sat at his table for a few more minutes before leaving. There was no need to follow the men. He had studied reports on Robert's habits. The investigation of Robert started moments after Tate identified him as the person who received the copied files. By backward mapping cellphone and credit card activity over months, his team had developed a solid predictive profile of Robert. The visitor probably knew Robert's behavior even better than Robert. Alex was now simply a complication. However, from the few seconds of communication between Robert and Alex, it did not seem like Robert was going to tell Alex about Tate, and it certainly did not seem that Robert had said anything about his findings.

The visitor paid his tab. His tip was simultaneously generous without bringing unwanted attention to himself. He exited the restaurant as unnoticed as he had entered.

Chapter 22

Robert had no scheduled appointments to visit various companies to drum up business for WebMark. Only a week ago, he had opened the files to discover a new world which he had previously dismissed as science fiction—with a far greater emphasis on 'fiction' than on 'science.' He sat at his office desk, staring unconsciously at a computer screen.

He heard the outside door to the office suite open. *Who's that?* With no receptionist for the company, anyone who first heard the door open would greet the visitor. This mainly was Robert's responsibility. Since only Kathy Hollander was also working at that time, and her office was furthest down the hall, there was little expectation that she would answer the door this time.

"Hello. Is anyone here?" came a call from the entering visitor.

Not a voice I know. "Hello. Can I help you?" Robert exited his office into the front room to greet the strange voice. Before him stood a tall, thin, well-dressed African American. *Never seen him before.* Robert was instantly taken aback for a moment. The visitor wore a suit. *Ha, don't dress like that in Boone. Has to be from off the mountain.* This was an anomaly in Boone. Some lawyers wore suits, but few others. Since Robert had spent almost his entire life in Boone, he knew most locals. It was more likely that this well-dressed man was in the wrong business establishment; he was probably looking for one of the lawyer offices on the street.

"I'm looking for Robert Forsythe."

Hmm, okay. "I am Robert. How can I help you?" Robert automatically stuck his hand out toward the gentleman. Quite graciously, the stranger reciprocated. *I like firm handshakes. Makes a good statement.*

"My name is Marcus Peters. I'm starting a new company in Greensboro. I have heard of your work, and I need your expertise to get a top-notch web presence and marketing and advertising strategies up and running."

"Why, this firm?" asked Robert. "There are many excellent firms in Greensboro." *How'd he hear of WebMark?*

"Yes, but again, I have heard of your excellent work. My business would take me to the high country quite often. So, I would rather work with a firm of this size where I would get personal attention from someone I know, rather than some man hidden behind a curtain." *Convincing. He's hooked.*

"Well, Mr. Peters . . . "

"Marcus, please."

"Okay, Marcus. If we get your business, I guarantee that you will have personal attention. Would you please come into my office?"

"Certainly," said Mr. Peters as he followed Robert to his office.

"Please sit down."

Robert's office was of a comfortable size and efficiently appointed; nothing was extravagant. In one corner was his old-fashioned L-shaped wooden desk—invented far before there were any concerns for ergonomics. It wrapped him into a small region in the room. On the short section of the L was a laptop computer connected to a monitor as large as the space could accommodate. The one large window in the office was directly behind the desk. In the daytime, it adequately illuminated much of the office. Since Robert's work was primarily at his computer, the daylight from the window allowed him only rarely to turn on his ceiling lights. When he worked into the evening, he would forget to turn on the lights, as his computer monitor sufficiently illuminated his workspace. Opposite the desk were two chairs for visiting clients. Beyond the chairs was a table for collaborative work surrounded by four chairs. On the walls were framed pictures of screenshots of his work for his most successful clients. The office was primarily illuminated by some ceiling lights, which were overly focused on the table and insufficiently diffused elsewhere.

Mr. Peters sat down in a lightly upholstered guest chair across from Robert's desk. Robert sat at his expected place behind his desk. "Can you tell me a little about your business?" *The more I know, the better.*

"Well . . . " There was a little hesitancy in Mr. Peters' voice. *I'm in his wheelhouse now. Must be convincing at all times.*

Robert misread Mr. Peters' hesitancy as mistrust. "I know that distilling the nature of an entire business into a few sentences is difficult." Robert knew that building an effective company website and advertising and marketing plan often requires intimate knowledge of a company. Some company owners were leery of providing another company with this intimate knowledge. "Plus, you might not yet quite trust me with your ideas. You can tell me as much or as little as you wish. I'm only trying to determine if the firm can help you. Every new client is cautious. They worry about the possible theft of their ideas. Or they are concerned that we use a cookie-cutter model which works as a one-size-fits-all. We do not do that. We see each client and business as unique. Our job is to sell a company, your company, to a wider audience and get you the visibility that you need. I guarantee that, as soon as I think that I can help you and your company, we will complete a non-disclosure agreement—unless you want to do that first."

"No," said the visitor. "I have no reservations. We can talk openly about my company. Well, more than discussing my particular company, let me tell you what I need. Beyond a web presence, I need the facility to disseminate information as rapidly and broadly as possible. I need to hit as many platforms as possible."

"Well," interjected Robert, "we can give you quite immediate access to FaceBook, YouTube, WhatsApp, Messenger, Instragram, SnapChat, WeChat, QQ, Tumblr, Qzone, TikTok, Rumble, Parlor, and a few more. And not just access to these. We know how to get your ads seen by millions. Granted, how we market on these platforms determines if people will see what you have to show. But, in the flip of a switch, we can give you access to more people around the world than you would ever imagine."

"Whoa, slow down," said Mr. Peters. "I'm not sure that my business, or any other business, could handle that number of customers so immediately."

"Yes, yes, I know. We'll set up a plan, a schedule, pick some immediate platforms, and then roll out the others at a scheduled time. We have the infrastructure and planning to do this one site at a time or all at once. We can target from as small as Greensboro, to all of North Carolina, to the East Coast, to the US, and beyond. So, we can adjust the dissemination of marketing by the platform as well as by location."

"That still seems like much work," said Mr. Peters.

"Yes," continued Robert, "but it can be set-up work that we do here at the firm, and then the work can be more automated. We can make it seem like it comes from you—even personalize some communication. The system can monitor hits to your website, know from which social media platforms, and target the audience from which hits originated. By monitoring the hits, we can see business wax and wane in any location and platform and automatically go in other or additional directions."

"So, you can send out any volume or any type of data as fast or slow as you wish." *This guy knows his technology. He could be a real problem.*

"Right," answered Robert, in a manner which he hoped could clarify his points. "For data-heavy information, like videos, we can store them on cloud-based platforms and send out hyperlinks attached to attractive and inviting pics. This takes far less data and is easier to disseminate." At the mention of 'cloud-based' platforms, Mr. Peters' attention peaked. "So, you don't keep the servers onsite?" he asked. *Of course not. That would have been too easy.*

"We keep copies of everything on servers onsite, but we do most of the work in the cloud. It is more efficient that way, and while I know that this seems difficult to understand, if we have copies of files all through the cloud, they are far more secure. If our servers here ever went down, the files are stored on a myriad of servers elsewhere in the cloud. So, the redundancy gives us security. We have algorithms such that our sever goes out and regularly verifies the files and file fragments in the cloud to ensure that these remain correct and unaltered. If they are corrupted, our server will resend the files and correct them. Also, which may sound a little too sophisticated for our discussion, we can have the cloud correct the cloud. Finally, if our server ever gets corrupted, we can use other algorithms to reconstruct everything on the server from the cloud repositories. It is almost foolproof."

He's too good at this. "So, how do you delete or destroy files saved everywhere?" asked Mr. Peters.

"Well, it is certainly easier to replace existing files than to actually delete them, but, again, we have algorithms for that."

"So, it can be done?" *It may get done.*

"Yes."

"And," continued Mr. Peters, "can the algorithms for saving or deleting files be sent only from here or from any computer on the web?"

Don't get that question often. "Well," cautiously continued Robert, not wishing to give away secrets regarding algorithms developed and implemented by WebMark, "it can be done from any internet-connected computer, but we have encrypted passwords and two-factor authentication. So, while it can be done from anywhere, only a very few have the authority to do so."

"And when the files are on the server and cloud, are they password protected as well?"

"Yes and no," responded Robert. "You see, we need passwords to place the file on the server, but how we put them there—password protected or not—is up to the person who uploads them. I sense your hesitancy, but I assure you that your data will be safe."

"I know, I know," replied Mr. Peters, raising his hand as if to say, 'it's ok. I don't need all the details. I expect that you know your craft.' Mr. Peters regretted that he had broken character even for a moment. He knew fully well of servers, files, passwords, two-factor authentication, cloud storage, and the like. His goal was to see what Robert knew—and he knew what was expected of an owner of a website development business connected to marketing and research for their clients. "I mean," said Mr. Peters, quickly correcting himself, "I believe in YOU. I am certain that, if I work with your company, my data and ideas will be safe." Mr. Peters looked about Robert's office. Quite prominent was a picture—now three years old—of Robert, his wife, and his two daughters. "What a beautiful family," he acknowledged. "I'll bet that they are the joy of your life." *Don't make these into collateral damage.* "I like seeing a man who values his family."

"Indeed, Mr. Peters, they are." Robert brimmed with pride. Clients only occasionally referred to his family pictures strategically placed throughout the office. Emily, his wife, had often told him that people valued families, and that picture humanized the office. For a moment, Robert remembered Emily's words and silently thanked her for her work in printing, framing, and locating the pictures in his office.

"Now, if you don't mind, I have to ask a delicate question."

"Sure. Go ahead," replied Robert.

"Have you ever had to work with a company's file which was, ah, um, legally or morally questionable?" Mr. Peters coughed into his elbow. "No, no, I do not mean for my company. Please don't worry about that." He chuckled. "I mean in the hypothetical."

"In the hypothetical?" *Where is he going with this? Does he have questionable stuff, or is he testing me?*

"Yes. I mean, like, if a person or company dealt with pornography, or some other data or files which were at least morally reprehensible, let alone possibly illegal, depending on the age of the people involved. Have you ever served those types of businesses?" *He's going to think that I am some type of a pervert. Nonetheless, I need to know what he knows.*

"No, never." *Strange. No, weird.*

"Well, maybe nothing so blatant. Maybe some kind of gambling sight which was, hm, how can I say, bordered on possibly being less than completely legal?"

"No. Never."

"Because they haven't yet come to you for business, or because you wouldn't if they did?"

"The latter. Well, kinda both. Probably the former because they deduced the latter very early on."

"Great," responded Mr. Peters. "I have little interest in giving my business to someone who always needs to look over his shoulder to see if the cops or clients are coming after him because of what he knows. Sometimes the few files on a flashdrive can cause a great amount of difficulty. Plus, I vet all my employees carefully and even do annual background checks. I hope that those with whom I contract also do the same. This might be overkill, but I want my business to be on the up-and-up." Mr. Peters observed Robert for any change in face, posture, or tone. None occurred.

Robert ran a relatively simple business with four employees. He had never encountered immoral, illegal, or dangerous information in any form. *Until Tate...* Before a week ago, Robert had never contemplated that either he would stumble upon dangerous materials or that he would be asked to cover any up. He had personally worked with hundreds if not thousands of clients over the years. He had spent a good part of his career on the road, meeting new potential clients, promoting his company to others, and gleaning more business. He would bring this business back to his group, and the person with the best experience with that type of business would take the lead on that particular contract. Thus, his employees worked on a greater number of contracts than he had the opportunity to handle personally. Nevertheless, none of his employees ever found themselves in a compromising position. And now, after all these years, Robert had Tate's files in his possession, and Robert had to consider how and when to disseminate them. *I'm being a hypocrite.*

Looking at his watch, with no forewarning of his plans, Mr. Peters immediately stood up, offered his hand to Robert, and announced, "Well, I'm sorry, but I need to run."

Taken by surprise by such an immediate change, Robert took his hand and said, "Um, Mr. Peters, will I be seeing you again?" *Not sure how this worked out. Client or runner?*

"You can count on it," answered Mr. Peters as he was already halfway out the office door. "Probably sooner rather than later." Robert considered this an optimistic salutation.

Before Robert had even made it around his office desk, he could hear the outside door opening and closing. The visitor had left so quickly that Robert never even had an opportunity to provide him some promotional material regarding his company and the services he could offer. Robert had not yet determined what type of company Mr. Peters owned and how best he could serve him, but, most disconcerting, he never even obtained the name of Mr. Peters' company. *Can't do business without knowing about the company. Can't even develop a draft of a plan.*

Mr. Peters returned to his car and sped away. He acquired the information that he wanted. He realized that Robert had the technological sophistication to instantly and broadly disseminate information.

Chapter 23

DAY 14: THURSDAY

I T had been a long day at work for Robert. He had split his day between his work office and traveling to three businesses seeking advertising contracts for WebMark. It was now evening. Robert had skipped the previous evening's goings-on at church. As his previous week's attendance was very unusual, his absence this week was more commonplace. Emily and Grace had attended church without him, and Abigail had participated in her group independently of the family.

Robert remained tortured by what he had viewed on the flashdrive. *If this is true . . .* , he began to process again for what seemed like the millionth time. His cellphone rang. It was Alex. *Alex . . . at this time? Strange.*

"Hey, Alex. What's going on this evening?" It was unexpected that Alex would call in the evening. Unfortunately, too many pastors seemed to always be on call. The larger the church, the less free time a pastor would have. Only when a church became large enough to employ multiple pastors might one occasionally get an actual day off. Pastors always felt the pressure. They heard the admonition from caring congregants and elders that pastors needed to guard their days off for their sanity. Then, the same congregants would expect the pastor to be at their beck and call 24-7-365. Pastors knew that the common perception of them having much time off was born from a significant percentage of their jobs taking the form of private or semiprivate counseling. Other than the pastor's administrative assistant, no one ultimately knew how busy the pastor was. Even when the pastor got a rare golfing outing with a group, he knew that every word was guarded and that he was always on duty no matter how much fun others had. Occasionally, a pastor had a very close friend—most safely when this person was from another church—with whom they could share unguarded quality time, but this was always a gamble.

"Hey, Robert. Got a minute to talk?"

"For you, of course." *I wonder what this is about?*

"You mentioned John Tate at lunch on Tuesday."

"Yeah?" Robert's attention immediately piqued. *He can't possibly know about the flashdrive.*

"Why did you mention him?"

"Just some information I received," Robert responded. *How do I get out of this? He brought him up. Strange.*

"Did you know him well?"

"Yes, quite well. But we actually got together just a few times per year."

"So, you weren't that close to him?" *I need to be gentle. His relationship matters.*

"Ah, more than casual acquaintances. Why?" *Where is this going? Ah?*

"Well, I thought it curious that you mentioned his name on Tuesday, and now . . . "

"Now what?" *He knows something. Maybe . . .*

"Well, Cindy Ashford called me. John was her brother-in-law. He died in a car accident."

"What?" *No, what?* "Died?" *Dead?* Robert sat down, his mind racing numerous times faster than he could articulate with words. No, he wasn't close to Tate but close enough for an occasional cup of coffee. *And I guess, close enough for him to have given me that flashdrive.* Not knowing exactly where Alex was going with the information, he was unsure how to further describe his relationship with Tate.

What? You sure? When? "When did it happen?" Robert was unsure if he should ask questions or wait for the information to come. Only the week before, he had met with Tate and had been given the flashdrive.

"On Friday, ah, Friday evening." Alex was ensuring that he got as many facts correct as possible. "On 421, toward Wilkesboro, going down the mountain. He went off the road before the first runaway truck ramp." Alex choked through the words. He cared for Tate, and recounting information regarding the loss of his friend was difficult.

"Tate knew that road well," Robert interjected. "He's been on that road—I'll bet, a thousand times." *An accident there was possible for tourists, but rarely someone who was experienced driving that stretch of road and within ten miles of his home.*

"It was very foggy and wet. We had rain on that side of the county," Alex said. Both men had lived 'on the mountain' long enough to understand how different the weather could be even from one side of Boone to the other. Rather than tearing up, Alex wore his emotions in his tightening throat. His voice shook under the straining.

As an involuntary empathetic reaction to the tension in Alex's voice, Robert's voice took on a raspy tenor. "What time?" Robert interrogated.

"Between five and six, if my facts are correct."

"Anyone else involved?" Robert asked, somewhat embarrassed that this vital question had not come up first in the conversation. Without asking, it made it look like he only cared about Tate and no one else who may have been involved. *That would be selfish.*

"No, it was a single-car accident, and no one else was in the car."

Robert furrowed his brow with a sense of disbelief. "Hmm . . . 'single-car?'" he wondered aloud. *We have all ridden in the fog. Dangerous. But Tate? Single car?*

"The recovery backed up traffic to the 221 exit to West Jefferson," Alex continued.

"Were there any witnesses?"

"Witnesses?" Alex wondered. *Why are you asking about witnesses? Oh, yeah, because cars can go off some heavily forested mountainsides and not be found for days or even weeks at a time. A witness would know where to look and greatly expedite the recovery.* "No, I don't think that there were witnesses. Well, I take that back. I was not told whether there were witnesses or not."

Both men struggled to dispassionately discuss the death of their mutual friend. They attempted to bely their feelings and robotically communicate facts in as manly a style as they could muster. Independently, each could later deal with emotions.

As strange as Robert's question was to Alex regarding witnesses, so was Alex's response to Robert about Alex not being told whether there were witnesses. This seemed like a typical accounting of any accident.

"Almost a week ago . . . Why didn't we know anything before this?" asked Robert.

"I truly do not know. Something about the investigation, I suspect. I agree that it is strange. I told you almost as soon as I heard. It seems that the family was informed late Friday evening or Saturday morning. Not sure why there was more delay before it got to Cindy Ashford and then to me."

"Do they know how it happened?" asked Robert.

"Not that I know of. They pulled him and the car out Friday evening. I'm not sure where they took the car. It was loaded on Stewart's truck." Stewart had a well-established towing service for the high country. Along with his two regular tow trucks, he owned a flatbed truck on which they loaded cars that were too totaled to be dragged by a tow truck. "I'm sure that they took it away and will examine it," Alex continued.

"Sure," said Robert. He had little else to say. "It reminds us that these mountains are not always friendly to even those of us who live here and love them."

"Quite."

"Maybe I'll see Stewart tomorrow and get some more information."

"Why?" asked Alex.

"Oh, hmm, just curious." Robert was trying to redirect the conversation.

"So, are you OKAY with this?" Alex asked. *Will he tell me the truth? Most people pretend things are better than they actually are.*

Both men wished to end the conversation as quickly as possible. Feeling intense emotions over the loss of a friend was far from what each would want. As best as they could, they tamped down their discomforting feelings, and when they could not, they simply attempted to conceal the depths of them. Fortunately, a phone call cloaked all visual cues regarding their extensive passions.

"Well, it will take a couple days, but I will have to be good with it," responded Robert. "I don't have a choice. God is sovereign over all things, right? This must have been His will. And all that He does is good, right?" There was more than a touch of sarcasm in his words and tone. *I should not be so rude. He personally called to give me info and see if I was okay.* "Hey, I'm sorry. You do not need my attitude right now. Just venting."

"I understand."

Robert did not necessarily believe this, any of his complaints against God. On the other hand, nor did he not necessarily disbelieve. Alex knew well that Robert was more verbalizing his pain than rhetorically goading him. This was his reserved way of lashing out against the God Who took his parents when they were just in their fifties, and he was in his twenties. He enjoyed placing people in what he believed impossible positions—when raw human emotion intersected with esoteric knowledge. While Alex would often engage Robert in these debates, this was not an appropriate time.

"Okay," said Alex. "Good night."

"Good night." Robert was both sad for the call and glad that it had been short and avoided the most central issue—that he recently received the flashdrive of files from Tate. *I'll see Stewart tomorrow.*

After his cellphone conversation with Alex and being informed about Tate's death, Robert returned home and sat down at his old laptop. He thought that working on business could distract his mind from the awful thoughts of Tate's car going off the side of the mountain. Robert wondered who this Mr. Peters was, whom he met the day before. He sat back at his computer and started to google 'new companies in Greensboro' and 'Peters.' Even with these delimiters, too much unusable information arose. Peters was too familiar a name, which showed up as owners, investors, CEOs, CFOs, and countless other positions in brief articles describing new entrepreneurial ventures. But none had pictures resembling the man in his office.

The Colonel's cellphone sounded an announcement. Someone was texting him. It was Rabbi, his nervous tech expert in D.C.

> We are monitoring Forsythe's computer activity. He is searching for Peters in respect to new companies in Greensboro.

> He find anything?

> Too much to be useful.

> All sending him down rabbit trails.

> How quick to push out Packet Q?

> In just a few minutes.

You sure he will get it?

We can make sure.

Do it.

We are already ghosting his computer and can monitor and add keystrokes as needed.

Good. *Glad he's good at his job.*

Robert continued his Google search but found nothing useful. Countless new companies had recently started up, and there was no short supply of people named Peters associated with those companies. After an hour or so, the search seemed pointless. He could find neither evidence providing him information regarding Peters nor evidence denying Peters' claims. He found this both strange and understandable—it would be easy for a small company with no real web presence to be challenging to find.

Making no headway on his search, Robert decided to call it a night and shut down his machine. He closed out of Google Chrome and closed the cover. Immediately, he heard a slight ding sound come from the computer. It was not any of the usual alert notices he had programmed on his laptop. *Why would it go off when the cover is shut? Automatically goes into hibernation mode.* He opened the laptop's cover and noticed that it had not gone into hibernation mode. "Broke?" he wondered aloud.

As soon as the laptop cover was fully opened, Chrome popped open on the screen. The first listing was of Mr. Marcus Peters as the head of the new Greensboro Packaging and Shipping, Inc. Robert clicked on the hyperlink. The listing prominently showed a picture of Mr. Peters with a full biography: originally from Tampa, he relocated only in the last year to Greensboro; married for 38 years with a son and a daughter. The article discussed the formulation, purpose, business model, and location of the company. It all seemed aboveboard and promising. The report was sufficiently up to date that it stated that GPS, Inc. was still in the process of developing its web presence. This was verified when Robert tried a Google search on 'Greensboro Packaging and Shipping, Inc,' and nothing came up.

As a competent businessman, Robert immediately began imagining what he could develop for Mr. Peter's company. Within minutes, he had formulated some beginning notions and a marketing strategy. This would doubtlessly evolve as he got to know both Mr. Peters and GPS, Inc. more completely.

He opened package Q.

He spend sufficient time?

Yes. Cover is secure

Chapter 24

DAY 15: FRIDAY

U NANNOUNCED on Friday morning, Robert entered Stewart's shop. It was little more than an old garage with a couple of bays and a large lot in the back for storing junk cars, from which Stewart could sell parts. When he had salvaged all usable pieces from each dilapidated metal cadaver, he would then sell the skeleton for scrap metal. The shop was mostly a one-man operation. Occasionally, Stewart would bring in his friend for help on larger jobs. Overall, however, Stewart could handle most of the work.

Robert went directly to Stewart's office. He knocked on the doorframe, and Stewart looked up from his computer screen, glad to have any human interaction at work. Stewart stood up and offered his heavily calloused hand for a shake, which Robert gladly took.

Stewart was in his mid-sixties, six feet tall, of average weight, and with a semblance of lost athleticism. Thirty years ago, he was a college football lineman in a small private university before he abruptly quit after his second year to take over his ailing father's towing business. While he had let his musculature go, a strength unusual for his age remained. On his still well-chiseled right arm, he had an appropriately massive tattoo of an eagle superimposed on the background of the Old Glory. Beyond being patriotic, the tattoo was a genuine art piece worthy of being displayed in any gallery of flesh.

He and his dad shared ancestry of dirt and oil-stained tee shirts, jeans, and coveralls—the latter only when more formally dressed. Within this lineage was one of short marriages and divorce. His father was left with one son, and Stewart was left with one daughter, now in her twenties. People would often state how much he looked like his father. Depending on his mood and how the person said it, Stewart could take this as a compliment or an insult.

While his father, Bruce, lasted into his mid-seventies, in his fifties, Bruce's health declined dramatically after a jack slipped, and he was pinned under a car for an indeterminate amount of time before a customer found him and called pararescue to free him. He was never the same. Previously extremely obese, he deteriorated within two years to a man of average size and, after another year, to a feeble skeletal form. Bouncing repeatedly back and forth from a cane to crutches to a wheelchair, his demeanor became dour, with no one and nothing able to ignite his enthusiasm. He died a sullen and despondent man who looked two decades older than he was.

Stewart loved this type of work. His hours were both flexible and continuous—he was always on call for another accident. He had grown accustomed to being busiest during the morning and evening rush hour—although only the locals considered a one-light delay at the intersection of Routes 105 and 321 as traffic congestion. The light on 321 at the Walmart entrance was even more frustrating, timed year-round for the very busiest tourist season. It was unnecessarily long during the off-peak season. Tourists welcomed the comparatively light traffic and the low-keyed nature of the town. Icy or foggy evenings also brought their share of business. Often Stewart was conflicted. He enjoyed the money associated with each tow, but he was often vexed for the families now suffering the loss of time, money, vehicles, health, and occasionally, even life. He was buoyed by the fact that there were so many fewer fatal accidents than thirty years prior. The safety systems in the newer cars had made a remarkable difference.

"Hey, Robert," greeted Stewart. "Strange seeing you in here." *No money here.* Stewart knew that Robert's vehicles were relatively new and that he probably would not have anything to tow or even any parts from Stewart's heap of older model carcasses.

"What can I help you with?" Stewart nodded toward the single chair in the room directly in front of his desk. Both men took their appropriate seats. From the groans of both chairs, Stewart's, inherited from his father, had done a lifetime of heavy lifting, and Robert's should have been junked long ago as scrap metal.

Robert answered as tactfully as possible. "I heard that you towed Tate's car last week." *Ask, but don't hint. Don't hint.*

"I did." Stewart immediately became very leery. Possibly too often and always inappropriately, people were curious about the condition of the person who had died in an accident. Were the victims caught in the wreckage for any amount of time? Were they decapitated? Was the body . . . ? Stewart never engaged in these discussions. *Hope he doesn't go there. Some of these people are sick.* He always directed the questioners to the police or medical experts for official statements. Whether truthfully or not, he informed inquirers that the body was always extricated from the wreckage before he could get involved with the vehicle. Only a few times was there a need for him to winch a car a few yards up from an embankment to provide the rescuers an opportunity to safely gain access to the deceased. He had once looked into the driver's compartment; once was enough. He had vowed never to look in again. He left this to EMS. He was the wrecker man, and that was enough for him.

"Can I see the car?"

"Well, normally, I might let you, Robert, but not this time." *What does he want? A twisted wreck is a twisted wreck.*

"Look, I'm not interested in how Tate died or his body. I'm hoping to see the car itself."

"I can't. It is not here."

"Did you bring it somewhere else?" Robert knew that if there were nothing salvageable, there was no need for Stewart to park the wreckage in his lot. *Where did it go, and why so quickly?*

"I brought it here, but then they took it," Stewart responded.

"Who?"

"I'm not exactly sure . . . government types. They flashed a badge. That was enough. They had an empty semi already here. I took the car off my winch, and they hooked up their own and hauled the car in. As soon as it cleared the door, they lowered the cargo door. There were a couple of guys inside the truck strapping down the car, I believe. Within just a minute or so, they knocked on the inside of the door and were let out. Then, the semi took off."

This is curious, Robert thought. *Is this usual?* "Do you know where they took the car?"

"No idea. They paid me well. I think some was for the car and some was to . . . "

"Shut you up? Hush money?" Robert asked.

"Call it what you want; I wasn't ashamed to pocket it," said Stewart.

"So, this was unusual?"

"I'm sorry, Robert, but I don't know how much I should say. Again, I really think that I'm not supposed to talk about it. They had official government badges. They said they were taking the car for some kind of official investigation that THEY could not discuss. I just read between the lines that maybe I wasn't to discuss it either. They didn't tell me specifically not to tell anyone. I just assumed that they preferred that I didn't speak about it. However, it has been a week. I guess that it should be okay by now." *But I probably still shouldn't say too much.*

Stewart continued, "Yes, this was unusual. None of it ever happened before. Thousands of tows. Maybe ten thousand. Nothing like this."

Robert recognized that Stewart had always been great at his job but far less so at keeping secrets. It was probably derivative of his career. He communicated with few people who were not in the difficult position of either just being in an accident or being a family member of someone who had just been taken to the hospital or morgue. When he captured an opportunity to speak to someone, he often said too much and far too loosely.

"Did you notice anything unusual about the car?

"Tate's car?"

"Yes."

"Like?"

"Well, kinda like," Robert equivocated. *How do I say this? Don't want to say too much.* I have trouble believing that this was a single-vehicle accident." Robert did not want to lead the witness too much.

"Who said that it was?"

"The person who told me about Tate's accident. I didn't have a chance to look at the news for some days. So, I didn't even know about the accident until last night." Robert wondered if it sounded strange that he had not heard about Tate's death. For more than a week, he had been so absorbed in thought regarding the material on the flashdrive that he had not even briefly looked at the news.

Stewart attempted to change the direction of the conversation. "Well, work must be busy for you."

"Indeed," replied Robert. He was, however, not so quickly sent off the scent. Did you see ANYTHING that might indicate that another vehicle was involved?"

"Well, there was . . . " Stewart hesitated. He recognized that the large sum he was given for others to take away that car under the dark of night was certainly hush money. While he was not explicitly told so, it was all too apparent. He wondered what he was allowed to say or not—particularly after a week.

"What?" prodded Robert, wondering if his tone was too forceful.

"Well, ah, there was black paint on the back quarter panel of the car. Tate's car was forest green. A green Subaru Outback." Both men knew that this mountainous region was Subaru country. Green Outbacks were laughably popular. It was not unusual to see two, three, even four closely and randomly packed in a parking lot.

Slowly, filling some blanks but not wanting to proceed too quickly, Robert responded, "So you think a black car was involved?"

"Well, there is the possibility that he had hit another vehicle, or another had hit him before the accident, but I can't say for sure. I don't even know if this potential fender bender happened before his accident."

"Any chance that he was forced off the road?"

"Hmm." Stewart cleared his throat. He had considered it a possibility but no longer had the evidence to prove it. However, probably more possible was that there was a fender bender of sorts days or even weeks before the accident. He paused, using another throat-clearing to buy him a second or two more to concoct the best response. He could have put the notion out of his mind if Robert had not unexpectedly raised the issue. "It could be. Maybe yes. Maybe no. I just can't be sure. The car was in really bad shape." While Stewart thought that Tate could have been forced off the road, he imagined that, if the government people returned, his equivocations regarding such would suffice to keep him out of trouble.

"So, your professional judgment is, 'I don't know?'"

"No, Robert, I don't want to know." Stewart stood up, rounded his desk, and placed his hand on Robert's arm, half lifting him out of his chair and turning him toward the door, providing a strong hint that the conversation was over. "And maybe you might not want to know either. Just let it go. The man . . . " Stewart immediately halted his sentence.

"What man?"

Knowing that the cat was out of the bag and Robert had heard his utterance and would tenaciously interrogate him, Stewart decided to continue his statement while ushering Robert out simply. "There was a tall, thin, Black man who did all the talking. Well, he really didn't talk much at all either. But he seemed in charge." Holding up his hand toward Robert, he continued, "Don't even ask me anything else about him. I don't know anything. I know he wasn't from around here, but I don't know anything else. Since this has only happened once, I don't expect to see him again. I wouldn't mind, though, if he had another well-paying job for me. Plus, it was dark out." Stewart wondered why he had added that last sentence. Of course, it was dark out; it would have been well into the evening when he had gotten the car up from the bank, out from the scene, and to his shop.

Robert wondered if Stewart had added the tagline to pretend that he could not see well and, thereby, could provide no more details. However, Robert knew that Stewart's lot was well-lit at night. In addition to the streetlights, security floodlights illuminated the lot. Additionally, he had already provided enough eye-witness data that it was impossible to believe that the dark blinded him.

Robert walked—no, was escorted—out of the shop and guided in the direction of his car. Stewart went only as far as the door of his shop. Robert sat behind the wheel and closed his door. Stewart went back inside. Robert sat there for a few moments, wondering what was going on. *What's the big picture? Could Tate's death possibly be connected to the flashdrive files? Would someone care enough to kill to keep this a secret? Is this the government? Why did Tate give ME this flashdrive?*

Overly deep in thought, Robert paid less than adequate attention as he began to pull out of the driveway to Stewart's shop. Within milliseconds of hearing a truck horn, he slammed his brakes, bringing his car to an abrupt stop partly in the road. A large truck swerved into the left lane to narrowly avoid hitting the front end of Robert's car. Robert's heart, shot with adrenalin, had instantaneously tripled its beating rate and had taken the form of pounding. Taking a deep breath to calm himself, Robert recognized that he could have been killed. He thought of his wife and daughters. *Every day, people die of accidents*, he mulled. *I need to take care to make sure that this is not me.* Turning on to the road, he continued toward his office. He wondered if the people whom Tate feared and who may have been involved in Tate's accident could, or would, kill him if they knew he had the flashdrive.

There were far too many concerns to all be coincidences. Tate had the flashdrive and now was dead. The accident was on a road that Tate knew well. It is difficult to believe that he had lost control. There had been 'possible evidence' of 'possible paint' 'possibly from another vehicle.' All possibilities, but no certainties. This evidence was now lost. The car had been taken away in the middle of the night to who knows where. Altogether, this puzzle led to suspicion, but conspiracy theories rarely had any validity in time.

Robert picked up his cellphone and dialed Alex's number. It rang a couple of times, and then, on the other end, came the voice, "Hey, Robert, what's up?"

"I need to meet with you," Robert demanded with little decorum.

"Ah, well, when?"

"Now, if possible."

"Ah, I guess I can move a meeting," responded Alex, realizing that Robert's tone indicated both necessity and immediacy. "How about 10?"

"Perfect. Thanks. I'll be there."

Chapter 25

ROBERT walked directly past the church receptionist, Astrid, and into Alex's office. He immediately closed the door and sat down on a loveseat, slightly distanced from Alex's desk. Alex recognized the closing of the door and the privacy it connoted, came from behind his desk, and sat in a wing chair opposite Robert. Robert did not need to say a word. Alex could see he was distraught.

"What's going on, Robert?"

"I'm not sure that I can tell you everything. It's all messed up in my mind. I'm confused."

"I know," replied Alex. "I, too, struggle sometimes to understand the will of God."

"The will of God?"

"Yes, Tate's death . . . "

"No," interrupted Robert. "I mean, yes. No, I mean no. Wait. I'm not struggling concerning God's will. I confess that I do not understand enough about God's will to either understand or misunderstand it. I'm even so below God's thinking and ways that I rarely feel that I know enough about God's will even to question if I understand it in any manner."

"In this, I wish more people were like you. In fact, I admire your humility on this issue and wish I was more like you as well—at least regarding this issue. In most people's minds, my job requires me to better understand God's will and an ability to explain it to others. The only thing

I know is that God is completely sovereign. Nothing can happen apart from Him ordaining it. So, the only thing that I really know about God's will is that whatever has happened has been in His sovereign will and part of His purpose—a multi-modal purpose that I could not adequately comprehend."

"No, no," again interrupted Robert, waving his hand to indicate that this topic was not what he intended. Alex could feel Robert's frustration rising.

"Okay, I'm sorry for high-jacking your concerns. Take a breath. Relax. Tell me what is confusing you."

"I'm not sure where to start," Robert continued.

"At the beginning."

"Hmm, I'm not sure that will work." Robert pondered how best to develop the story in a lucid manner. Suddenly, without sufficient forethought for the ramifications of doing so, Robert burst out with, "I think Tate was killed." *Is he gonna think I'm crazy?*

"What? No. It was an accident." *What's he mean? We all know that it was just an accident—a one-car accident.*

"I think that it was made to look like an accident. Who would take the car away like that?" Robert said.

"What? 'Take a car away' like what?" *He's not making sense.*

"Stewart towed Tate's car from the accident scene. When he got it to his place, he was met by people with badges who paid him so that they could take the car away in a large box truck. No, a semi. No. I'm not sure. I can't exactly remember what kind of truck, but it was an enclosed truck. I have no idea where they brought it. And Stewart doesn't know either."

"Why would someone take a wrecked car, particularly on the night of an accident?" asked Alex. "Usually, the car must be kept intact for follow-up investigations." *This is not how this is supposed to work.*

"Right. Why indeed?" asked Robert. "Unless they wanted to cover something up." *I don't have a reason. Sounds crazy, even to me.*

"Cover-up? Cover up what?"

"This," Robert replied while waving a flashdrive. "I think that they want this."

"What is that?"

"A flashdrive. Information that Tate gave me. He got this information from work."

"From work?"

"I'm not sure."

"Tate did tell me that he had taken some files from work," said Alex.

Robert was shocked. "He told you?" *Why would he tell anyone? He knows that it might endanger them.*

"He said something like that he copied some files accidentally. Then, when he knew what they were, he copied them purposely. He may have mentioned a flashdrive; I just don't remember." Alex fumbled around, wondering if he should reveal much about Tate's confession—most likely his last—or ask any more questions. He did not want to be involved in illegality, nor did he want Robert to get into trouble. *But Tate's now gone. Facts about the cause or reason are not necessarily to be kept under pastor/ congregant confidentiality.* "Do you know what is on the flashdrive? He never told me."

"Yes. But that's what scares me." *Should I tell him? Tate already broke the ice.*

"Scares you?" inquired Alex. "First, why do you think that this is connected to Tate's accident? Second, why does the content scare you?" As soon as his question left his lips, Alex thought, *Tate worked at CCTech with classified documents. Maybe I shouldn't know this either.*

Robert hesitated. He knew that if he went further, he could jeopardize his friend. "I'm not sure that you should know."

"Okay. Well, I trust your judgment. Why did Tate give that to you?"

"I've been scratching my head for days wondering that. I know that he put it together on Friday, two weeks ago. He gave it to me on the following Monday. The more that I have thought about it, I think that I was the first person that he saw who he trusted. I think that he just wanted to get this out of his hands and to someone completely disconnected from CCTech. I think that he wanted to avoid his family as well."

"Why?" interrupted Alex.

"To keep them safe. I think that he knew that they would figure out that he had the files and that whoever got hold of them would also be in danger. Later that day, he seemed to think that we could make . . . umm." Robert waved his hands before his face as if erasing a chalkboard to write notes to go in another direction." "I'm not yet sure what he meant. Then, by the next day, he seemed to think that we were in far more danger than the potential money would be worth."

Alex nodded with less than complete agreement.

"When he gave it to me, Tate told me not to be connected to the internet when I opened the files. That's why I asked to use the computer in the library," said Robert, as he nodded his head in the direction of the library down the hall.

"You used our church computer to open files that you thought were dangerous?" Alex protested. *That's not right. You shouldn't have. You should have told me.*

"Yes, and I apologize about that."

"Wait," Alex continued, "isn't that computer on the internet."

"Yes. Well, it is, but I didn't know. When I got on the laptop, I pulled the ethernet cable to get it off the internet, but after looking at the files, I realized that it was still on the Wi-Fi network. I don't know for sure whether governmental entities can actually determine if some files are opened on some computer. But Tate knew much more about technology and secret stuff than I ever will. He certainly seemed to think so."

"So, the congregation could be in jeopardy?" asked Alex.

"Yes. Or, well, not necessarily so. I can't say no. I just don't know. The more I know about everything, the less I think I know about anything."

"Look, Robert," began Alex, "I feel like you have taken our friendship for granted. No, I believe our relationship has been taken for granted. No, to be blunt, I feel like you have betrayed our friendship. You brought potential danger into these walls."

Robert cringed at the word 'betrayed.' He remembered that he felt betrayed by Tate giving him the flashdrive. He knew how deeply his actions possibly affected Alex. "I am so sorry," stated Robert. "I never intended to bring harm, or even the threat of harm, to the church. It wasn't until I considered that Tate had been killed—just a few minutes ago—that I realized the possible full extent of my actions here at church. And I looked at the files a couple days before Tate's accident." Both men were more comfortable calling Tate's situation 'an accident' rather than 'his death.'

"Robert, I accept your apology. I fully believe that you had no understanding of the possible ramifications of your actions. However, there are ramifications with which we must all now consider."

After a long, silent, contemplative pause by both men as to what to do, Alex asked, "This is a crazy situation. Should I talk with Tom Cleef at Samaritan's Purse?" Tom was retired military, retired police, and retired from the prison system. He had many years of law enforcement experience. He was valued at Samaritans Purse for his talent at securing the facilities and training and supervising the rest of the SP security. He was respected outside of SP for his understanding of legal matters, particularly involving violent offenses. On many fronts, he had maintained connections with various law enforcement entities from the community, the state, and even on the national level.

"You can, but I'm not sure that it will help. I would be shocked if anyone would come here to the church—such a public place. The more I think about it, I expect that no one is really in danger if they do not know what is on this flashdrive."

"I'm glad, then," said Alex, "that I don't know either."

"Exactly," replied Robert. "But now we are both boxed in. You don't know how with certainty if you need to protect your congregation or how, and I don't know how to protect myself and my family. I believe that Tate was killed over these files. And I believe that if they know that I have them and that I have opened the files, they will come after me."

Both men, still stinging from recent betrayal, contemplated next steps. Alex knew that forgiveness was an active act—an ongoing act that needed to be repeated with every reminder of the sting. He could forgive without forgetting. The memory of the act would eventually become disassociated from the pain of betrayal. Over time, trust would be rebuilt. Until then, two less than trusting people would need to work together toward the end of protecting as many people as possible.

After the pause, Robert said, "I need to ask you a spiritual question."

Alex was taken aback by such an immediate change in direction. However, with automaticity, he reverted to the role of a pastor and welcomed the opportunity to answer any spiritual questions from his friend.

"What if there is undeniable evidence of sentient extraterrestrial life on Earth?" Robert blurted out.

"What?" asked Alex, shocked that the conversation had gone so quickly in such a bizarre direction. *From Tate's death to aliens in a split second? Maybe he's in shock.*

"So, what if?"

"What do you mean?" *Is he serious?*

"If there was indisputable scientific evidence of alien life, how would that affect your view of Jesus?"

"Woah," Alex responded. "I certainly wasn't expecting this?"

"I know."

"Wait," said Alex. "Isn't Tate's potential murder of far greater priority than space aliens?" Alex was attempting to direct the conversation about what he believed was most important at that time.

"Please," responded Robert. "Just trust me, and if you can't trust me, just indulge me." Robert parried Alex's maneuver and brought the conversation to where he needed to go. He knew that Tate's death was important, but he also knew, or believed deeply, that Tate's death was somehow associated with the flashdrive. He needed to learn more about the aliens to know more about Tate's death, not to mention the potential fate of anyone else associated with the flashdrive.

While Robert was not a committed believer in God, he believed sufficiently to be angry at Him. Robert often thought *it would be tantamount to insanity to be angry at an impotent drogulus incapable of interacting with the physical world.* Alex perceived Robert's anger at God for the young deaths of his parents and grandparents as his tacit belief of God—a belief which Robert could not admit to even himself. Alex saw in Robert an embryonic belief in God which would eventually grow into faith in Him. Only time would tell. Alex hoped that God would woo Robert to Himself by circumnavigating more pain rather than drawing him to Himself through it.

Robert's belief of at least the possibility of God was sufficient to make him consider that the finding of sentient extraterrestrial life on Earth may rock the world of many he knew well and cared for deeply. He cared more for them than he did the philosophical discussion itself. As little as he genuinely believed, he did not want to see harm come to so many others through the possible fracturing of their faith.

"Well, what type of scientific evidence?" asked Alex, seeking clarification.

"That doesn't matter. Let's just say indisputable evidence confirmed by the best scientists."

"Well, let me begin by saying that I certainly don't believe in little green men," stated Alex.

"I know. I know. Just humor me."

Alex paused to carefully consider his thoughts and words, still distracted by Tate's death and the flashdrive. "I can begin by saying that there is only one God and Creator of all. You heard my sermon on Sunday. There is only one God. So, if there are alien beings, they, too, were created by the One True God."

"But even you read in the Bible that Paul said, 'even if there are other gods, for us there is one God.'"

"Well, that is a rough translation with some significant omissions," responded Alex, "but I'll work with it."

"Go ahead," prodded Robert.

"Orthodox Christianity—and Judaism and the Muslim faith, by the way—have monotheism as a central tenet. Christianity recognizes that there is only one God, albeit in triune form. And Christ is the Creator of all that is."

"Of all?" Robert probed.

"Yes, even of little green men. Even Zoot, if he exists, would have been created by God." Alex remembered the name 'Zoot' from a Monty Python movie he had seen more than twenty years ago, but he could not remember Zoot's gender.

"I don't know who Zoot is, but what if Zoot disagreed and believed that another god created him or her?" Robert pushed forward.

Alex was prepared for this maneuver. He responded, "The Christian position would say that either Zoot is incorrect or that he has a different name for the same God. By the way, Robert, this is not a new question. Hundreds of years ago, theologians debated whether human life could be on distant islands only accessible by sailing ships. The debate raged on, with some arguing that life on the 'antipodes,' as they called them, was impossible because how could they have come from Adam. And, if they were not from Adam, they could not be saved through the Savior come through Adam's human lineage. Altogether, and through the implications of what we now know were weak arguments, they tried to convince Christendom that antipodal alien life was impossible. Similar arguments have been raised over the more recent half-century regarding alien life from other planets. It is actually quite sad that philosophical arguments have not become more sophisticated."

"But how do we know that we are correct and Zoot is wrong?" asked Robert.

"We must believe the revelations that were given to us by God. These are what we are bound to."

"I know we have the Bible and all," Robert replied, "but more than about God, I'm wondering about Christ and salvation." Robert often demonstrated exceptional knowledge of theology for someone who had not committed to believing in Christian dogma. He was a classic example of 'head knowledge' without application to the heart. Alex would occasionally mention the eighteen-inch gap between Robert's head and his heart. Quite often, to the surprise of Alex and Emily, he listened carefully in church and could often recite several significant points from the sermon—sometimes even weeks later. Of course, he would often recount the most controversial aspects of the sermons, which struck his intellect most forcefully. While he did not accept the tenets of the Christian faith, he was fully aware of them. He had never stopped thinking about the implications and ramifications of Christian theology. While often silent in church meetings, his mind was rarely still. On numerous occasions, Alex had said to him, 'You know enough to be very dangerous,' but he never elaborated upon whom Robert would endanger.

"Ah, I understand. Does Zoot need Christ? That is your question," directed Alex.

"That certainly is a great part of it."

"Well, I guess we need to look at some cases. That is what we seem to do often in theological discussions."

"I've already been wrestling with that," offered Robert. "Maybe Zoot is not fallen."

"Yes," interjected Alex. "That is one option that we need to consider, but that might be the easier one."

"What is a tougher one?"

"What if Zoot is fallen? That's a tougher question. But we should probably handle the easier question first."

Robert's cellphone ring abruptly interrupted the discussion. The two men had been so deep in thought and conversation that they were both startled. Robert looked at the phone. The caller ID announced that it was a work-related issue.

"I'm sorry, but I need to take this," Robert said. He answered the phone, and he seemed concerned. He asked and answered a few questions to the person on the other end. The call took only a minute or so, but it was apparent that he would quickly have to leave.

He ended the call and announced, "I'm so sorry, Alex, but I need to leave. I need to get to the office. We have a problem with a client, and I need to be there. It seems that they are pretending that they might leave for another firm like ours out of Charlotte. I think it is a bluff, but I want to head this off."

"No worries," responded Alex. "I understand. We can continue with this later."

"Thanks, Friend," said Robert as he quickly arose and left.

Alex was pleased that Robert left with such a salutation. He did consider him a valuable friend. But now, Alex had to wrestle with two concerns: the safety of his congregation concerning Robert opening Tate's files and the theological implications of Zoot—to better answer Robert's questions in the future.

Alex took a moment to further consider Robert's question. *More likely than the possible existence of aliens is that Satan—'the deceiver' and 'the father of lies'—is trying to deceive some, and the church in particular. Satan can deceive scientists into seeing what he wants them to see. He would have no greater goal than to take our attention away from God's work on the cross. Satan would love to make us wonder if God's way is the ONLY way. He would love to draw some away from the church through contemplations of endless possibilities and pretend that salvation could be provided in some manner differing from by God's grace through our faith in Christ's work of substitutional atonement. So, even if the scientific evidence looked realistic, it could be, and most possibly is, a ruse by the Devil. I need to share this idea with Robert as soon as I can.*

Chapter 26

DAY 16: SATURDAY

IT had been a long two weeks. Robert had received the flashdrive from Tate. He and Tate had texted back and forth. Robert had opened the flashdrive at church and seen top-secret files about alien life. These files seemed to be part of a government coverup of alien life on Earth. He had taken a second look at the lexicon of human-alien words. He had struggled through church service regarding a message that troubled him. He had been out to lunch with Alex. An unannounced Mr. Peters had dropped in at WebMark with the potential of becoming a future client and, after being investigated, was found legitimate and found promising. Robert came to know John Tate's death and the possibility that it was not an accident.

Now, he was facing another Saturday morning since his world had been shaken to its core by information that would dissolve the stoutest person's constitution. At this relatively early hour, he sat at his kitchen bar, enjoying a hot cup of coffee, looking over the morning news from various newsfeeds on his iPad. The political news was demoralizing in its divisiveness. The financial news was encouraging but barely enough to overcome political depression.

He did not yet have plans for the day. Emily was up and getting ready in the bathroom. While unsure about what the day would bring, he knew that he could barely escape a moment of wrestling between recalling what he had come to know and fighting to forget it so that he could accomplish required tasks. Even in reviewing the news, his mind flashed between politics and visions of the top-secret files he had seen. He was slowly trying to reconcile innumerable topics: the history of UFOs and extraterrestrial life on Earth; the long-lasting government coverup; that some humans had learned to communicate with some aliens; the fact that Zims lived and Gitts died on Earth; and nuances of the Zim language, which seemed to imply a connection among the Zim words for 'God,' 'all,' and 'live.' He desperately wanted to ask the Zims, 'Can a Zim live without God?' but he did not know how to construct the notion of 'with' and 'without,' although the latter was simply the negation of the former.

It was to be another beautiful September day in Boone. For this day, the weather forecasted a high in the upper 60s. This seasonal temperature drew many to Boone from the surrounding regions to escape the still sometimes oppressive heat off the mountain. Unexpectedly, Robert received an alert on his burner cellphone for a text message. The alert came from an unknown caller.

> Tate no accident.

> > Who is this? *My burner phone?* How did you get this number?

> No accident.

> > Who is this?

> No accident.

> > I suspect that. *Who is this, and why is he being so cryptic?* Paint on car. *Enough said. I'm not giving any more away without knowing more.* Who is this?

> Protect you.

> > *He's going to protect me, or I have to protect myself . . . or is it my family?* Why?

> Know much.

> > About? *I 'know much' or 'know too much' or he does? Too cryptic to be sure.*

No time.

> *??? No time for whom? Him, me? He doesn't have time to explain, or I don't have time?*

Zims. Gitts.

> *Who could know those words? Only someone deep inside CCTech, the government, or . . . someone who had previously seen the files. Tate? No. He is dead. Buried. Did he show the files to someone else? Might the flashdrive have been copied . . .* (Robert began texting, but then stopped.) *This person knows a lot, but he might be fishing for what I know.*

Know much.

Danger.

Protect youself.

> *'Protect youself'? Maybe 'protect yourself.' From? Grammar is weak. Hard to understand, but can't be someone pranking me.*

Some want hide information. Next Tate you

> *'Next Tate you?' Is he saying that I could be the next Tate? That I could also be killed?*

Be smart. Many want see. No could. President no could.

> *Seems like top secret. Even higher. Above top secret.* (Robert hesitated.) *Above top secret? Above Top Secret? ATS? I've seen that.*

Start understand. Know much. (after a pause) too

'Know much too' or 'know too much?' He or me? His grammar seems to be of a non-native English speaker. Or is he just trying to hide his identity? How can I protect myself?

Use you tech.

Not keep information.

What is he saying? 'Use you tech?' Maybe 'use your technology' or 'use your technology skills.' Does he want me to get rid of the files? Destroy info?

NO.

Don't keep and don't destroy? Disseminate the information?

YES. Fast.

How can I protect myself?

Get info everyone. Fast. Everyone. Only way safe people.

Grammar poor. Still has to be a foreigner. How do they know about Zims and Gitts? Who is this?

Protect youself

Protect family

My family?!?!

Why should I trust someone who won't tell me who they are?

No trust.

THIOP

*? No trust? 'Do not trust him' or 'do not trust anyone?' If
I'm not supposed to trust anyone, how can I trust him? ??*

(There was no reply.) What is THIOP? (Still no reply.)

Immediately after reading 'protect family,' Robert became visibly shaken. He could understand that someone might be after him. *But my family? They don't know anything. Why would anyone hurt them? Maybe it meant 'protect yourself and your family?'* A feeling of panic crossed him. A stabbing pain made Robert aware that he had been clenching his jaw. His shoulders tightened, and he could taste fear in his mouth.

As difficult as it was to believe that someone may be after him, even to the extent of Tate's fate, it was appalling that his family might now be in the crosshairs. He would do anything to protect them. He continued to text questions of various sorts, but there was no further reply. After four or five texts, his messages became undeliverable, as if the number had never been available.

THIOP? THIOP? An acronym? But for what? An acrostic? HI? HIgher Order? OP? OPeration? Higher Intelligence Operation? Part of the government?

Speaking into his phone, Robert inquired, "Siri, what is THIOP?"

The phone responded, "Here are my findings for 'THIOP.'" Robert read the findings . . . 'Archaic for Ethiop', 'Ethiop archaic for an Ethiopian or any dark-skinned person.' *Robert pondered if this was code to indicate that the person texting was a Black man or woman. What can this mean? So many things. It could be the object providing the warning or the target of the warning.*

Who could have my burner number? Only Tate. No one else knows the number. No one else knows I have a burner. Robert tried to dismiss that the text was meant for him, but the texts could be meant for no other. 'Tate,' 'No accident,' 'Protect youself,' 'Know much . . . too', 'Zims' and 'Gitts,' 'hide information,' and 'Next Tate you' all attested undeniably that the texts were meant for Robert—and for Robert alone. *But from whom?* Robert thew his forehead into his open hand and rubbed forcefully between his temples. *I have to know the 'from whom' before I can know the 'why.'*

Now visibly shaking from a combination of fear and confusion, Robert held his phone in one hand and his cup of coffee in his other. His burner phone was placed before him on the bar.

"Hi, Hon." Emily's voice burst into the room. Although soft and sweet, it pierced the silence associated with panicked thought. With a jerk, Robert quickly flipped his burner phone face down on the bar, nearly spilling his coffee. Unfortunately, his actions were all too revelatory.

"Are you okay?" Emily inquired.

"Ah, yes. Yes."

"Cut it. What's going on?" She sat at the bar beside her husband. She could see his distraught countenance. "This has all gone long enough," she said, expecting that this was part of his secrecy over the last week or so." "Just spill it."

"I can't . . . "

No longer willing to tiptoe around the bush, Emily asked, "Is this still part of whatever you kept quiet about last week?"

"Ahh, umm."

"Is it? What's going on? We don't keep secrets?"

"This is different," Robert defended. "There is something that I just can't tell you. You are safer if you don't know."

"Don't know what? Safer? What is going on?"

"Honey, please."

"No," insisted Emily. "I need to know even more now."

"Do you want to know if it might place the girls in jeopardy?"

"Safer? Jeopardy? ROBERT?"

"Okay. Look, I saw some computer files that I probably should not have seen."

"Computer files? Porn?"

"No, no," Robert responded with a slight chuckle, glad that alien videos would now seem tame in comparison.

"What files?"

"You won't believe me."

"Try me," Emily demanded.

"Okay, okay," Robert insisted in return, holding up one hand as if to slow down the conversation and give him more time to think.

"Don't do that. Just go for it."

"Aliens. Files about aliens."

"Excuse me?"

"I'm telling you. Aliens. Extraterrestrials."

"Look. Cut it out. What's going on?"

"John Tate."

"What about John Tate?"

"He's dead," replied Robert.

"I know he's dead. And I'm sorry about that. I know that he was a friend of yours, but you became disconnected from me and the girls before you knew about Tate's accident. So, I'm not seeing the connection."

"I don't want anything to happen to us. I don't want you or the girls to be endangered."

"First," interrupted his wife, "it was safety, then jeopardy, then dead Tate, and now we may be endangered? I need to decide about the danger."

"But you won't believe me. And I can't show you."

"Try me."

"Okay. Okay." Robert again raised his hand toward his wife to better control the pace of the conversation. Half teasingly, she slapped down his hand as if to say, 'get on with it.' This was unsuccessful as, that instant, she recognized that Robert had a cellphone in his hand and another face down in front of him on the counter. "Whose phone is that?"

"Mine." Robert knew that her observation would lead to trouble.

"Yours? You have two phones?"

"Just since last week," Robert replied, hoping that the short season of having two phones would not look too damning.

"Why do you have two phones? Only criminals have two phones."

"Tate and I communicated on this burner phone last week."

"Why use a burner phone?"

"So the government would have more difficulty tracking us and listening in."

"Like I said, criminals."

"Well, in a way, possibly. Maybe not really, though." Robert was very confident among friends and with business colleagues and clients. However, he rarely could long endure the pressure of his wife's interrogations. Further empowering her inquiry was Robert's deep longing to fully confess all. They were a marital tour de force. He knew that together they could accomplish much more than they could independently.

"Maybe a criminal? The government?" Emily's concern was at a fever pitch. "There better be a good—and complete—story out of this. Now."

Robert took a deep breath. He knew this would be painful. It would be even more painful if she did not believe him. "Tate gave me some files that he got from work. They were on a flashdrive. He did not tell me how he got them, and I didn't know what the files contained. He insisted that I open the files on a computer that is not connected to the internet. I took my first look at the files in the church library last week on that Wednesday night. He warned me not to use an internet-connected computer to open the files, or some government entity would know the files were opened and could track down that computer and possibly then me. Then Tate got killed."

"Wait . . . what?" interrupted Emily. "It was an accident. He didn't get . . . " Robert nodded his head as to affirm that it was not an accident.

"I believe that he was pushed off the mountain by someone wanting the files."

"Pushed off the mountain?" a panicked tone was growing with each of Emily's questions.

"I really think so."

"Who is the 'someone??'"

"I don't know. Before his death, I was really not that concerned for our safety. Other than at church, I was careful not to be on the internet when I looked at the files. So, I wasn't too concerned that someone would come after me."

"Come after you?!"

"Even after I suspected that Tate was killed, I did not really think that anyone would come after me. Until I got some text messages this morning."

"When?"

"Just now."

"From whom?"

"I don't know."

"Let me see them." Emily reached out her hand, obliging Robert to give her his phone. To her astonishment, he did not hand her his personal phone. He handed her his burner phone. She read the texts, muttering some of the words audibly: 'accident,' 'paint,' 'Zims,' 'Gitts?,' 'protect yourself,' 'Tate,' 'President?,' 'use you tech,' 'safe people,' and 'Protect family.'

"Robert," Emily was now raising her voice in fear. "What does all of this mean? What have you gotten into? Wait. Why are these texts on your burner phone? How did someone get your number?" Fearful tears were starting to roll down her cheek. Robert grabbed a sheet of paper towel from the dispenser on the bar and handed it to Emily. *I hate that she is so scared. My job is to keep her safe and feeling safe.*

"I have no idea on earth how anyone got my number. More than that, we were using a texting app that we thought encrypted the texts so that only the recipient could read them. It seems, though, that this person had some insight into our texts. I would imagine that only someone with pretty high government clearances could do that. I didn't know what the files were. I didn't know it was about aliens and a government coverup since the 1940s. I had no idea that it was this big, and I certainly did not expect to be caught up in all of this."

"You 'didn't know' and you 'had no idea,' but here we are," she stated in what Robert interpreted as an accusatory manner.

"I know. I know. Not by my planning." Robert's head sank a little as he considered the reality of her words. It stung that he had placed his family in such a precarious state.

"Do you think that we are really in danger? Should we call the police?" Emily asked, trying hard to hide her sheer terror. Sensing her trepidation, Robert put his arm around her and held her tightly. Although she was frustrated with him getting the family in potential jeopardy, she appreciated his act of kindness and sunk deeply into his shoulder and chest.

"No, we can't call anyone. This is way too big for any local or state police. This is a federal government issue, and I have little doubt that we could trust anyone there either. I have to plan as if we are in danger. I think that I only have one plan. Both Tate and this text seem to say that my protection comes from letting as many people know this information as soon and as broadly as possible."

"Do you know how to do that?"

"Yes. I can have this material sent to dozens of platforms at one time. I think that sending it to as many platforms as possible simultaneously will be needed. If I send one or more files to one platform at a time, the government might be able to catch those files before anyone could see them. Also, I might need to send it from multiple computers at the same time, so they can't block files from only one computer."

Emily pushed herself upright and out of his arms. It was not the push of rejection but of wanting to think more clearly about the problem. "Do they have the technology for all of that?" she asked.

"I don't know, but I am planning for the worst."

"Planning?" inquired his wife.

"Yes, as soon as I heard about Tate's death and figured out that it was probably not an accident, I've been thinking about how to disseminate these files quickly and broadly. I think that I have figured it out."

"How long will it take?" Emily asked.

"Two or three days to do it right . . . I did not do this on purpose."

"I know, Hon," Emily assured. She was always swift to go from being in a traumatic situation to being a problem solver and forgiving when needed. She knew that if anyone could get them out of trouble, her husband could. *Or at least die trying. Oh . . . shouldn't even think that.*

"Can I see the files?" asked Emily.

"I really don't think that is best. The less you know, maybe the safer you and the girls may be. Plus, as soon as I disseminate the files, everyone will be seeing them."

"When can you get started?"

"I have more planning to do. So much will need to happen from so many different sources to many different platforms. I need to set up as many computers as possible on as many different networks and servers. It's organizational work first. Then I need to set up the algorithm."

"But it is doable, right?"

"Yes. I just need some time to get it done. Much of the planning just happens in my head. Then, I will implement it. Until then, we need to be careful and protect ourselves the best we can . . . I need to talk to Alex."

"Why?" asked his wife.

"He knows that I had a flashdrive of data that I opened on the church computer, but he doesn't know what was on it. And now that we have some threats against us, he should know that it could possibly affect the church."

"Yes," she acknowledged, "if there is any possible danger to anyone in the church, you need to let him know."

Emily left her husband at the kitchen bar. She had a list of chores that she had to accomplish out in town. Often, Robert would accompany her, but today, she knew that he had to plan his technology work. She made a mental note, *have to try not to burden him with too many minor household concerns so he can be free to solve this. Losing him for a couple days is worth it to keep us all safe.*

Robert grabbed a paper towel and a pen from a cup and began drawing a diagram. It included codes such as 'C1,' 'C2,' 'C3,' 'C4,' 'C5,' 'FB,' 'YT,' 'WA,' 'Mess,' 'Insta,' 'SC,' 'WC,' 'QQ,' 'Tr,' 'Qz,' 'TT,' 'Rum,' 'Par,' and a few more. From each 'C,' arrows were drawn to each of the other lettered codes. 'HB' was centered on the diagram with dashed arrows to all the codes with a 'C.' Robert was planning how several computers could pull the files from his 'home base' computer and then immediately send those files to numerous platforms simultaneously. He needed the file transfers to be automatized. Twenty, thirty, fifty, or more computers all sending files to all these platforms simultaneously would be far too much for any government agency to be able to stop. Even if they took the files down as quickly as they could, someone would inevitably find at least some of them. This would take much planning. Finding this many computers to send files all at once would be his greatest challenge.

Chapter 27

ROBERT arrived at church about an hour before the service would start. He was alone and would soon be followed by his wife and younger daughter. He knew that Alex would be in his office putting final touches on a sermon that he had been preparing all week. A few deacons were roaming around, making sure all was ready, and the worship team was in the sanctuary practicing for the service. However, the rest of the church office staff were not yet in the building. Robert walked straight through the foyer and down the hall to Alex's office. Unannounced, he burst in and immediately sat down in the chair in front of Alex's desk. Alex instantly understood that this was not a social call and that whatever brought Robert in with such steam was a priority. Alex looked up from his computer, Bible, and notes.

"Hey, Robert, what's going on?"

"Alex, we might have a grave situation. I think that some in the church could potentially be harmed."

"Harmed?" asked Alex. "Who might be harmed and how?" Alex cared greatly for his parishioners and often went to great lengths to protect them from harm and assistance to get them out of trouble.

"I got a text warning me that what happened to Tate could happen to me."

"What?" Alex remembered—indeed, found it impossible to forget—that only two days before Robert told him about the flashdrive and that Tate's death was possibly not accidental.

"And I truly don't know if the same warning would apply to people in this church."

"But, why? What is on that flashdrive that is so important that you and Tate could be killed and someone else in the church hurt?"

"Look, I know that you won't believe me," Robert continued with a hint of embarrassment that he was going to say his following words. "The files are about . . . about . . . space aliens." *Gonna think I'm whacko, but worth it to protect some people.*

"Excuse me?" Alex tried to chuckle, but there was a serious tone to Robert's words and the situation. "Did you say, 'space aliens?'"

"Yes," Robert gulped, realizing that he would need to repeat it. "The files are about a government coverup regarding observed extraterrestrial life on Earth." *Still sounds really whacko, even to me. Not as crazy if I don't say it out loud. Not crazy when you see the files.*

"No. Wait. You're not kidding, are you?" Alex sat up a little straighter, trying to determine that this was not a poor attempt at humor. Looking into Robert's face ravaged by days of worry and lack of sleep verified that, whether Robert's ideas were valid, Robert believed it so.

"Nope. Dead serious."

"Someone is willing to kill and hurt to protect information about space aliens?"

"I have a feeling," responded Robert, "that they—whoever 'they' are—are willing to do even more. And I believe that they think that they are untouchable." *They got away with Tate.*

"So, how many files are on that flashdrive?"

"Hundreds."

"No one in the church other than you saw those files."

"That's true, but they don't necessarily know that. They don't know if there weren't more people with me when I opened the files."

"How can we protect the church and the people?" *So many innocent people.*

"I was told that the only protection is to disseminate all the files as broadly and quickly as possible. That's what Tate told me and what I interpreted from some cryptic texts I received from someone."

The last phrase piqued Alex's attention. "Texts from whom?" he asked.

"I have no idea. Maybe someone inside the government wants this information out. I just don't know."

"Is that possible? I mean, can you disseminate the information in a manner that would keep people safe?"

"Yes . . . or, at least I think so," replied Robert. "Well, let me put it this way, I believe that I can get the information out very broadly. I hope that this does protect everyone. I'm working out a plan. I can have it finished in a few days, but I just wanted to let you know what was going on."

After a brief pause, Robert put on a wry smile and asked, "Hey, can I use the computer in the library again?"

Instantly, Alex responded, "No! Haven't you done enough?"

"Just kidding," Robert responded as he was already making his way out of the office. "Just kidding."

As was often the pastor's life, Alex was left to his thoughts. People would often 'dump and run,' and the pastor was left to ponder. Often issues required much study and even more prayer. Robert's confession demonstrated how the tentacles of one man's misdeeds could spread far, wide, and quickly to affect many others, even the truly innocent. Tate's theft of files made his family fatherless and husbandless. Moreover, Robert's family was now in danger, along with possibly other members of the church and Alex and his family. Alex recalled a sermon he heard that 'sin is rarely a one-person operation, and, when one thinks that he has gotten away with sin, sin may not have gotten away with him.' Misdeeds could affect lives, sometimes for generations.

I don't even know how to advise him. Completely lost on this one. To protect him and his family, he would have to disseminate classified information—another crime. Better pray for wisdom about all of this.

Alex's prayers were interrupted by the thought that Tate's original sin and Robert's opening of the files possibly placed many in harm's way. Alex fought the temptation to be angry at how the acts of a few could bring harm to many within his congregation. He well knew that prayer frequently resembled the wrestling of flesh against spirit—between desiring God's will and wanting 'God's will MY way.'

Robert's interruption, combined with Alex's contemplations and prayer, made the hour before the service evaporate more quickly than Alex would have wished. He was prepared for the sermon but not as over-prepared as usual. He looked back at the hour lost to the morning's events and forced himself to remember that people were the purpose of his ministry. *People are more important than time. Time was made for people to use, not fret over when we seem to lose it.*

Robert and Alex were both tense during the service. Alex lacked his common verve in the pulpit. Indeed, he could hardly process anything beyond robotically reading his prepared sermon. *Got to get through this. They'll forgive me if this isn't my best. Wow. Good thing I have my notes for hand gestures, claps, and nods.*

As disinterested as Robert usually was during any sermon, he was utterly disconnected from this one. He continued to mull over ideas about wrangling as many computers as he needed to guarantee the job's success. He considered using computers from work and church. Even if that would compromise more people, it would only be for the moments it took to get the information out to a broad audience.

Robert felt a sense of unease. He wondered if he was getting paranoid. He thought about his cellphone. *Could they track him everywhere? Were they able to listen in on his phone conversations? Even more, were they able to use his phone as a microphone? Did they know everything he said to anyone?* He wondered if they knew where he was at every moment.

The congregation rose to sing with the worship band. Robert conformed, albeit with a distant mind. The service was over, apart from the last prayer from Alex. Alex mechanically mouthed a sufficiently automated prayer that allowed him to still share part of his mind with the concerns of the day. As in the week before, while all others had their eyes closed, Robert and Alex met gazes. Uncertainty was written on the face of each.

The prayer ended, and the congregation was dismissed. Robert reached back to help Emily put on her jacket. As he turned to grab his coat, he saw a glance of whom he believed was Mr. Peters dart out the back door. *Could that be him?* he wondered. *Didn't say anything on Thursday about church. Didn't know I came here, and he's not from around here. Hmm.*

Robert, Emily, Alex, and Jenny met in the foyer near the exit door. Robert announced, "I think that I am taking the family off the mountain tomorrow, or even tonight."

"Where to?" asked Jenny.

"I'm not sure," answered Robert.

Although surprised by Robert's spontaneous announcement, Emily immediately recognized that he was in the process of devising a plan to take his family out of harm's way. She immediately interjected, "We're going to Winston-Salem for a couple of days. A shopping trip. A couple of restaurants. Maybe a movie." Emily was always much better and faster at thinking on her feet than was Robert, and this time he appreciated it.

"That sounds like fun," Jenny interjected. "We need to do something like that soon," she said, pretending to punch Alex's shoulder. Alex, while understanding full well the coded conversation before him, also knew that his wife was naïve to its completeness. "Yes, that sounds like a great idea. Sometimes it is good to get away for a couple of days. It keeps us out of trouble." Robert and his wife immediately knew about what Alex was hinting.

"What are you doing with Grace and Abigail?" asked Jenny.

"Ah," hesitated Emily. "We can call them out sick."

"Sick?" interrogated Jenny. "They don't look sick."

"I know," answered Emily, but we need to take them with us." Emily looked at her husband as if to say, 'You need to follow my lead on this.'

"Ah, yes, ah," continued Robert, desperately trying to get on the same track as his speeding wife. "We have not been out of town with both girls for a long time. This will be good for our family, especially before Abigail leaves for college."

"But isn't she going to AppState here in Boone?" asked Jenny.

"Ha, probably," replied Emily. "But we never know for sure where she is going. We might even take off this evening."

Jenny was simultaneously disappointed with the Forsythes' willingness to lie to the schools and confused why this was coming about so quickly. This was certainly unusual for them. Furthermore, this decision was abrupt at best. Emily and Jenny had talked on Wednesday evening, and nothing regarding the multi-day trip had been mentioned. The Forsythes potentially leaving as early as that evening was even more confusing. *Is there something going on here?*

"Will you be able to get your new work accomplished as you travel?" asked Alex. *Glad he knows what I'm saying, and my wife doesn't.*

"Yes," I expect that I can get it completed sometime tomorrow?" *I hope.*

"Good," said Alex and Emily simultaneously. This again caught Jenny off guard. She wondered if both knew something about Robert's business that she did not know.

Perceiving some curiosity on his wife's face, Alex added, "At least that will give you the rest of your time in Winston relaxing." He hoped that this would lead Jenny to temporarily lose the scent of the trail, but his obvious dodge only led her to be more convinced that she was being kept outside of a secret. In his role as a pastor and counselor to many families through the years, Alex necessarily kept many families' secrets. While Jenny found this discomforting, she accepted it as necessary. Nevertheless, Emily, Robert, and Alex recognized it would be a greater ill to inform and possibly endanger Jenny than either lying or circumnavigating the truth.

Attempting to cut short the conversation, the Forsythes made eyes toward the line of people behind them, waiting to meet and greet Pastor Spencer. The foursome noticed this, and hand-in-hand Robert and Emily made their break.

"I hate lying," stated Emily.

"I know," replied her husband. "Bugs me too. But we need to circle the wagons to protect everyone we can."

"I'll text Grace that we are out in the car. She will come right out."

Rather than going out to lunch after church, Robert, Emily, and Grace went home. Robert texted Abigail about the family plan and asked her to come straight home.

But I have plans for later today.

I expect that.

But this is important.

How so?

I am sorry. I know this sounds vague. But I need you to do this.

Not fair.

What's going on?

Please, honey. Just trust me. I need your help with this. (pause)

We need this.

I'll contact my friends and get back with U

No, I need this. Please.

It doesn't matter what your friends say.

?

I can't explain now.

Maybe in a couple days.

What? A couple days?

Yes.

Dad. I'm 18.

I know.

When do you need me?

ASAP.

Really? We were going out to lunch.

Really.

I'll see what I can do.

No more texts were sent in either direction. Robert hoped that the message had been received.

Abigail arrived home about thirty minutes later. With a biting attitude, she slunk to her room to pack for a few-day trip. While the family was packing, Robert continued to construct a mental picture of a diagram and algorithm for file dispersion.

The trip almost due east on Route 421 South would take about ninety minutes. The parents hoped it would be relatively uneventful. While Abigail was outwardly pouting for not being with friends, she hoped that a couple of days in Winston would lead to some fun shopping. Grace was her usual upbeat self. Although she knew that something strange was happening, she could always put a positive spin on everything. She was a great student but enjoyed the notion of playing hooky for a couple of days without getting into trouble. She liked that she could feel like she was doing something 'bad' or not approved of by the school. Her parents would handle any ramifications.

Emily was quiet, in a nervous manner. She worried for her family but did not want to alarm her daughters. She kept glancing at her husband. Through unconscious movements of his fingers on the steering wheel, she could tell that he was 'working the problem.' He was developing an invisible diagram of how he would disseminate the files and protect the family. Every few minutes, she would ask a question of the girls to engage in small talk. She strategized which questions would evoke responses from the girls without distracting Robert from his task.

An hour into the ride, about a mile before the Yadkinville exit, Robert pounded the steering wheel, startling the three women. The action was so abrupt that they were unsure if this was an act of anger or happiness. There were no context clues in the past hour that would indicate either.

"Dad, what's up?" asked Grace.

"Oh, I'm sorry," Robert said with a smile. He looked over at his wife with a reassuring smile. "I've figured out a problem I've been working on."

"All of it?" asked Emily, returning the smile.

"I believe so."

"From anywhere? I mean, can the project be done from anywhere?"

"It can be set up anywhere with a computer online."

"What are you guys talking about?" asked Abigail.

"Nothing special," answered Emily. "Your dad has been working on a project for his work. He wasn't quite sure how to accomplish it. He just figured it out."

Emily turned her attention back to her husband. "Do you have to be at a computer to execute it?"

"I can set it up to do it automatically at a particular time."

"But what if you change your mind? Or need to change the time? Move it up or back?"

"Well," pondered Robert. "What if I'm not at a computer when I need to be? That's your question?" *Now that's a great question.*

"Yes," she replied. Then thinking about the girls and their cover story. "We might be out shopping or something when you need to do the transfer."

"Right." Robert kept his eyes on the road and began tapping again.

Abigail's phone rang with an alert for a text. She was forever texting with her friends. And today, since she was not attending a previously scheduled meeting, the rate of texting was even more furious. However, Abigail's texting was fortuitous as it stimulated Robert's thoughts. He again drummed with his fingers on the steering wheel but somewhat softer this time. He glanced over at his wife.

"An app. I can develop a straightforward app so that, with the touch of a button, everything could happen immediately."

"You sure?"

"98.73 percent sure."

"I'll take it."

Chapter 28

DAY 17: SUNDAY

A RRIVING in Winston-Salem, there was an opportunity to eat before reaching the hotel. The restaurant meal was delicious, but the family mood was tepid, with the potential for Abigail to erupt at any moment. However, she did not. She remained cordial, recognizing that she could get her pound of flesh in shopping the next day. Emily understood this of her daughter all too well. The purpose for this trip, however, trivialized all possible costs.

The atmosphere lightened once the family recognized that Vesuvian Abigail would not spew molten lava on everyone within familial proximity. The three women joked and giggled, often at the expense of Robert—indicating that all was relatively normal, even better than expected. Abigail and Grace did not realize the effort their mother put into the comic distraction. Emily was overwhelmed with grievous concern for the family, and humor seemed the best substitute for visible worry. She could not let on what was happening.

Robert appreciated what appeared to be a distraction. While he too joked and laughed, he continued replaying events and cognitively developing the technological infrastructure needed to disseminate the files using an app on his cellphone. Once, when he appeared a little too distant and distracted, Emily grabbed his hand below the table and, with a squeeze, indicated that she had complete faith in him and that he could accomplish his task. He looked into her eyes, thankful that he had such a loving and supportive wife. *She's amazing. No hint of fear in front of the girls. Calm and collected. Simply amazing. Wish she understood computer architecture and coding. She could do this so much better. Thankful that she is supportive. I hope that I can live up to her expectation.*

When they arrived at the hotel, the girls noticed that their father had ordered two rooms. The parents would be in one and the girls in another. Abigail recognized that her dad's act was to appease her for the day's inconvenience. The hotel had Wi-Fi; she would be fine.

The four went to their respective rooms.

"There's a free continental breakfast in the lobby," Emily informed her daughters. "The stores open between nine and ten. Be ready at nine for some fun shopping."

"Okay, Mom," came an immediate response from both girls.

While the girls were excited that they had a room, Abigail was less thrilled that it was immediately across the hall from her parents. *Not like I was gonna wander out anyway.* They would make the best of it. Wi-Fi would allow all the connectivity that teenagers would want with their friends.

Robert and his wife entered their room. Not waiting even to take care of his luggage, Robert was on his computer at the small desk in the room. Emily recognized that what he was doing was of utmost importance to the family. She resigned herself to the notion that he would probably spend a long evening building the infrastructure to support his project.

"So, what's your idea?"

Colonel Peterson's cellphone announced a text message. It was Rabbi, his tech expert in D.C. The Colonel looked upon this lowly-positioned person as someone who had simultaneously reached the highest level of his potential and performed his duties well. Rabbi understood the nature of security and was accomplished at scouring the internet to find real-time information.

Team F just checked into the Hilton. Garden Inn in Winston-Salem.

Forsythe family. Book me a room.

I'll be there in a couple hours.

Already done.

Any idea what you are going to do?

Whatever needs to be done.

Right.

Good luck, Sir.

(No response.)

Randy knew well the Colonel's disdain toward him, but he had a good job—one which most people would covet. Completing a bachelor's degree, he was only qualified for a position ranked at GS-7. He was given advancements due to his skill. But, without more advanced degrees—which he had no interest in pursuing—he could never advance to GS-9 nor need to. He and his family were comfortable as they were. His $60k salary was added to his wife's $90k salary, and they did just fine.

The Colonel's supercilious air was not singularly pointed to his messenger. Colonel Peterson had disdain for anyone he felt did not reach what the Colonel secretly esteemed as that person's fullest potential. By the Colonel's measuring rod, few apart from himself were deemed 'successful.' He would often devalue even his superiors, those with positions to which he would need to report. Their worth to him was measured by the extent to which he perceived that they could boost his career and position him among the highest in authority.

Unbeknownst to him, however, most above him paid him little respect. They saw his continual manipulation and clawing to rub shoulders with those at the top. They despised it. It was ugly. Nevertheless, just as he tolerated his messenger because of his excellent work, so too did his bosses appreciate him—although they would far more have appreciated someone else, anyone else—as skilled as he was in that position.

"Okay," Robert began answering his wife's question. "Here's my plan. My company has accounts with hundreds and hundreds of businesses. Each has its own website on many different servers. I can write a script and push it out to each website. At a particular time, each website will pull all the alien files to their servers. Then, all at the same time, each of these will send the files to Facebook, YouTube, Twitter, Snapchat, Parlor, and a dozen more sites. That means that, for instance, hundreds of servers will be sending all these files to dozens of sites simultaneously. Even if the government saw the files from one computer going to Facebook and could block it, they could not possibly block hundreds of computers sending files to FaceBook all at the same time. In addition to hundreds of computers sending files to FaceBook all at once, they will also be sending these files to over a dozen social media sights all at once. Hundreds of computers sending files to dozens of sights give you thousands of simultaneous transfers. This is almost impossible to stop. So, the files will be available to everyone. No security system could stop all these computers from sending all of these files to all of these sites at once. It's nearly foolproof."

"Wow, that's great." Emily thought for a moment. "So, you'll set it up on some kind of timer? But, again, what if we want it to go off earlier or later, and we don't have a computer with us? What about the app?"

"Yes, so I'll set up the app on my phone. With one click, I can start the process."

"What if you don't have your phone."

"We always have our phones with us." *She's being paranoid and freaking out. Ah, but maybe justifiable.*

"But . . . " *We need redundancies. Backups. Things can go wrong.*

"I know," replied Robert. "I'll put the app on your phone as well." *Great idea, actually.*

"Good. That will give us more security."

"There is only one problem," Robert continued. "The app won't work until we get home.

As soon as we get home, I will hook up the flashdrive to my work computer. I won't transfer any files, but it will be ready. So, as soon as I get the flashdrive plugged in, the whole thing should work."

"So, we can't do this TODAY?" Emily was notably concerned.

"No, I'm sorry, but less than five minutes at home, and we will be set."

Emily sat in the bed and turned the TV on low. She texted her daughters to ensure that all was okay. The few-second delay in their responses let her know that they were frenetically communicating online with friends and saw her text as hindering their conversations. She ended her texting with a perfunctory, 'Good night. Sleep tight. I love you.' She did not bother to tell them to 'go to bed.' They were too old for that parental oversight, particularly during a shopping trip to Winston-Salem.

While Emily did not want to distract her husband from his work, she needed a distraction from continual worrying. She looked at her husband. He was deep in thought. She appreciated his dedication to solving the problem and protecting his family. He was a good man and a great husband and father. She was proud to be his wife and partner.

Her love for him and her great fear of what could transpire seamlessly led to a time of prayer. She had prayed many times regarding this situation over the past couple of days. However, witnessing his strength being diluted by the depth of his concentration led her again to beseech her heavenly Father for help.

After prayer, she watched one show after another, paying only a quarter of her attention to whatever was on TV. Another quarter of her mind was on her Bible reading. The remaining half of her thinking was on her iPad going through social media. She would then return to prayer and then again to TV, Bible reading, and social media. She continued this circular orbit until, silently, she was overtaken by sleep. Robert noticed her nodding off. He turned off the lights and covered her with the blanket. He could efficiently work in the dark, illuminated only by the laptop screen.

Robert looked at this wife. He wished that he could be under the covers with her. He generally loved the time together with her. *We don't do this often enough. Get away. Together. Alone. I don't tell her often enough how much I love her. Can't imagine life without her.* Robert looked at the clock on his computer screen. *Tempus fugit. Gotta keep pushing on. Focus. Focus.*

Chapter 29

T HE morning light cracked through the hotel room window. Emily opened her eyes to see her husband still at this computer. He also had his cellphone in his hand. He heard her rustle.

"I'm in the final testing of the app," Robert announced. "If this works, we should be all set. I'll download it to your phone as well."

"Okay," mumbled Emily, not fully awake. She rolled around and decided it was time to get up. "I've got to get ready to go shopping. Are you coming?"

"I don't know. I'm exhausted. I really need some sleep."

"Well, why don't you at least get in bed while I get ready." Robert did not argue. He poured himself into the spot where she had been, stealing the latent body heat to warm himself. His wife caressed the hair on his head. *He's been working so hard at this. To protect us. He's a good man.*

Emily texted her daughter to ensure all was well.

> You girls ok?

> (After a long pause) Yes, Mom. We're fine.

> Sleep well?

> Yes.

> Just checking up on you.

228

We are fine. Just got up. Will go to breakfast soon.

Ok. See you after.

After showering and primping, Emily went to wake her husband in time for him to get ready to go. He got up and stumbled into the shower.

Emily heard his text ding on Robert's burner cellphone. Curious, she picked up the phone. The text came from an anonymous person.

Today do.

Is this the same person who previously warned Robert?
(She decided to respond.) What?

Do FILES

It's ready

Today do

It can't be done. Who are you?

Today

Tomorrow. When we get home. *I hope that isn't too late.*
Who are you?

Enemy close. Today do. Protect you family.

WHO? How close?

No know who. No know when. Know too late.

Does he not know who, or will we not know who? Does he not know when, or will we not know when? This is almost impossible to decipher. English is either poor or purposely bad. Does he mean 'know too late' or 'now too late?' How will we know? How will we know when, and how will we know it is too late?

Know when too late only.

Who are you?

THIOP

?

(The text was undelivered. The other end seemed to simply disappear.)

Loudly but not loud enough to be heard in the adjacent rooms, Emily called out to her husband still in the shower. "Robert, Robert. You got a text."

Robert was startled by her urgency. "What? What kind of text?"

Emily walked into the bathroom. "It says that you must send the files today before it is too late."

"Too late for what?" *Doing a Tate?*

"It does not say. But it says to 'protect you family.' Get out of the shower, and I'll show you." Emily was petrified. Any fear which escaped the act of wrenching her gut attacked her mind. *I'm really scared. That's weird. People who are scared don't think, 'I'm scared.' They just are. But I am afraid, and I can think that I am. Maybe this is what real panic feels like. This is insane. Over UFOs and aliens? Nuts.*

Robert rushed to grab a towel and get out of the shower. Still dripping wet, he took hold of the phone and scrolled through the texts. "This must be the same person," he said. "'THIOP.' I Googled 'THIOP.' It is an archaic denotation for 'an Ethiopian.' This may explain why the grammar is poor—not a native English speaker." The two looked at each other. "Since this is a burner phone, I don't think he knows where we are. Um, I wonder . . . " *They have all the technology in the world at their hands. If they want to know where we are, I'm sure that they can track us. And maybe even listen in on us.*

"What?" *Don't tell me there is something else!*

"Do you think that they traced us using our credit card to check in to the hotel?" Robert involuntarily spoke an expletive. *Of course, they can.* A shudder of alarm ran through both. Emily immediately texted her daughters, who responded as annoyed by her hovering. The girls were safe. Temporary relief came over the parents.

THIOP? THIOP? Robert pondered. *Maybe not a name. Maybe a salutation. Or maybe still an acronym or acrostic for some governmental agency overseeing the investigation of extraterrestrial life on Earth?*

A novel type of exhaustion—emotional exhaustion—was setting in from wave upon wave of trepidation over the past two days for Emily and two weeks for Robert. They continued to get ready for their outing. Robert was exhausted but temporarily adrenalized by the text from the secret person. *Don't know how long I'll last today.* In fifteen minutes, he, too, was completely ready.

The four jumped in their car, ready for the girls to have an adventure. Attempting to camouflage his bone-deep exhaustion, he put on a brave face. Even if he weren't tired, shopping was among the last things he would ever wish to do.

"Did you guys get breakfast?" asked Abigail. Both parents realized that they had been so preoccupied with the project and text that they had not considered breakfast.

"No," said Emily. "But we're okay. We will get an early lunch." She hoped that would be the last question about breakfast. The parents did not want to alarm their daughters by revealing what weighed heavily on their minds.

Robert's mind went to the possibility that their credit card was tracked when they registered at the hotel. *I don't see any government people around*, he thought. Then he scolded himself. *Duh, not that I would know who is and who isn't."*

"Let's go to Target, first," offered Grace, sufficiently starved for shopping experiences while living in Boone. Boone had Walmart, Belk, Old Navy, T.J.Maxx, and Mast General Store. In the Boone Mall, a very tiny JCPennys had been replaced by an extended Hobby Lobby. As a mountain tourist spot, there were abundant opportunities to buy camping and hiking apparel like the Mast General Store, Mo's Boots, WayPoint Outfitters, and Footsloggers. If one did not go to a store specifically for AppState clothing and memorabilia, such as Mountaineer Mania, there were some racks of AppState apparel in seemingly every store. All these stores together still provided a limited selection for those shopping for trendy fashions. Elite shoppers were forced to go 'off the mountain,' east to Winston-Salem or south to Hickory, or further, in the direction of Gastonia and Charlotte.

"That's fine," negotiated Emily. "Abigail, you get the next choice." All were appeased, so they headed off to Target.

After an hour and a half—and a respectable cart-full of clothes and accessories—the women exited to find Robert napping over a laptop in the family vehicle. He was fine in the car; it was better than 'girly shopping.' Robert prided himself as a 'man shopper.' When necessary, he would enter a store, go directly to the one item he wanted, purchase it, and leave. Often this would involve less than five minutes in a store.

"Dad, are you okay?"

"Sure, sure," responded Robert, in a voice that was diminished by fatigue. Unsuccessfully, he tried to put energy behind his voice to sound convincing.

"You didn't shop."

Robert lied, not wanting his daughters to feel badly regarding his exhaustion. "I did. I ran into BestBuy to see any new technology."

"How long did you spend in there?"

"About fifteen minutes. That is enough time in any store." Robert smiled, knowing that his worldview of shopping was antithetical to that of the girls.

It was now time for Abigail's choice, the Hanes Mall, with dozens of shop-worthy stores. The family now knew that it was no longer to be the 'early lunch' that Emily had mentioned, but this mattered little; Abigail and Grace were having a wonderful time. Emily was doing an impressive job at 'faking it.'

Robert's stamina waned. His goal was to continue his nap, but he felt self-imposed pressured to join them. He knew that he lacked the cognitive fortitude to continue testing and refining the app. He decided to leave his computer in the car when they arrived at the mall. *It will be safe. Plus, my app is automatically copied to my cloud drive.*

The four entered the mall, and Robert went toward the food court, not because he was hungry, but because there was more available seating. He parked himself on a bench, expecting to be there for a while. This was a valuable time for him to at least pretend to check email and surf the web for business opportunities—companies with less than adequate websites and marketing strategies. In short, he was seeking some mindless endeavor that, unlike recreational games, still provided some positive opportunity. The women knew his centralized location and could drop off bags of purchased items with him to guard as they entered other stores hands-free.

Robert was slightly refreshed from his previous nap and knew that he had to conserve his energies as they would quickly ebb. With relief that his file dissemination project was nearly completed and would be set to run within minutes of being home, his time on the bench was his first minutes to unwind without having something particular which needed to be completed in the past two weeks. He wondered if his calmness were rational. He and his family might still be in jeopardy, but a semblance of solace emanated from knowing that there was little more that he could do until he got home. Additionally, whether or not sensible, he felt a little comfort from being out of the Boone area. All his recent problems were centered on Boone. *I might be too tired to be making sense, but hard to believe that I would be followed out of town. I'm sure they can track my cellphone, but they would not expect me to do anything an hour and a half from home. I should be in more fear than I feel, but I might be too tired to feel.*

He decided that it may be interesting to investigate the internet's information about UFOs and extraterrestrial life. He remembered that the third presenter on the video mentioned that Zims were named after some observations by students at some school in Zimbabwe. In seconds, his smartphone searched for articles about the 'Ariel School in Ruwa in 1994'. The aliens depicted in the article indeed physiologically resembled the Zim he had seen in some videos.

He continued searching for credible information regarding UFOs and extraterrestrials. Unfortunately, sources that showed even a modicum of credibility seemed only a small subset of all the garbage proposed by conspiracy theorists. *How's anyone supposed to make heads or tails of this material. Tons of crazies out there.* After an hour or so of documents and videos, Robert again fought sleep and almost dropped his cellphone. *That could have cost me one of my lifelines. Better rest.* He returned his cellphone to his pants pocket, bent over, cradling his head in his hands, and closed his eyes—and hopefully his mind.

His nap was first interrupted by Grace, who left him some shopping bags to guard. Fifteen minutes later, a mall security guard checked on him to see if everything was okay. *Haha. He probably thought that I was homeless and just entered the mall for a nap. Oh no, do I really look that bad?* "All is well, officer. My girls are shopping, and I know my greatest value is on guarding the spoils."

After a total of two and a half hours of Robert napping, surfing the net, stretching, pacing, napping, and more internet searching, the three women returned together. Robert knew the sign: it was time to move on. The grazing had been exhausted in this location. It was now time for lunch and already after the noon-time rush. The family decided to go to Firebirds, one of the family's favorite restaurants. They were seated in one of the booths by the window. Before the waitress even came for their drink order, the conversation began.

"Okay," began Abigail, recognizing the unusualness of the day, "what is going on? You took us out of school on a school day and insisted that I come also."

"I'm almost sixteen," interjected Grace, seeking to support Abigail's argument. "We aren't stupid. We know something is going on."

"Yes, girls," replied Robert. "Something is indeed going on. We are having a great time in Winston-Salem." *They can't know. No matter how hard they try. They aren't ready for this.*

"We appreciate the shopping trip, but we realize that this is a diversion." Abigail continued her inquiry. "And look at dad. He obviously did not sleep at all last night. He's wasted."

"I'm fine," insisted Robert in a very unconvincing tone. *Wish I could hide the exhaustion.*

"Are WE fine?" asked Grace. "Did you sleep on the floor? Is that why you are tired?"

"The Johnstons had a day like this just before their parents informed them that they were divorcing. And the Dunagans, just before they told the kids of her cancer. And the Millers . . . well, we know about the Millers. Parents are not very good at keeping these kinds of secrets."

"No, no," Emily stated emphatically, raising her hands as to halt the direction of the conversation. "We are not getting divorced. All is okay. No cancer. No illness."

"Then, what is it?" inquired Gracie.

Their teenagers had cornered Robert and Emily.

"Yes," admitted Robert, looking to Emily to ensure that it was okay to provide some version of what was transpiring. Emily gave him an acquiescing nod. Robert continued, "There is a situation at work that I had to get away from."

"Are you losing the business?" asked Abigail.

"No, not at all. A friend of mine recently died. It seemed to be connected to his job. I needed to get away for my health."

"But you look really bad today, Dad." Grace had some concern for her father.

"I know. I did not sleep well. I had that project on my mind that I needed to complete."

"I thought that you were trying to get away from work." Abigail revealed some frustration with her father's decision.

"I know, Honey. But when you own a business, you still have to get things done, even when away from the shop." *She probably knows all too well that my work never really ends. Maybe sometimes it should.*

"Believe me, I know," replied Abigail with a mocking tone, as if she felt she had been without a father far too many times. Robert read her implication and simply dismissed it as communication consistent with an eighteen-year-old.

"I may seem distracted today, but it is only because the project I'm . . . " Robert stopped abruptly. A figure passing by the window caught his eye. He was walking in the direction of Brixx Wood Fired Pizza. *Was it? Was it Mr. Peters? Strangely coincidental. Not really. His business is in Greensboro, only twenty minutes east on I40. But there are hundreds of thousands of people between Boone, Winston-Salem, and Greensboro. Probabilities are low of seeing him just a couple days ago in Boone and then now again here.* Thoughts poured through Robert's mind, interfering with his conversation with his family. "Only because the project is not one hundred percent completed, but it will be as soon as we get home." Looking at his wife with the hope of comforting her, "It's actually completed, but I need to test it more and tweak it to improve it. We can't afford anything to go wrong."

"It's got to be today," Emily stated in a tone that the girls did not understand. However, Robert recognized that the tone indicated some level of concern and immediacy. Although unsaid, Robert clearly understood her to mean that the project would be completed today and that the project must be completed today.

The sighting of Mr. Peters surprised Robert. It affected the remainder of his day. The women were shopping, but he was lost in thought—the files, the app, and now Mr. Peters. *There's too much going on. Can't focus.* He decided that Mr. Peters and his business was a sideshow distracting him from the greater concerns of the day. *If I can only find one more hour, the app will be finished. If I get a contract with him, I can start working on his business sometime next week.* The women wished to go into Hobby Lobby. This did not make sense to him, as Boone now had its own Hobby Lobby. But this was Robert's big chance; he could use the Wi-Fi still accessible in the parking lot and complete his task. The girls would spend at least an hour in the store, and the app would be completed.

The Colonel texted Rabbi.

> I have eyes on the package.

In WS?

> Yes. Shopping. Dining.
>
> Nothing out of the ordinary.
>
> Don't seem to suspect anything.

Find the FD?

> Not yet.
>
> Had Martin check the room while they were out. No FD, but not expected. He wouldn't leave it out of his sight. I think that they still suspect T's accident.

Where will the project occur?

> At their home. Home invasion.

When?

> 30min after arrival. Using Martin. (after a pause) You in DC?

Rabbi began to respond but never sent the text. Then the ellipses disappeared. The Colonel found this curious. Certainly, whether Rabbi was in D.C. would be a strict binary response of 'yes' or 'no.' The delay continued for a minute or so.

Yes

Ok. I'll be in touch for flight tickets as soon as this is
over.

10 4

When his wife and daughters returned to the car, Robert asked for his wife's cellphone. She immediately obliged.

"What do you want with mom's phone?" interrogated Abigail, as if her mom's privacy was being violated.

"I just found a cool app that she should have on her phone."

"What's it do?" asked Grace.

"It simply transfers files from one device to another," answered Robert. Emily understood completely.

"You'll need to show me how to use it," she responded.

"Yup. Easy peasy."

"Dad," interrupted Abigail. "You didn't just say, 'easy peasy!' No one has said that in thirty years."

"Yes, he did," chimed in Grace. "What a dork."

"But he's MY dork," emphasized Emily with a loving stroke of Robert's neck. "He's my dork." *Glad my dork can protect our family.*

The App was loaded on each of Emily's and Robert's cellphones. "See Hon," Robert explained. "You really don't need to do anything. Simply touch this app icon twice. Tap tap. That's all you need to do. Everything will be automatic, and it won't go off automatically. You had your fingerprint programmed into your phone. As long as you use the same finger for your ID and tap this twice within three seconds, it will run the algorithm. Let's not use it until we are sure that we need it."

"It said, 'today,'" Emily interjected. The morning text was unforgettable

"What said 'today'?" asked Grace. Emily recognized that she said too much in front of her daughters.

Robert ignored Grace's question. "I think that we will know. I don't know how. But I think that we will know when the best opportunity will be."

"I hope so," replied Emily. "I hope so." Although her eyes were open and she was attentive to her environment, Robert could tell that his wife was almost continually praying as the day progressed.

After a few more stores, a dinner out, and a movie, the Forsythes poured themselves into their hotel beds. Robert was exhausted from losing sleep the previous night and more than thirty-six hours of continual planning, work, developing, and testing—not to mention accompanying his wife and two daughters shopping, a feat exhausting in and of itself.

Conversation with Robert was becoming increasingly impossible. He was nearly comatose in sleep. Emily was left to her thoughts. She had suppressed them as best as possible all day while feigning that all was okay in front of her girls. She now had the time to process what no person ever should need to consider. It was inconceivable that the family could be in jeopardy from the knowledge of governmentally decreed top-secret space aliens, *little green men*. She sat on the end of the bed and sobbed, not knowing what the immediate future may hold, fearing for the safety of her family. *What on earth was Tate thinking? Oh, Lord, please help.*

Chapter 30

DAY 19: TUESDAY

T HE Forsythes opened their eyes in the hotel on a beautiful Tuesday morning. They all knew that their excursion was over and they would need to return home to Boone. The girls were ready to return to their friends, and Emily was ready for Robert to insert the flashdrive into his home computer. *Lock and load, Robert. Lock and load.*

The drive home had a strange feel to it. Robert and Emily felt they were driving to safety—they could implement the last step to make their app fully functional. Grace was returning to friends. Although not one to avoid an opportunity for brooding, Abigail was notably quiet. She did not laugh at the family jokes and only grunted the simplest and shortest possible responses when necessary. Her eyes were puffy from seemingly a lack of sleep.

"What's wrong, dear?" Emily asked Abigail. "You've been very quiet. Is there anything wrong?"

"No, all good," came her three-word response.

"I think that she argued with a friend," chimed Grace. "Last night, she was texting with someone and then went into silent mode. I don't know who." With that, Grace felt the sting of her sister's backhand on her shoulder. The weight of the blow was purposive—not too light to imply humor and not too heavy as to cause harm. Grace knew that gesture meant an unequivocal 'shut up.'

Seeing that there was no real damage, Emily asked her eldest daughter, "Is that right, dear? Did you argue with a friend?" Waiting and then hearing no response, Emily let it go. Sooner or later, Abigail would respond in private. There was no privacy with four people in a car driving on 421 North.

Grace continued to explain, knowing that a more forceful strike could follow. "Just after we got in bed, she received a text that seemed to upset her. Then another. Then another. Not sure what is going on, but she's been a zombie since."

Abigail glowered at Grace as if to scream. Grace received the message and dropped the explanation. Emily also halted the inquiry. She knew that time would do its work and eventually pry the complete truth out of Abigail. At the age of eighteen, many issues which seemed severe would eventually be contextualized as much more trivial and occasionally even laughable. Feeling trapped by secrecy, Abigail was frustrated that her family could not rightly interpret her mood and silence. Nevertheless, she knew that this was not the time to share. She swallowed hard and sank back into the din of silence.

By 10:30, they were home. All grabbed their respective luggage and bags of purchased items. The girls were busy caring for their stuff. They did not notice their father ducking immediately into his office.

Robert pulled out a six-foot USB cable and ran it from a semi-concealed USB port in the back of his computer around the back of his desk and into the back of a lower desk drawer. To the cable, he connected a four-port USB hub. He inserted the flashdrive into the hub, covered the hub with a few sheets of paper, and closed the drawer. In less than three minutes, he exited his office and approached his wife. The girls were out of earshot.

"It's ready. Just need to use the app."

"But they will know that the files were transferred from here, right?" asked Emily. "Might that be dangerous?"

"Even if 'they' know," Robert comforted, "the files will be everywhere in a matter of moments. It will be too late. The app directs my computer to send out a seemingly trivial nondescript file to hundreds of servers belonging to WebMark clients. This will go under everyone's radar. This file will then have each server copy the files from my computer and flashdrive to the servers. Since these servers are all over the place and always active, this will probably go unnoticed as well. Then, the servers will send out the files to dozens of social media sites. This will all be done in seconds. They may block some of the files from some of the servers, but it will happen so fast and so simultaneously that I suspect that they will only be able to block a very few of the transfers. Once the files are on the social media sites, they will be again open for attack—or elimination—but there will be far too many of them. And once any file is opened by anyone out there in the internet universe, that file belongs to the person or machine that opened it. They might want to stop us from sharing the files, but once it is done, they will have no concern about us."

"Are you sure?"

"96.39 percent"

"Okay. I hope you are right." After a moment of thought, Emily asked, "Why are we waiting to run the app and send out the files?"

"Who is THIOP, or what does THIOP mean?" Robert answered with a rhetorical question. "If indeed, THIOP is a person, we don't know who he is or what he wants. It may seem like he wants to help us, but I don't trust him. He won't even tell us who he is. We don't know if the strange grammar in his texts is intended to confuse us or to conceal himself. We know nothing about him. We can't put our lives in the hands of someone we do not know. We need to take control. With the app, and the fact that we can employ it instantly, I believe we have the upper hand. This way, more than just controlling if we do or don't, we control when. Additionally, I was thinking about this yesterday; it could be that THIOP is not at all a person. It could be some type of salutation. It only appears at the end of texting."

At that moment, Robert realized a new panic. *What if THIOP is a setup? What if someone in the government wants me to do this for some reason that I do not know? What if I am being played, set up? What If . . . ?* Robert righted himself, recognizing that guessing, second-guessing, and third-guessing himself had no value. His knowledge was limited. *I can only do my best. This is my best.*

As straight-faced and comforting as he could be, Robert took his wife's hands into his, looked into her eyes, and stated as confidently as he could muster, "I truly believe that if we do this, we will be okay."

"I hope you are right."

The Colonel's cellphone buzzed with a call from Martin.

"Yes," answered the Colonel. "Are you close?" The Colonel had great respect for Martin. He was an expert in his field—a hired gun, an assassin.

However, his skills were multifold. He could make a murder look like a home invasion gone wrong or keep the area pristine with no evidence apart from a corpse. He could assassinate in a manner that would mislead investigators regarding a cause of death. He had studied how to kill with similar dedication to a pre-med student learning how to heal and save a life. Some wondered—and dared not ask—if Martin were not previously in the medical field. While he understood trauma, he also knew about chemicals, poisoning, and misuse and overuse of medications.

Unfortunately, the Colonel and Martin made an efficient team. They both shared almost a pleasure in brutality—the Colonel through coercion and Martin through, well, whatever means necessary. They had previously partnered in a few 'eliminations.' They knew how each thought and worked. Few events were unanticipated.

"Five minutes out."

"Park down the road. I'm fifty yards from the house. Just off the property and in the woods. Northwest side."

"Be there soon."

"Home invasion—robbery—gone wrong."

"Copy, but won't that be unusual around here? Quiet part of the county."

"Maybe so, but necessary. Make it look like druggies looking for money?"

"Ten-four. Can do."

Within minutes the family's dirty clothes were in the hamper, luggage was put away, and Abigail and Grace tried on some of their new clothes. They were on their cellphones with their friends showing off their new garb. Robert and Emily could hear them making teenage girl sounds. The parents remained in the kitchen and shared a deep comforting hug, celebrating that they should now be safe.

Robert's burner cellphone announced a text from, again, an unknown caller.

You not do.

No. But it is ready.

Do now.

It's my only security. I don't want to blow it too soon.

Wait not safe. Do it safe.

It can happen in an instant.

Enemy there.

Enemy there? Who is the enemy, and where is there? Who? Where? Here?

Enemy there. THIOP.

A knock came on the door. It startled Robert and Emily. Their guts immediately tightened. *Who can that be?* In an instant, Emily felt tension climb up her spine, strangle her shoulder blades, and settle in her neck. They were not expecting any company. *We just got home. Who could know? Be careful. Could be 'them.'* They both went to the door, cellphone in hand. Robert kept his finger near the button on his app. It was ready to deploy in less than a second.

Cautiously opening the door, they saw Alex awaiting entry. Emily and Robert simultaneously thought, *is the warning about him? Is he part of this?*

"Hold on, Martin. Stay in position. The pastor showed up. He's in there now."

"Ten-four. This may be lucky for us. We might have had to take care of him later anyway, particularly if Tate or Forsythe had told him anything."

"Agreed," continued the Colonel. "But home invasion for drugs may be more difficult to stage."

"After we finish, we will decide what it should appear as."

"Hey, Alex," inquired Robert. "What are you doing here?" *Doesn't make sense. How does he even know we are home?*

"If I told you, you might not believe me."

"Try us," answered Emily. "We've been through a lot of 'unbeliev-able' in the last couple of days."

"The last couple weeks," embellished Robert.

Alex followed their lead and entered the house. He had been at their home numerous times before. Without further coaxing, he took a seat in one of the chairs around the kitchen table. Robert and Emily did so as well.

"Emily, I don't know what you know," opened Alex.

"She knows everything," reported Robert.

Alex continued, "Emily, I know about Tate and the files. I know that it is about extraterrestrials. Robert told me this much, but I really don't know anything more than that."

"I knew he told you," Emily replied. "But why are you here? And why now?"

Alex continued, "Do you know what THIOP means?" Both Emily and Robert gulped, recognizing that the mysterious texts ended with 'THIOP.' However, they remained uncertain as to whether these texts were lifesaving or threatening—or both. Furthermore, they were unsure if 'THIOP' were a codename, a denotation for an African person, or some unfamiliar salutation, such as 'good luck.'

Before they could answer, Alex continued, "I could only find that 'THIOP' could be 'seven' in Chaldean numerology or 'five' in Pythagorean numerology. Mind you, I find numerology detestable and antithetical—no, more so, heretical—to Christian theology. However, that's all I can guess about it."

"Where did you see that word?" asked Robert. He was surprised that Alex had found other possible meanings for 'THIOP' that he had not encountered. *If 'THIOP' is a number, even is constrained to five and seven, this could introduce a far greater number of possible interpretations and meanings. When I get a chance, I need to think about this.*

"At the end of some strange texts I received yesterday and today. I don't know who they were from. Very cryptic. Strange. Not English as a primary language. Foreign, I suspect. Possibly someone in government or some non-governmental organization who knows about the files. Seems to be trying to protect us and you, your family—at least I think so. The last text, less than thirty minutes ago, told me to go immediately to your house. It was very emphatic—at least that's how I interpreted it. Each phrase seemed to be strained for interpretation."

"I think," added Robert, "that we have been receiving texts from the same person, but only a minute ago I got a possible warning, 'enemy there,' and then you showed up."

"'Enemy there'? Who? Where? Here? Me? I don't think so."

"Nor do we," supported Emily with a trusting look, "but we still don't know who, when, or where."

"Enough time. Move in. Meet just below the front porch."

"I'm ready," Robert said to Alex. He nodded to his wife, who reciprocated. "We're ready." Robert held up his cellphone a little indicating that the solution may be somehow connected to his phone. *Not letting this out of my hand.* "I've prepared a way to protect all of us."

Another knock came on the door. All were startled and jumped to their feet. Robert held up his hand toward his wife, indicating that he would answer the door. The combination of the geometry of the kitchen and the position of Robert and Emily completely obscured Alex's view of the new arrival. On the doorstep were Mr. Peters and a tall and very powerful-looking Caucasian man in a suit that did little to camouflage his massive neck, shoulders, and arms. Robert immediately recognized Mr. Peters, but he was numbed with surprise and confusion to see him at his home. *Doesn't make sense. How'd he know where I live? Just saw him in Winston. Completely strange. Unprofessional—to come to my home.*

"Yes, Mr. Peters. How may I help you?" Robert asked. Emily was taken aback that her husband knew someone she did not know and that this stranger was at the door.

"Honey, this is Mr. Marcus Peters. He came by WebMark to inquire about us doing business with his company. It looks very promising. And who is this with you, Mr. Peters?"

Without being overtly invited, Mr. Peters and his associate inserted their way into the house. Upon entry, Alex caught a glimpse of the visitor. *The guy from church who I didn't get to meet. He snuck out too fast. Now here? What's going on? How's Robert know him?*

"This is Martin Burns. He's my associate."

"Um," Robert awkwardly hesitated due to their forwardness, "what do you need?" *Unprofessional. What's he want? Why's he here? So*

unexpected was Mr. Peters appearance—a possible business association—at his home that Robert disconnected the two men from the threat
of approaching danger. Emily felt her husband's fear dissolve and be replaced by confusion. She followed suit.

Alex was not so quick to divorce the men from the threat. *'Enemy
there.' 'Enemy there?' They the danger? Don't think I've seen Burnes before.
What kind of enemy?*

"Hello, Mrs. Forsythe," and, turning toward Alex, "Hello, pastor
Spencer. I saw you in church."

Alex was confused by Robert's attitude altering so quickly from
fearing the knock at the door to annoyance that a client would come to
his home rather than his office. Alex, less trusting and still mulling over
'enemy there,' stood up and haltingly reached out his hand to the stranger,
offering a handshake. He felt like he was reaching out to pet an unknown
dog and wondering if he would be licked or bitten.

To Alex's surprise, Mr. Peters did not acknowledge the attempt at
a friendly greeting. The dining area felt small, with five adults standing
around various sides of a centrally located table. All silently noticed Mr.
Peters' failure to reciprocate a handshake. It made the crowded room feel
confining without escape.

"Well," began Mr. Peters, "First things first. My name is 'Colonel
Peterson.' I work for the U.S. government." With that, he immediately
took authoritative control of the environment.

Emily, Robert, and Alex were civilians with proper respect for the
military and law enforcement. The title 'Colonel' seemed worthy of attention. For a fleeting moment, the three were somewhat comforted. Robert
thought, *whew, government . . . 'Colonel' . . . to help us with all of this. They
must know that someone is threatening us.*

"I thought that you worked for . . . " Robert was at a loss for words.

"Cover story," the Colonel responded. He was not concerned with
revealing the entire truth since the Forsythes and Alex would soon be
'eliminated.' "I am here for one thing. Give it to me, and you and your
family—and now families—will be safe."

"What?" Emily asked, not yet making all the necessary connections.
Robert, convulsed with ping-pong thoughts and emotions, swinging back
from fear to confusion to an instant of security and immediately back to
terror. He swallowed deeply and could almost sense a metallic taste.

Noting a threat which now included Emily, Robert and Alex simultaneously took a step toward the Colonel. "Don't be stupid," interjected

Martin. With the slightest, nearly imperceptible motion, the Colonel indicated that Martin's skills with physical intimidation were not yet needed.

"The flashdrive, Robert," stated the Colonel. "Just give us the flashdrive, and we will be gone." The Colonel planned that if Robert handed over the flashdrive, Martin would dispose of the witnesses in a few seconds; if Robert did not produce the flashdrive, each family member would be tortured in front of Robert until the flashdrive appeared. Nothing would deter them from their goal.

"I don't . . . " Robert fumbled for words. Terror paralyzed his motions, comments, and reasoning.

"Stop," replied the Colonel. "Please don't. I don't have time for lies." Looking toward the kitchen ceiling in a manner indicating that he was talking about Robert's daughters, "they don't have time for this. Please keep them safe."

In the blink of an eye, something seemingly supernatural came over Alex—something even he did not anticipate. With an authoritative tone, he stepped in front of the Colonel, pushed his hands toward him, and raised his voice in a manner that Robert had never before heard. "Get out of here and leave them . . . " and with equal verve, Alex found himself sprawled on the floor, from a single dismissive blow from the Colonel. Authority was immediately retained by the Colonel, who relished it.

Robert looked down at a dazed Alex, who already had a bloody lip. Alex was not accustomed to contact sports—particularly a blow to the head. For a few seconds, while Alex was devoid of thought, Robert and Emily had difficulty tracking the everchanging scene before them. Easier to imagine were considerations of what could occur in the next few moments. None of the thoughts was attractive.

"I'll get it. I'll get the flashdrive." Robert was cornered. He needed to protect his family, but the flashdrive was their only protection. Attempting to implement his plan and take the offensive, he clutched at his cellphone and tried to awaken the screen to implement the app. With cat-like reflexes, the Colonel slapped the phone away. The phone hit the floor hard, cracking the screen.

"We don't need that now, do we," the Colonel stated in an eerily controlled voice. He did not seem to know about the app on the phone. He simply did not want any calls to 911.

"And I don't think that you need yours either," Martin stated while forcibly taking Emily's cellphone out of her hand.

Robert and Emily silently panicked. Robert thought, *our defense, our only defense, is gone. It's gone. Mine might be broken. Need hers if I can.*

"Now, get it," the Colonel ordered Robert, in a voice made more potent and alarming by its controlled and soft nature. "I'm right behind you. Please don't try anything. We don't want anyone hurt."

Alex attempted to stand but was wobbly. He used a nearby chair for balance. Mr. Burns kicked the chair out from under him, and Alex fell to the floor, hitting his head on another chair on the way down. "Stay down," Burns ordered. The order was not necessary. Without a few minutes to recover, there was no alternative. Emily felt sorry for Alex but understood that the situation could quickly devolve to much more severe consequences. Alex prayed silently; *God, please help us. Protect the family. Please get this evil out of this house without the family being harmed. Lord, give me strength to help in any manner I might. God, please . . .*

Robert walked toward his home office. He approached his desk and began to open the left lower desk drawer. The Colonel moved in close to ensure that there was no weapon hidden in the drawer. None was seen. Robert repositioned himself to reach into the drawer and remove the papers piled on the USB hub and flashdrive. As he moved the papers, he noticed that the light was blinking on the flashdrive. He paused for a moment, unclear why the drive was activated. Files were being transferred! *What's going on? Doesn't make sense. I didn't . . . she didn't have the opportunity to activate the app! Is this an automatic backup from the computer?* He reached down and purposely fumbled in getting the flashdrive out of the hub. His hesitation was sufficient. The blinking had stopped. Robert was quite sure that the Colonel had not noticed the flashdrive blinking. He pulled the flashdrive from the computer and handed it to the Colonel.

"There," Robert declared, "you have it. Now go."

"I'm sorry," said the Colonel, "but it doesn't end like this. You know that. Remember Tate."

"My family?" Robert understood too well that someone willing to kill Tate, even after they knew that he no longer had the flashdrive, would undoubtedly be willing to kill him. His wife and daughters would only be collateral damage. *What can I do? No more leverage. Out of cards. Fight or flight.*

"We will make it easy on everyone," the Colonel stated confidently. The two men walked back to the trio, who had been left in the kitchen. The Colonel gave Robert a hard shove in the back to position him with the others. This was enough. Off-balance, Robert used the momentum to plow full-weight into an unexpecting Martin, sending him careening forcefully into a china cabinet, shattering the glass on the upper doors, and sending goblets and china crashing to the floor. The loud crash punctured the previously quiet room. In an instant, however, the tide was changed. Martin's training had the two men turned with Martin pinning Robert to the wall beside the china cabinet.

"Stop," barked the Colonel, at a volume which could only be heard upstairs by ears if they were purposely listening—which would be quite possible after the crashing of the dinnerware to the floor. "That is enough." Emily looked upon her husband with a conflicted eye. She appreciated that her husband was willing to fight for his family but recognized that the visitors could easily overpower him.

As Martin released Robert, brushing broken glass off the back of his jacket, he whispered into Robert's ear, "It will be a pleasure doing you last." Robert grabbed Martin's suit jacket as if to keep him from advancing toward his family.

"Enough," the Colonel ordered. The two men separated, neither significantly affected by the three-second skirmish. "Martin, take care of the girls."

"Yes, sir," Martin replied, turning toward the staircase. He knew his responsibilities.

"NOOO," screamed Emily, forcing herself in front of Martin's path. Martin brushed her aside with ease, and, like a rag doll, she bounced off the wall and to the floor. Ungainly sprawled out on the floor, she shouted, "God, please help us. Protect the girls from . . . "

Her prayer was interrupted by Martin's foot to her nearest body part, her thigh. He had kicked her with the right amount of force to hurt and demand requisite silence without actual harm.

Robert squeezed through the quickly congesting hallway to also block Martin's way. With the option of flight removed, only fight was available. In the ill-timed instant when he contemplated whether to assist his fallen wife or use all possible force to stop Martin from proceeding upstairs to harm his daughters, Martin's heavy backhand across Robert's face sent Robert semi-airborne to the floor, almost landing on Emily. Only adrenaline kept Robert from passing out. Recognizing that Martin was only following orders, Robert yelled toward the Colonel, "No! Leave them alone! You have what you want! GO!"

That exact moment, two more men stepped in the front door, both carrying pistols at the ready. One was in a military uniform and the other in a suit. Thorough training led them to quickly scan and assess the situation and the occupants. Alex was trying to stand—injured, but not irrecoverably so. Emily and Robert were clearly more freshly incapacitated, but they would be all right.

"Stop right there, Burns," ordered the man in the uniform. Seeing the pistol of the suited man already pointing at him, Martin Burns complied.

"Ah, Colonel Poriss," said Colonel Peterson, surprised by this unexpected interruption. "You have come at an interesting time. I have the flashdrive."

"I expected such, but at what price?" asked Poriss. Turning his attention to Alex, Robert, and Emily, he asked, "Is everyone okay?"

"Yes, yes," confirmed Emily after glancing toward a weakly standing Alex. "We are all okay." Nodding toward Martin, Emily reported, "He was just going upstairs to the girls."

"Agent Mays, put cuffs on Burns," ordered Colonel Poriss. As the suited man took a step towards Burns, Burns reached for his gun in his jacket holster. A shot rang out, and Burns fell into an unanticipated position—sitting on the floor but propped up against a kitchen cabinet. Colonel Poriss had pulled the trigger.

"Anything from you, Peterson?" asked Colonel Poriss, still refusing to call Peterson 'Colonel.'

Poriss' calm demeanor connoted his extensive battle experience in a military career. He had feelings but had learned to position them in submission to completing a mission. He would again grieve taking another life—but this would come later, when there was time for such emotions. Only his wife had seen his feeling of guilt and his wrestling with questions regarding whether the mission could have been done in any other way to protect one more life—even the life of one whom he was certain God would judge. Even his killing of the vilest of offenders bothered Colonel Poriss. While his wife would again partner in his inner turmoil, she would do it willingly, lovingly, and compassionately. Never asking nor answering any question, she would hold him as he writhed during the infrequent but dramatic climax of his internal battles. Eventually, minutes, hours, days, weeks, or even months later, he would answer his questions with the realization that the mission had been done well and as carefully as possible. He knew that every mission had possible unexpected results—most often based more on the person's threatening actions at the other end of his gun than his own. For the moment, however, he demonstrated a poise that revealed the change of command from Peterson to Poriss.

Peterson stood motionless with his hands semi-raised to indicate his submission and compliance. The suited man squatted to verify the death of Burns, stood, and reached in and confiscated Peterson's gun. While Poriss had his weapon trained on Peterson, the suited agent patted Peterson down for additional weapons. Although none were found, the flashdrive was located in his pocket. Peterson was immediately handcuffed.

Robert, Emily, and Alex instinctively trusted the man who shot and seemingly killed a person threatening their daughters. Robert thought *the enemy of my enemy is my friend. Or at least, is friendlier.*

Robert helped his wife and then Alex to their feet. They were unsteady but would be fine.

"You are under arrest," stated Agent Mays to Peterson. He was an agent from the FBI, CIA, or NSA. The fact that he was with uniformed Colonel Poriss provided additional validity.

"On what charge?" asked Peterson.

"Ha," almost joyfully cackled Colonel Poriss. "We have so many charges that it would take too long to list them now. Decades of charges."

"You don't have the authority!"

"Hold on," Poriss said to Peterson. At this, Colonel Poriss tapped a redial button ready on his phone. "Mr. Attorney General, this is Colonel Poriss . . . Yes, Sir . . . Yes Sir . . . We did, Sir . . . It was, Sir . . . In his pocket, Sir . . . All safe, Sir. No one injured. No family member. Burns went for his gun . . . Yes, Sir . . . No, Sir. No choice. We have a video record, Sir . . . The President, Sir? Yes, Sir . . . You have our, no, MY, word, Sir. He won't be harmed. He will be delivered to you . . . Yes, Sir. Thank you, Sir. And, Sir, I want to say how greatly I appreciate Marcia Commander reaching out to you and the President. None of this could have happened if she had not bypassed the chain of command. She should be recognized as making this all happen. Yes, Sir. She saved a lot of people. Yes Sir, I agree; gutsy, the real heroine in this saga. And, Sir, we need a special commendation for Rabbi, ah, I'm sorry, Sir. We all affectionately and respectfully call him 'Rabbi.' I mean Randy. Excellent job . . . Yes, Sir. I'll write that up as soon as we return to Washington . . . Yes, Sir. You will get to meet him soon. You have already met Marcia Commander . . . No? Not yet? Only by phone? Well, I'll make sure that I bring her by as well. Thank you, Sir. See you tomorrow . . . Yes, Sir. Same to you, Sir."

As quickly as Peterson's objections had been raised, they were silenced by the call. *Commander and Rabbi . . . stabbed me in the back, cut my throat, teamed up against me. Should've watched her more carefully, and the little weasel too. She ratted me out, and he gave her the technical support. She probably knew everything I was doing, where, and why. He had the means to know. Collusion. Collusion. I'm the fool for trusting that they would keep their places.* Peterson unwillingly donned the downcast persona of defeat. His power was stolen, and he morphed from conqueror to vanquished. He still held his head up and face firm, as if in control—but this was more of habit than certitude. All could see the shell of a man he had always been and had always cloaked from others behind a façade of intimidation.

Hearing the shot and then that the commotion was over, Abigail and Grace burst into the house from the back door. They had escaped out the second story of the house using a large tree adjacent to the house. Leading the way down the hallway toward the kitchen, Abigail hurdled over Martin's legs, jutting into the room. Grace was not so fortunate. She did not see the obstacle and tripped. Falling headlong, her father caught her and protected her from a possibly serious injury. Propped up in his arms, she looked back to see what tripped her and saw the open-eyed dead body on the floor. She screamed with revulsion. Her father held her tightly and turned her to face away from the sight. "It's ok, Hon. It's ok. We are all safe."

Grace and Abigail observed the participants in the room. Alex had a fat lip and a good-sized knot on his head. Their mother seemed disoriented and disheveled, but okay. Their father only showed the sign of a reddened cheek from Martin's blow. It looked like he would soon be sporting a lovely black eye.

Emily looked at her daughters. The family hugged tightly, unwilling to let go and even less willing to look toward Martin's body, sullying the environment. All were ecstatic about their mutual safety.

Colonel Poriss placed a hand on the shoulder of each of Robert and Emily and said quietly and confidently to the family, "This is all over. You will all be okay now." Looking down at Martin's body, the Colonel continued, "Let's take this outside away from this mess." All obeyed and stepped out on the front porch. Robert positioned a still-woozy Alex to sit in a chair on the patio.

"Take Peterson out of here and send up Randy," Poriss ordered the agent. Within seconds of Mays sternly placing Peterson in a parked car, Randy stepped up on the porch.

"You are Randy," stated Abigail, running over to give him a big hug. "Thank you, thank you."

Emily and Robert were confused, not knowing 'Randy' and how their daughter knew him. "You know him?" asked Emily.

"Well, yes and no," responded Abigail. "Randy has been helping me since last night, letting me in on some of what is going on and on what I needed to do. Telling us to escape from upstairs was his idea."

"Thank you, Randy," said Robert with a firm handshake which transitioned to a heartfelt hug. "Thank you for protecting my family." At that moment, Robert remembered the flashdrive and the files. "Wait, are we safe?"

"Yes," said Randy. "You are all safe." Looking toward Colonel Poriss, Randy continued, "An algorithm that I created and used is showing me that about thirty-two percent of all the file transfers went through. 'I3' intercepted about sixty-eight percent, but enough got through." Turning toward Robert, he stated, "Since you had hundreds of computers simultaneously transfer files to dozens of social networking sites, all files got through to one site or another. It was a brilliant strategy." Returning his attention to Colonel Poriss, Randy confirmed, "Within minutes, almost every file will be opened by someone around the nation and the world. There is absolutely no way for even I3 to get them all back."

"Additionally," continued Randy toward Robert, "I hope that you don't mind if I improvised a little. I modified your app. I enhanced it in one way."

"What do you mean?" asked Robert. *What did you do?*

"Well, I was given clearance by Colonel Poriss to look more deeply into the SETL files. I noticed the codes on the screen."

"I noticed those also," added Robert.

"Well, I recognized those as referencing particular decryption codes. These codes would allow anyone to see EVERYTHING in the SETL files. Nothing blurred and nothing redacted."

"Yes?" Robert was intrigued.

"Well, again, with the Colonel's authorization, I was able to locate a hidden spreadsheet aligning each SETL file to a respective decryption key."

"And?" The information was not coming quickly enough.

"I sent a copy of the spreadsheet with each batch of SETL files."

"So, anyone can open each of the files completely?"

"Yes. No more secrets."

"Excellent," replied Colonel Poriss. "Excellent. It is about time that the world knew. Even the President wanted this but did not know the best way for this to happen." Randy nodded in agreement.

"Because these files are now the property of the entire world," the Colonel stated to Emily and Robert, "everyone is safe. We had the permission of the President and the Department of Defense." Turning his attention directly to Robert, the Colonel continued, "By the way, since some government officials will not be happy that their secrets have been made public, the President has already crafted a complete pardon for you regarding any of this. And, since all of your actions regarding this were done in North Carolina, the President is also currently working with the Governor of North Carolina regarding the same on the state level."

"And what about Tate?" Robert hated that his friend had paid the ultimate price for his malfeasance.

"We are working on a plan. While we can't undo his death, I can tell you that his family will never have a financial concern."

While Robert was pleased with these last words, the entirety of the moment was sinking in. "Wait, so the files WERE transferred?"

"Yes, they were," replied Randy, "and quite effectively."

"But I didn't get a chance to use my app."

Robert looked at Emily. She shook her head and confirmed, "I didn't either."

Then, with cellphone raised, Abigail proudly pronounced, "I did. I used the app on my phone."

"How did you get the app?" Robert asked his daughter.

"Randy sent me a link to download the app. He told me to use it when he texted me. He explained that it was an issue of life and death."

Randy nodded in agreement and filled in the blanks. "I used our technology—um, a secretive technology—to clone your app and send it to Abigail's cell. You had the right idea to give your wife a copy, but I thought that one more level of security could be useful."

"And it was," acknowledged Colonel Poriss. "If it had not been for Randy being in contact with Abigail and cloning the app, we might not have had such a happy ending." Poriss placed the flashdrive firmly in Robert's hand. "This is now yours. You can have it as a memento. The files are both in governmental servers and throughout the world. This flashdrive won't be needed again."

"Except possibly in the Smithsonian," interjected Randy. "This might be worth money someday. This changed the world and how we see it."

Robert willingly received the flashdrive. He looked at the small device and marveled that it was a participant in changing the world. He held it up to the family, and all let out a victorious yell.

Alex returned home to explain to his wife and children the wounds he could not conceal. He was glad that almost any Google search would provide evidence of the alien files—soon to be known as the 'Forsythe Files'—making his story more believable.

Within thirty minutes, a 'cleanup crew' descended upon the Forsythe home. Burn's blood had pooled beside his semi-propped body on the tiled kitchen floor—far less blood than the family had expected from their TV crime-drama education. Within minutes, the body was removed, the floor cleaned, the kitchen and dining room inspected with a hand-held fluorescent light to find any remaining body fluids, and the crew disappeared. It was almost like nothing had ever occurred in the home.

However, unlike in movie fiction, the family's recovery was far from complete within minutes of such a traumatic event. They were still visibly shaken in a manner that might take days or even weeks to dull. Even though the house had been returned to a pristine state by the cleaning crew, Robert decided that the trauma in their home warranted that the family should spend the night elsewhere. A hotel in Boone was selected, and the family grabbed the barest essentials to escape for the evening.

The Forsythe family sat crowded together on a king-size bed in one of their hotel rooms. Abigail broke the ice. "Randy texted me from some kind of a blocked number. I could not read the number or the ID. After he texted me a few times to get my attention, he told me his name was Randy. He told me what had happened, about the flashdrive, and what he expected was going to happen. He explained that the only way to save the family was to follow his instructions. I told him that I did not trust him. He told me that I had no choice. He told me that it was important for the family to go home. Some people would come to our home, but others would also come to protect us. He told me to act naturally. When we got home, we went upstairs. Grace and I pretended to be talking to our friends on the phone. He told us when to go out the window."

"We had some texts also," Robert said, and Emily nodded in agreement, "but we do not know who sent them. We probably would have died without them."

Abigail's cellphone buzzed with a text.

> This is Randy. If you or your family ever need help of any kind, just let me know. The entire nation owes your family more than we can ever repay. If you need to contact me, use my personal cell number. 703-555-7742.

(after a pause)

> Oh, BTW, you may also want to save your cellphones for the Smithsonian. Within a day or so, when people realize what they are seeing, this will be a very different world.

By morning, the world would know what had happened, and the Forsythes would need to fight off onlookers and crowds for the fame the events would bring. In the following weeks, their house would become a tourist attraction for passers-by and news crews hoping to see where events unfolded which changed the world. In the following years, their super-celebrity status required security and a business manager for bookings and interviews. The world had changed in unimaginable ways, and whether they wished it, so too did the lives of the Forsythes.

DAY 21: THURSDAY

After a day of rest and trying to wrap his head around all the events, Robert met Alex at the church office. The two met with a hardy handshake that seamlessly flowed into a heartfelt hug, ending with exactly three pats on the back by both.

"Welcome, my friend," stated Alex, walking back behind his desk and nodding toward the chair. Robert followed his lead and took a seat in the chair opposite Alex's desk.

"How are you doing, my friend?" Robert asked.

"Very well. So glad that is all over. Well, at least most of it." Both men knew that Alex was commenting on the unending barrage of newspaper and cable news reporters who wanted interviews from those involved with 'changing the world.'

"Hey, I've been thinking," opened Robert. "I've been thinking a lot about God. It's irrational to be angry at God if I don't believe in Him—I mean angry at Him for taking away my parents and grandparents so closely together decades ago. So, I realize that, all along, I really have believed in God. I have just struggled with this forgiveness thing and salvation through grace and faith in Christ. I am certainly not saying that I am okay with this now, or at least yet. However, a couple weeks ago, I didn't believe in 'little green men' either. I think that the universe may have always been a little larger—ha, or a lot larger—than the confines into which I had boxed it in."

"I'm glad that you seem willing to reconsider these faith-centered things," added Alex. *There is hope for him. Thank You, God, for this work that You have done, and I pray will continue to do with Robert.*

"Well, I really came over to share something else with you," said Robert with enthusiasm. "Something came up last night that I wanted to bounce off you." Robert pulled his cellphone to the ready to prepare to show something to Alex. "Remember when we wondered about the meaning of THIOP?"

"Of course," responded Alex.

"Well, I texted Randy—haha, I still think that it is cute that they call him Rabbi—and asked if he had written those texts."

"And?"

"He categorically said 'No,'" Robert continued. "I don't know how your THIOP texts were, but mine were bizarre. After the conversation was over on their end, my texts were undeliverable . . . Undeliverable—not even like being blocked. It was as if the number had never existed."

"I got the same thing," replied Alex. "So, did you figure out what it means?"

"I'm not completely sure, but I have a working hypothesis—as of about 2:30 this morning."

"Go on."

"Well, as I was looking at alien videos almost two weeks ago, I found a video with two men interviewing and carrying on a simple conversation with an alien. On the board behind them, there were words written out in English and—I suppose—in the transliterated language of the alien."

"Okay," encouraged Alex.

"Let me show you a pic of one part of the board." Robert pulled up his cellphone, found the correct picture, and began spreading his thumb and forefinger to zoom in on a particular line of writing. Here, take a look."

Alex grabbed the phone and looked at the picture. He saw:

$$\text{Zim} \Leftrightarrow \text{Z} \Leftrightarrow \text{T't}_\text{h}\ddot{\text{i}}_6{}^\text{P}$$

"What is 'Zim?'" asked Alex.

"'Zim' is the name of that type of alien."

"Are you sure?"

"Yes," confirmed Robert. "I got that through several other videos." Pointing at part of the picture, Robert asked, "Does it seem to you that 'T't$_\text{h}\ddot{\text{i}}_6{}^\text{P}$' looks like 'THIOP' if you are texting?"

"Certainly does." After a thoughtful pause, Alex asked, "Do you think that . . . "